Bard   FICTION PRIZE

Bard College invites submissions for its annual Fiction Prize for young writers.

The Bard Fiction Prize is awarded annually to a promising, emerging writer who is a United States citizen aged 39 years or younger at the time of application. In addition to a monetary award of $30,000, the winner receives an appointment as writer-in-residence at Bard College for one semester without the expectation that he or she teach traditional courses. The recipient will give at least one public lecture and will meet informally with students.

To apply, candidates should write a cover letter describing the project they plan to work on while at Bard and submit a C.V., along with three copies of the published book they feel best represents their work. No manuscripts will be accepted.

Applications for the 2011 prize must be received by July 15, 2010. For further information about the Bard Fiction Prize, call 845-758-7087, or visit www.bard.edu/bfp. Applicants may also request information by writing to the Bard Fiction Prize, Bard College, Annandale-on-Hudson, NY 12504-5000.

Bard College PO Box 5000, Annandale-on-Hudson, NY 12504-5000

COMING UP IN THE FALL

Conjunctions:55
URBAN ARIAS

Edited by Bradford Morrow

Some people hate them. Others are terrified of them. Still others find them filthy, noisy, congested, ugly, and downright uninhabitable. But those who choose to live in cities often have a complex, almost loving relationship with their stone, steel, and glass environments—an attachment that often mingles irritation with affection, fear with calm, a desire to leave with the imperative to stay. It is this bond between city dwellers and their metropolitan milieus that lies at the heart of *Urban Arias*. Downtowns, uptowns, midtowns. Financial districts, ethnic neighborhoods, warehouses, waterfronts, skyscrapers, townhouses, parks, ghettoes, museums. The very rich gamut of what constitutes one of the oldest experiments in human habitation.

Included in *Urban Arias* are Paul La Farge, Karen Russell, Elizabeth Hand, Charles Bernstein, Brian Evenson, and Lynne Tillman, among the more than two dozen contributors, along with a previously untranslated major interview with Thomas Bernhard. In it, the uneasy relationship between urban and rural life is discussed with typical Bernhardian hilarity and insight.

Subscriptions to *Conjunctions* are only $18 for more than seven hundred pages per year of contemporary and historical literature and art. Please send your check to *Conjunctions*, Bard College, Annandale-on-Hudson, NY 12504. Subscriptions can also be ordered by calling (845) 758-1539, or by sending an e-mail to Michael Bergstein at Conjunctions@bard.edu. For more information about current and past issues, please visit our Web site at www.Conjunctions.com.

CONJUNCTIONS

Bi-Annual Volumes of New Writing

Edited by
Bradford Morrow

Contributing Editors
Walter Abish
Chinua Achebe
John Ashbery
Martine Bellen
Mei-mei Berssenbrugge
Mary Caponegro
William H. Gass
Peter Gizzi
Robert Kelly
Ann Lauterbach
Norman Manea
Rick Moody
Howard Norman
Joan Retallack
Joanna Scott
David Shields
Peter Straub
John Edgar Wideman

published by Bard College

EDITOR: Bradford Morrow
MANAGING EDITOR: Michael Bergstein
SENIOR EDITORS: Robert Antoni, Peter Constantine, Brian Evenson,
J. W. McCormack, Micaela Morrissette, Pat Sims, Alan Tinkler
WEBMASTER: Brian Evenson
ASSOCIATE EDITORS: Jedediah Berry, Alice Gregory, Jessica Loudis, Eric
Olson, Patrizia Villani
ART EDITOR: Norton Batkin
PUBLICITY: Mark R. Primoff
EDITORIAL ASSISTANTS: Charlotte Benbeniste, Jared Killeen, Eimear Ryan

CONJUNCTIONS is published in the Spring and Fall of
each year by Bard College, Annandale-on-Hudson, NY
12504. This issue is made possible in part with the generous funding of the National Endowment for the Arts,
and with public funds from the New York State Council
on the Arts, a State Agency.

SUBSCRIPTIONS: Send subscription orders to CONJUNCTIONS, Bard College,
Annandale-on-Hudson, NY 12504. Single year (two volumes): $18.00 for indi-
viduals; $40.00 for institutions and overseas. Two years (four volumes): $32.00
for individuals; $80.00 for institutions and overseas. Patron subscription (life-
time): $500.00. Overseas subscribers please make payment by International
Money Order. For information about subscriptions, back issues, and advertising, call Michael Bergstein at (845) 758-1539 or fax (845) 758-2660.

Editorial communications should be sent to Bradford Morrow, *Conjunctions*,
21 East 10th Street, New York, NY 10003. Unsolicited manuscripts cannot be
returned unless accompanied by a stamped, self-addressed envelope. Electronic
and simultaneous submissions will not be considered.

Conjunctions is listed and indexed in Humanities International Complete.

Visit the *Conjunctions* Web site at www.conjunctions.com.

Copyright © 2010 CONJUNCTIONS.

Cover design by Jerry Kelly, New York. Cover photographs by Stephen Berkman.
Front: *The History of Dread: A Guide for the Perplexed*, undated, albumen
print from a wet-collodion negative, 11 x 14 inches; rear: *Obscura Object*, undated, albumen print from a wet-collodion negative, 11 x 14 inches. Reproduced
by kind permission of the photographer.

Available through D.A.P./Distributed Art Publishers, Inc., 155 Sixth Avenue,
New York, NY 10013. Telephone: (212) 627-1999. Fax: (212) 627-9484.

Printers: Edwards Brothers

Typesetter: Bill White, Typeworks

ISSN 0278-2324

ISBN 978-0-941964-70-8

Manufactured in the United States of America.

TABLE OF CONTENTS

SHADOW SELVES

Edited by Bradford Morrow

EDITOR'S NOTE

A MANNEQUIN, decorated with the colorful fishing lures of injured anglers, takes on a life of her own. A father filming his seven-year-old daughter's birthday party on the front lawn happens to capture on video, inadvertently in the grainy background, a man on his way to commit a heinous crime. A literary memoirist, invited to meet a famous and famously difficult novelist, enters into a life-changing dialogue that may or may not be imaginary. Doppelgängers, clones, sleight-of-handers. Hiders and seekers, the deluded and the deluders. Ponzi-scheming tricksters, identity thieves, dead ringers and living ones.

This issue gathers a kaleidoscopic array of fiction and poetry that investigates the venerable themes of self and other, appearance versus reality—the very tenuous nature of identity itself. As Stephen Berkman's compelling cover image, *The History of Dread: A Guide for the Perplexed*, so succinctly asks, Who exactly are we looking at when we gaze into the eyes of another? Is it ourselves we see in a varied guise? When we look into a mirror, do we see an other? And is that other a falsehood or some complex extension of a truth we don't quite grasp? The theme of the doppelgänger has preoccupied the likes of Dostoevsky and Abraham Lincoln, Shakespeare and Buffy the Vampire Slayer. *Shadow Selves* offers a spectrum of permutations on this theme that is central not just to classical literature but to postmodernism and post-Freudian psychoanalysis from Lacan forward.

I want to offer special thanks to my intrepid group of editorial readers—Micaela Morrissette, J. W. McCormack, Jessica Loudis, Alice Gregory, and Eimear Ryan—who helped me find a number of the astonishments in this issue.

—Bradford Morrow
April 2010
New York City

Elizabeth Thug
Jonathan Carroll

SHE WALKED INTO the place and without saying a word, handed the man the wrinkled yellow slip of paper she had worked and fussed over for hours the night before. There were only two words written on it in careful block letters. After glancing at it (she watched his eyes closely to see his reaction but his face remained blank), he looked at her and then once more at the paper to be sure he'd seen correctly. Then he asked, "Where do you want it?"

Her shoulders drooped. Her whole body relaxed at his question. She had imagined so many scenarios of how this scene was going to play out, but what the man had just said was not one of them. She'd anticipated derision or perhaps stunned surprise from him; maybe some suspicion, questions like "You want *this*? Why?" Or, worst of all, a mean little smile that said, You're an idiot, lady, but hey, money's money and if you want to pay for this, I'll give it to you.

"On my hand." She stuck out her right one, palm up. With her left index finger she pointed to the middle of the right palm. "Here. I want it here."

"OK." He handed back the paper. "You want it in block letters or in some kind of special script? We've got a book of fonts that you can choose from."

"Comic Sans."

"Excuse me?"

"I want it done in a Comic Sans font. Can you do that?"

He pointed to the paper. "Like it's written there?"

"More or less. I brought along a Comic Sans alphabet in my bag that I could show you. Can you do it?"

He chuckled. "Easy. I just spent three hours doing Hokusai waves on a skinny guy's forearms. I guess I can write two words on your palm, right?" The sentiment was snarky but his voice wasn't—it was only stating a fact. "Are you Elizabeth?"

"No."

He scratched his cheek and looked at her with more interest. "Are you a thug?"

8

She grinned and shook her head.

"But you want this on your hand forever?"

"Yes."

He spoke wistfully, musing to himself. "People want the strangest things on their bodies."

"I can imagine."

"One guy wanted a strip of *bacon*. Another had me do a car battery over his heart. But what do I know, huh? The guy's got money, I give him a car battery."

She nodded.

"Delco."

"Excuse me?"

"It had to say DELCO on the side of the battery. He wanted it specific."

"Specific." She didn't know what else to say.

"And you want ELIZABETH THUG tattooed on your palm?"

"Yes."

"Who's that, your girlfriend or something?"

This moment and question she'd expected. She was not a brave woman but would have to be brave now. She spoke quickly because she wasn't used to being rude and it was difficult for her. "I'd rather not say." She spoke firmly—the subject was closed.

He put up both hands in surrender. "OK, I'm cool with that. You want to get started?"

He was finished in less than an hour and did a great job. The new tattoo on her palm looked exactly as she had imagined—maybe even a little bit better.

As he worked they talked. He told her stories about people who'd come to his shop. Like the man who wanted the car battery tattooed on his chest was a long-haul truck driver who was going blind. He was terrified of what was happening to his eyes and how he would cope with the rest of his life. He wanted the battery tattooed over his heart so that he could touch it whenever things got really frightening. It would remind him of the good times and that life could be good as well as bad.

"But why a *battery*? Why not a truck if he's a truck driver?"

The tattoo artist wagged a finger in the air. "Good question. I asked that, too. He said trucks couldn't run without a battery. They're the heart of the machine."

She wished she hadn't asked. She liked mystery more than answers. Both as a child and an adult she never asked or wanted to know how magicians did their tricks, how special effects were done in movies, or why men gave her flowers now and then. Her life was unmysterious so much of the time that any chance she got, she avoided clarification and hungrily embraced the unknown. Part of that was because *she* was so unmysterious. She had almost no secrets. Nothing naughty or fishy was hidden away under her bed or stuffed deep into the closet. Anyone could walk through her apartment with a 1,000-watt flashlight and a magnifying glass, snooping everywhere, but find nothing that would cause her even to blush. Just that thought alone made her despondent. She looked at people around her, friends and work colleagues, and was certain most of them had secrets or secret lovers or secret stashes of stuff that both mortified and delighted them when no one was looking.

One boyfriend she broke up with said he knew things were going wrong between them the same way you know your shoelace is untied before you look—a sort of loosening and slight shoe wobble that makes you check. "I basically knew it was over when I started feeling that same kind of loose wobble between us, you know what I mean?" She was hurt more by that description than by the fact that he no longer wanted to be together. More mortifying, he was right. Shoes have no secrets and neither do shoelaces, tied or otherwise. No passionate other woman ever lurked in *their* shadows, ready to leap out and scream, Ah ha! No operatic cris de coeur that led to wrenching emotional scenes in which the truth finally flooded out because too many dark secrets and words had been left unsaid until that moment. No, to him all their relationship added up to was an untied shoe and, by extension, she was a shoelace.

That was the reason for her tattoo.

While buying coffee one morning, she'd chanced to glance at the hand of a well-dressed middle-aged woman standing nearby. A photorealistic blue accordion was tattooed on the back of it. She was so taken both by the image and the mystery of why anyone would choose to have *that* drawn on their skin she covered her mouth with her hand because she didn't know if she was going to laugh out loud or splutter in glee.

At once she realized a person didn't need to be mysterious at all—only their skin did. From then on she studied any tattoo she saw. She sidled up to people on the subway, and once sure they weren't looking, peered closely at their arms, their legs in shorts, the backs and sides of their necks, their forearms thick with muscles or thin as chopsticks, so long as they were inked.

Most tattoos she saw were dull, dismal, or trite—cartoon characters, Celtic or Maori designs, advertising logos like the Nike swoosh or once even the McDonald's hamburger arch. Why? She constantly wondered why people volunteered their skin as a billboard to tell the world they were clichés, unoriginal, or, worst of all—they just wanted to be like everyone else.

In contrast, the mysterious blue accordion on that woman's hand was enthralling. An accordion? Why? What did it mean? Was the woman a musician, or was there a deliciously recondite meaning to her tattoo that only she and a few select others knew, but the world would never discover. How could anyone see that tattoo and not wonder about the person who owned it? Mickey Mouse or a dragon on a bicep? Snore. An accordion across the back of a delicate female hand? Brilliant.

She was so smart yet uninspiring. She worked in magnetic bubble technology. When she told people that, their eyes either turned off all the lights or else got jumpy and nervous, wanting to escape. If you were interested in vortex dynamics of high-temperature semiconductors, then she was your girl. But let's face it—nobody was and that was perfectly OK. She knew in the world's eyes she was like a store that sold only one rarefied thing like Iranian caviar or antique French needlepoint. But she *did* have other interests. Come on—give her some credit. She liked to go swimming, line dancing, and absolutely loved to kiss. When she created a profile for online dating services, just trying to describe herself in an interesting, original way was a challenge. What she wanted to say was, I am smart, have a great sense of humor, like sex, and am up for more or less anything. But you probably wouldn't think that if you were just to look at me. So here's the deal—Get in touch, let's talk, and maybe we can dance. In the end, after much soul hemming and hawing, that's exactly what she did say but the results of her candor were unfortunate, to say the least. The only men who responded were creeps, bores with dubious issues, or guys who started whining in their very first e-mail to her.

But seeing that accordion tattoo revived her. It changed her attitude from three-quarters hopeless to hopeful by giving her a concrete plan that she'd put into action as soon as she walked out the door of that tattoo shop.

How happy she would have been if she'd been able to glance in a rearview mirror and see the look of puzzled admiration on the face of the tattoo artist as she left his place that day. Whoever she was, she must be cool to want that tat on her palm, no matter *what* it meant. He even wrote the enigmatic words down on a scrap of paper so he would remember: Elizabeth Thug.

A few nights later at a popular downtown bar, a stranger glanced at her hand. After doing a small double take and narrowing his eyes, he reached over and took hold of it. A nervy gesture and she winced slightly because it still hurt from the tattooing, but she didn't mind. This was the beginning.

"Elizabeth Thug." He said the name without a question mark at the end. He was decent looking. His tie was pulled to one side and his shirt collar was open.

She looked at her hand as if to make sure they were talking about the same thing. Then she smiled at him and nodded once.

He waited for her to say something. When she didn't he asked if she was Elizabeth Thug.

She shook her head.

"But it's tattooed on your hand."

She nodded again. "True."

"Why?"

"Why do you think?" Her voice was soft and friendly but gave nothing away.

He looked at her as if she'd just spoken to him in a foreign language. "What do you mean?"

"Why do you think 'Elizabeth Thug' is tattooed on my hand?"

He smiled but it faded. He smiled again but it was different this time: confused, quickly gone. "Is that you, or a relative?"

She said nothing and made a sour face. It said come on; you can do better than *that*.

"No?"

She sighed and withdrew her hand from his so she could lift her glass. "No."

He sat up straighter. "Are you Rumpelstiltskin? Do I have three guesses and if I get them wrong, you'll put a spell on me?"

"You never know," she winked.

"OK. You're a feminist and Elizabeth Thug was the world's first female boxing referee."

She tipped him a nod for his clever answer. "Not bad. Wrong, but original."

He rubbed his hands together. This was fun; he liked it. Liked that she got his humor and hadn't pushed his answer away like it smelled bad.

He guessed two more times and was wrong, of course, because the secret was "Elizabeth Thug" meant nothing. They were simply two words that had come to her out of the blue when she was showering one morning. But moments after they arrived in her mind she knew exactly what to do with them. Once she was sure she wanted two disparate words that signified nothing, she tried out many others just to be sure. But she kept coming back to those two and they were the words she had tattooed onto her palm.

That first evening at the bar with the man was useful and sexy. The guessing game opened things up between them and although she never revealed the secret of the tattoo, he was clearly interested in her. When he asked for her telephone number, she wouldn't give it. She teased that if he had given the correct answer she would have, but oh well—maybe next time. He asked if there would *be* a next time. She said she came to this bar fairly often. Maybe they'd see each other here again. And then she left. On the cab ride home she stared at her tattoo and knew she had made the right decision.

Scheherazade was so wrong; she had it all backwards. For 1,001 nights, she told her king new stories to keep him interested and spare her life. But men don't want to hear stories—they want to *tell* them. They want to talk; they want to hold the floor. Males want the world to listen to whatever it is they have to say. That was the single thing she learned from her dismal period of Internet dating—most men really only want to talk to someone who listens. Some want to download while others want your sympathy. Some want admiration but not as many as she had originally imagined. More often than not, men just want to tell you what they're thinking or how they see the world. They prefer an appreciative audience but willingly settle for an attentive one. She realized after meeting so many men in a short period of time that the best way to start things going on a date was to give the guys a little verbal push and off they'd go—talking about themselves, their world, their take on things.

"Elizabeth Thug" was a natural outgrowth of that discovery. She presumed correctly that most men preferred guessing what her tattoo meant rather than hearing the truth. If Scheherazade had done it right, all she'd have had to do was get her king talking about a subject that intrigued him and she wouldn't have had to tell a new story every night for three years.

A dog, a cat, her sister, her mother. A friend, a car, her favorite bar. These were some of the guesses men made about her tattoo. In the beginning, when she was just getting used to the attention those mysterious two words created, she was coy or ladylike in her denials.

No, I'm sorry, that's not it. Oh, that's an interesting guess but you're wrong. Some men tried to charm the answer out of her. Others were derisive and taunting. Why would I care what it means? She was sweet even to them. She smiled and purred, Because you *asked*. If you're not interested, that's fine. But of course they were interested and all their gruff was a bluff.

However, as time passed and more and more men guessed wrong, she became impatient. She knew that was ridiculous because how could anyone get it right when there was no right? Still, she grew irritated and positively snapped at some of them when they guessed.

"The family *boat*? Are you joking? Would you want the name of a boat tattooed on *your* skin?"

This man took a long drink of his double Jameson and then wiped his mouth with a scrunched-up cocktail napkin. "I was just kidding," he said defensively.

She looked at him like a teacher who's just caught a student cheating on a test.

No boat, no best childhood friend who died tragically, no title to her unpublished first novel. She sort of liked that last guess and considered giving the man her telephone number but in the end said no.

Her sister came to town and two minutes after they had hugged hello, noticed the tattoo. "What the hell is that?" When she heard the explanation she slapped her hands against her cheeks and hooted, "I love it! You're out of your mind."

The two women went to a bar that night so she could show her sister what happened when men noticed her hand. They were there forty-five minutes and three men struck out guessing.

"Ooh look—see the really handsome guy at that corner table? Go over and ask him."

She looked over and saw a hunk with short hair and a three-day-old beard sitting alone with a beer mug held between his two hands, staring intently into the distance.

"But I've never done that—gone up and just asked."

Her sister nudged her shoulder. "Come on, be brave. It's like cold-calling in telemarketing. Let's see if you can get him to bite."

After finishing her drink for courage, she walked over to his table. He looked up at her slowly and smiled, but it wasn't warm or welcoming—only a hello-what-do-you-want smile.

She put up her right hand like an Indian chief going "How!" The good-looking man saw the lettering on her palm and squinted to decipher it.

"Elizabeth Thug?"

She nodded.

He took a sip of beer. "Am I supposed to guess what it means?"

She nodded again, feeling awkward and uncomfortable now so close to his handsomeness.

"I don't want to."

She took a sharp breath, a little gasp of humiliation, and turned quickly to go.

"But wait a minute—can I ask you something?"

She stopped but didn't turn around. The bastard could talk to her back.

"Do you ever scare yourself on purpose? I must do it five times a day."

She frowned and half turned to him. What was he talking about?

He addressed his beer mug but loud enough so that she could hear. "For some absolutely unknown reason, I need to scare myself at least a few times every day. Maybe it's just the adrenaline rush, right? Maybe I just dig that body buzz you get when you're scared or nervous. But it's insane.

"ATM machines, right? *They* scare me."

She thought he was joking. "You're scared of money machines?"

"I am." He nodded and tapped the table for emphasis. "Worse—I *make* myself scared of them. That's the big difference, you see. As I'm walking up to one to get some money, I think this machine is going to eat my card and then what? How am I going to get around without any cash?"

She stared at him. "But even if that happened, just go into the bank and tell them to get the card out for you," she said reasonably, still not believing he was serious.

He shook his head. "Not on Sunday, or ten at night, which is when I usually end up needing money.

"Or how about this one—I'm riding alone in an elevator in the middle of summer. It's a small car and not air-conditioned. Every time, *every* time I'm halfway to my floor, I suddenly think, what if this elevator broke now and stopped? What if I had to stay in here for hours because nobody came to get me out, or no one was in the building? And as soon as I think that, I get boiling claustrophobia. So I say to myself *shut up*—just stop it. Stop being stupid, but it does no good. Being reasonable never works. It's like I create demons to eat me alive from inside out.

"Or I'm on line at the post office . . ." He began to go on but stopped. "I do it to myself, understand? An ATM machine is just a machine. They're tested a zillion times before they're installed, so they never fail. But that doesn't make any difference—it's gotten so bad that just about every time I go up to one, I get nervous. Sometimes I almost physically lose my balance because I'm so worried.

"Why do we do these things to ourselves? Life's hard enough, right? Why make it worse by scaring ourselves? Or making ourselves miserable by creating stupid imaginary scenarios that never happen anyway?"

She could think of nothing to say. Instead she just opened and closed both hands and then pushed them against her sides. How did she get into this? She just wanted to go back to her sister.

He rubbed his head with both hands. "It's not even masochism; it's weirder than that. The things we do to torture ourselves, you know? I used to think I liked me, but not so much anymore.

"Do you know what I was thinking about before you came over here? I'm going to name it. So that every time it happens to me from now on, every time it comes, if I have an actual name for it I can say, 'George, go away.' Or 'George, go back to your room now and quit messing with my head.' Treat it like a bad little kid who needs to be disciplined."

He lowered his eyes and for several moments stared at her hand. "Elizabeth Thug." His eyes moved up her body. When they reached her face he was grinning. "Elizabeth Thug! *That's* what I'll name it. Thank you. That's perfect. The next time it happens I'll say, 'Elizabeth—get out of here. You can't do it. Not this time.'" His entire expression and body language radiated how much he liked the idea. "Get lost, Elizabeth *Thug*. I'm only getting some money from the machine, so leave me alone."

He raised his beer mug to her, a toast. "You don't mind my borrowing the name for this, do you? I will worship you for the rest of the week. Elizabeth Thug. That's exactly it." With a triumphant voice, his glance dropped to the table, dismissing her. But he did look sort of transformed.

There was nothing else for her to say or do but return to her sister, who'd watched the whole thing from the bar. What could she tell her? What had just happened? Walking back, she glanced down at her right hand and saw a bit of the tattoo there, the name he would remember and use. The name that actually meant something now, but not to her.

Freak Magnet
Julia Elliott

IT'S A BALMY SUNDAY in March. Daffodils glow. Normal folk stroll back and forth, chirping of normal things, and though I've slipped into a pair of rumpled khakis and an olive polo, though I graze my pregnant wife's elbow with the tips of my fingers, guiding her along the sidewalk, whistling even, with a hint of strut in my gait, inside I'm a lurker, have always been a lurking freak, my face filmed with sweat, my smile tainted with twitches, my heart fat and riotous in my chest. And sure enough, when we're tucked into our booth, munching our whole-grain muffins, a madman swaggers into the bakery. I can instantly peg him as a failed artist, megalomaniac type, clutching his notebook of ravings, demanding that the hipster behind the counter produce a bucket of fried chicken, because in the 1980s this place was a chicken joint.

You're still a fucking chicken joint in your greasy little heart, says the maniac, spitting on the floor and swiveling his gray pony-tailed head around to leer at the bourgeois bohemians.

My wife is trying to smile. The gentleness of her gazelle eyes creates certain palpitations in my heart, a weird mess of love and panic attack. Our frog-sized fetus floats inside her, the essence of fragile hope. And the nutcase is, of course, headed our way. Even though I sought out the darkest corner of the room, and we're blocked by a plus-sized goth goddess in a vampiric muumuu, the madman, guided by unknown forces, swoops down on us like a bat on a pair of moths. I study the spongy texture of my broken muffin. My wife asks me, with flamboyant nonchalance, if we're going down to the land trust to see the emus. The lunatic does not like the idea of our idyll with exotic birds.

"Pet the fucking emus," he says, his mouth toxic with sarcasm.

"We're not going to see the emus," I say, and my wife picks up her plastic fork, holds it like a weapon, making me feel ashamed.

The madman has gathered all kinds of evidence against me: (1) I was staring at him with my beady eyes; (2) I was talking about him with my "big, fat, dick-sucking mouth"; (3) I'm sneaky and arrogant and think I'm better than people like him. He wants to fight me, right now, outside, where petunias sway in window boxes and several pampered, overbred dogs are leashed to a polka-dotted park bench. I sigh and slump, feeling the precise distance between my amphibious offspring, a tender bundle of flesh and nerves, and this leathery, stinking danger. The distance is way too close and I stand up. A cop arrives to escort the man out. You'd think I'd be able to relax in the biochemistry of relief, but panic percolates through my system. I gnaw my fingertips. The restaurant is freezing. And my wife has vanished—must be puking her muffin in the bathroom.

We're finally walking in the sun again. My spine has not exactly relaxed, but no longer twitches like a chopped-up snake, is more or less one unit, flickering nervous energy. Though the robins on lawns look old and matted, they twit among dandelions. A squirrel with a boil on its elbow is chewing a Styrofoam packing peanut. Adults bark orders to dogs and children. And flowering trees spew their sweet, soft pink. I take my wife's hand. I'm just getting into the business of swinging our arms casually as we stroll along in the spring afternoon when the voice of a shell-shocked ape croaks in my ear.

"Going to pet the emus?"

I know without spinning around that the maniac is dogging us. I know that his eyes will be blood webbed, his pupils huge, his mouth crusty, agape with a carious grin. Rivulets of gray sweat will be streaming from his head, down his nape into the unspeakable depths of his flannel shirt. I can feel his misery, licking at the back of my neck. But I don't turn around. We quicken our stride. My wife's perky waddle makes my heart feel sprained. I tug her down an alley. The best thing to do is stay in public, move back toward the little strip of shops.

We dip into a candle shop called Paradise. A thousand gaudy smells swirl, and colorfully dressed ladies dawdle, sniffing the wax lumps. My head throbs in the sick sweetness. My wife's face looks greenish white—such a hell of scents for her wolf-sharp nose. And the madman has slipped in after us, mumbles something about kicking my ass, seems a little disoriented amid the purple swells of scent.

"Fucking candles," he hisses, and I understand. He voices my sentiments on candles precisely. I want to tell him this, but I don't. We exit the shop and scurry into Hemp Dreams, where the dim lighting, tapestries, and tribal drum recordings capture the essence of our primal predicament. My wife's pretending to try on sandals that we can't afford. When the crazy man sneers at her, I want to tell him that we're not really the people he hates. That we're brittle and scared. That spring, with its pink chaos and onslaught of pheromones, upsets me.

"We can hide in the back of Tiff's shop," my wife whispers, her nauseated frown spiked with accusation, for this is not the first time a freak has felt an inexplicable attraction to me, and I know that it will not be the last. It must be some kind of desire that the maniac feels. He wants physical contact. He wants to roll with me on the new grass and pound my face with his cracked fists, to smear himself with the red reality of my blood.

We hustle down the sidewalk toward I Wanna Be Your Dog, a doggie gift shop run by a trust-funded lesbian couple we know. In a renovated feed shop decorated with portraits of dogs in Victorian finery, they sell vegetarian biscuits, canine horoscopes, and hand-knit, berry-dyed, organic-wool pooch sweaters. They stock gourmet-diet kibble for bored dogs driven to obesity. They conduct seminars on canine massage for all the shivering, nervous housebound hounds in the area. A dog psychologist does stints on Saturdays, combing out the tangles of the master-pet power struggle.

Today Tiff's promoting an herbal flea shampoo, and my wife can't handle the combo of wet dog and essential oils. Her hand flies to her stomach. Tiff, who's bathing her girlfriend's Italian greyhound in a claw-footed tub, runs to my wife's side. "We've got to hide, right now," my wife snaps, waving off Tiff's *whys* and *wherefores* and stomping right back to the stockroom. In the darkness, at a Formica diner table piled with vegan raw-bone treats, my wife breaks down.

"He's lured another maniac," she cries, pointing at me.

"How do you know it was . . . ," I mutter.

She stops this idiotic defense with her glare, a firm jab of a self-righteousness that she'll probably use to discipline our child.

"I mean, what do you do? Do you wink at them or something?"

"I swear. Nothing. I was hiding this time. He came right to me."

Tiff shushes us. Someone's rustling around in the shop, which is separated from the stockroom by a mere curtain of paisley linen.

"Oh my God, Brutus," hisses Tiff, referring to her girlfriend's dog, "out there alone with that lunatic." And she rushes out into the shop, assaulting the madman with an aggressively genteel, *Can I help you with anything, sir?*

Our crazy does not appear to be in a conversational mood. As he grunts and shuttles, the constant flow of baby talk Tiff's directing at Brutus reaches a hysterical pitch. My wife's studying me, rubbing her stomach defensively, invaded from within by my freakishness, the strangling vine of my DNA slithering through the weave of her own lovely code. I can feel the dirty bomb of a panic attack scattering its filth inside me. My hands are shaking. My knees jump. I'm a clammy, quivering mess with a boiling heart. The fear that rips through me on such occasions often increases my attractiveness as a freak magnet. Drawn to the current of my panic attack, the freaks come stumbling, ignorant themselves of what beckons them.

Sure enough, the madman stops near the stockroom door and starts bellowing something about every dog having its day. This guy thinks he's fucking clever. But what can I say? I, too, am a wit narcissist. My father was a wise guy, as was his father before him. If anyone carried the legacy of freakishness within his blood, it was my grandfather. I recall summer afternoons at Pawpaw's river house in South Carolina. Meemaw fried catfish. Pawpaw messed around in his shed, the magical locus of his amateur taxidermy and electronics experiments. He'd mail-ordered these taxidermy kits that enabled him to transform squirrel carcasses into miniature sportsmen, and the room was decorated with mummified squirrels throwing footballs, shooting hoops, and playing golf. Stuffed deer wearing bow ties gazed down from bare plank walls. And the room crackled and glowed with Pawpaw's machines: depth sounders and scanners and homemade seismographs. Just after my twelfth birthday, Pawpaw took me into the pungent steam room of his shed to measure my animal magnetism with his electromagnetic frequency machine. He had a stylus on a wire hooked to a screen with an oscillograph on it. Stinking of cigarettes, fish guts, and Aqua Net, the old man leaned over me, took my hand, and pressed the tip of the stylus into my sweating palm.

When the wave representing my electromagnetic charge shot through the graph's roof, Pawpaw hemmed and hawed. He searched my pockets and peered into my nostrils and ears. He scrutinized my tongue and shone a penlight down my throat. He tried the experiment a few more times and got the same outrageous results. In a gruff voice, Pawpaw asked me if I had anything—*scrap metal, refrigerator magnets, electronic doohickeys*—stashed in my underpants. I assured him, with tears in my eyes, that I was clean. Then he stared at me for a full minute. Told me I was a *freak of nature*. Said,

Meemaw's got a Co-cola with your name on it waiting in the fridge.

I've never told my wife about this incident. If she knew about it, she'd immediately start making appointments for me—with neurologists and new-age magnetic therapists. She'd try to cure me. She'd be delighted that what's wrong with me can be quantified, and thus, in her eyes, adjusted. A believer in biochemical fine-tuning, she's the one who got me hooked on Xanax, Clonazepam, Lexapro, and Risperdal. When I resisted, she called me a psychopharmaceutical Neanderthal. She said drugs would save me from myself. She said drugs would help me manage the complicated system of myself and allow me to behave like a *normal person*. She doesn't seem to notice that I've become a pill-popping maniac. She doesn't seem to notice that before performing any act of moderate importance (calling my parents, for example), I'm now required to prepare myself pharmaceutically. And it can take up to two hours to hit the right groove.

I also enjoy holding off on pills for several days and then treating myself to a night of chemical stimulation hyped by alcohol, marijuana, and strategic sips of Robitussin. In fact, I was planning on engineering such a state of bliss this very evening, listening to music while enjoying the brief period in Atlanta's temperate months during which I won't be imprisoned in an air-conditioned cube. And that's why I have no pills on my person right now. That's why I can't even enjoy the comfort of holding a dissolving Xanax in my clammy paw. That's why I'm sweating and quivering and biting myself in the back room of a dog trinket shop, sending particulate farts and pheromones and huge gusts of electromagnetic energy out into the atmosphere where madmen lurk, flicking their snake tongues and twitching their ant antennae.

"Gotcha," screams the madman, who has swished aside the paisley drape, and whose look of triumph is so childish I feel sorry for him. It was only a matter of time before the bastard sniffed me out.

"Shit," screams my wife. My wife has reached a certain point. It's a state she enters when our arguments become so fierce that, as she describes it, she feels she could levitate from the sheer force of her anger. She has stood up, and though she clutches the little mound of her belly defensively, her green eyes are throwing off sparks. Her soft pink mouth looks like it could spit venom. My only thought is: *Thank God this is not directed at me.* I'm actually smirking at the nutcase, who's now backing away from my wife, now colliding with some codependent poodle fanatic, now knocking over a display of doggy sunglasses on his way out.

"We are going to see the fucking emus," says my wife.

"Fine," I say. "We can have our little frolic with those disgusting birds, but this is an adventure that requires Xanax."

"Did you forget to take your medication this morning?"

"I don't know."

"You don't know?"

I don't answer her. We're walking down the sidewalk with Brutus. Tiff begged us to take the poor thing to the land trust and the little freak is so spastic it keeps tangling its Bambi legs in the leash I'm holding.

"Let me do it," says my wife. "You can't even walk a dog."

The second my wife takes the leash the dog calms down, trotting along like a circus grunt. My wife smirks. Her sleeveless dress is crisp and yellow and her legs are long and brown. Her sunglasses, a gift from her parents, cost fifty dollars. The creased white skin on the back of my neck is getting that sunburn tingle, all because the ozone's shot to hell and I refuse to wear sunscreen, even though my wife begs me to wear sunscreen, perhaps *because* she begs me to wear sunscreen (I'm not really sure what my motivation is), but we are home, at last, and I may toss a festive bouquet of pills into my mouth and add a hat to my ensemble.

My wife ties the dog, unlocks our front door, and heads for the pisser. I stumble around in the dark chill of our duplex, bewildered by the light gushing from every window as though stage managers have strategized to illuminate our squalor. This morning we were in the process of transforming my computer lair into a nursery when my wife said she had to have a muffin. This muffin run turned into an idyll with the emus, then into an escapade with a stalker, and now I'm facing the rude prospect of post-emu exhaustion followed by an endless evening of furniture moving at the beck and call of a pregnant goddess. I swallow a fistful of pills and slip out back for a smoke.

I gaze upon my landlord's kingdom of junk. My landlord is a millionaire slumlord who can't stop himself from amassing junk, which he stuffs into various sheds and garages that belong to his many ramshackle properties. The shed affixed to our duplex is crammed with rusty lawn furniture and battered mannequins. In keeping with the major theme of my life, our landlord himself is a freak. When we first met him he seemed like a normal guy. He had a background in veterinary research, he said. And we thought: *ah, a gentle lover of animals.* Turns out he made his bundle by patenting a method for infecting lab rats with human gonorrhea. And he collects junk. He also likes to build crappy sheds and workshops and add strange architectural additions to his existing properties. For example, on top of the dilapidated garage of a neighboring yard, he has built a rustic log cabin. Sometimes he hangs out up there on the deck, pretending he's in the mountains. Sure enough, he's up there right now, donning his navy dress uniform, smoking his antique pipe, and, it suddenly registers, saluting me. I salute him back and notice that someone's rustling through the shrubbery next to our own beloved shed. A bandannaed head pops up from a bush. In keeping with the algorithm of my day, I recognize the man as none other than my homeless doppelgänger.

You see, my wife and I have a doppelgänger couple that we see all over Atlanta, in the most unlikely places. This doppelgänger couple, we have joked with twitchy smiles, represents what we'd be if we sank to a state of homelessness and drug addiction. They've become an allegorical force in our lives. Their presence *always* signifies discord, and *may or may not* (depending on how paranoid we're feeling) portend disaster (my burst appendix, for example; my wife's miscarriage; my father's diabetes, etc., etc.).

The man's a wheezy hypertensive creature with facial boils and a mangy beard. The woman's a frog-eyed sinewy thing with a yellow wolf leer. Their voices are cracked from nonstop arguing. They stumble through life in a drunken haze. Nevertheless, we somehow get the sense that they were once a normal couple, working normal jobs, living in normal apartments. I've never seen them this close to my house. My heart is sputtering. And now my landlord is walking toward me, across a junk-jumbled lawn dotted with bird shrieks, grinning and holding a digital camera in his hands.

"Will you take my picture?" he asks.

"Uh, OK, why?"

"I've got to post something on my college reunion's Web site."

He hands me the camera. My landlord, pinching what looks like a tiny capsule between two fingers, poses in full military regalia, rather pompously, in front of a stunted dogwood tree. The capsule, he informs me, is his invention, the insert scientists use to infect lab rats with human gonorrhea. I'm feeling too nervous to ask about where the thing is inserted. As I snap pictures, my eyes keep straying to the shadow-shrouded shrubbery where my evil double lurks, and none of the pictures satisfies my landlord.

"Harry," he screams, "come 'ere for a minute."

My doppelgänger's head appears again, and then the uncomfortable bulk of his sweaty body lurches into the open air. He's entering the field of my official yard. He, too, is wearing khakis (albeit a filthy pair). His fat torso is stuffed into a tattered polo that looks exactly like something I threw out. He's tubby in the exact same spots that I tend to gain weight whenever I quit exercising and allow myself to lapse into despairing sloth. His consort, looking like a postnuclear-disaster version of my wife, follows.

"Yeah?" says my double, casting me a knowing smirk.

"Know how to work a digital camera?" asks my landlord.

"No."

As my landlord conducts a crash course on digital photography, my wife bounds from the back door, the picture of spring beauty, freshened up for our jaunt and sporting a fetching green tent dress. When she sees our evil twins she actually shrieks and retreats to the safety of our kitchenette. The screen door slams. She stares at the freaks through the metal mesh, no doubt blaming me for luring them. The wolf lady is grinning at her, inching closer and closer to the door, where she will grab my wife in her bruised arms, and they will meld into one person and then teleport to a very sad parallel universe. This parallel universe feels closer than I can bear.

"We've got to go," I shout. I'm about to back into our apartment when our doppelgängers finally return to the shrubbery from whence they came.

"What the hell are they doing here?" I hiss in my landlord's face.

"They're doing some odd jobs for me, so I told them they could keep a cooler for food behind the shed. You know, lunch meat and bread."

"Behind *our* shed?"

"Well, technically it's my shed. What's the problem? Do you know them?"

"Definitely not. We don't know them at all. I've never seen them until today, but I'm not sure it's safe to have people like that . . . lurking around."

"People like what? They're just down on their luck. They both used to teach school, you know. Try to put yourself in their place."

24

After uttering these ominous words, my landlord walks away, thumbing his camera to flip through his glamour shots.

In the kitchen my wife is crouched down on the warped linoleum, sucking on an unlit cigarette and whimpering. Even though I'm the evil magnet that draws darkness and chaos from their hidden places, into the light of her life, I'm the father of the child inside her. I'm the human she's put all her energy into fixing for the past seven years. Our bodies fuse in a convulsive hug. We shiver and nuzzle in the afternoon's evil vibe. When my wife starts scraping a scab of spaghetti sauce from the floor with her fingernail, I know the crisis has passed. I kiss her soft brown hair.

"I guess we're not going to the land trust now," I venture.

"We will have a wonderful day, you motherfucker," she says.

Hell-bent on a picnic, my wife's in the food co-op gathering high-dollar grub. She's convinced that having a wonderful afternoon is the only way to counteract the evil sorcery of our morning, and only a full-fledged picnic will appease her. I'm waiting outside, sitting on a bench, holding Brutus's leash and enduring his invasive sniffing. He wants to plunge his sharp snout into the musky paradise of my groin, but I'm uncomfortable with this level of intimacy. Whereas my wife has a calming effect on him, he's a total spaz around me.

I'm gritting my teeth and smiling and watching the door for my wife when a woman emerges, eating raw seaweed straight from the package, struggling to chew the tough stuff. She's wearing an acid-washed denim jumpsuit with puffy black Reeboks. Her hair is this curly wasp nest out of which random clumps appear to have been cut. She's about to mosey on down the sidewalk when she picks up my vibrations and jerks her head around to get a good look at me. She staggers over with a cracked smile on her face.

"What kinda dog is *that*?" She kneels down to handle the unbelievably willowy Brutus.

"A miniature Italian greyhound," I say, careful not to make eye contact, searching the horizon for something to fix my powerful laser gaze on, lest this freak receive my beams and ignite.

"I want to breed him," she says, rubbing the dog's back. Brutus does not like her. He's sniffing and whimpering and skittering about.

25

"Do you have a dog?" I fasten my eyes on a mysterious smoke-belching pipe that protrudes from the roof of a distant coffee shop. A group of pigeons takes to the air and speckles us with shadows.

"*I* want to breed *with* him," she snaps.

I think I know what she means, but I dare not acknowledge it.

"He's been fixed," I say. "He's no longer, um, breedable."

"Like hell he has!" she screams, directing all her fury and disappointment with life at me.

I stand up and simply walk away. Brutus shoots ahead of me, collars himself, and yelps.

My wife strolls out of the co-op, excited about organic goat cheese encrusted with raspberries, and I'm mumbling prayers under my breath. She's wearing a frilly dress and holding an actual picnic basket, another gift from her parents. Her parents' gifts always seem to suggest that we live a life of endless leisure, and this old-fashioned picnic basket, straight out of a European fairy tale, mocks me.

"Come on." I take my wife's arm and tug her away from my latest fan.

"I want that dog," screams the crazy woman, laughing, and, thank God, walking the other way, down the hill toward a dark industrial area from which, on certain days, the smell of a poultry-processing plant blows into our sunny neighborhood. My wife turns to look.

"Who's that?"

"I don't know. Some lady."

"Did you talk to her?"

"No. She likes Brutus. He's cute. Let's go."

I take the picnic basket and hand my wife the dog leash. We stroll along in the perfumed air, a happy young couple enjoying the stunning day.

At the land trust, amid neurotic dogs and yelling children and Frisbee-throwing trustafarians, I slump in a dark electromagnetic funk. I scan the horizon. I toss olives and panini and dirty balls of brie into my mouth. My wife's looking self-satisfied and well fed, sprawled in the sun, her lips slack with a lazy smile. We've had an hour of normality and she's gloating. She's the intuitive know-it-all who understands how to banish the darkness from our life. Magic and light emanate from her sun-kissed limbs.

"I want a dog," she says, "once the baby gets old enough." She's watching a blond imp torture a cocker spaniel with a stick.

I don't say anything. It seems like every apartment in our neighborhood contains at least one restless, pacing canine, and I don't want to add to the misery. I don't want some imprisoned, sycophantic wolf becoming obsessed with my every move.

"Neither a master nor a slave be," I pronounce, sarcastically yet pompously, and my wife rolls her eyes.

"Why can't you just relax and be normal?"

"Most master-pet relationships are complex codependencies, hardly what you'd call normal."

"Only somebody like you would *see* it that way."

"That boy over there. Look. Did you happen to notice that he's actually trying to insert that stick into that dog's nostril? And the dog's getting annoyed."

"He doesn't know what he's doing. They're just having fun."

"He knows *exactly* what he's doing. And yes, *he's* having fun, but the dog's getting worried, look. Young children torture animals all the time."

"That's a horrible thing to say."

"Well, it's true. You have to train the little savages not to do shit like that."

My wife's mouth flies open but no words emerge. She pops in an olive, closes her lips, and chews furiously.

"We will have a nice picnic," she says, "despite your subversive instincts."

I describe reality and that's subversive. Does she want me to talk about how pretty the Japanese magnolias are?

"The Japanese magnolias are beautiful," I say.

"They are beautiful. If we ever manage to buy a house"—do I detect a flicker of contempt in her glance?—"I'd like to have a big Japanese magnolia in our backyard."

"That would be lovely, assuming that the small, shady yard of our three-hundred-thousand-dollar ghetto shack will get enough sun."

"You can't even let me have a fantasy?"

"We're having your fantasy picnic right now, aren't we? And I was just joking."

"Us buying a house is definitely a joke."

My wife fixes herself a gourmet sandwich and turns away to commune with Brutus while she eats it. He's staring hard at the sandwich, a sly glint in his eye, growling with lust. That's when I notice that no more than ten yards from our plaid, plastic-bottomed picnic blanket (another gift from the in-laws), our doppelgängers are enjoying a romantic outdoor lunch of their own: what appears to be a bag of Sunbeam, a pack of baloney, and two tallboys in paper sacks. The woman, just like my wife, is sitting Indian style. The man, just like me, is lolling on his side.

I'm out of touch with myself. I don't understand where the moods I slip into come from. Deep in the compressed suboceanic freak show of my being, bioluminescent tentacles squirm. I'm smiling. I'm tugging my wife's shirt hem. I'm pointing out our doppelgängers. I'm raising my eyebrows and shrugging my shoulders and watching my wife's face grow fierce. She clutches her stomach and I feel like a shitbag. My next urge is to strangle our evil shadow couple and steal their tallboys, because I'm in dire need of a drink.

"Let's go check out those emus," I say, quietly and solemnly, and I'm sincere. There's nothing I'd like more than to take my wife's soft, manicured hand and guide her down the gravel trail to the pond where the emus dwell. She stands up, wipes the crumbs from her butt, and packs our gear with astonishing efficiency. She frees Brutus from his tree and hands me the leash, which symbolizes the second chance she's giving me. I'm grateful. I will not let her down. I will walk a dog in the sunlight with a mindless smile of contentment on my face.

Brutus hustles along, turning back to eye me every ten seconds.

"Look, butterflies," my wife crows, pointing at the confetti of yellow insects that suddenly floats in the air just when the pond starts to stink. I smell fish slime and dark aquatic flowers. A delicate robot lands on my arm, inserts a microscopic needle, takes a slurp of my blood, and darts off into the humid muck. Life, with its blossoms and fangs, has come back to the land. Plants are thriving, fat with green. Pregnant rodents scheme in their musky holes.

"How would you feel about butterflies if they stung you?" I say.

"They don't sting you."

"But *if* they did."

"They don't."

"I'm just saying."

"I know exactly what you're driving at, mister."

We're bickering about butterflies. We've mated, and our love has become flesh, and we're bickering about butterflies as we wait for our child to grow. We bicker with restraint. We don't raise our voices. We're almost whispering. Though I'd like to yell, I don't. And when, behind us, some couple explodes into loud, jangling discord—fierce, fucked up, and primal—I feel that my secret passions have been given a voice. We look back and find our shadow couple hobbling down the trail behind us, swigging from tallboys and screaming at each other. My double's face is pink as ham. His sweetheart is all teeth.

"Just ignore them," says my wife. And we stroll down into the swampy realm of the emus. Emus naturally live in flocks, but these two have been isolated, trapped in a hippie paradise, just the two of them milling among cattails. Wisteria chokes the treetops, dangling its purple. And someone has planted canna lilies along the bank.

"Cute birds," says my wife.

Brutus's giving them the look over, the sniff test, and he doesn't like what he picks up. He's barking. He's quivering.

The emus are not cute—with their shaggy brown torsos, their snake necks, their greasy prehistoric heads tufted with black frizz. Their smirking pterodactyl beaks and piercing eyes bother me. But seeing my wife's girlish love for the big birds softens my mood. Our doppelgängers have shut up, are creeping up on us to get a closer look at this marvel of nature. And a whole group of people is shambling down the path behind them, young people with skittish gaits, kids escorted by some kind of official uniformed personnel.

"Did you know that the male sits on the eggs and then watches the chicks when they hatch?" my wife informs me. Her smile puts such faith in my paternal gentleness that I'm overcome with affection for the being marinating in her belly's mysterious hormonal brew. I put my arm around her. The doppelgänger couple is walking our way, but I will protect her. Danger and filth and failure and despair are walking our way, but I will conquer them. A fireball rolls up my spine and explodes in my head. My face burns. Around a clump of yellow forsythia what appears to be a group of mentally ill teenagers comes scampering. Touched by the delicious spring weather, they dance and shriek and run: girls and boys with wild eyes and hyperbolic smiles; girls and boys with unkempt hair and drug-addled bodies; neglected and damaged girls and boys; girls and boys at the cusp of manias that will, when they're finally back in the antiseptic chill of their air-conditioned cells, plunge to terrifying depths. I can see nurses, in the distance, dealing with the more difficult among them.

A pale girl with mad-princess hair shrieks and giggles and points at me. A boy with a flaccid Mohawk and innumerable arm scabs screams, "There he is, I told you; what did I tell you? Can you fucking believe this?" He's gesturing toward me and slapping himself on the head.

29

Now all the wild children are pointing at me and high-fiving each other. They're crowding in on us with their hysterical hormone levels ignited by insanity and spring. And our drunk doppelgängers are lurking on the other side of us, grinning as though in on the joke. My wife is trying to escape the madness, but there's nowhere to go but down, into the habitat of the emus.

The birds are flapping their stunted wings. Their serpent necks writhe and whip. And now these strange reptilian creatures, these bumbling feathery primitives from the dawn of time, are booming their inflatable neck sacs, charging the placid air with dark, contagious percussion, something my gentle scholarly wife has read about in her bird book but has never heard them do, until now.

The Society for the Veneration of Bernard Madoff

Rick Moody

1.   THIS FIRST ITEM in our display is an example of the celebrated genre known as the *trading-floor photograph*. Our protagonist stands in the foreground, right hand oddly concealed beneath left, bringing to mind the passage from Matthew 6:3: "But when thou doest alms, let not thy left hand know what thy right hand doeth." The left hand, perhaps, is the hand in which Madoff giveth, while the right hand, which, in the photograph, could conceivably be massaging a rather private area of the Madoff physique, is the hand *which taketh away*, verily, which *plundereth* from the citizens of New York and Miami Beach. His lower half is cut off, cropped, but his dark tie, fit for a mortuary director, is here for us to interpret, and the fluorescent illumination in the room renders a pale shirt almost purple, though purple is, as you all know, *the hue of the unmasculine*. Madoff's expression in this photo has been much remarked on, as have his photographic expressions generally. Here we find the *slot mouth*, derivative of former president Bill Clinton's funereal mien, in which lips are lightly *insucked*. Madoff's *slot mouth* gives like amounts, which is to say nothing at all. His nose, large and noble, if severe, also tells us nothing. But what of the eyes? Are not these eyes the amphitheater of the soul? We may assume, since we are in the business of the veneration of false idols, that there *is* a soul in there somewhere, and that this soul of Madoff, this sociopathic soul, is tortured, anguished, doomed to numerous counts of eternal damnation. Do the eyes betray this torment? On the contrary, Madoff has the eyes of a little boy, at once wounded, desirous of approval, and slightly skeptical. Withal, the expression of Madoff in the *trading-floor photograph* admits *I can crush you like a bug* at the same time it offers *Please allow me to invest your hard-earned savings, but do not ask me for the particulars of my investment strategy.* Again the double trust, the inconclusiveness of Madoff, so bracing, and not unlike the action of capital itself. As we move further on in the second year of the Society for the Veneration of Bernard Madoff, I expect that I will be polling

to see if we have enough interested parties for a lecture series, perhaps downloadable as podcasts, *on the action of capital itself*, and the ways in which Madoff, by perpetrating fraud on such a basis, creates a new opportunity for those who would critique the supplementarity and artifice of the American hedge fund and its apologists. A question for further study might be: *If a client in Madoff's fund is able to cash in on a portion of his earnings so as to pay for the education of a child, is it possible that this education, once it is clear that the funds advertised did not in truth "exist," is invalid?*

As for the trading desk depicted *behind* Madoff in this photograph, which is among the first photos that I encountered when I began spontaneously collecting materials relating to Madoff, what leitmotifs do we there encounter? And what can we say about the empire as depicted in the distance of this image? Of course, it is true that the *trading-floor photograph* is among the important lexical units of fiduciary mendacity, and in the case of the Enron Corporation, e.g., the ruse of the photo will be expanded to include *trading-floor video footage*, or even *tours of the trading floor*, the latter complete with employees shouting down the phones about the electrical supply in the state of California, and so on, but Madoff must have felt that a still photo of the trading floor in his offices was *essential* to the amassing of fictions at the heart of his operation, and if he did not handpick the photographer and carefully control the circumstances of this photograph, I would be awfully surprised. For this exegete, however, it is important to speak to the *books* in the image. They are rearmost in the flattened pictographic space, just to the left of the venerable Madoff's head (and I have not described his hair, as yet, though there is so much to say about his hair, entire treatises could be devoted to the hair of Bernard Madoff). His books. This chamber in which the ostensible trades took place—which might, instead, have been a room in which imaginary monthly statements were spit out of computers, or a room in which actual trades were taking place to *disguise* the absence of other trades, in either case a *simulated* space layering over a fraudulent space—this room was, let's say, forty by forty. In the rear of the image, as I say, farthest from the venerable Madoff himself, there is a shelf of books, and it would be possible that what resemble books at this remove are in fact just empty ring binders, or, worse, are books detailing regulations adopted by the Securities and Exchange Commission, which Madoff was short-listed *to govern* at one point, and we can only wish that he *had* governed that stuffed shirt of a government agency, because then we might have seen it for what it is, a figment of governmental regulation of the financial industry, a dream of what government might still be, in a moment in which banks and other dealers in exotic financial instruments are adrift, like subatomics, in a murky sea of unregulated corporate endeavor. At any rate, let's say the books *are* in fact *books*, then what kinds of books are they? Clearly there are some *red* books there, and what would it mean for there to be *red books* on the shelves situated on the fraudulent trading floor of Madoff's enterprises? I would like to submit to the Society for the Veneration of Bernard Madoff that until I am told otherwise, these books, both the red ones and the ones to the left of the red ones, which just might be *green* ones, I would like to submit that these are titles in the Loeb Classical Library, so familiar to all of us who read the classics in robust translations when sent away to school at an early age. I want to invite members of the society who are gifted with online sleuthing and digital enhancement to go out and take a close look at these photos and see if those books are in fact translations of Plato or Seneca or Aristotle, such that we might observe that a *classical education*, even when you are born and bred on the mean streets of New York City, must undergird your mendacity. A classical education makes fraudulence more elegant, more spectacular.

There are seven men in the photograph, each of them with dark hair, and there are no women and no children. The interior space of the *trading-floor photograph*, the pit, as it is sometimes called, is a place that is without women and children, though Madoff's children, as they came of age, did become part of his professional family (fraud is passed down along the patriarchal line); however, let us posit that none of these people on the fictitious trading floor are actually Madoff progeny, but are, rather, other employees pressed into service for the purposes of documenation. Does the existence of the photograph not indicate that a feral and cutthroat maneuvering for position in the photograph must have broken out among employees of the honorable Madoff? And how did he officiate among the persons who wished to be nearest to him in the photograph? Were there hazing rituals, including nude wrestling and self-inflicted brandings or maulings new employees suffered in order to indicate a serious need to appear nearest to the excellence of Bernard Madoff? As our society has observed at various moments, it is impossible to imagine the depravity that needed to coexist with comity and rectitude in order to permit the ship of Madoff to remain seaworthy through its manifold shoals. Many of these men have receding hairlines, and you would think they had the resources to procure topical treatments for a male-pattern baldness, *or perhaps they could have purchased a rug*, to use common parlance, such that these traders might appear more presentable, that is unless Madoff preferred that they did *not* get treatment for their thinning locks, and I will note that I myself have allowed my hair to thin considerably, in an effort to venerate Madoff more perfectly and to understand his example, which is to say the American example, the example in which will and domination lead to vulnerability and failure and imprisonment, and that's not all: The last thing I would like to say about this photograph is that it seems to me that some of the traders in the image are almost certainly playing *online solitaire*. Why is it that I cannot look at this photograph without being convinced that there are people playing *online solitaire*? And the telephone handset that is off the hook just out of reach by Madoff himself? With this telephone Madoff must be calling someone to ask what can be done about the fact that the men of his trading desk are all playing *online solitaire*, would it not be possible, at the very least, Madoff must inquire, to get these men to view some pornography, preferably some of that Brazilian stuff, *Why must I have employees*, Madoff seems to be saying in the photo, *who play online solitaire*, when they should instead be spending their time trumping up monthly statements, or perhaps ordering dinner tonight from one of those very expensive delicatessens, and oh, one other thing, there is so much *light* at the right-hand margin of the image, light, to remind you—all of you who think that this is *just* a story of lying and profligacy—that there *is* the possibility of light. Madoff's offices were not such as to be directly bordering a river, and yet you can tell that those windows are windows of *power*, that power is where the light is, and all of you who, like me, are out in the cold in this oligarchical present, you are often finding yourself held in *exile* from the light, but what the venerable Madoff is telling you (I will make available to you the secrets of Madoff) is that you must make your way *toward the light*. First, conceive of the light, second, know that the light can do for you what you cannot do yourself, third, make your way toward it.

2.   This next is certainly one of my favorite Bernard Madoff images in the pantheon of images that we have assembled here in our gallery, but before I speak to this, I want to remind everyone that I have posted a calendar on which we might arrange some of the potlucks;

I found a really excellent calendar program that makes it easy for groups of persons to plan events, but as yet only a couple of you have signed up and made yourselves available, and in that case neither of you suggested bringing any particular dishes. Certainly, some local favorites should be on the menu, like knishes, or pierogies, or you could also propose other comfort foods that would be welcomed by those among us who have fallen on hard times recently—mac and cheese, pigs in blankets. And if I want to eat steak and frites and to use that kind of food to talk about the peculiar philosophical lessons that are embodied in the career and accomplishments of Bernard Madoff, not a soul is going to tell me to do otherwise, and I'm thinking of course about my wife, who originally felt that it was good that I was interested in *something* when I told her that I had been collecting images of Madoff, cutting them out of various papers (*The New York Post* was particularly helpful in this regard); initially she felt that this was a *net positive* since I had been let go from my position; well, in any event, let's not dwell on my wife, but let's turn instead (while you ponder what you might bring to the potluck) to the photo of Madoff and *his* wife, Ruth, from the charitable dinner, the photo that clearly has a red, white, and blue theme to it, giving this photograph a patriotic veneer, which reminds us that Madoff could have not effected his fine bit of performance art had he not been in these United States where the lust for reliable return is at its most acute; now, it is true that in the latter days of his empire Madoff had felt a need to move abroad and to attempt a globalized solicitation of new capital, but Madoff was raised up in New York City, USA, and during his incarceration he will have plenty of time to think about what it is that makes the United States unique in the area of return on investment. I am betting that during the era in which this photograph was taken, he just didn't have time to think, to philosophize about his station and his accomplishments. Instead, he had to spend his time trying to manipulate the tendrils of his deceits, and as any chronic liar will tell you this is a time-consuming approach to life. Madoff likely had to travel a lot to look after his simulations, and you can see that this fact informs the photograph I am discussing today, because it's clear that Bernard and Ruth, his wife, who apparently smokes Marlboro Lights, are somewhere *in the desert*. I would like to propose that Bernard and Ruth have flown west very briefly, to a land where patriotism still thrives, to think about the recruitment of new clients. While Bernard did give to the *blue party*, as we know, to Democratic candidates, he must have felt that it would also be useful to move in Republican circles, and thus the trip out west, the Libertarian West, where Ruth would be able to smoke without having to inconvenience anyone. She seems to have a small compact in front of her, indicating that keeping up appearances is essential. This is probably why she wanted to keep that one fur coat, too, after the court-appointed functionaries began seizing assets. In this image, she is also wearing a rather large watch, but is it a jewel-encrusted watch—perhaps another of the baubles that Bernard tried to protect from the prying eyes of those who would have laid claim to it? We cannot say. It is a square watch, however, and I will digress here to tell you that I once patronized a psychiatrist who put forth the proposition that all persons wearing square watches were homosexual. I myself have avoided square watches ever since. One wonders, meanwhile, if Ruth Madoff's botox injections were encouraged by her husband, as part of her duty to be the presentable wife, or if it was something she undertook on her own, in order to preserve the semblance of youth. There is also the possibility of a face-lift, if you examine those prominent cheekbones shown here.

How shall we describe Ruth Madoff's smile? She holds her fingers like pincers around some flatware, unclear whether she is about to seize this implement in order to polish off whatever substandard dessert item she is still eating, or whether she intends to throw the knife at the photographer who is immortalizing the moment. Such complexity is also in the nature of the smile. No smile by *any* Madoff, now that the scale of the fraud is clear to us, can serve as a simple act of social grace. All Madoff smiles have many tonal colors to them (which is why Bernard's *slot mouth* is more honest than Ruth's facsimile of affability). Dyed hair, heavily depleted eyebrows, Botox injections, face-lifts, earthy lipstick, and that tan all give the sense of a woman no longer at ease with her late middle age, and this applies to the question of whether Ruth did or did not understand the felonious nature of Madoff's operation. Did Ruth push away the accretions of money and success like the plate on the table that she has shoved toward the middle, which seems to have some residual green grapes thereupon, the better to keep her wine at hand? Was it the wine that sustained Ruth and that sustains her now when Bernard has gone off to the hoosegow? We need not dwell upon her excessive thinness either, since it tells us about how easily Madoff could have crushed his wife, if he'd had a mind to crush her, and this is never a generous thing, crushing one's wife, and perhaps my own wife felt the same sense of discomfort about my own ability to crush her, and that is why she felt that she had to *file separately*, if you know what I mean. I don't want to dwell on these details in this online forum, but I do feel like when we have the potluck we should talk a little about this, about Madoff's marriage and whether it was barren, and that was why he had the long affair with that *other woman* whose funds he theoretically managed, not to mention the inappropriate comments to his female employees that we have been compiling. Because Ruth was somehow shut out? He shut her out of the business, in order that she would know nothing and would be protected from criminal charges? But at the same time did this not make his life with her a sham, or a mere *appearance* of marriage? Anyway, back to the Diet Cokes in the image. Bernard Madoff seems to have not one but two Diet Cokes. No alcohol at all. This is so he wouldn't be tempted to discuss details of his organization while intoxicated. Ruth's generous glass of wine, on the other hand, *does* suggest that she knew nothing.

I have not yet fully explicated the symbolism of the sand dunes in the rear of the shot. Undoubtedly, this is the kind of sand dune that we associate with *golf*, and were I to tackle this subject, the simulation of sand dunes in golf courses, and the fraudulence of golf courses in general, I would probably make some kind of equation between unrepentant wealth and simulation, and the fact that one form that this simulation always takes is *golf*, which is to say that there is a reason that the wealthy now favor this pseudosport with their leisure dollars, erecting exclusive beach clubs and country clubs largely dedicated to keeping the riffraff away, and that is because golf depends on *simulation*, on a kind of landscaping that repels all natural growth and can only be accomplished with metric tons of dangerous weed killer that runs into streams and lakes and causes mutant species of fish. This kind of landscaping brings to mind a very particular historical dynamic. This landscaping calls forth the British Empire and the aristocracy that was part of that empire. No simulation, among the oligarchs of our nation, is as welcome as the kind that promises the complete cultural dominance of the late British aristocracy, and perhaps our venerated Bernard Madoff, in this moment of posing before the sand dunes with his surgically enhanced wife, was trying to promote the notion that he should have a seat in the House of Lords, and I realize that I'm just sketching this out now, but I do have to *take a break* in order to *attempt* to find work, after which I may file for fortnightly unemployment benefits.

37

3.   How lucky are you, the members of the Society for the Veneration of Bernard Madoff, because today we are running a special discount for new associates, through which you can forgo the cost of a yearlong membership. Instead, you can just sign up for $19.99 right now, flat rate, by sending me the number of your credit card, including expiration date, and that little security code thing, and you'll get all the benefits that the more expensive yearlong membership would include, excepting the trading cards signed by Madoff's secretary, which are for premium members. There never was a better time to join the Society for the Veneration of Bernard Madoff than today, because today is the day that Bernard Madoff's residence was first listed with a prestigious Upper East Side real estate broker, all proceeds doubtlessly to be disbursed to those defrauded by Madoff, but that is of no consequence to yours truly, the editor of this site, because I personally need to follow a narrative of intrigues to a spot where it *viscerally moves me*, almost as though there were a carnal, or even prurient swelling that I feel in me, the thrill of taboo and disgust all admixed, and never have I felt such a thing quite as strongly as today when I came upon the set of images of the interior of the Bernard Madoff residence. This apartment does, in fact, beam us to the edge of the known universe (and, for those who do not already know, I locate my server for the Society of the Veneration far out into the wilds of Brooklyn in a rent-stabilized apartment that has plenty of room because my wife is no longer residing at this address with me, which is probably my own fault, and yet I am close enough to see my son at the close of the school day; that is, I occasionally go down to the school, and sometimes I will wait across the street and watch as his mother picks him up; on these days, I don't involve myself directly in the fetching of him, because on these days he is not my *official* responsibility, and I suppose I feel that *unwarranted fetching* would entail some kind of trampling of the visitation agreement, and I don't want to put my son in a predicament that I personally knew well, since my parents were among the first to divorce on our street) and this edge of the known universe is a thrilling thing, especially when one of the images that you can see, among these ten available images of the Madoff interiors (most stripped of personal effects, though it's tantalizing to wonder aloud if Madoff actually lived without the display of effects), is the diagram of the layout of the apartment, which allows you to assemble the photographic evidence into some kind of real estate jigsaw puzzle. Especially as regards the terrace. That is some terrace! It seems to wrap around the

entire apartment! I have to say: The horticulture that can be seen on
the terrace is not especially delightful, and one wonders that the venerable Bernard Madoff was *not* more concerned with being seen out
on the terrace, because, after all, as we know from the gallery of
images here on the site, he did prefer to control the circumstances in
which he was *seen*, wishing only to profit from the possibility of
expanding the client base whenever a camera was available; didn't he
want something more Amazonian, the kind of canopy of rain forest
that would completely prevent residents of nearby buildings from
looking out at the terrace and saying, *There he is! That's Bernard
Madoff! The financier who guarantees his clients fifteen percent
rain or shine! Let's fire a poisonous blow dart into his hide!* But,
no, the plantings are rather ho-hum, of the sort you might see anywhere in the region. Why, if I had the resources myself—and it's possible someday, what with some original Web content that I have in
mind (a site pertaining to Alan Stanford, e.g.)—it's possible that I
might enjoy an apartment such as this, with a terrace on it that
wraps around on the order of 280 degrees, facing in all relevant directions, and since many has been the time that the housing situation
in this city has left me in a position where I was in need, and on one
occasion it was true that I was turned down from renting in a cooperative building because it was not felt that my employment
record was substantial enough to merit the *subtenancy* that was my
wish, I would like to volunteer that when I collect my inevitable
millions and purchase the sort of apartment that the venerable
Madoff once resided in, I will, just as he did, assume the chairman-
ship of the co-op association, and I will make it a living hell for all
such persons as attempt to relocate to our building. I will ask if
they've ever entered a tattoo shop, I will ask if they have ever been
treated for any sexually transmitted diseases, especially herpetic
ones, and let's see, what else, I will ask if they have ever been friendly with any persons who had children with autism or an autism spectrum disorder, because children with these afflictions can disrupt
things in a lobby or foyer with all their yammering. I will ask if these
applicants have autistic children or know any autistic children or
are liable to be visited by any, and I will ask if they have any hearing
loss, because hearing loss encourages people to play their televisions
and radios at alarmingly loud levels, and I'll ask if they can have a
testimonial letter composed attesting to the fact that they have
never quarreled and that their marriage has always been devoted and
loving; in particular, perhaps they could have a letter composed

attesting to the fact that the women in the relationships do not experience *fickle moments* but are devoted to the husbands, especially if the husbands for reasons that are not clear cannot seem to establish comfortable professional relationships with other persons. If these testamentary letters can be produced, then perhaps these applicants will be allowed into the building, as long as they are not now or never have been or never will be on television. Television news reporters cause horrible things to happen in front of buildings, and I'm sure I'll have more occasion to talk about that soon, when we post some of the photographs of Mr. Madoff after his surrender to the authorities.

I want to say a few things while I have time about Madoff's office. For example, I need to say that the venerable Bernard Madoff certainly did like representations of livestock. Bulls, for example. There are a great number of bulls in there. Well, perhaps some are horses (racehorses, I should think, based on their physiques), but there is at least one bull. It is certainly a bull. Unless it's a cow. If it is a bull, is it the sort of bull that is meant to be a symbolic representation of the *bull market*? Or is it something altogether more interesting, an expression of masculinity, as indeed are the horses in the windows. Because what do we know about bulls and racehorses (most of them geldings), we know that they are celebrations of phallic potency. Of course I can hear some of you saying out there, and you know who you are, Oh, Phil, *cut the crap*, are you really going to say it's all about *cock*, actually using that word *cock*, because the word *cock* has such a potency itself, and, in fact, not that I want to belabor the point, your updater of bulletins, your recording secretary, does know a few things about the weaknesses of the flesh, the obverse of phallic potency, if you will, and there is no shame in this, there is only shame in persisting in feeling weak, notwithstanding mental acuity, or what have you; in any event, if we were to use the disreputable word *cock*, then we would have to conclude that there is a lot of *cock* in Bernard Madoff's home office, especially in those animal likenesses, those idolatries, and we are reminded, naturally, with all this *cock*, of the Sin of the Golden Calf, wherein, while Moses is off fraternizing with that on-again-off-again Old Testament God, the Israelites need some graven imagery to keep them from becoming too restive while stalled at the outskirts of the promised hectares of milk and honey, and so Aaron fashions his golden calf, which signifies the fetishism of wealth, above all; on this site, our constitutional referenda indicate that we agree that the pursuit of wealth, which is

40

also called *abundance,* is not a sin, or perhaps it is more accurate to say that Bernard Madoff admitted in his statement to the court that he'd made some awful mistakes, and that the pressure of money management was such that he could not perform as well as he liked, and thus was born this guarantee of *unrealizable returns.* The admission of this failing, which was probably composed by his lawyers, this is where we begin to take an interest in Bernard Madoff, though we are interested in his apartment, too. Don't get me wrong. It's often possible for me to get *very* interested in a person's apartment, especially when they have a spiral staircase, and when their office has that much wood paneling, and *bulls,* which certainly are suggestive of the thousand-year reign of *cock.*

And what about that schoonerish naval scene above the mantel? Perhaps we should pause to admire the fireplace itself, but I'm more interested in the schoonerish naval scene, which is a replica of some painting brought in by the realtor after everything was sold and the proceeds salted away with the other funds that will one day be disbursed to injured parties. But let's suppose that Bernard Madoff really did favor this marine imagery. Frankly, I can't believe it. No one loves the sea who does not love the riotous anarchy, the sheer Rabelaisian helter-skelter of shipboard life, and Mr. Madoff couldn't afford to, because he needed to maintain the external simulation of Bernard Madoff, the construct of Bernard Madoff. You know, my father had a yacht when I was young, and I will tell you a story about my father's yacht, which I detested. When my father had the yacht, and I mean the sailing kind, not the big steroidal powerboat kind, he tried to get everyone in the family interested in his yacht, but the problem was that my mother was sorely afraid of the yacht because of how much it heeled when the gales were blowing hard. The thing that made the yacht go was also the thing that made it terrifying, and my mother tried hard to honor my father's love of the yacht, but her heart was not in it. On one occasion when their bond was beginning to fray, my father asked my mother to oversee some cleat or line, I can't remember which, and my sister and I were sitting on the yacht, and my mother failed to observe the chain of command, and my father, in remonstrating with her, referred to her as a "stupid bitch," he actually said, *What is it with you, you stupid bitch,* or some similar remark. I said nothing at the time, because I was acutely aware, as any shipmate ought be, that my father could easily *throw me overboard,* and I would drift out to sea, and in becoming aware of the psychodynamics of the moment, and of my potential as flotsam, some

41

hatred began to smolder in me, never rightly to be extinguished, and though I admire Bernard Madoff, and could easily see founding a religion on him, I also see a painting like that one with the yacht, and for a moment I am filled with disgust.

4.   The famous *hat photo*, which our friend Maurice L. has argued should be air-dropped from the American fighter planes on areas controlled by radical Islamists when the next world conflagration begins, is going to be the last of the *before* photos of Madoff, and then we will move on to the period of martyrdom; as you know, I have been attempting to map Madoff's confession and initial confinement onto the narratives of other great martyrs, such as Socrates or MLK, and the fact that the numbers are so off, that there is no reliable numerical congruence, is just plain irritating. Be that as it may, the *hat photo* is monstrous, is bracing, as anyone will admit, and partly this has to do with the hirsute qualities of Madoff's arm in the photo. I suppose the first thing I ought to do is to describe the hat. It's some kind of paper hat, suggestive of *puritans*, of the sort you could easily get at any store that stocks party favors, and it's *gold*, of course, which suggests yet again the monetary symbolism of all photos having to do with Madoff, and then there is the blue of his attire, some robin's-egg blue slacks that look like they might be poplin, and then a pale blue shirt, and he's reclining on some kind of chaise longue, and the blue, and the reclining posture, and the absence of socks, all frankly describe a Hindu religiosity, as if Madoff is receiving adherents who would beseech of him answers to the abiding questions relating to *Samsāra*, and then there are the flowers behind. I will admit that though I come from a well-to-do family, I never did get any horticultural lessons as a child, but I am almost sure that the flowers behind Madoff, some of which are rather predictable, include those plants such as the *Venus flytrap* that consume insects and other carbon-based life forms. I don't see the corpse flower, or *Amorphophallus titanium*, although it would be gratifying to think that the *hat photo* was somehow taken in front of the corpse flower, and there are more of them blossoming these days, so you never know, but let's say we do instead find the common *Venus flytrap*. If Bernard and Ruth don't have any of these out on the terrace, at least they have them in the apartment, so that they might be displayed at holiday celebrations. Before they are going to settle down to a holiday repast, they release the plant's meal, just a few flies or arachnids,

and then they relax and wait. I'm wondering if in fact we might give away some kind of *Venus flytrap* as a bonus for people registering for the Society for the Veneration of Bernard Madoff, and I know I have already tried kitchen implements, I tried giving away kitchen utensils, which I thought were homely, but also useful, for example, that implement that I believe is called the mandoline with which you could certainly slice off your finger; I happen to possess some extras, because there are certain kinds of kitchen implements that are now mine, because my wife and I separated so quickly that we didn't really take time to divide all the kitchen implements, and before she gets a chance to ask that I return these items I would like to give some of them away to new registrants, and I could make some labels with one of those labeling devices, and I could put your monogram on the kitchen implement, I also have mashers of various kinds, with which you might mash potatoes or yams, and a mortar and pestle. I could send these along, especially since I am mostly eating takeout right now. All of this gear could be available to new registrants out there, just let me know what would make you happiest.

I have commented elsewhere about Madoff's lipless smile, and have wondered if there manifests in Madoff some psychoanalytic obverse to the Angelina Jolie phenomenon, viz, lips as a sign of fertility, and maybe Madoff, with his corpse flower (his *amorphophallus*) and his tiny lips, somehow signifies a masculinity in the absence of proper lips, and maybe the smiling is harder for him since the lips, physically, need to be *pulled back* into a rictus shape, and that display may be too uncomfortable for some people. Has anyone definitively declared this photo to be taken on New Year's Eve? I'm thinking that the image was taken on a New Year's Eve. Though I personally wish it had been taken on Thanksgiving, because then we could refer to the image as having relevance to the national character. New Year's Eve, on the contrary, is an international holiday, and so the hat is some kind of international sign of the turning over of the years, which is disappointing. Perhaps if we could verify that the image was taken at the turn of the *millennium* it would somehow bring about the interpretive zeal that is necessary for this writer to continue, when his own economic circumstances are so dire, but, unfortunately, the image appears to have been taken more recently (by the girlfriend of a close friend of Madoff's, I believe) and on some unimportant off-year New Year's Eve. Let us hope, however, that the thoughtful expression that Madoff appears to be sporting has to do with the fact that he has only hours to go before putting into effect his New Year's resolutions, and because we have mostly agreed to endorse my personal *at-war-with-himself* hypothesis about Madoff's inner struggle, it is likely that he is struggling with contradictory impulses with respect to any upcoming New Year's resolutions: On the one hand, perhaps his New Year's resolution is to plunder Monaco, perhaps he has not yet moved his lieutenants into Monaco, awaiting introductions to the royal family, Grace Kelly's relatives, or a few owners of thoroughbreds and manufacturers of luxury yachts, and he is thinking that the plundering of Monaco will enable him to cover some of the redemptions of earlier clients that he so desperately needs to cover; then at some point in the evening it is likely he must get up from the chaise longue and go to the bathroom where he will spit up a little blood because of the bleeding ulcer that has been troubling him for some time and for which he will not let himself see a doctor, because he imagines that the bleeding ulcer keeps him *honest*. He hasn't even told Ruth about it yet. The bitterness of bloody stomach acid tastes like *paradox*, and perhaps, just after the photo is taken, he also imagines that he could go ahead and alert the feckless husband of his niece, the SEC kid who in the past he successfully persuaded to kill any investigation into his operations, he could alert the lackluster and federally employed husband to the fact that it has all been a *sham*, because *sham* is always a powerful, energized word to use in a New Year's resolution, and, by the way, in the rear of the image, on an occasional table beside the great money manager is, I believe, a small disposable camera, so that the camera taking a picture of Madoff is also taking a picture of *another camera*, and this would imply a circularity of gazes in effect, in which Madoff, despite his legendary taciturnity and his reclusive desire to avoid appearing in public, is in danger of being trapped in a systematized circularity of gazes, as when one is prey to a lynch mob of photographers, so that this image, unlike many others, though very private, and less composed than the Madoff we know from many images in our gallery, this one *does prefigure the arrest*, and if we look at the image this way it's also possible to imagine that Madoff *knew the day was coming*, and his impassive demeanor is not unlike Christ's at Gethsemane.

Obviously, I'm putting my heart and soul into these posts, and I can only think that none of you is replying to what I'm posting here because you fear the prying eyes of those who would condemn you for finding common cause with my obsession. Can there really be no one out there who has found fit to post for a week, and I'm not talking about the posts I had to delete because they amounted to libelous statements about myself, who, as I have repeatedly said, had no dealings with the Madoff family at any time, nor contributed to any of its subsidiaries or feeder funds; yes, I have traded privately online now and again, and I can tell you that I have not had very good results, I have lost some real money. You know, you should never invest more than you can afford to lose in a rough-and-tumble market. My personal feeling is that one of the things that really sets me apart from other commentators in the business sector is that I am not agitating for an instantaneous uptick on my trades. I feel like it's fine to wait ten years for a stock that's lost eighty percent of its value to come back. I like waiting. I have found myself in a waiting posture many times in life, imagining that the golden ring I did not manage to secure, that golden ring of opportunity that others got without breaking a sweat, would one day be mine, whether it was love, money, health insurance, my very own automobile. So I don't mind wading through libelous remarks and deleting them, and I don't mind if there are periods when many people are busy and are unable to post, not really. Maybe it's the holidays and that means that people have other business.

5.   Can you not hear the ducks quacking faintly on the pond? Do they not now chortle and scrape as though a dire storm brews in the East? Are not the foghorns faintly tolling? Is there not a pause in the urban traffic? On East Sixty-fourth Street? Is there not a collective inbreathing of anxiety as the inevitable transpires? I can hear around me the faint sounds of organ music from a distant parish, funereal dirges that indicate that the eulogy must commence. For months now we here at the society have watched the desperate gyrations of the stock market, and we have heard of fortunes lost and economies in free fall, and we have heard, over all of this, some stately song of the heavens that indicates that there is pity and sympathy in the world even as the very worst transpires. By which I mean: In the opera of the life of Bernard Madoff we come now to the part of the story in which we find him alone on the terrace of East Sixty-fourth Street, coolly placing his last calls trying to make the new deals in Brazil and Indonesia, trying to place calls to the Burmese junta asking for their business, the Russian oligarchs, and what I would give to hear some of these conversations. He has lived with the inevitability of discovery for so long, and yet he has always

slipped the noose. This time he will not slip it. From the terrace, Madoff again repairs to his bedchamber to sleep but finds himself unable to rest. What a moment! I come back to this moment again and again, as if it's my own life. I'll be doing something humdrum and routine. For example, I will be fetching my medication from the pharmacy up the street, where they are in the habit of trying to prevent me from fulfilling my prescription because of a lack of appropriate health coverage, and while I am undertaking this rather mundane activity, I'm thinking of the night in which Madoff realizes that he has come to the end of the line. Perhaps I'm often thinking of this moment because I have not lived a life of consequence. I have Googled my high-school classmates and therefore I know. The days in which I go to the pharmacy or I go to the grocery store, and so on, these are the days on which *the most happens*, simple events, encounters, meetings with unremarkable people, and while I don't wish to be arrested and carted off by federal authorities, as is about to take place for Madoff in our reconstructed story, the mug shot, the first mug shot that was to be released, *does* indicate that Madoff lived (and I'm using the past tense just because we know he hasn't much of a life now—as I understand it he shares his cell with a convicted drug offender, and may recently have been given a *beat down* by fellow prisoners) *grandly*, even if it was at the expense of many other people, at the expense of their hard-earned savings. Though, in fact, when is *profit* not at the expense of others? I'm just throwing this question out there.

Nature abhors Bernard Madoff, but it also feels pity for his suffering, and for the suffering of other sociopaths. The night is long. In this night there is time for reflection. And since none of the telephone calls Madoff has placed have produced the hundreds of millions, if not billions, he needs to cover redemptions, he recognizes that the first thing he will have to do in the morning is to speak to his sons. He will, we know now, tell his sons that he wants to pay the in-house bonuses *now*, rather than in the first month of 2009, as had previously been the habit, and this conversation will set into motion the gruesome course of events. Does he have breakfast on this morning? Which of the blessings of great wealth and power—hot milk with his coffee, fresh salmon served by a domestic aide, a massage before work—will he forgo, as he prepares for what is to come today? Does he start by telling Ruth to stash her jewelry? Does he try to clean, assemble, and load a pistol in his office? The morning hours tick by in Madoff's penthouse. He tells Ruth, when she pads by the office in a dressing gown that *it's true—he hasn't been himself lately*. Does he say Kaddish, does he read *The Tibetan Book of the Dead*, which has occasionally pleased me when I have considered the un-varying consistency of my own difficulties? After checking the for-eign markets on television, or perhaps watching a bit of CNBC, he knows he has no choice, there is a car waiting for him—it is the last time he will pay for his own car service—and he goes and gets into the Town Car, and heads for *the lipstick building*, and then a great void comes and swallows up our story, and this void may begin, per-haps, as a glimmering of nothingness at the extreme margins of our field of vision, as in the tunnel vision of those having been bitten by the black mamba, and the periphery, in which our story is produced, this periphery falls away, and we no longer see Madoff in relation to his clients, we no longer see the breadth of his deceit with respect to particular clients, and instead we see the world closing in and then violently stripping the layers of his fiction from him, and Madoff can hear himself telling his sons that it was *one big lie*—though it has often occurred to me that his empire can better be described as a great conglomeration of tiny fractal-style lies, not *one big lie*—and that he will turn himself in to the authorities (as soon as he pays the bonuses), but we can't hear this discussion clearly, despite the fact that this meeting of the generations will be described over and over in court documents and in accounts in the newspaper, but it will be difficult for us here at the society to possess this moment for our own, though we can intuit the darkness coming to spread its wings, and we can see how the darkness is like a lover. How sustaining are its caresses. We can delight in giving ourselves over to this darkness of the amorous. Just as we are ready to lie down with the truth, the federal agents arrive.

Is there an *innocent explanation* now, I ask you, before addressing the mug shot, which is today's featured photograph, the last in the series, and about which I know there has been a lot of speculation. I ask you: What is an *innocent explanation*, is it not oxymoronic? Once the splintering that assails credibility has taken place, the fer-vor of an unrepentant Madoff can never be gathered in again.

And so the special agents descend on his house, and they seize this and they seize that, and the news begins to rear up, and to spread, and soon the investors, the many thousands of investors, are beginning to become aware of *all that is lost*, and though the darkness that precedes calamity is blissful, it must in the end be followed by the arc lamps, and as Madoff is carted off to a holding cell, and the mug shot is snapped, the investors begin to see *the way of the world*. Madoff is deprived of his tie, in booking, because they are worried that he will hang himself with it, and maybe they have taken his belt, too, but we cannot know this in the photograph. Many of you have spoken of the gray backdrop in the mug shot. I keep thinking Avedon, Avedon, by which I mean of course the celebrated fashion photographer who inclined toward a white backdrop for his photographs. Madoff avoided being photographed, generally, but naturally I have been busy trying to learn whether there was ever any attempt to photograph him by the legendary artist. The gray here is a disconsolate variation on Avedon's white, and it represents the intrusion of the authorities, and what the authorities are doing, of course (as they did in my own case, when they restrained me from having unsupervised visitation with my son), is extinguishing the flame of liberty.

6.   Everyone knows of the tabloid photos of Madoff—when he attempts to go out into the crowds, after his arrest. Everyone knows of the bizarre, and admirable, attempt to smile with all these no-account jackals circling around him. Occasionally, in some of the television footage, he also attempts to batter the photographers. Sometimes while smiling ludicrously. The society deplores the rush to judgment, though it also welcomes throwing the book at Madoff. His jacket, in these street-level photos, is something like a quilt as you might remember it from the seventies, the big plush covering that makes it possible that no night is ever again cold. These tabloid photos have no background, because where there ought to be a background there are instead photographers *walling you in* wherever you look, so that the cameras *are* the subject, as much as Madoff is himself. He's a *dog*, the photographers say, *how can he be human*, he's a worm, *he's a snake*, he's a shark, he's a curiosity, he's not human, the photographers say, and what's of interest is that the people around him *thought* he was a human being but subsequently his nonhuman-mammalian status became clear, and that's why the photographers become interested, because he *looks* so much like a human, but evidently he's not, and that's why these images depress me horribly, and what with the fact that I am unemployed, and am divorced, and have been spending a lot of time alone or online, I just don't have the time to look at photographs that are going to depress me horribly. I need to be looking into some of the software that others use for social networks. I think it might be nice if we had a

social networking possibility here on the site, so that when people wanted to get in touch with one another, it would be easier for them to instant-message. Or maybe there should be some kind of automatic notification when other Madoff-informed people list interests similar to your own. Perhaps some persons interested in Bernard Madoff, like myself, are also interested in Egyptian antiquities or astrophysics. You could have a profile on our site, and a photo, and you could quote your favorite line from Bernard Madoff. We haven't really talked much about the possibility of romance among members of our society, but it would be wise to prepare.

Anyway, I say this because I find these last photos too depressing, and I would rather speak of something else. And so now the tale of Madoff draws near to its terminus. When we get on the bus, freshly spattered with snow and mud from some taxi that has driven gleefully into the puddles nearest us, we are Madoff; when we are being treated for our bleeding hemorrhoids, we are Madoff; when we have delirium tremens, we are Madoff; when we pad our résumé, we are Madoff; when we keep the ten that the cashier overchanged us, we are Madoff; when we lean out the car window, swollen with drink, and puke out our insides on the side of our friend's brand-new vehicle, we are Madoff; when we attempt to stem the professional advancement of others in order to secure our own, we are Madoff; and when we have lost everything, job, house, wife, child, we are Madoff; and when we dream of having it all, when *all* does not just refer to some reasonable but greedy portfolio of items, a second house, a third house, but to *everything*, entire countries, diamond mines, arms-smuggling operations, oil tankers, stars and galaxies, when we want it *all* in this way, we are Madoff. But that's easy, it's easy to see how when we are villainous we are living close to the ideal of Bernard Madoff, and often I have told myself, in my deprivation, that I am Madoff, that I could have done a better job at being Madoff than Madoff himself, but what about when I am good and kind and reasonable? Is it impossible now to see that we are all Madoff, even when we are helping the proverbial blind woman across the street? Are you so certain we are not Bernard Madoff then? When we try to insure that our children have money for college education? When we volunteer? Madoff volunteered, you know, he volunteered his time and money for many charities, and while it is true that he defrauded most of them, that doesn't mean he didn't believe in their mission. Here's the thing, I defy you to say of Madoff that he was incapable of human feeling at all times and in all places; I think it's more likely that he compartmentalized the lying, sociopathic part of himself from the part that actually did, for example, *appreciate children*, and when we make him into the sociopath, and forget, for example, that wherever he is now he is a miserable wretch (with broken ribs), and that in suffering we are all most conventionally human, then we forget our own capacity for good, and in delighting in his condemnation, we assume in ourselves the reluctance to sympathize that is *characteristic of the sociopath*, and I'm thinking back, for example, to the kinds of things that my wife's lawyer said about me during the divorce, and I really don't believe those things, and I can't forget, for example, watching this brisk I-am-unaffected-by-your-worthlessness stride that she affected the last time we traded off my son, over by the school, and off she went, and I looked at her curvy figure and remembered that once it was lying beside me in bed, and I know that her idea of me is not my idea of me, and my idea of Madoff is not your idea of Madoff, and if you can't even be bothered to post anything on this site, if you can't even be bothered to take up these questions with me, then how is it that I am to persuade you of anything?

Essay: The Chinese Shirt /& The Human Body
Eleni Sikelianos

I wear this Chinese shirt in honor of the human body.

You move toward the bricks.

What moist noises of the deer.

You make shade on the river, a small folded shadow-boat that floats and
    floats.

Your shadow-finger fingers the tiniest wave.

Strips a leaf in sunlight.

You shoulder another bit of dappled water.

I think of night and exclaim so. It comes out no. Night no.

You thesaurus the fire.
You stoke it, you bank it. The words arc
the world, we all know that. But the body
refuses to let go
of the body, seaweed
at its rock clutch. You look onto the split
scene, reality & reality. You are a machine
& you take me
into the cave with tiny robot bears where men & machines teach
men & machines to flay
each other alive. You lead me down
a ramp to escape the destroying world. When we get back every bird
has changed its wing clip, every phoneme has adjusted
its leathers toward a newer color, every restaurant has shifted its menu
(lamb chops are lamp shops), every home has fractioned itself toward a

new silk sidewalk or street. Thank you.　　　　In the new old world order
I'm a time refugee. I will never intercalate the new clock. Prestidigitate me.
You do magic me.
You help me overhear a dream about a 21st birthday with 22 candles & you
help me escape from the Chinese buffet. Who are you? You say
buffet *boo-fey*.

We're sitting at a dinner table. I prefer not to recall
the exact company. A few stars dust
themselves across the sky. Put a little gauze on it. I am trying
to ingratiate myself. More stars fly up like a stinging shower. Sparks off the
millstone, daughters of sand & time. You know how to operate the flywheel,
the sun bounces
toward earth & our shoulders glow. I grab someone's hand but it is not
someone I love. Is this the new way to live, or
the end of the world?
Back in the house, flesh has been stripped of its bones.
Lightning pulses at the windows like a TV screen licking the glass,
television is trying to enter the house, where we collapse,
rubbery, without our bones.

Where have you put my old poetry head?

You point to my old poetry head nestled among the dust. It looks like a
chewed-up rattle or a stick lying in the corner.

You do all these things, with *opus spicatum*, with ashes, lime, & ammonia.
You bleach & you starch using the ancient methods, you do it for sizing,
you preserve the liquid in vats near the loom weights, you are washing a
Roman sheet with lavender seeds, you make the linens crisp with rhizomic
liquids—this is for a trick you will perform later using teasels and dye fixers.
Hematite for red.
Saffron for yellow.
Woad goes blue.
Alum, lime, & piss near the frigidarium.
Dolia for *garum*.
This is your salted fish factory & you have me.
Do Spanish men ever cry?

They cry golden bone shards in long hollowed cheeks.

You cough radiculopathically & your ligamentum flavum glows.

Oh my myelogram. Here is Our Song:

When it says "fragile" above a body sleeping in the doorway
When it says "fragile" above a body without a home
When it says "fragile" above the exhibit, a pile of bones
You teach me

to clothe a dream in new words
to drape a dream in a new form of words
to put flesh back on the bones and bones back in the body

not *es muerte* but *esta muerte*
because we are not always dead
First we live & *then* we die, processual verb.

A fat girl lighting a crooked cigar.

Using reality goggles, a camera
& a stick
prod the body.
It will leave

in sensory streams. Vision, touch,
balance, body positioned in space
& time

You say, the brain abhors an ambiguity

You say, next is the rubber hand trick
Stroke it with a stick.
Whack it with a hammer
You'll wince
You'll cry out

"The next set of experiments
will involve decoupling
other aspects of sensory embodiment, including
the felt sense of the body
position in space

"and thus
do I [assert] the error that asserts

that one soul on another burns in us"

near heaven's equator
fragile above the body slum

invaded by [heaven]
drinking a dragon in a cup

Humans, I offer you an angel
for every object on earth, an angel &
the angel's gleaming stream
of piss

this

is how we radiograph the head's history
to revel in/
reveal

Aristotle's true & dirty fingers, the Lord's
long hours

Now to receive your daily ration from a sparrow

make my see-through cherry

my cherry see-through

like a see-through dress
of bones & flesh

made & worn by that witch
of time who teaches
corners to be corners
& rounds to be rounds

Eleni Sikelianos

You learn a leaf to wiggle a little in wind
a bird learns the ways of the worm
a stick learns to lie still
a man pisses behind a bush

who haunts the
witch of the cherry tree & teaches a tree this:

& if in the hour of death we find ourselves in the same field
get hold of the hay, haywain
hayhead, hey, hell
is to the right

& heaven's there, too, a happy
memory ground

Heaven and hell haunt each other
my Master of the Half-lengths
of light, sewing the eyes
shut then

shouting like a blackbird when the sun comes out an hour

if you want the blood to phosphor
you've got to let the bones phosphor   phosphoresce
throw bright crayons down the veins

don't split   don't slit
    the skin,   human

                    of her cherry dress

Eleni Sikelianos

Coda

I'm wearing a blue-black dress with little silver-lining window-pockets
—our trouble, our
patience, our woe, each of our gifts sewn into its own private pocket

I'm a girl whose name is boy, that's trouble, that's a
pleasure

I phosphoresce near a lemon tree

You could and you did get a new
heart, a not broken
one—see
photograph of not
broken heart with air
pump, yellow & clean
plastic heart   a heart
chamber   chamber with
bright orange dots made
by a German
woman

You put on your bottle-cap coat
made by a man
from Ghana & learn
to make something of what's left
(here on earth)

Sailing by Night
H. M. *Patterson*

PERHAPS IT WAS SOME childhood backmind cinema of the snowpack that had been melting from the top of Roan Mountain that spring-like winter—two whole *fainéant* feet of it lollygagging its way down to the Doe River like a little girl picking mountain flowers—that caused me to dream my dream so deep: Our kitchen pooled with the oaky aqueous collection, then the hall, then my room, and in I slipped from my bed's edge, sank down opposite bubbles breaking away from my cowboy-clad pajamas. I breathed in the mountaintop's sweat. My lungs waxed with the earthy wet of it.

Meemaw's antiques grew. Her mammoth cupboard contents bobbled by. I clamored aboard a colossal ultramarine-colored teapot, hefting myself up, trembling and coughing, by its swan-neck spout. There were others inside the porcelain vessel, peeking out from beneath the half-fluted lid, neighbors, and some folks I didn't know: a flannel-shirted man holding a writhing, venomous serpent, a boy in Mac-Alpine tartan—redheaded, with a crescent-shaped scar on his chin—playing cat's cradle, and a stunning, big-busted lady working her wavy auburn hair into a bun. Our helmsman, an orange-toothed beaver, rode the handle and steered us with its waffled rudder tail.

A pirate, ocular socket patched and velvet vested, stood balanced atop the baluster kettle in stereotypical high-seas freebooters pose, pointed his sword in the direction he required we travel—he had a peg leg, too! . . . no parrot—and he winked at me with his exposed eye. We wove through the misty, swollen gorge before the real-life cloudburst sluiced in, and Meemaw nudged me awake and whispered . . . *flood*.

*

Strange, how a hide whitens then puckers and bloats. When eleven inches of surprise rain fell on Carter County and the seasonal accumulation of snow joined in the saturation of our barns and homes and roads and land, hogs and cattle washed by, the live ones snorting

57

and wheezing and clambering on top of the lifeless ones. The Highlanders' football bleachers filled with sheep and rabbits, and Colonel Thomas, cack-handedly postured on his hands and knees, hollered *Over here!* to us from his rooftop as it drifted toward a dizzy round of floodwater over Bee Cliff Road.

My buddies and I trolled around in the aftermath, hoisting up lost belongings now surfaced: a tackle box, a viola, a taxidermied gray fox, plastic bags of carded wool, canteens and flasks, a telescope, a Nitty Gritty Dirt Band record, granny-square afghan, swollen photo albums with pictures of fishing trips and graduations, of the Toomer-Gill family reunion, of babies with spaghetti faces, tots waddling around the kitchen in their parents' boots. Amid a huge field of floating debris, in a clawfoot tub, Eliot Grub sat crying. Her face was scratched. She grasped a prosthetic arm and wailed and shook. The arm had a hook. Where was the man who belonged to this arm?

*

After the county no longer served as reservoir for what the mountains refused to hold, our recovery effort lay drying on the Cloudland Elementary parking lot pavement. Toomers and Gills picked up their albums—both photo and Nitty Gritty—and Ms. Maisy Kathleen Wayne gathered her wool sacks. Into a pickup bed went gray foxes and mounted antlers, silver trays and tackle boxes. Someone's pappy kissed his soggy viola and plucked its strings. Off went all the claimable treasures. Everything went. Except the arm. I wrapped it in a rag and snuck it back up the mountain home. Underneath the privacy of bedspread, as Meemaw fiddled with her crackly kitchen radio, I rubbed the cool, smooth length of the limb, scratched an itch on my head with its hook tip. I slept with the arm in my bed. Held it tight. Mine.

*

One early winter I attended—with reluctance—an auction with Meemaw round about a year after garnering the first member of my terminal device collection. Bid on and won a "peg leg" (to her mortification), a three-quarter-inch steel rod with a socket for a stump crafted by a local blacksmith for his brother-in-law. As it was easier for Meemaw to imagine my eccentric collection stemmed from a boyhood fascination with pirates and high seas buccaneers, I told her at a Thanksgiving Day dinner table, performing in a briny voice, squinting an eye so she could imagine a patch there, stories of the Howard Pyle–esque corsair of my flood dream. The maritime theatrical—how handy, my remembering that dream!—was an elaborate ruse to spare her the worry of having an adopted grandson who collected (and cuddled) prosthetics and orthopedic devices—such oddities. But so well worth the deception, since Meemaw gifted me a new limb at every Christmas, every birthday: a finely carved wooden antique prosthetic hand with *SiZE 8* written near the thumb in graphite pencil, its fingers wrapped in wire coil—nail holes at the wrist (the nails once fastened a leather strap for attaching hand to arm)—and a jar she found while junkin' with her best girlfriend, Eugenia Bibby, of blue, brown, green glass eyes—and oh, *baby*—a rare circa-1890s capital amputation saw with hard rubber-handle scales Eugenia discovered in a flea market bin of odds and ends. *Mostly odds,* she'd said as she relayed the tale of the find. *Or maybe mostly ends,* she chuckled, standing in front of the Christmas tree, holding up the saw for the cousins to see, then drawing it back and forth a hair above Meemaw's thigh.

*

Meemaw often asked me about my postflood dreams. She began to think of me as a diviner, reading into them—as if images depicted on Tarot cards—prognostications of events happening around the mountain. Through her tales to Eugenia—blabbermouth supreme—word got out about my collection—and my powers, gee-whiz—and soon enough folks were rapping on the door, asking: *Is-er-it true he can scry river rocks? Is-uh-it-true he can dream-predict deaths, disease? Accident, fire? Like the flood? Can he?*

Eliot Grub came to call. *I know all about that pirate, and you ending up with that hook arm and all. I heard about how you take that arm into the trees and gaze into it and see what's gonna come. And I figure I had it first and I want it back now,* she said. And I said, No, now it's a part of an anthology and did she want to see my collection, and she yelled, *You're a freakazoid and your hobby is plain freaky* and ran out the door. I was heartbroken, and maybe I should've given her that wonderful arm, because I believe— still do—that I loved beautiful Eliot Grub. I bolted to the porch, watched her kick rocks past the mailbox, and spent the evening reading *Overmountains Antique Emporium—Elizabethton, TN* over and over from a sticker on an old prosthetic lower right arm (with hinged wooden hand) in the cerulean of pre-night.

And—it figures—until I went off to college in Georgia, I wasn't too big with ladykind. My buddies were interested in my parts, though. Charlie Close, Basil Timmons, and I often sorted through the pieces together, studying with magnifying glasses serial numbers and markings, supposing how scratches were made, what the original owner was like, personality, ability to manage, to navigate, how he lost his leg, why she had two fingers lopped off, talked about Civil War soldiers with gangrenous feet, thalidomide babies, neuromata, prosthetic socks, cups, thumbed through catalogs, wondered about the end of loss. Charlie, a waterfowler, had buried Goose, his favorite retriever, thanks to that darned flood, and I turned away when he teared up recalling it. Basil patted him once on the back and sighed, *I think that was maybe worse for you than how I felt when my baseball cards got ruined.* I changed the subject to astronavigation and oceanic brigandage—as had become a habit—sculling, swabbies, argonauts.

*

Something changed. If I had to describe the alteration of the usual design as sound, I'd declare the day Meemaw fainted in her sewing room to have sounded like a tiny hand-painted box clicking shut, the way, according to Miss Fancy Lammon, the pulchritudinous new twelfth-grade English teacher from Nashville, poems are supposed to end. And space got lighter on the mountain, flower petals lifted as if they would love-me-not up into the sky with the slightest touch of air—everything was fluffier—and everywhere I went, I moved like some balloon, freewheeling and drifting on puffs of breeze. I felt thin and dizzy. I sought anchors to hold me down, anchors to hold. I held an antique prosthetic corset in the night like I'd snuggle a girlfriend if I had one, nuzzling into the metal frame, sniffing the leather straps, whispering, *I'm gonna go to college . . . and I think I'll be a prosthetist and a doctor* and *Are you applying to college? I want you to be proud of me. You could go to Georgia, too. You'd make a wonderful teacher.*

I began to heft cherished pieces of my collection in an old Pro-Sport backpack, trotting around, sweeping off the porch, mending fences, gathering up yard twigs before mowing, mowing, with that pack of prosthetics cinched in place like a turtle's shell. And if I could've withdrawn into the pack when I sensed danger or a whack of fright befell me, I would've. But Meemaw said, with a furrow of concern between her sparse white eyebrows, *You look a little green behind the gills these days*, and I bucked up and worked. Last time Meemaw accused me of looking seasick, she obliged me to talk about my mom and dad for over an hour, and I didn't need to kindle any speculative lore about that meth-headed pair.

The pirate hars and arghs that I *better shape up or ship out*, and even in my dream, I chuckled at his pun, though I felt fizzy and slight, unable to swab the fo'c'sle as I'd been tasked, wobbling as the boat wagged, my mop only skimming the fishy surface of the deck. *Do I have scurvy, you think, Stede?* I ask one of my hearties. *You look about as pale as a blowfish's belly . . . and I think you're gonna fall*, he says. I slip into my washbucket and lie on the wooden bottom, gawp up through the dingy water, brown and gray, a little blue from the sky churning in with dapples of light popping left then center then left then right, and Stede calling down to me, his voice bubbly and garbled, *I think you are sick there, bucko, in need of some cackle fruit. He just needs t' crack Jenny's teacup!* a faraway matelot prescribes.

*

As Eugenia dials for the ambulance I stand over Meemaw, who places her hands on her bulbous belly and stares at the china cabinet. I notice her socked feet and purple ankles as they twitch in her loafers. Splatterings of cobbler streak the kitchen floor, peaches splayed around her head like a sunburst. *Just fainted. Be back on my feet if you and Eugie'd just give me a minute or two*, she wheezes, still gazing at the plates. *You lie still*, I tell her, and then ask, *You see something over there?* I'm looking at you in the glass, she says.

She tells me she's just been on her bum feet too long, and as she offers excuses for her fall one after the other like items ticked off on a list, the paramedics hoist her onto a gurney and siren her away to the hospital with me in the back of the van holding her cracked hand and her enormous macramé pocketbook.

I see. Everything in the hospital is shiny, patent, reflective. I see Basil Timmons in a jar of gauze, gurgling blood at the steering wheel of his Nova, its faded frame wrapped around a willow oak on Bee Cliff Road, Eliot Grub in a metal tray, waiting cross-legged and sighing next to a dog box in a truck bed as her boyfriend's dog rips an ear from its opponent near a tree line. I see Miss Fancy Lammon in a fluorescent tube light, wringing her hands over papers on a mahogany desk. Colonel Thomas winces in a burnished bedpan as he bends for his slippers. In the white linoleum, Charlie Close takes some cash from a register.

Meemaw's in bed made up with sheets cinched to the mattress with nurse's corners, and I leer at her like someone I hate. I imagine I'll have to care for her now—forget getting away from the mountain—and feed her mashed things, wipe her dribbling mouth, sponge her sagging body, and help her in the toilet. Any why shouldn't I? She took *me* in, burdened herself with the little orphaned weirdo grandbaby, fed him mashed yams, wiped his sloppy face.

In the lens of Meemaw's glasses, I see my dad chase my mom from a concrete slab patio into a field of cow thistle, a skull-and-crossbones Jack Tar bandanna on his head. Meemaw moans and stirs, and I hear my dad growl, *Aaarrrrrrrrrrrrgh!*

*

In stones, glass, mirrors, fire, smoke, water, pools, puddles, each one of the eyes in my jar, the lacquered sheen of an arm, the catoptric thigh of a leg.

*

I tell Meemaw, *Hell—sorry—but* hell, *I gotta leave this place.* She has never asked me to stay—with words, that is—but she communicates in moist doe eyes. Her lips quiver. She holes up in the kitchen with her radio and her Crock-Pot. She begs me to sit at the dining table and talk about my folks when I'm not working. She has my number. So I work.

When I lick the stamp on my college application, she takes off her spectacles, wipes her brow with a dishrag. I slap the stamp on the envelope hard, pound it with my fist for extra measure, and run it out to the mailbox. Meemaw peers out from around the front door. I get mean, smirk at her, flip up the red flag.

Before bed she says, *I'm sorry I'm so mopey. I want you to go to school. You're a smart boy. You're gonna make a good doctor, and I'm gonna brag about you.*

I can't remember the last time I didn't feel guilty.

*

I'm in my dorm room, highlighting a passage in a thick, raggedy, used *Atlas of Human Anatomy* when Meemaw calls me up from home. *How's Athens?* she asks, and just as I open my mouth to answer I'm still liking it just fine, she asks about my dreams. Meemaw's been ill for quite some time. Diabetes, she found out. Eugenia Bibby has it, too. *We're lovers of pies so it figures we got the diabeetus. Good eating, being belly-satisfied all these years. Worth it. Comfort foods, they call it on tee-vee,* she says. *Been sailing any?*

In a possum skull, on my last visit home ages ago, I'd seen Meemaw having her foot sawed off.

Nope, I think all of that seafaring's through. I tell Meemaw I'm coming home as soon as I ace all my finals or as soon as summer ends or . . . as soon as I can.

*

Unaware of an injury due to neuropathy causing numbness, Dr. Jarvis says, *your grandmother failed to notice her foot'd been infected.*

Meemaw's foot rotted like a plum left too long on the branch. The withered walker was amputated. She chooses to spend her days in a wheelchair rather than utilize prosthetics, and I lament my introduction of all those artificial limbs into her home. But, no! When you lose a leg, you go get a leg! I've read the case studies. You get a recovery team—a physical therapist, a prosthetist, a shrink—and you develop strength, and range of motion, balance, coordination. You don't jump on someone's back and ride them to the grocery, around the garden, through the thrift shops. People shouldn't ride on backs like copepods.

Here's something random I learned, Meemaw, I say to her on the phone when she calls, before she has a chance to ask me when I'm coming home, *Did ya know that the word* parasite *is derived from a Greek word meaning one who eats at another's table? Didn't know that,* she says, *that's interesting. And the one who's paying up, like the shark, say—the one who's being* robbed—*is called the host. It's like the parasite levies an energy tax on the host. Good parasites do not typically overextort their hosts, and that's how they guarantee their own sustained survival. You sure do know a*

63

lot about scientific things, she says. *I'm learning*, I say. She tells me what she's had for supper. She asks me when I'm coming home. I tell her, *As soon as I can*. I want to take back my parasite talk. *Take care of yourself, OK?* I say. *Love you. Love you, too*, she says. I get teary eyed, hang up the phone, and take a Sleepy-Time Softgel.

I dream the pirate vessel hits land and a million sandpipers scuttle away from us seamen as we push ashore. Stede scoops some of them up for dinner and pops their necks, collects the birds in a basket he carries on his back. He goes to snatch up a gull and it squawks at him before taking flight. The gull circles Stede all day and he makes a friend of it, names it Tew, tosses fish heads to Tew, who catches them midair. Tew is content to linger with Stede, later to rest with Stede through his snoring in a hammock, later to follow our ship when we shove off into the great briny, to become Stede's familiar forever.

*

The governor calls for a ban on open burning to reduce wildfire risk. A meteorologist informs on the radio: *The inauguration of a drought is tricky to determine. Several weeks, months, or even years may pass before people recognize that a drought is in the works. The end of a drought can end as gradually as it began. Dry periods can last for ten years or more. The initial evidence of drought is typically seen in rainfall records. Within a diminutive period of time, the amount of moisture in soils can begin to dwindle. The effects of a drought on flow in streams and rivers or on water levels in lakes and reservoirs may not be noticed for weeks or months. Water levels in wells may not reflect a famine of rainfall for a year or more after a drought begins.*

I wake from a sweaty late afternoon nap and realize my bed has stopped bobbling. I don't pack. I get in my car. The twilit roads home—dried-up sea lanes, withered riverbeds. My lips are chapped. I lick them often. Airy, moistureless clouds cloak the stars, ruling out astromarshaling, and I hunt for Tew, some friendly conduct to steer me, to bowsprit me toward the mountain. Though I should be familiar with this route, some heatstroke-like disorientation handicaps me. Blips of sparkle in my peripheral. Wooziness. I am on the shriveled road home, an ineffectual voyager, and not a thing around me holds water. Leaves crackle. The trees beg dogs.

Gathering any energies this blistering cosmos has to offer, I muster up all my espial abilities. Argus-eyed once again, I brake, pull over, pick up a turkey flight feather I spy—as if through the aperture of a pinhole camera—on the Loop 10 roadside. Brilliance, as if viewed via hagioscope, illuminates a killdeer plume near a pine right outside of Spartanburg, South Carolina. I take the feather. Nuthatch feather, cardinal feather, scarlet tanager in Hendersonville, wren, chickadee, warbler, hermit thrush in Avery Creek, mourning dove in Enka, screech owl, grosbeak, oriole, red-shouldered hawk, cowbird in Asheville, kingfisher, waxwing in Woodfin. I collect all the feathers in light-grasp until my hatchback storage spills into the backseat, until too many feathers begin to swirl around the searing air, and I'm forced to roll up windows and chug along in the hotbox the rest of the way home.

*

Meemaw struggles to breathe as she dreams, still in her wheelchair, in the kitchen, that old radio playing music, crackling in and out. Her throat emits gravelly sighs and snorts, her mouth agape. She looks like a fish in a soup, and I want to kiss her, touch her face, to smother her—no!—but, not intending to wake her, I pad-foot up to the attic and sit Indian style near rolls of pink insulation I should've installed like an indebted grandson should. I notice a ship in a bottle on one of the shelves I'd never glimpsed before when lugging up all the boxes containing my infamous boyhood collection— THE BATTLESHIP "POBEDONOSETS" BY ARTEM POPOV, reads the brass plate on the wooden base—and I whisper, *No more ocean for exploring, Stede; this is where our ship should be.*

I gather the boxes, ones labeled LOWER EXTREMITY DEVICES, UPPER EXTREMITY DEVICES, BONE PLATES, SOFTGOODS FOR HANDS OR FINGERS, BREASTS, BRACES. . . . Now and then I remove a piece, close my eyes, touch with my tongue tip, explore wood and metal with my fingertips, sniff. I take down the lightest box first.

Meemaw's eyes closed. Meemaw's breath shallow now. She's dreaming, her fingers twitch.

I haul down all the limbs, the entire huge collection of parts, the collection that, no matter how Frankensteiny I assembled them, would never make a person, and I line them up outside the front door from the ramp there, like a garden path of "ends" as Eugenia Bibby'd called them. I line them up as far out as they'll go—and wow did they create a span end to end.

H. M. Patterson

In the shed, I assemble my newest collection into pinions, place them at the end of the line after adding a carved wooden plate for them, its lettering says TEW. I admire my craftsmanship. I think, *I'm gonna be good at this.* I fall asleep at the shed window, staring at the path to the flight device, my first creation as prosthetist.

*

Who's done this! Meemaw weakly wonders aloud as she rolls her chair down the ramp, pushing herself along the procession, out of breath, chest heaving. She stops in the sun at the end. *Tew,* she says.

*

When I wake: Meemaw's empty chair at the end of the line. The wings, gone. I run inside, call out to her. *I didn't mean to frighten you! I was compelled!* I didn't know what I meant by "compelled." Compelled by heat, drought, dream. I've done it. What have I done? Outside I am frantic, witlessly dashing to check behind trees, behind shed. I look in the mailbox, I look—I've done it now—under a water trough. I look up and see a speck, a tiny speck that is not buzzard or weather balloon, angel or kite, floating up, up, then down slightly, then up, then up, then up, then up, down, then up up up up up.

Jean Takes a Moment to Respond
Michael Sheehan

WHAT IS SEEN

IT WASN'T UNTIL LATER, when we learned what had happened, that
I noticed it. In the background of the tape. The tape of my daughter
Jean's seventh birthday party. It's way in the background, kind of
small, out of focus. But it is there. He. He is there. And then he is
gone.

Children play in the foreground, my daughter is crying out—
they're playing a version of hide-and-seek, I gather, where the looker
(Jean) has to cover her eyes while the other children dance and move
all around her. Then she opens them, and they must all freeze. I
think they were all playing statutes, statues that come alive when
their owner is away. When she is looking at them, they must remain
completely frozen. When she looks away, they all move. The last one
to be caught moving is the next to count and play looker.

"Eleven, ten . . . ," Jean says, and there in the lower left-hand corner of the frame a blue Chevette pulls up to the curb. A man gets out
and is immediately hidden by the swinging, simian arms of a statue
come to life. ". . . nine, eight, seven . . ." Jean peeks a little, though
none of the other children notices. The arm has swung through its
arc. I have to play this part of the tape in slow motion to even see
that he is there. He gets out; the arm blocks him. The arm moves
and he is on the sidewalk, walking—an argent streak striding meaningfully and yet without definition from the lower left-hand corner
to where he disappears behind Jean, her hands now free of her face,
the statue children all frozen in my yard. A moment passes, another.
Jean has moved, and there again in the background: a man. Really no
more than a silver streak with a dark tip, a sort of match-head figure
standing on the front steps of 1547, three houses down from mine. It
is January 27, 1978. Roughly 10:00 a.m. I remember the air was cool,
though the tape shows everyone in shorts and tees. It was warm for
January. The breeze coming inland off the Pacific smelled just the
slightest bit like oysters. Perhaps not.

The man knocks, waits, knocks again. A curtain is pulled aside—a graphite smudge appears in the otherwise completely white bay window—and is returned. He waits. Perhaps he knocks again. The door is opened, just a slight darkness along the edge—and with nothing more than a tidy silver sunburst (reflected off his shirt?), he has forced his way inside. The door is shut so quickly, you have to pay close attention to see it ever opened. If not for the disappearance of the man's shadowy head, you might say it never did.[1]

Jean cries out as she catches the first of her statues, this one her little friend Gregory, who years later would sue me for malpractice. Jean wears a floral sundress, a birthday present. She is so small in this video. So small.

THE BEGINNING OF THE TAPE IS EARLIER

The beginning of the tape is earlier. The tape starts with my wife as she is lying in bed, and then after that me waking up Jean. "Good morning," I say to the tape as I zoom in on my wife's face. The tape is filmed on a VBT200, which was an early RCA recorder. I had gotten myself one for Christmas that year. She has those wrinkles people get from sleeping, those lines across her cheek. Her hair is greasy and her forehead mottled with old sweat. She looks more sick than angelic when she sleeps, as though her nights were filled with terrible dreams.[2] I nudge her a little bit, but she doesn't wake yet. "Sleepyhead," I say. "Wake up, sleepyhead."

---

[1]When I found this tape, it was just a curiosity; when I realized what had been captured that day, and all the many things lost, it was to face something back from the dead. I knew, had read about, what happened across the street. He left and then the police came and then we read about it, went to the funerals, were interviewed on the news, and for weeks no one would go outside, even in broad daylight. Doors were not opened to strangers. But by the time Jean had moved out of the house, somewhere around 1989, we had pretty much forgotten anything had ever happened. It is troubling, finding this, because it was so forgotten. I knew that date, and recalled that for a couple of years after we had the uncomfortable association between Jean's birthday and the "vampire" killings. But I didn't watch it to see that. I didn't think consciously that he would be there, that I would have seen him that day and never even realized it. That, maybe, in some way I am still uncomfortable thinking about, I am to blame, I am guilty. It is an uneasy burden, this tape. Something is seen on here, something without a name.

[2]I can't say exactly how these things relate, but my wife, years later, suffered from insomnia and anxiety. These, as I said, don't necessarily relate to the things on the tape and whatever was lost. I don't think anything is that simple, that reductively basic and straightforward. It's like something—maybe what happened, maybe something else,

My wife groans a little, and rolls over, turning her head away from me. I follow her for a moment, tracking with the camera by climbing onto the bed a bit, leaning over her, maneuvering the camera over her shoulder and around her so I can see her face where it is half buried in blankets. Our comforter was a galactic blue-and-pink weave—supernovas bursting in brilliant pastels here and there, this one larger this one smaller—the Egyptian cotton of our sheets a scarlet color. Her tiny fingers loosely wrap a corner of the wrinkled sheet, and the whole right side of her face is occluded by blue and pink—perhaps salmon is the color. I must have moved the camera too close, because suddenly the screen is a close-up of the threads of the comforter, bordered by the almost silky texture of the scarlet sheets.[3] They were a very high thread count, I remember. Very nice sheets. I pull the camera back and it shows my wife's head is now completely buried under the covers. "Sleepyhead," I say again, this time perhaps a little naggingly. She does not respond.

MY DAUGHTER JEAN

My daughter Jean's room is marked by a poster she drew of a mountain and beside that a lake. I think it was supposed to be Lake Tahoe. We had never been to Lake Tahoe. I open the door to her room, saying, "Jeanie," in a kind of expectant singsong. There are many tapes just like this one. I am recording Jean's seventh birthday, as I must have recorded more or less all her preadolescent birthdays. Jean is still in her bed, though stirs quickly when I enter. "Happy birthday," I say. It is funny, though everyone knows it and everyone observes it all the time, that your voice on a tape sounds nothing like your

---

maybe many things, maybe nothing—took away her confidence in the most basic parts of life. She was tormented in her sleep, almost desperately possessive of Jean, and more often than not silent, evidently brooding on a dark sort of shadow image (as she once described it) that she felt was just behind everything everywhere all the time.

[3]Several of the early tapes I made were actually filled completely with things like this. I was fascinated by capturing textures, really close up, filming for even as long as an hour just a bunch of different textures and things and objects. Although I know some of these were a kind of technical trial and error with the camera itself—zooming in and out, adjusting the focus, shaking my hand to create a sort of cosmic vibration effect—others were meant as abstract art, which I can't explain even now. I would put on records—Shostakovich, Schoenberg, Bartók—and you could hear them in the background as I spent three, five, ten minutes focusing and unfocusing on the folds of a lampshade, the skin on my arms, the glare of a lightbulb, the stains and cracks in the sink, the rotting mulch of leaves in the rain gutters.

voice. When you hear it when you speak, you don't hear it the way it really is.[4]

Jean sits up in her bed, and I walk toward her and zoom the camera in. "How does it feel to be seven?"

"Good," she says.

"Yeah? Do you feel older?"

"Yeah," she says.

Her eyes don't look into the camera. She is attempting to peer past it to where I am, but she cannot see me. She looks up, as though over the camera, and then her eyes seem to flutter to the side. Perhaps she glances at the window. She is smiling, a kind of nervous smile she had; she is missing a tooth. Her hair, as always when she woke, was knotted and tangled. It catches light from the window and seems for a moment to luminesce.[5]

"Tell everyone how old you are today," I say.

"You already said it."

"Do you know how old you are today?"

"Seven."

"Say your name."

"Jean."

WHAT IS SEEN

The tape is pretty old, as I've said, and so the colors are faded and the images look washed out—something imprecise to the quality of the light that gives the distinct impression of dust motes floating everywhere—as though the camera were picking up some atomic image of existence happening, something invisible to the human eye. In this way, as I zoom in, Jean's face is grainy and little molecules or effluences or whatever float across the space between where

---

[4] I think generally this is said to be because of how we hear, how our ears are built, built so we can't get a clear audio on our own speaking as it reverberates through our head. But I think too it is because there are sometimes two of us, one inside our head and one outside. I don't mean in any complicated metaphysical sense. I just mean we are a sort of two-way mirror, seeing inside and seeing outside at once, and when we hear what others hear of our voices, or see what others see of our faces, we tend to feel a strangeness, the strangeness of recognizing this dualness.

[5] I miss my daughter terribly. I know I am lucky to have been able to watch her grow— the tape reminds me of this—but I miss this little girl, I miss this daughter. In some terrible way when I think back to that day and what happened I am somehow almost relieved that he killed the mother, too, because to have lived knowing what he did to her children would have been a pain far worse than dying.

the camera must be and her, sitting there, looking not at the camera but again toward the window. The light forms a kind of triangle or tilted square on her right cheek, and the left side of her face looks somehow different, as though the right and left didn't match. Actually it looks as though the left side of her face, in shadow, is an older version of the same face.

I AM

I am scrambling eggs with one hand while taping with the other, and Jean is standing in front of me, her hand on the spatula, mine on the pan; the lights are off in the kitchen and so the shot is uncertain, the early morning light (as before) leaking into the frame, and Jean looks up at the camera once or twice. She is too small to be cooking at the stove. I am letting her do this because my wife is asleep. She is telling me something unintelligible about her birthday party. I wonder if the tape was damaged by water or dirt, because the audio for much of the early part from here on is garbled, as if someone was speaking through a fan or maybe someone was speaking while gargling mouthwash.

Jean is at the table, which in those days was a kind of radish-colored plastic apostrophe with white bentwood chairs, themselves decorated with the same apostrophe shape. She sits along the inner curve of the apostrophe's tail. The sound is still going in and out and she is talking and I am as well, I say "presents you want" and she responds, but I can't tell what she's said. I remember she wanted a doll: I had gotten her a My Friend Mandy, which had just come out instead of the usual baby doll, Mandy is this basically noseless, hydrocephalic blonde in a straw hat and rose-printed sundress. Jean is talking with her mouth full, and the sound is rising and fading.

I RETURN TO MY BEDROOM

I return to my bedroom—the tape cuts from the kitchen to me fumbling with the camera at the door to the bedroom—and my wife is still covered in blankets. I turn the camera on myself and hold a finger to my mouth and whisper, "Shhh" as though the camera and I are sneaking up on my wife, as though we are a team. I had a sort of sandy mustache and still had my hair. The man on the tape is shocking the first time I watch this, because that is so long ago, and it doesn't seem like he and I are even the same person. We're not the same person. He is young and has a new camera and a wife and a seven-year-old and a mustache, and as the camera turns quickly on him and then quickly is spun back toward my wife, he is only there for a moment—just enough for my shock at not recognizing my own face to register—and then as quickly the camera is searching confusedly over the room again as (I guess) I get my eye back to the viewfinder and refocus the aim on the bed and the sleeping wife buried there.

I say, "Honey," and the sound is better now, though the word still comes out a little like "Hnnghee" and sounds kind of distant. I think these old tapes were only supposed to have a shelf life of a couple of years, ten tops, though I didn't know it then. Who would have thought then how long the tapes would last? I guess you assume these things will last forever, once captured on film, but the film doesn't last, and you forget the things and the films of them, and one day you just throw all the junk out. I have no idea what tapes I might have lost or thrown away. It's still odd to think I have this one.

My wife groans a little, quietly. There is a new static sound that enters the tape at this point and the sound takes on a further kind of warble as she moves in bed. An ambient static hum, basically. "Hrnn-ai," I seem to say, and she rolls over and sits up a little, props herself up on her elbows. "Grt mnn-eng," I seem to say and the tape quality is pretty bad at this point—her face is an indistinct pink area in the middle of the bed, and then I zoom and focus and there she is, my wife. Her hair was short then, short and in a permanent. She looks tired, bags under her eyes, sweaty, but she smiles a little. Her look is mostly blank, expressionless, and her smile seems more confused than happy.

"Oh, leave me alone," she says, the sound kind of a radio static but understandable.

"Jean," I shout, off camera. "Hey, birthday girl," I say and my voice still sounds too thick, or maybe just too slow, too deep. It is not my voice.

"Let me get out of bed at least," my wife says, and starts to sit up straighter.

"Jeanie," I call again. She comes into the room and runs to jump on her mother in bed. My wife says, "Hey, birthday girl," and sighs with the weight of Jean on her. Jean hugs her mother and is telling her details about the party. Jean is now lively and awake; my wife is wiping at her eyes (my wife's), brushing the sweat and hair out of them. My wife settles Jeanie a little, moving her off, and sits up further in bed. Jeanie gets to the floor, and continues narrating her party to come. My wife rolls onto her side, grabs a cigarette from a pack on the table, and lights it. "What time will they be here?" I ask Jean, zooming in first on her face as she turns to answer and then after moving the camera to my wife's as she sits smoking, watching our daughter, disappearing volutes of her smoke slowly passing across her face.[6]

MY WIFE SINGS HAPPY BIRTHDAY

My wife sings "Happy Birthday" to my daughter, who sits expectantly on the edge of her twin bed, her little feet kicking against its footboard, her hands clasped in her lap. I am singing behind the camera, too. I do not have a very good singing voice. The package she hands Jean is small and wrapped in pink and blue tissue paper wrapping. Jean holds it a moment before she opens it. My wife is saying, "for your party, but you have to wait for the rest, OK?" Jean tears it open, and I say, "What is it?" before she's quite gotten the wrapping off. She sheds the tissue paper, letting it fall to her floor, and pulls from it the floral folds of her sundress. My wife stoops and picks up the paper. "Do you like it?" I ask, and my wife claps quietly. Jean smiles, and lifts up the top part of the dress, unfolding and holding it as though it were a child. "You can wear it at the party," I am saying, though my wife has already said this. "Thank you," Jean says, her voice too adult for me to hear.

THE CAMERA MUST HAVE BEEN OFF

The camera must have been off while everyone was arriving.[7] The next scene, after the obligatory insertion of static and that silver

---

[6]Already she was a stranger to me. I wished she'd not smoke in the house, asked her to only do it outside, said it was bad for Jean. What brand did she smoke then? I watch these silver curls of cigarette smoke obscuring her features as she watches Jeanie and I can see now that what I thought I was seeing was not really there, that she was already someone else, someone I did not know and would not yet know for some time. She was already leaving.
[7]That's the thing about these old tapes—I don't know if memory works the same way, like a movie screen across which play the fractured reels of images remembered—

snow between shots or frames or whatever, is on the lawn. Several children are playing in the background and the adults sit near at hand, around a white metal table, smoking and drinking coffee and talking. There is a lot of sound on this part of the tape, a cacophonous song of speech and the refrain of ambient hum, and it recalls a little the chorus in some manic opera. I don't know of any operas, but it's as if all the singers were on stage at once, singing different harmonies. Children in the background run here and there, in and out of the frame. It must be only half past nine or a little earlier. I am on the porch near the house, moving the camera around from the adults to the children, though not getting much of what the children are doing. They move in and out of the frame and are impossible to quite fix in the shot. Jean chases and is chased.

My wife sits with her sisters and smokes and laughs. Her sister Eileen is a loud talker and the rush of her alto voice crescendos above the rest. She is a soloist stuck in a large choir. I zoom in on my wife; she doesn't see me at first, then looks up, and gives me a look, a sort of widening of the eyes. "Turn that thing off," she says, and waves her hand before her face. Her sisters turn and either smile or stick out a tongue or wave or simply stare. My wife repeats, "C'mon, take a break with that thing." Then she turns her head away.[8]

---

you get moments of time, separate and without all their context—I am not even in these scenes, though I am the watcher seeing them all—and you watch them and start to notice there are a host of things not on the tape, there are many moments never yet recorded that were and that are no more, like things you must have done in your life, moments you've lived and yet no longer remember even a little bit even at all—who arrived first to the party or what Jean was like as we anticipated our guests, these things are lost now to both my memory and my newly restored image of this day—I do not know if you kept a recorder on the whole time something was happening what you would tape and what you would miss. I think even had I never turned the camera off during this whole day, I still would have missed so much of what was happening and I still would not have known all the many things recorded here but not seen at the time.

[8]Later on and much later still we would fight, and then stop fighting and I would beg her desperately to talk to me, and then we would go to sleep—as we must have this night—silently and without contact, then we would go to sleep in separate rooms, and finally we would only speak across visible distances—tables, through screen doors, in courtrooms, and finally only here and there over the telephone. When she looks at me, she shows she hates me watching her with the camera. I remember her saying that. She hated me hiding behind the camera and she hated me watching her with it. I can understand now, I think, what she must have been seeing when I was watching her with the camera, but I did not then know or even think what it was she was looking at when she widened her eyes like this.

WHAT IS SEEN, WHAT IS NOT

Now is the part where I am filming the kids in the yard and he pulls up. He is in the house for something like an hour, until Jean opens her presents. He disappears behind the swinging arm, and then reappears at the door, waiting like a courier. The door opens, and is shut.

IT SEEMS IMPOSSIBLE TO TALK ABOUT
WHAT WAS HAPPENING AT THAT ONE MOMENT

It seems impossible to talk about what was happening at that one moment, where these two terrible worlds aligned suddenly and irrevocably, twin planets on opposing orbits colliding in some unexpected accident. Some breach of some kind between something like what we know and what we cannot ever name.

On my lawn the children continued playing their statue game and for some time I continued taping them. Some minutes passed as they froze and unfroze repeatedly. The air was cool and their cries and calls ringed through the front lawn and overmatched the quieter adults. Eileen can still be clearly heard on the tape. Jean won repeatedly, managing to remain extremely still and thus to be the last to get caught. She would stand and stand and stand and never once move,

It seems impossible to talk about what was happening at that one moment, where these two terrible worlds aligned suddenly and irrevocably, twin planets on opposing orbits colliding in some unexpected accident. Some breach of some kind between something like what we know and what we cannot ever name.

Inside her house, he struck her, the mother, and then dragged her by the hair into the living room, where her two children played. He shot the two children where they played. From behind him came a scream. Still with the mother's hair in his hand, he shot her through the temple, and chased after the retreating screamer, a friend who had been in the kitchen. The friend ran to the back door, was shot once in the shoulder and a second time through the left eye. He then got a

75

barely breathing; whichever of her friends was at the time the watcher would create elaborate spin moves and feints, whirling round toward her in hopes of catching the moment when she would move. One of her friends cried, "Unfair" and suggested Jean did not move as prescribed by the rules, but this was not so. She moved, and would move again. She did so at the precise moments when the watcher's eyes were averted and somehow, through some preternatural insight, she always knew just when the watcher's gaze was about to come her way again and she froze just in time. Then when it was Jean's turn to be the watcher, somehow she was aware just when someone was moving, of the motions of every one of her friends at just that moment.

knife from the counter and dismembered the man's body, using the knife with artless zeal, his hands almost uncontrollable in their passion, movement more like spasms or reflexes, born somewhere deep within the muscle. He carried the knife to the living room, and began disemboweling the mother. He then had sex with the corpse, her dead children some short distance away. Allegedly he drank her blood. Somehow all of this happened within something like an hour. He then did the same, maiming and disfiguring the older boy. The boy was two years old. Supposedly he heard a sound while cutting open the chest of the younger; he was startled and fled the house with the body of the infant in his arms, his shirt soaked with blood, blood also on his chin.

HOW TO USE THE RCA VBT200

Some more of the kids playing. Then a skip and the camera is focused on my shoes and the stained wood of the porch. I am explaining the camera to Jim Sebring, who worked with me at that time, and who had a young daughter, too. His daughter went to school with Jean and we often met at a park nearby and let our daughters play.

"No, you can pretty much just look. Point and shoot. Zoom with this." The chipped white paint of the porch rail suddenly lurches toward the camera as I move it to show him how the thing works.

"This is the mike," I say and evidently tap on the camera's external microphone, bringing on a moment's residual buzz.[9] The camera turns on Jim's face as he is saying, "What'd that run you?" and I tell him and then he says, "Be great for recording the kids," even though I have only one kid. Jim asks can he see the camera and I let him see it and he fiddles around with it—the images are at first of a telephone pole and then of the children still playing their statue game—too close up to see who's who or what's happening—and then he zooms in for moment on his wife, and even—laughing and then wolf whistling as he does it—focuses the zoomed-in camera on his wife's cleavage. He hands the camera back to me, or I take it from him.

JEAN TAKES A MOMENT TO RESPOND

A circle of little kids rings my daughter and behind them, mostly still sitting at the white metal table, are all the adults, friends I no longer even recognize and family I never hear from. Jean sits regally in her floral dress, a gift in her lap, something I cannot quite recognize. Her feet swing with excitement in the chair. She is very happy with the gift and seems for a moment to forget she is there with others, to forget she is being watched.[10] "Say thank you, Jean," I say and she does, quietly. She smiles and the adults clap politely and one of her little friends asks can he see it, and is told "That's her gift, Robbie," by a voice I assume is his mother's. "It's OK," my wife says,[11] and I lean the camera her way for a moment, the last look at her face on the tape.[12] Then I return to Jean, who is being handed the next present by her aunt Eileen. Jean accepts it tepidly, perhaps still

---

[9]You can tell from my voice, though it does not sound quite like me, that I am impatient with Jim and do not wish to be showing him the camera. I am sure I am worried he will ask to see the camera. I don't know whether this was from some jealousy or pride, some fear of Jim's clumsiness, or whether it was from some combination.

[10]This is not just the camera itself, for it is easy to forget someone has a camera. This even though I know, were there to be a camera recording me recording, it would show a man with a large black device held before him, completely hiding his own face, an eye that watches but is not itself seen. But in this moment, as in many others of her early childhood, Jean managed somehow to escape somewhere where she was alone in a moment, as if she lived it alone, as if no one else was witness.

[11]My wife's voice is my wife's voice. It is only your own voice that sounds so foreign, that you cannot know or name.

[12]Unlike getting a glimpse at my own face, when my wife's face appears on the tape—here as in all other places—she is immediately my wife. The recognition of her resonates at once and thoroughly and lasts for some time. It is not just her face I know but it is *her*.

77

thinking of the gift before, and then peels the wrapping off with a delicate relish.[13] She removes the paper in long strings, setting these before her on the ground. Her feet no longer swing with excitement in the chair. I am standing and the camera looks down upon her as though from much farther above than my height. Jean opens the gift and looks up. She looks right at the camera as I zoom in on her face. "What did you get, Jean?" I ask and she looks off to one side, away toward the street, and stares. "What is it, Jean?"

---

[13]I can recall from watching my children and dealing with their moping after the thing was done and also from my own childhood how poignant the moment when one recognizes there are no gifts after this one, this is the last. It is a recognition that somehow undermines all the happiness that may have come before, a recognition that somehow destroys the happiness even of opening that last gift. It is the realization that this, too, will end.

Cowgirl

Susan Steinberg

; IT WAS VIRTUAL, the killing; it was conference call, the killing; it was party line, a party; it was everyone talking at once; it was everyone talking and me in charge; it was nearing morning, almost light; it was the doctor begging me, come on already; it was the doctor begging me, do it already; it was me saying, you do it already; it was my brother laughing into his phone; it was my mother sighing into hers; it was my mother saying, this isn't funny; it was my mother saying, you kids are monsters; it was my mother saying, I'm hanging up; it was the voice she used when we were kids; we hated that voice when we were kids; my father hated that crazy voice; he called her crazy with that voice; he called her crazy, that way she got; it was his fault she was crazy; it was his fault everything went the way it did; it was his fault everything in the world: like planes falling from the sky, like suns exploding into dust, like the whole world how it was; but it was too easy to blame the father; I was done with blaming the father; I would take the blame from this point on; I would take the blame for the world how it was; the world was in a state of collapse; the world was collapsing in my hands; the world was my mother and the voice we hated as kids; it was my brother saying to my mother, take a fucking pill; it was my mother laughing too hard now; it was my brother laughing again; it was funny because we were on the phone; it was funny because we were in different rooms on different streets in different states; it was funny because it wasn't funny; it was funny because it was nothing even close to funny; but it was totally ours; it was no one else's but stupid ours: like words you made up as kids, like things you watched through a keyhole as kids; it was my tv on when it shouldn't have been; it was my brother saying, turn down the fucking tv; it was me saying, no fucking way; it was my brother saying, this is serious shit; it was me thinking you don't know serious shit; it was rain for the tenth day in a row; it was twelve spiders in twelve corners in three rooms in the house; it was a different time zone where I was; it was a different altogether time; it was the doctor saying, I need you to focus; it was never just,

I need you; it was never just, let's have a good time; it was the doctor saying, I need you to pull the plug; it was never that; it was softer than that; it was more like, I need you to do the right thing; it was more like, your father would want it this way; it was me not knowing what he would want; it was no one knowing what anyone else would ever want: even if he said it to your face, even if he wrote it down, even if he carved it into a tree, into the sidewalk, into the softest part of your arm; it was the doctor saying, this isn't funny; it was the doctor saying, this isn't life; it was the doctor saying, trust me; it was hard to trust a person I couldn't see; it was hard to trust a person I could; it was like watching though a keyhole as a kid; it was long ago that one day; it was no big deal that one day; it was no big deal looking in at him; it was no big deal walking in on them; my father screamed; the lady screamed; my mother was out of town; I called her; she came back to town; she kicked him out; the end; it was not the thing that did me in; it was the conference call that did me in; it was the conference call why I had issues; and here I was on a date in a bar; here I was on a date with a guy and I told him there was no way; here I was in a lovely skirt, my knees exposed, his hand about to touch my knee, and I told him no fucking way; now was always no fucking way; now was always no fucking; now was the luxury of years passed; now was the luxury of the bartender's serious face; now was his serious eyes as he described this wine or that; and it was me drinking way too much; it was the date saying, I think you've got issues; it was me saying, I think everyone's got issues; it was the date saying, I think you know what I mean; it was me saying, bartender; it was the date saying, what's your deal; it was me saying, there's no deal; it was no big deal my deal; it was too easy to blame the father; it was too easy to blame a father dying on a terrible narrow bed I never saw; it was stupid to blame a terrible plug I never saw; it was unclear if the plug was a literal plug or not; it was possibly a switch one flipped; it was possibly a metaphor; it was easier to say a plug; it was something I never saw, the plug; it was virtual, the plug; and it was virtual, the terrible narrow bed; and it was virtual, the father; and it was crazy how he got that way; it was crazy that way he got; it was clichéd that way he got; it was too many drinks; it was too many pills; it was rock star how he was; it was hotel room how it was; it was calling me in the night; it was singing stupid songs to my machine; it was, wake up little, etc.; it was, wake up little, etc.; it was never funny; and then he got sick; and then he got sicker, and then, and then; it was never once funny; it was never me laughing;

it was me looking for the bartender; it was another round; it was another round; it was me feeling slightly better; it was a shame of course, ever feeling better; it was the worst shame ever, killing one's father; it was the worst shame ever, really killing him really; it was the worst shame ever the virtual way I did; it was me lying on my bed; it was me and the phone pressed to my ear; it was me watching some actor on tv; it was some familiar face that shouldn't have been familiar; it was my brother and mother in my ear; it was all the voices I didn't want in my ear; it was all the voices telling me to do the right thing; it was all the voices somehow knowing the right thing, and I didn't even know the exact time; because there was no such thing as exact time; because it was one time where I was, one time where they were, one time where he was; it was me saying, wait a second; it was me saying, just wait a fucking second; it was me saying, just shut up a fucking second; it was wrong to say this to my family; it was only an actor on tv; it was only the actor saying something funny; it was only the actor saying a really funny joke; it was me needing a really funny joke right then; it was a shame to need a joke right then; it was me waiting, everyone yelling; it was me about to laugh my ass off; it was my mother complaining weeks later; it was my mother complaining, you shouldn't have called me; it was my mother complaining, you put me in a hard place; it was my mother complaining, he was a monster; it was me thinking who put who in a hard place; it was me saying, who put who; it was me saying, you had me; it was me saying, you put me in the worst hard place: the oldest kid, the only girl; I said, who put who; she said, who put whom; I said, exactly; my father put me in a hard place; my father put my mother in a hard place; my father put the lady in a hard place; my eye was pressed to a hard place; my father put the lady in front of him; he stuck her there in front of him; she was younger than my mother; it was a hard place to be; it was probably love; it was probably total love; it was her laugh that waked me; it was her stupid laugh; and there was no keyhole; it was only a metaphor, I think; it was only me opening the door, I think; it was only me screaming, I think now, something awful; it was my father screaming something too; and it was me screaming something else; and it was shameful the lady screaming something too; it was shameful how trashy just screaming like that; it was shameful being a lady like that; it was my brother hiding in his room; it was my mother out of town; it was my mother still able to dream something lovely; it was my mother about to dream something lovely; it was me running out to the lawn;

it was me standing under some dumb moon not knowing what next: like maybe I could run away, like maybe if I were a guy, like maybe I was not that girl, like maybe if I were I wouldn't care; but I went back inside; and it was not the beginning of the end; it was the beginning of something else; her purse was on the hallway floor; and it was my floor, that hallway floor; meaning it was my purse on the hallway floor; meaning it was my stuff in that purse: meaning her comb, meaning her ten dollars, meaning her ID; it was the beginning of the beginning; I deserved something that night too; and her picture looked nothing like me; and her name was impossible to pronounce; and I memorized the spelling of her name; and I memorized her address; and I figured out her sign; and I styled my hair to look like hers; and I made a face that looked like hers; and the ID worked for many years; meaning I was a piece of trash for many years; I was a piece of trash walking into bars; it was me before I had issues; it was me before no fucking way; it was me before no fucking; it was me before, I'm too fucked up; it was the date giving that look dates gave; it was me thinking try killing yours, motherfucker; it was me saying, drink your drink, motherfucker; it was just shut up shut up shut up; it was a shame to make a virtual decision; it was a shame pulling a virtual plug; it was a shame my ear pressed to a hard place; it was only voices in my ear; it was only some actor on tv; it was half my brain waiting for the punch line; it was half my brain pulling a plug from a wall; it was pulling the plug in my brain like a pro; it was swinging the cord like a lasso; it was me like a cowgirl, swinging the cord around my head; it was the date saying, you've got issues; it was the date saying, serious ones; it wasn't always like this though; it was a good time with that ID; I was a good time with that ID; I met guys and it was a good time back then; it was the ID always getting me in; it was the ID always getting me what I wanted; but there was a night a bouncer said, ID; I looked around like no big deal; there was a guy in the bar; there was a guy in the bar I wanted; the bouncer looked at my ID; he said, what's your name; he said, where do you live; he said, what's your sign; I was ready for this; I was well rehearsed; I said, Virgo; he said, no way; he said, you're a Capricorn; he said, and a liar; it was true; I was a Capricorn; I was also a liar; the whole point of the story is something else; the whole point is I wasn't always this pent up; the whole point is I wasn't always; I said, you caught me; the bouncer said, get out of here; he said, liar; he said, get; but I wanted to go into the bar; I said, come on; I touched his leg; I said, I'm a Capricorn; I said, you guessed it; I could not hide what I was; I said, I'll buy you a drink; he shifted; his leg was too warm; another bouncer walked up; then there were too many men in the picture; then there were too many men I needed to please; there were often too many men; some nights I just wanted to kiss the softest part of my arm; some nights I just wanted to think of some guy I thought I loved; some nights I waked, my mouth still pressed to my arm; some nights I could stay there and fall back into dreams; some nights, though, the phone rang through the night; some nights were songs on my machine; some nights were rain on my machine; some nights were dead air on my machine; some nights I should have said, no and no and no; some nights I should have fallen back into my arm; I was in love with myself some nights; but there were often too many men in the picture; there were often too many men I needed to please; and there was no way to shut it off; there was the date wanting something I didn't want; there was my father singing, wake up wake up; there was the doctor saying, do it already; there was my brother saying, do it already; there was a plane past the window; there was sun past the window; and there was me saying, mother, to nothing there; there was me saying, mother, but she had hung up; because nothing was left but, shut it off; because nothing was left but, do it already; then it was a hum from some machine gone dead; then everything went dead; all the voices in my ear went dead; then the plane; then the sun; then light; then air; then the punch line to the actor's joke; then another joke; then another joke;

Six Poems for Jackie
Jason Labbe

WHERE

From the hotel window above the courtyard
              one might not miss the pool
     or the canal
     for that matter
If one were to search for disappearance this
would not be the leap

*

We could drive out to the northwest corner
where the roads get confusing and follow
instinct into a mountain We would not notice
our bodies thrown
upon themselves and each other

*

         at which point I could say
I am addicted to little

When sleep took on too raw a texture
I thought *call me Jackie* and our shame may vanish
I was not woken

There was little to do at night but
drive the outskirts

*

If your ring never slipped into the pond
If a puddle could only be circled from its center

84

If the accumulation of fieldstones
didn't cause the wall's intensity

If the street didn't facilitate the trespasser
If I'd never driven by and admired the horse

If it were not the practice of the addict
to pay/beg for a strange bed in which to withdraw
If you knew the practice of the insomniac
If practice knew only the desired result

If your ring never dropped from the rowboat
and I drove us home without headlights

Dawn was when
there is no then

                                    *

There is little to drive some nights but the canal
rushing
Quiet is as
close as I get
                        to a pond
                        that other town
where the craving can but does not dissolve

Each strip moved along
or across is a shining black wash

Jason Labbe

WHAT

the left hand that itches to introduce
a warmth
to the side of a horse

the pasture daily driven past

by the right hand as an extension
of grass
and the infinitesimal divide
of touch

the grass as measure of sky
or the degree of green
in the brown horse's mystique

further and farther across the fields
hang stars hardly watched
by the city where

no starlight falls on a cooling hand
and
there is no affectionate animal only

what takes and takes until
your call
the warmth tonight does not deserve

obscures the swirl
the print on the hotel sill

Jason Labbe

WHY

your hair is damp
black in the picture
thin snow on the slick steps
and anticipating rain
the conversation already
emptied and the truck
loaded with approaching
spring's junk

no ledge ever high enough
to talk us down
without the ring did you think
the nickel is lost
and the dime
sure to be discovered
you are so surprisingly
tall and always lovely

a week away renews
the distance this mood
depends on every edge
of the city I visit
softening through wayfarers
allow me another
encounter with your stature
that windy effect

Jason Labbe

HOW

With one hand behind my back
and the other ready
             to coast toward my side
of our epic duet sung
across an indescribable boundary
Or

for you I'll remain
             stationary and awake
in the decision the difficulty the

parapet
the quiet around the window

*

With a record playing
with rolling drums rolling me
I don't fucking care
I exhale on the upbeats

*

Via the elevator that rises out of the hotel
Pretending we
can climb so many flights is

impossible
The railing can't save us

*

In another picture
you are hilarious
with the indescribable way you shape
             a past of little use
around that contorted face

So many visible ways to say *need*
and always mean it

Jason Labbe

WHEN

Between waking and never,
only cattle graze the pasture.
The delusion of the horse
is another way to say ghost.
I wake with the feeling not the image.

Every night I spend driving the outskirts
comes before the church service,
a morning of visible rain.
Where I will travel the weather
does not follow. South is sunny

and your phone off or eaten
by the bottom of the canal.
Tomorrow is *your* answer,
my best suit pressed and laid out.
Do not imagine the mites in the creases.

WHO(M)

what else but waking
to your face and fluorescent corona
wearing new dark frames
new enough
not to have appeared before

what else but waking
to you reading a magazine
to me a sort of blurry sister
what else but waking
again

the curtains drawn
or a wall grown across
the window
near some surface far from sterile
transport to infection

the syringe you could not bear
the book you could not bring
the narcotized
whom you could not locate
what else but the window was

concealed a line around
your forehead
what else but straight above
what else but not quite dead
what else was waking again

The Nordic Soul
Joyce Carol Oates

THOSE OF US, POSSESSED of ancient souls. Yet we move among you as if we were merely of you.

In the beginning was the Word. And the Word was with God. And the Word was God. This, he believed. Passionately. With the Word at his fingertips—that is, his writing effort—aimed at the minimum goal of eight thousand words a day, a discipline he initiated in his young life as an undergraduate at the City College of New York—he would make not converts to the smug Caucasian Protestantism of his rich grandparents but a true revolution in the souls of Americans.

It was so, much that he'd tried to hide from his beloved wife, Meta Fuller, and his admirable friends Jack London, Clarence Darrow, Florence Kelley, with whom he'd founded the Intercollegiate Socialist Society in 1905—his mother's father was John S. Harden, a "high official" of the notorious Western Maryland Railroad; yet more egregiously, his father's grandfather was Commodore Arthur Sinclair of the U.S. Navy, a hero of the War of 1812 rumored to have "profited considerably" through his military connections and to have gloated, *There is no war that is not a rich harvest—for some!*

Such blunt truths of the capitalist spirit, such *facts*—somehow did not repel the majority of Americans, as one might expect. Why?— young Upton Sinclair yearned to know.

He had himself firsthand experience of the rich—from time to time pitied, in his threadbare Baltimore home, with a failing salesman/drunkard father and a helpless and overwhelmed mother, and invited to spend time with his Harden grandparents; he had no illusions as to the higher quality of the intelligence of the rich, as of their moral condition; it is true, the rich can be "generous"—"charitable"— no one more kindly, in an ostentatious manner, than rich Christian women at such times of year—Christmas, Easter—when their hearts are swayed by the pathos of the poor!—this is true, but not relevant to the cause of social justice. *When private property is abolished, the true spirit of Christianity will emerge. But not until then.*

Sinclair felt a stab of shame, that his weak, often ailing mother took pride in the sorry fact that her Harden ancestors were Protestant landowners in Northern Ireland, said to be of the very highest rank of breeding, wealth, and influence. How ashamed to be told, with a reproachful squeeze of his hand, *In your veins their blood flows, even now! The blood of aristocrats.*

These painful biographical facts! Never to be published in any "profile" of Upton Sinclair, if he could prevent it.

Though he passionately opposed censorship, of course. Any infringement upon the freedom of others—the rights guaranteed by the Constitution of freedom in speech and in print—the *natural rights of man*—Upton Sinclair would oppose with his life.

*

"Thank you—but *no*. There is only one man for this office—that is Jack London."

It was flattering, and very tempting, to be offered the first presidency of the Intercollegiate Socialist Society, in the fall of 1905. But with a grave smile for the nominating committee, Upton Sinclair declined in favor of the popular and far more famous young Socialist author from San Francisco.

"Though I don't know the man personally, I have read such remarkable work of his—*The Call of the Wild, The Sea Wolf, War of the Classes*—above all, that masterful chronicle of slum life, *The People of the Abyss*—I can vouch for his genius. And from what I've heard of our comrade—his efforts in the cause of Socialism—I would stake my life on it, that Jack London would present our cause to the world more admirably than any other individual of our time."

He was utterly sincere! This was not false modesty—this was not modesty at all, Upton would have insisted. The vision of Socialism presented by Karl Marx—and refined by Friedrich Engels—was impersonal, and shorn of individual ego; all that was *ego* was of the past, condemned to decay, wither away, and vanish within a few generations; this Upton Sinclair believed passionately and meant to inculcate into his daily, moral life as the most effective antidote to his quasi-bourgeois background.

At this time Upton Sinclair was twenty-seven—about to publish the most challenging work of his career, *The Jungle*, already the author of numerous articles, plays, and books since his first novel, *Springtime and Harvest*, in 1901. Jack London was two years older and had not published nearly so much—yet *The Call of the Wild* and *The Sea Wolf*, bestsellers in several languages, had made him famous—as popular a writer as the legendary Mark Twain, whose prime was now past.

Upton had yet to meet London. He had yet to shake London's hand and to gaze upon the young Yukon adventurer face to face—though he'd seen London's rugged photograph in numerous places, including *The New York Sun*, where the "socialist-seditionist" author was anathema to the editorial writers.

How handsome London was! In secret—for his wife, Meta, would not have understood such a predilection—Upton examined photographs of the adventurer-writer hoping to see in his comrade's smiling gaze some sort of—mystic connection, or kinship. . . . Upton could not have articulated what he sought but knew it to be the identical *ravishment of the soul* he'd experienced when first reading Byron's *Childe Harold's Pilgrimage* and Blake's *The Marriage of Heaven and Hell*; intellectually, it was Marx, Engels, Feuerbach, and Nietzsche whom Upton most admired, but he could not feel the sort of zealous passion for these thinkers he felt for the poets, and for Jack London, who was not only his contemporary but a sort of brother, or soul mate. . . . Guiltily aware of himself as the privileged son of a genteel family, he found fascinating the details of London's very different background: London was the illegitimate son of an itinerant astrologer, born in San Francisco in poverty, forced to quit school at the age of fourteen to work as a sailor, gold miner, and manual laborer; as a young man he'd begun writing for newspapers, and had been bold enough to campaign as the Socialist candidate for mayor of Oakland in 1901. (London had lost, of course—but newspaper accounts spoke of the power of the "Boy Socialist" to "captivate" the crowds that gathered to hear him speak.) In Upton's dreams London appeared not wraithlike, like most dream figures, but solid, earthy, muscled, lively, and livid faced; as he'd been rumored to be in actual life, London was quarrelsome, yet charming; so very charming, it was impossible to turn away from him, or to shake off the effect of his personality. . . . *Here is my deepest self*, Upton thought—*far deeper than I myself can realize.*

For there was, as Upton had come to believe, following the shrewd cultural analysis of Nietzsche, a *deep, true, primitive self*—most often betrayed by the moral cowardice of the public man.

93

At Upton's instigation the men had been exchanging letters for the past year—voluminous letters—doggedly earnest on Sinclair's side and fervid and florid, on London's—extolling the crimes of capitalism and the virtues of Socialism. Upton had urged London to accept the invitation of the Intercollegiate Socialist Society to be its first president, and London had declined initially, but allowed himself to be cajoled, and eventually won over. Each young writer had sent inscribed copies of his books to the other—Upton seemed to be the more impressed, rapidly reading the stirring pages of *The Sea Wolf*, London's new best seller, only just published and already in its eighth printing; he'd written to London in San Francisco—"You are a 'real' writer—I am but a 'muckraker.' But I hope I can recognize literary genius when I confront it."

Weeks had passed, without London responding. At last, when Upton received a scrawled card from London, he'd been dismayed by the bluntness of London's remarks: "The Socialist sentiment of your work is faultless but I am afraid that your temperamental lack of touch—your 'sex attitude'—is anathema to my own view of the subject."

Lack of touch! Sex attitude! Upton Sinclair was utterly baffled what this might mean, and had no one whom he dared ask—certainly not his wife.

How busy September 1905 had been for Upton Sinclair! Having agitated for Jack London to be president of the Socialist Society, he'd felt obliged to help organize the plenary meeting in New York City at Carnegie Hall; his cofounders, Clarence Darrow and Florence Kelley, though supportive of the effort, did not live in the vicinity of New York, and were too busy with other matters to participate. Upton had only just recovered from the ordeal of correcting galleys for *The Jungle*—and very crude galleys these were, as riddled with typographical errors as worm-ridden wood; in a marathon stint he'd stayed up three nights in succession completing what he believed to be a major article for the influential journal *Everybody's*—"The Gospel According to St. Marx"—completed in record time, even for Upton Sinclair. (Yet, fast as Upton could write, typing so rapidly he was in danger of wearing out a new typewriter ribbon within a week, and developing cramps in both his hands, he was uneasily aware that Jack London could write faster, as well as far more successfully—though London hadn't begun publishing until 1900, by 1905 he'd already published ten books, each of them having created an extraordinary "stir" with the public.) In his rented quarters—a rough-hewn cabin on Rose-dale Road in the countryside southeast of Princeton, New Jersey—he was accustomed to working as long as twelve hours at a stretch, with only brief breaks for meals; he saw little of his wife, Meta, who was teaching in a local private school; he was obliged to commute to New York City several times a week, by train. In his late twenties, Upton Sinclair more resembled an adolescent male of seventeen or eighteen: He was just less than six feet tall, painfully thin, with a slight stoop of his shoulders, an alert manner that verged upon the nervous, a somewhat shy and enigmatic smile, hopeful eyes. His skin was sallow, and often reddened with a mysterious, mild rash. His eyes, which were nearsighted, watered easily. His health was a chronic worry to him despite his strict diet and habits of cleanliness; a Socialist specialist in nutrition had advised him to fast as frequent-ly as possible, avoiding meat, fish, and eggs, as it was now known that such a regimen led to an increase in the metabolic rate, or ener-gy—though Upton had to confess he felt no more energetic than ever, and often felt enervated and even discouraged—a predilection he had to fight against, vigorously. Set beside his hero Jack London—in his own eyes, at least—Upton envisioned himself as a sort of quasi-male, or stunted male—as London had so uncannily perceived, Upton lacked the temperament for *touch*—for human contact.

Yet Upton had married an attractive young woman, a fact that often bedazzled him. *How*, and *why?*—he would have said that he loved his young wife, and hoped to be a reasonably good husband to her, yet, when they were apart, as they were so frequently in the late sum-mer and early autumn of 1905, Upton had difficulty remembering what Meta looked like.

Suddenly in Upton's life there were so many young women—so many people! And many were recent immigrants to the United States, or the sons and daughters of immigrants, like the Lithuanians Upton had interviewed in Chicago, as background for *The Jungle*; in New York City, residents of immigrant neighborhoods in the Lower East Side—"teeming" and "lawless," as the Hearst newspaper called them—were drawn to the Socialist cause, and impressed Upton Sinclair with their vitality and passion. They were German, Italian, Polish, Hungarian, as well as Lithuanian and Russian—their heavily accented English was frequently incomprehensible to him, even as their emotions were vivid and direct and so very different from the veiled and obscure emotions of the class to which he and Meta Fuller were born.

"You won't accompany me to the rally, Meta? I wish you would— it will be a historic event."

Upton did not want to plead with his wife, whose political sentiments, he'd thought, were near identical with his own, and whose methodical, meticulous editing of his manuscripts—often line by line, and hour by hour—was invaluable to him, but his voice expressed a sort of wistful yearning and childish hurt.

"You would meet Jack London! It will be quite an occasion—all the newspapers will write about us. We are hoping to take up a collection afterward—this will be a unique opportunity. 'Revolution Now' is the title of Jack's speech—he has sent a telegram."

Meta, preparing to leave for the Chapin School on the Province Line Road a few miles away, where she was a young instructor of English, murmured a vague reply. For Upton had asked her numerous times to come to this "historic" rally—many times, very many times, he'd extolled the virtues of Jack London to her. She could not possibly go to New York City with him, she said; it was the conclusion of her workweek, and she was expected to be at the school well into the late afternoon. She was not a *freelancer* like Upton, but a *salaried worker*.

"But, Meta—the opportunity to meet Jack London—!"

"But, Upton—I've had the opportunity to meet Upton Sinclair. And what of that?"

Meta's nervous laughter rang in his ears for some time after she hurried from the house, utterly baffling to him.

In his journal for September 20, which was the eve of the rally at Carnegie Hall, Upton Sinclair grimly noted: *In a time of Revolution, private lives are of no significance. Marriage, family, tradition—all bourgeois customs, propagating hypocrisy and capitalist exploitation—are doomed.*

*

"He will be here. He will not let us down."

Yet by 7:45 p.m., on the evening of September 21, Jack London had not yet arrived at Carnegie Hall for the program that was scheduled to have begun at 7 p.m. Since he'd joined the Socialist cause Upton Sinclair had discovered that it wasn't uncommon for Socialist rallies to be delayed—sometimes canceled at the last minute—as it wasn't uncommon for the rallies to be haphazardly organized—but the audience awaiting Jack London this evening was unusually restive; there was a tension in the air resembling the tension before an electrical storm. Many individuals refused to be seated but were milling about in the foyer and the aisles—these were excitable, bellicose men who bore little resemblance to the young students from Columbia University, New York University, City College, and other area universities and colleges for whom the society had been organized. Belatedly the organizers were realizing that a good portion of the audience had come expressly to hear Jack London speak, not as the president of the fledgling Socialist society but as the handsome young author of the enormously popular *The Call of the Wild*, which had sold more than one million copies in hardcover; in spite of London's reputation as a writer of adventure stories, there were a number of well-dressed women in the audience who didn't appear, to the cursory eye, to be likely Socialists.

On Fifty-seventh Street, outside Carnegie Hall, as if unwilling to pay the small price of admission until they were certain that Jack London had arrived, were men who, judging by their rough-hewn clothes and their air of masculine aggressiveness, might have stepped out of *The Sea Wolf*, London's new, wildly best-selling novel of a tyrannical sea captain in the mode of a Nietzschean *Übermensch*— a novel that, to Upton Sinclair's astonished envy, had sold out its initial printing of forty-thousand copies *before publication*.

Amid all this commotion, and the mounting anxiety of the rally organizers, Upton Sinclair yet had to marvel—what a wonder it was, a writer of his generation had so swiftly attained such stature with the masses, of a kind he could never dream of attaining! Though his commitment to the masses was absolute, and in his most private fantasies he dreamt of being a martyr to the cause like Eugene Debs, brutally beaten by strike-breaking police, thrown into prison . . . emerging with renewed dedication. . . . "The Socialist cause has found its great poet-visionary—and he is my age, or nearly! My brother, and my friend."

It was nearing 8 p.m. Jack London had not yet arrived. When the acting president of the society addressed the audience, with a plea for just a few more minutes' patience, he was greeted with jeers and boos amid scattered applause. Clearly there was a division in the hall between those who were committed Socialists—for whom the rally was the principal draw of the evening—and those who had come to hear Jack London speak—for whom the rally, if not the Socialist cause itself, was incidental. Some of the roughly dressed men who'd been milling about on the sidewalk outside had now found their way inside, and were jostling individuals in the aisles. With an air of wonderment Upton Sinclair murmured aloud—"We are approaching chaos—catastrophe! How has this happened?!"

In fact the blame might lie with Upton himself—he'd been so adamant with the nominating committee, insisting that Jack London was their man; he'd tried several times, without success, by mail and telegram, to convince London that he should arrive in New York City on the day before the rally, or, at the very least, early in the afternoon of September 21. But, for some reason Upton could not comprehend, since it suggested a reckless confidence utterly absent in himself, London had assured him that he wouldn't have the slightest difficulty in arriving at Carnegie Hall "precisely on time"—if his sea voyage from San Francisco to Miami wasn't delayed beyond a few hours, or the train from Miami to New York City . . . which was, as Upton discovered to his horror, due to arrive in Grand Central Station at 6:35 p.m. By telegram, Upton had pleaded with London to move back his travel time, by at least a half day; to arrive in New York just twenty-five minutes before he was scheduled to address the society seemed very risky—"You will make us all very anxious, and yourself as well. Please reconsider!" London's reply had been blithe, bemused: "Spare yourself 'anxiety,' comrade—Jack London guarantees a *juggernaut of a performance.*"

Upton had been so chagrined by this exchange, he couldn't bring himself to tell his fellow organizers the exact time London's train was due. Some measure of guilty embarrassment prevented him, as he'd hesitated to confide frankly in his wife about London as well. It was a principle of his Socialist vow—as it had been a principle, previously, of his Christian character—that he made every effort to be *positive;* that is, resolutely to avoid *negation,* as a self-defeating strategy of action. From the great American pragmatic philosopher William James he'd taken the admonition to simulate faith, where faith might be flagging, in order to revive and resuscitate faith; as a young undergraduate at City University, he'd been impressed by no philosopher more than James, in the matter of "pragmatic truth"— *Truth is not something that resides in a principle. Truth is something that happens to a principle.*

This, Upton had tried to explain to his wife, whose knowledge of philosophy was limited to those fragments of "great thoughts" she'd been taught at Sweet Briar College—"As Darwin has taught us, the species are ever evolving, as specimens within species must evolve, to survive, so too truth must 'evolve'—it can't remain fixed."

" 'Truth must *evolve*'—how very convenient for liars."

Upton had frowned at Meta's frivolousness. Whenever he tried to speak seriously to her, she joked; whenever he tried to joke with her, she responded blankly.

It hadn't always been this way, he was sure—when they'd first met, only just a few years before. Then, Meta had been a very sweet, soft-spoken and amiable girl, if not uncommonly beautiful or striking—quick to laugh at Upton's jokes, quick to sympathize with his ideas, and eager to hear him speak, at length, on "The Gospel According to St. Marx" and its variants.

Naively, he'd thought the woman to be his soul mate.

A thunderous roar of cheers!—Jack London had arrived.

"He's here! At last—thank God. . . ."

It was 8:12 p.m. London was more than an hour late. But the bois-terous audience, which had seemed on the verge of anarchy, was immediately placated, like a great brainless beast. Backstage, where he'd been pacing in a state of extreme agitation, Upton Sinclair felt a wave of utter, ecstatic relief—not just the Socialist cause had been rescued, but Upton and the other organizers, who'd begun to fear for their physical well-being but could not bring themselves to flee the premises.

Upton hurried out to greet London, who was making his way down the center aisle of the hall, like a politician, or a celebrated prizefighter, his thick, dark hair attractively windblown; London was in an ebullient mood, very friendly, pausing to shake hands with admirers and autograph seekers. It had been understood that London would arrive at the rear door of the hall, on Seventh Avenue, to be spared just such a situation, but it was clear that London greatly enjoyed the scene, as did his female companion—a small Gypsy-like woman in colorful attire, clamped to his arm.

Hurriedly, in the melee at the front of the hall, Upton introduced himself to Jack London who, flush faced and enlivened, and smelling frankly of alcohol, shook his hand so hard that Upton winced; then, like a long-lost relative, grappled him in a bearlike embrace that left Upton breathless. " 'Upton Sinclair'—comrade! You are exactly as I'd envisioned"—London laughed heartily at this remark, which was meant as playful chiding, if not outright sarcasm. Upton too laughed, nervously—he felt a thrill of worry that one or more of his ribs had been cracked in Jack London's embrace.

"My woman—Miss Charmian. My loyal consort."

Again, London laughed heartily—though clearly he was proud of his companion, who was known to be not Jack London's lawful wife: In the gutter press, the caption beneath her photograph was "The Call of the Wild: Jack London's Other Wife." Charmian! Seemingly, the woman had no surname. Upton was surprised to see her for he'd been given to understand—by London—that London wouldn't be bringing her with him to New York, but—here she was, preening like royalty: a surprisingly squat little person with a garishly made-up pug face and a silk turban wound about her head, who took so little notice of "Upton Sinclair" that she might have thought him an usher at the rally, whose responsibility was to escort her to her reserved seat in the front row.

Upton's second surprise was that London didn't want Upton Sinclair to introduce him to the audience—"No, no! These people haven't come to hear you talk about 'Jack London'—they've come to hear 'Jack London.' And I'll oblige them now."

It was a measure of the man's high spirits and his consummate confidence in himself that he strode up onto the stage without hesitation, and to the podium, very like a prizefighter, shaking his fists in the air both to acknowledge the deafening roars of applause, and to evoke an even greater volume. Several minutes were required for the audience to subside to the point at which London could be heard, his mouth close to the microphone as he shouted, with no preamble: "Revolution now! Revolution now! And again I say unto ye— *Revolution now!*"

Again, the hall erupted in clapping, foot stamping, and cheers; again, London had to wait for the hall to quiet.

Upton had taken his seat beside squat little Charmian, in a bit of a daze. His temples throbbed, his eyes watered. He'd been so distracted for the past forty-eight hours he had virtually forgotten to eat and was now light-headed and weak in the knees. How close they'd come to pandemonium, if London had not arrived just in time! It was thrilling to Upton now, to hear his hero speak in a powerful, dramatic voice, hunching his broad shoulders to lean forward, gripping the sides of the podium. The audience that had been so restless was now hushed in reverent anticipation.

"'No Compromise' is the essence of the Proletarian movement. . . . Capitalism is the Sole Enemy. . . . If one Socialist comrade will bring another into the fold, and he yet another, the entire United States will be won by the year 1912. . . . We are witnessing the death struggle between the two great forces of Greed, the chiefs of the Beef Trust and the chiefs of the Standard Oil Trust, for ownership of the United States of America. . . . 'Big Bill' Haywood's motto, 'Good Pay or Bum Work,' will soon replace 'In God We Trust' as the motto of the United States. . . ." London spoke in a loud, incantatory manner, like one repeating memorized phrases, yet with great effect. Though his words were familiar ones—at least to Upton Sinclair and other Socialists in the hall—they were greeted with applause, as if they were highly original, and daring. Upton sat in the first row of seats, below the podium, gazing up at his hero with the unstinting admiration of a kicked dog for his master, who has left off kicking him for the moment and is being kind to him, capriciously, yet wonderfully.

When London's flushed face crinkled with schoolboy slyness, you could see that he was about to make a joke—"Far be it from yours truly, the much-derided 'Boy Socialist'—as my detractors have called me, in an effort to discredit the noble cause for which I stand—to deny that Socialism is a *menace*; why, our stated purpose is to wipe out, root and branch, all capitalistic enterprises of present-day society"—and all erupted with laughter, including Upton; when London's face grew sober, or seemingly sober—"Our cry is a simple appeal to the downtrodden, exploited workingman of America and of the world—*Organize! Organize! Organize!*"—the hall became hushed, as if London were uttering a prayer. Like the refrain of a ballad, these few words of London's returned, each time with more vehemence: "*Organize! Organize! And again I say unto ye—Organize! And the world will be ours! And human destiny will be ours! Revolution now! Revolution now! Revolution now!*"

In his fatigued and excited state Upton sat limp, like one basking in another's warmth. It had been said of Upton Sinclair as a public speaker that he was "earnest"—"inspiring"—but there was no comparing Sinclair and London, the one delivering prepared speeches in a dogged monotone, often dropping his gaze to his typescript, the other flamboyant, animated, gesturing with his hands and arms, interrupting his own words with shouts of laughter—"This'll stick 'em! This'll *stick 'em!*"—zestfully rubbing his hands together. London's astonishing charisma could carry all of New York City, if the city's residents had turned out to hear him; it could carry all of the United States. . . . Such a *juggernaut of a performance* deserved a stadium full of cheering spectators, not the mere twelve or fifteen hundred

101

who had turned out this evening in Carnegie Hall.

Upton could not comprehend how Jack London had done so poorly in his campaign for mayor of Oakland several years before. Had his Socialist message been premature? Had his personality not yet ripened?

Yet, as the speech continued, and London began to repeat his words, and even his seemingly spontaneous gesticulations, Upton began to notice that, in the unsparing spotlight of Carnegie Hall, the handsome "Boy Socialist" did in fact look older than his dust-jacket photos. And was he—shorter? Shorter than one would have expected? His romantic-masculine features had coarsened, his muscled body had grown perceptibly thick, and oddly clumsy. His speaking manner was to simulate a kind of confiding intimacy with his audience— as if he were sharing secrets with them; at the same time, his rhetorical habit was to raise his voice suddenly, and dramatically—so that, if you were leaning forward in your seat, listening avidly, you were likely to rear back, as if you'd been struck a playful blow to the face. And there was the hearty, bellowing laughter with its edge of— mockery? Or was this simply—Upton wanted to believe—the expression of a sort of *brimming masculinity*, which could scarcely be contained behind a podium, on a conventional stage?

Upton had not wanted to think that the first president of the Intercollegiate Socialist Society had arrived at Carnegie Hall in a drunken or semidrunken state, but this did seem to be the case. At the start of his speech, London had taken large swallows of water from a glass placed on the podium, but after some twenty minutes he'd begun to sip openly from a flask he carried inside his coat, to the merriment and approval of the more vociferous members of the audience. The more London sipped, the more flushed his face became, the louder his voice and the more sweeping his gestures. Of course—it was known that Jack London was a *drinker*; Jack London was hardly a *teetotaler*, like Upton Sinclair. Yet, somehow, Upton had not thought that London's drinking would impinge upon this rally, and this evening, Upton had not thought of this possibility at all. He didn't dare glance around at the lively, mesmerized audience but it wouldn't have surprised him if many of these individuals, too, were sipping from flasks.

(Any consumption of alcoholic beverages was expressly forbidden in Carnegie Hall!)

Upton was also dismayed by London's clothing. How peculiar it was—how unexpected—Jack London was wearing not the rough

102

seaman's clothing in which he was usually photographed, nor even work clothes, but an alarmingly "dandyish" costume—an English-style herringbone suit with a vest and a white—silken?—blouse and a flowing silk tie in polka-dot design. When you caught a glimpse of his footwear, you could see that he wore elegantly styled shoe boots of gleaming black leather. And, on his thick fingers, gleaming rings.

The herringbone vest fit London very tightly, like a sausage casing, and was becoming, as the minutes lurched past, increasingly stained from spillage from the flask. London's hair looked now more disheveled than windblown, threaded with a coarse sort of gray. More openly, London now sipped from his silver flask and smacked his lips with relish—drawing a raucous response from his audience.

Upton chided himself—"As I am a 'teetotaler'—often derided for my 'old-maid sentiments'—as by Jack London, for my deficient '*sex attitude*'—I am the last person to pass judgment."

It was clear by now that London had no prepared speech to deliver to the Intercollegiate Socialist Society, and seemed loftily indifferent to the fact that there were young university students in the audience; his remarks, like his increasingly ribald humor, were directed toward those who reacted with laughter, applause, foot stampings. It was clear too that London had forgotten, if he'd ever known, that his "presidential address" was but one of several speeches scheduled for the rally: He continued to speak past 9 p.m.—past 9:30 p.m.—and now nearing 10 p.m., without a hint of fatigue. Of the speakers who were to follow, Moses Leithauser, the martyr of the recent Garment Workers' strike, still on crutches after his ordeal at the hands of Pinkerton's strike-breaking "detectives," had come at Upton Sinclair's express invitation, and was becoming impatient, and annoyed, but there was nothing anyone could do, certainly not Upton Sinclair, for the audience would have been furious if their hero had been interrupted, and indeed London was very funny, at times uproariously: "The workingman of the world needs to take a lesson from yours truly, in that, if he wishes to 'make ends meet,' he should not lower his standard of living but—like yours truly—*raise his income*. There you have it, comrades: Revol'shun now!"

Even Upton had to laugh. This was very witty—worthy of Oscar Wilde—as, when you thought of it, London's playful/parodistic manner and dandyish costume were reminiscent of the notorious, lately disgraced and deceased Wilde. Yet how different the effeminate Wilde from the hypermasculine London!

Upton was uneasily conscious of the eccentric little woman seated beside him, who applauded Jack London as vociferously as anyone in the hall. He didn't want to seem—he didn't want to *be*—puritanical; he was sure that, like any radical-minded Socialist in the first, thrilling years of the twentieth century, he had overcome the outmoded strictures of the bourgeoisie; yet he couldn't help but regret that London so brazenly flaunted the conventions of the bourgeoisie, which overlapped with those of the proletariat in matters of morality and "decent" conduct. It was unfortunate that the Hearst papers had luridly latched upon "immorality" and "free love" as charges against the Socialist movement; yet more, that Jack London had "repudiated" his wife, Bess, for her failure to provide him with a male heir, and spoke in interviews of his new attachment to a "temptress of exotic breeding and beauty," known only as Charmian. Upton had been shocked to have seen, a week before, in one of the gutter tabloids, a front-page, blurred photograph of the turbaned, broadly smiling "Miss Charmian"—"Jack London's Other Wife"; now, seated beside her, close-up, he could not imagine how the squat little female was any sort of "temptress," let alone an "exotic" beauty.

Charmian must have been older than her lover by some years, Upton thought, judging from the harsh bracketing lines framing her rouged mouth, and the sunken though glittering nature of her small eyes: more than forty, surely! (London wasn't yet thirty, though he looked older.) Maybe the gas jets in the hall were unflattering to the gnome-like little woman who, flamboyantly costumed in a magenta silk turban pinned with a jeweled scarab, and a flowing "kimono"-style gown of crimson and black stripes, sat in a rigidly self-conscious pose, as if she were on stage herself; knowing herself watched by many in the audience, she made a show of gazing adoringly at the speaker above her, lifting her hands to clap fervently, and glancing from time to time, with queenly condescension, at the audience.

Must not judge her, and their love—"free love." As I am so conspicuous a failure along these lines myself.

For so it seemed to Upton Sinclair, what should have been obvious at the time of his honeymoon with Meta, spent at a Socialist campground at Bayhead, New Jersey: He had not a clue what *manliness, masculinity, any sort of "sex attitude" meant.*

Now he understood why Meta had ceased laughing at his jokes—why Meta had so little patience for him, and seemed always to be too busy, too distracted, to have time even to listen to him, as she'd had before they were married. She did not appeal to him to come to bed with her any longer—she did not mind how late Upton stayed up

104

working, or how many hours he worked through the day.

Initially, it was Upton's belief that marriage could be studied as a science, from a rationalist perspective; he thought he'd made the effort—yes, he had made the effort—but Meta had not seemed to know how to cooperate.

I, too, would like a male heir—of course! As any man would.

There was something thrilling—"primitive"—in the way that Charmian stared rapturously at her lover, and London, from time to time, paused in his speechifying to wink down at his beloved, and smile a secret sort of smile, wet teeth gleaming. For this was a radically liberated couple—a heroic couple, you might say—unashamed of the "illicit" nature of their passion, in defiance of the hypocritical disapproval of the bourgeoisie. It was known that Charmian—"Miss Charmian," as London called her—was no middle-class female but a courageous rebel, for whom the role of the "other woman" was a challenge to be met with zest, and with "dash"; as for Jack London, he'd lately advocated *natural passion* as the cure for most of society's ills, along with the Socialist Revolution.

Upton was roused from his reverie by a renewed uproar in the hall as Jack London, glowering red with exuberance, brought the audience to their feet, chanting lines from the "Marseillaise"—in loud, mangled French incomprehensible to most, though, to Upton, chilling in its robust brutality—

> Aux armes, citoyens!
> Formez vos bataillons!
> Marchons! Marchons!
> Qu'un sang impur
> Abreuve nos sillons!

Upton's sensitive nerves were such that the very thought of human blood "watering" soil left him weak, faint; as he was repelled by the finale of Jack London's juggernaut performance—striding about the stage, lurching as if about to fall, striking the palm of one hand with the doughy fist of the other while shouting furiously—"Revolution now! Revolution now! *Revolution now!*"

Truly now, Upton Sinclair *was* surprised.

For, before the storm of riotous applause and foot stamping had halfway abated in the hall, Jack London strode backstage, waving aside congratulations and offers of handshakes from Socialist comrades, declaring to Upton that he was "both ravenously hungry and uncommonly thirsty—for beer, and bored to high hell by the brain-addled sheep out front." His broad smile had vanished, as if it had never been; his eyes were bloodshot, and his skin sallow. He'd torn open his herringbone vest, which had too tightly constrained his torso and belly, and was freely perspiring. In vain Upton and the others urged him to stay for the remainder of the program, or at least to hear the revered Moses Leithauser, who had waited so patiently for London to finish; London refused even to meet Leithauser, and brushed rudely past several well-to-do Socialists who'd come considerable distances to hear him, and who were much valued as donors to the cause.

"I too have come a long distance, all the way from California, and must now refresh myself—Miss Charmian, come!—we are going to MacDougal's, should any comrades wish to join us—but do not attempt to restrain me now," the stocky man laughingly warned, "—for I want *meat*, and I want *drink*, and I want *my woman*—and there it is! Miss Charmian, come: The hackney cab awaits, and we are off."

Upton tried to plead with London not to leave so abruptly—but to no avail. Miss Charmian in her glittering silk turban had joined her lover backstage, marveling at his performance—"*Magnifique!*"—and clamping her arm tightly into the crook of his arm. Together the two made their way out onto the street, through the stage door.

Of course, Upton couldn't follow them. Not only did he feel an obligation to hear Moses Leithauser speak, and several others, but there were responsibilities he couldn't shirk after the rally ended: skirmishes between Socialists and New York City police officers on Fifty-seventh Street, and a quarrel among several of the organizers over who had misplaced a packet of valuable receipts.

When Upton returned to the hall, he saw to his dismay that more than half the audience had rudely left in the wake of their idol Jack London. Those who remained were scattered about the rows of seats and most of these appeared to be young men of university age—neatly dressed, with glasses—of whom a number uncannily resembled Upton Sinclair.

At last, at 10:20 p.m., Moses Leithauser was to speak! The delay had been unconscionable and humiliating—Upton could barely bring himself to look at the revered union man waiting backstage with pages of a speech clutched in his hand, his face a mask of wounded pride, indignation, and fury. Upton hurried to the podium to introduce Leithauser, and to urge the remaining audience—"Come forward, please! There are many empty seats at the front."

*

So late! It was nearing midnight when Upton Sinclair and the more reliable of his society comrades were free to leave Carnegie Hall, parting from one another in exhausted silence.

Upton thought, *I will go home now—of course.*

Yet, though he was exhausted, his nerves were strung tight; he was light-headed, and famished; he could not stop thinking of Jack London's *juggernaut performance,* and of the remainder of the rally—a succession of doggedly earnest Socialist speakers, lecturing to a gradually diminishing audience until, at the very end, only a few isolated individuals remained in the hall, of whom several were deeply asleep and could barely be wakened by ushers.

I will go home to sleep. And tomorrow—I will return to Princeton, and to Meta.

Maybe—it isn't too late. . . .

In his dazed state, Upton hardly knew what he meant by *too late.* Or, rather, that *it wasn't too late.*

Somehow, as in a trance, he was walking south—on Seventh Avenue—in the direction of Times Square. Though he hadn't ever patronized the notorious MacDougal's, nor even would have thought he knew its location, Upton found himself drawn in that direction—for hadn't Jack London invited him to drop by MacDougal's after the rally?—it would be rude for him not to accept London's invitation, under the circumstances. For he, Upton Sinclair, had invited London to accept the presidency of the Intercollegiate Socialist Society, and to speak at its inaugural rally—very likely, he was Jack London's closest friend in Manhattan, and the Socialist comrade closest to him in ideology, zeal, and temperament.

"It would be rude, certainly. After the sacrifice London has made, coming here . . ."

When Upton arrived at MacDougal's he had no difficulty locating Jack London and Miss Charmian in its crowded, deafening, and sulfurous-smoky interior—there, at a table at the very center of the bustling restaurant, was the conspicuous couple, surrounded by a pack of admirers. Hesitantly Upton approached—he'd been jostled by departing revelers, at the front of the restaurant—feeling as if he were stepping into something like a blast furnace—by the indraft sucked inside, shyly excited, intimidated, yet helpless to resist. He saw that London's table was strewn with glasses, champagne and beer bottles, dirtied plates and cutlery; on a platter in front of London was the remains of what appeared to be a raw hunk of meat, only the curving, tusklike bone and shreds of bloody gristle remaining. Upton would have thought that, after his energetic performance at Carnegie Hall, Jack London would be in a subdued if not exhausted mood, but, to the contrary, here was the famous man laughing loudly, sprawled in his chair, a railway cap perched cockily on his head, and the stump of a thick-ashed cigar clamped between his big bared teeth. His jaws gleamed with grease, his canine teeth looked particularly pointed. The elegant herringbone coat had been removed, the herringbone vest had been torn open, the white silk blouse was splattered with food and drink stains, pulled open also at the throat to show a broad, fatty, grizzle-haired upper torso.

Yet more astonished was Upton Sinclair that London, sighting him as he hesitantly approached, squinting at him through wafting clouds of smoke, reacted so suddenly, and so warmly: "Here he is! Here! We've all been waiting for—who's-it—Comrade Sinc'ler—hope of the twentieth century—author of the greatest novel since *Uncle Tom's Cabin—Jungle! The Jungle!*—that's it, ain't it?—*Goddamn Jungle!*—truer words were never uttered—this damn-cursed cap'list nation is a *jungle*—never mind *Wolf*, and *Death*—predators of the deep—here is where the cesspool lies, in these United States." As Upton paused a few feet from the table, stricken with self-consciousness as everyone at the table turned to stare at him, London lurched to his feet as if he were greeting a long-lost friend, or indeed a comrade-brother. He staggered toward Upton as if to embrace him, colliding with a waiter and with a gentleman in a tuxedo seated at his table—"Make way, make way, damn you—this is *Comrade Sinc'ler*—make way and let the skinny fella in—runt of the litter—shy!— 'the meek shall enter first'—or—is it 'last'?—no matter, if you enter—better last, if the first is trompled over—'survival of the fittest'—sit!—here, my friend!—beside Jack, sit—there is plenty of room—my woman on my left hand, my brother Sinc'ler on my right— now, we are all meant where we are to be, or—we are all where we are meant to be, and the hour is still young."

Upton had no choice but to sit beside London, who pulled him down into the chair beside him; his face was hot with embarrassment, and a wild sort of elation, as if he, too, were drunk. Yet more surprising than London's welcome was Miss Charmian's—the perky little woman, not to be upstaged by her lover, leaned across London's stocky, grizzled chest to kiss Upton on the cheek!—warmly, wetly— tickling him with one of the curled macaw feathers that adorned her bosom, to the amusement of the table of revelers.

"Wel-come! Wel-come to—wherever this is! If you are Jack's brother, you are Miss Charmian's brother. *Sit.*"

There followed then a confusing interlude during which, though Upton protested that he didn't drink, he had vowed never to drink following his father's tragic experience with alcoholism, London tried to press on him any number of highly potent beverages, including what he called his *postperformance libation*, a blend of champagne, whiskey, and dark beer; even more strenuously, London tried to press on him the remaining half of his *cannibal sandwich*, a pound of raw beefsteak topped with onions, pickles, and catsup, on a kaiser roll, which lay on a nearby plate, the hard-crusted roll showing the imprint of London's teeth. He'd had a sixteen-ounce plank steak, London said, as well as two of the *cannibal sandwiches*, and had not been able to finish the second, though it was delicious. "Comrade Sinc'ler—you are looking so undernourished and anemic, as if the women had been uncommonly rough on you, you'd best gobble down this sandwich at once, and bring a little color to your cheeks."

"But—I think I may have mentioned to you, Jack—in one of my letters—I am a vegetarian. . . ."

At the mere utterance of the word "vegetarian" the table erupted in laughter—even Miss Charmian, who'd been so welcoming to Upton, laughed derisively. Upton laughed too, or tried to laugh—he was a good sport, in such situations—as a Socialist he'd learned to parry and thrust when baited, teased, even threatened; apologetically, he tried to explain that his "digestion" wouldn't accommodate such rich food, for he had some sort of stomach condition—"colitis"; yet, at this, the table again erupted in laughter, as if Upton had said something even more witty than before.

It was a relief when, laying his arm across Upton's shoulders, London regaled the table with an account of his favorite delicacies of the moment—number one wasn't beef, in fact, but "two large male mallards—cooked for no more than eight minutes to assure the fowl sufficiently *underdone.*"

This ushered in a protracted discussion of favorite delicacies, from around the table, which gave Upton some respite. He'd managed to order, from a harassed waiter, a bottle of mineral water, which he drank as unobtrusively as he could manage, not wanting his vociferous companion to notice; beside London, as in the vicinity of a blast furnace, he felt both warmed and overwarmed, dazzled, wary. Naively he'd hoped for some time with London during which they might have talked frankly together of politics, literature, the future of Socialism, possibly even the vicissitudes of married life, and love; naively he'd hoped that London might have sequestered a private room at the restaurant, and rebuffed the invitations of admirers to treat him and Miss Charmian to drinks and dinner. For, Upton was surprised, London didn't appear to be acquainted with even the gentleman in the tuxedo, who'd been seated beside him before Upton arrived, and Upton was surprised to learn that, far from journeying to New York City principally to address the Intercollegiate Socialist Society, London had come here on the first leg of a trans-Atlantic journey—his Yukon books had become runaway best sellers in Great Britain, France, Germany, and Russia, and his publishers in these countries were eager to host him—"It seems that I have quite eclipsed old 'Mark Twain'—the Germans especially despise Twain, y'know—the old fool has mouthed some crude sort of criticism of them—in defense of Jewry—*he* is in defense of Jewry—the Germans will not forgive him"—London burst into laughter, as if he'd never heard anything so amusing—"and caricature him now, in the public press, with a *Jew nose*."

This crude remark initiated a round of *Jew talk* and *Jew jokes*, which were offensive to Upton Sinclair, as well as shocking—for wasn't Socialism a wholly nonsectarian movement, vigorously led and supported by Jews?—as a Socialist, Jack London would know this fact, surely. What would Moses Leithauser think, if he could hear. . . .

Yet more disappointing, London seemed to have forgotten Upton Sinclair. After the initial fuss, London turned his back to him, addressing others at the table in the hale, hearty tone in which he'd addressed Upton; nor did Miss Charmian give Upton a second glance. London had moved now from his champagne concoction to straight Kentucky bourbon, in shot glasses.

Sprawling in his chair like a pasha, his heavy chin several times brought to rest on Miss Charmian's plump shoulder in a way to make the excitable woman emit little cries of laughter, London entertained the table and patrons of MacDougal's who'd gathered in a semicircle, with a rambling and disconnected monologue—his "Life Philosophy"—about which, evidently, there was enormous interest across the States.

"In interviews it is always inquired—'Where does Jack London's stamina derive from'—where, his ability to compose never less than one thousand words a day, and often near ten thousand, and how does he hold an audience in the palm of his hand—as I did just now in Carnegie Hall—for more than two hours, without slackening? Where, in short, is Jack London's particular 'genius'? Where, indeed." London chuckled deep in his throat, like a stirring beast; he pressed his chin downward on Miss Charmian's shoulder, in a way to make her squeal and glance about the restaurant in shivering delight. "Such questions," London continued, in a graver voice, "strike deep to the heart of primeval Being itself, and can't be answered, except, perhaps, in terms of *racial ancestry*. That is, to speak bluntly—the superiority of certain races, and the inheritance of these superior traits by 'superior' specimens within these races."

Now, to Upton's extreme discomfort, London began to speak with drunken animation of *Nordic supremacy*—the uncontested superiority of the *Beast-man*—descended from the great icy wastes of the polar region and "taking the sickly little dagos of the Southern hemisphere by storm." Upton dared to interrupt, objecting that such a belief was in violation of the Socialist brotherhood—"Are not all men equal?—men of all races, skin colors, and classes?—that is, *men and women alike*, in the Socialist fold? No race can claim superiority—no skin color—though, at this perilous point in history, the proletarian is undoubtedly superior, morally. . . ." But London rudely puffed on his cigar, releasing a virulent cloud of smoke, swallowed down another shot glass of bourbon, and snapped his finger to summon a waiter, to order more bourbon. It was uncanny; London behaved as if Upton Sinclair had not only not said anything, but wasn't seated in the chair beside him; London merely continued his monologue as if he hadn't been interrupted. Nor did Miss Charmian, or anyone else at the table, take note of his rudeness to his friend.

"The dominant races of the earth came down, you see, from the North. From the great ice fields and snowy wastes, the tundras, of the North. From the forest primeval—the abode of silent tragedy. Yes, it is ever so: *noisy comedy, silent tragedy*. Once, we were forged of iron, and much that is greater than iron, in the blast furnace of the soul. For there, y'see, in the pitiless North, the struggle for survival continues as always—as if it were not 1905 but the very beginning of history, and our feeble, effeminate 'civilized' notions of right and wrong, justice and injustice, social welfare and social outrage, never conceived." London sighed loudly, stubbing out his cigar in the remains of his beefsteak sandwich, and signaling for a waiter to carry it away.

111

With surprising boldness, for one so temperamentally quiet and loathe to quarrel, Upton Sinclair dared to raise an objection: "I don't doubt the 'pitilessness' of the North any more than I would doubt the 'pitilessness' of the Sahara or the Amazon rain forest—but I contest its application to human history. Doesn't this lead to the very 'social Darwinism' advanced by our enemies? Think of the criminal Rockefeller publicly congratulating himself that God had given him his money—or daring to compare the fruits of his criminal trust to the 'exquisite flowering of the American Beauty rose.'"

Again, London failed to reply to Upton. It might have been that he was preoccupied in searching through his pockets for another cigar (which Miss Charmian gaily provided him out of a glaringly sequined purse), or London simply didn't hear his comrade's remarks in the din of MacDougal's. In any case he scarcely altered his frowning gaze, or modified the condescending tone of his argument, proceeding as if uninterrupted: ". . . *never conceived*. And, indeed, mere jests upon the wind! For in the land of the midnight sun, where the wolf pack trots at the flank of the caribou herd, singling out the weak and the aged and the great with calf, and pulling them down to devour with not a flicker of remorse, it's a foolish fancy to prattle of such effeminate notions. The Nordic soul is a man's soul from time immemorial. Wolf knew, and Death knew—predator brothers of *The Sea Wolf*—but all know, in our hearts—even the slant eyed, the Jews, and the dagos. For that, my friends, is the cauldron out of which Jack London has been forged and it would be false modesty to claim otherwise." London cocked his railway cap at an aggressive angle on his thick, disheveled hair, as if to dare anyone to knock it off.

But no one at the table contested his words or, except for Upton Sinclair, seemed upset by them. Jocose toasts were drunk to the "Nordic soul"—to Jack London's "Nordic soul" in particular—while Upton, blushing and nettled, refused to drink even his mineral water, unnoticed.

It was now nearing 1 a.m., and the din of hilarity in MacDougal's showed no sign of abating. How lurid, this nocturnal life!—this *underbelly* sort of city life, of which Upton Sinclair had had no notion, in his monastic seclusion outside Princeton, New Jersey, and in his fervent dealings with immigrant Socialists of the Lower East Side, who rose early to work fourteen-hour days, and collapsed into bed most nights immediately after their evening meal. Jack London, tireless, continued his slurred monologue, while Upton berated himself—

112

what a fool he'd been, how naive, to have imagined that Jack London expected him here tonight, to have entered of his own volition a fashionable "gin mill" like MacDougal's. If his mother could see him, in such a place! If Meta could see him!

(It might have been the lateness of the hour, and Upton's dazed and distraught state, but, so oddly, he'd seen, or seemed to see, a woman resembling his wife to an uncanny degree, elsewhere in MacDougal's, though a far more blonde, frivolous, and glamorous Meta Fuller, in the company of a portly gentleman in a tuxedo, seated in a booth bracketed by mirrors, on the farther side of the restaurant. Upton knew—of course—this wasn't Meta, yet, like one digging at a sore, he couldn't seem to resist glancing over at her, at the woman, that is, who resembled Meta. *She is in Princeton, sleeping. She is nowhere near MacDougal's. Even if she were in Manhattan, she would not be in MacDougal's.*)

Upton could have wept, he'd been so naive! So—hopeful! Since they'd begun their correspondence in the summer, Upton had been anticipating an intimate meeting with his brother-hero; he had so many things to discuss with him—the "anarchist intellectual" C. L. James's *History of the French Revolution*—Benjamin Tucker's *Instead of a Book*, the reformer William Travers Jerome's revelations of prostitution in New York City, aided and abetted by Tammany Hall, and future plans for the Intercollegiate Socialist Society—how were they to draw more undergraduates into the organization, apart from Jewish boys, and a smattering of Jewish girls, from the Lower East Side? Yet more naively Upton had hoped to bare his soul to another man—a married man—of his own generation; he'd hoped to speak frankly of his predicament. Not that Meta had threatened to leave him, or had made any move to do so, but—in their marital relations, she had sometimes . . . she had frequently . . . expressed dissatisfaction with him, and impatience. *Is it a fear of pregnancy? Or—a fear of barrenness? Do all women fear pregnancy?—and barrenness? How can a man hope to speak to a woman—do we share an identical language?* Jack London had no trouble communicating with the Gypsy-like Miss Charmian, Upton was sure.

He'd known that something was wrong when, after her initial pride in Upton, for having completed *The Jungle*, Meta had expressed only the most perfunctory interest in the rumor that President Roosevelt had been reading a pirated galley of *The Jungle* and intended to invite the young author to Washington one day soon. . . .

113

Meta, I hope you will come with me! It will be a historic occasion. . . .

But where was Meta? Drifted off somewhere, in the tall grasses behind the rough-hewn little cabin, amid trees, and a tangle of wild rose, where Upton, who suffered from mysterious pollen and plant allergies, could not follow. . . .

". . . Korean valet, we have trained—Miss Charmian has trained!— to call his master 'God.' So very funny!"

Upton was becoming ever more repelled by his comrade-brother— the fleshy, flushed face, the air of bellicose complacency—the way London swilled his bourbon, and had made a shocking mess of his white silk blouse, unapologetically; he was wondering whether, frankly, London could be only thirty years old?—had he falsified his birth date, as he'd falsified so many other things about himself, like his Socialist convictions? Here was the heralded Socialist warrior who had emerged from the West only a few years ago, in a blaze of glory: Early photographs of the author of *The Call of the Wild*, which Upton had kept, in secret, in a drawer in his study where Meta was not likely to find them, showed a dreamy young man of unusual handsomeness; rugged and masculine, yet touched by a poetic delicacy suggestive of Percy Shelley in certain of the portraits. Where had the Boy Socialist gone? Was it simply to be ascribed to an excess of alcohol and rich foods and the adulation of the public? Though he'd been—perhaps!—just slightly envious of London's audience at Carnegie Hall, Upton had seen how seductive it is to entertain such large, rowdy audiences; how hard to resist, to stir belly laughs, if one can do it; how much more difficult to hew to a prescribed line of persuasion, and the rhetoric of logic; to uphold one's ideals, not to stoop to the level of vaudeville and burlesque. . . . A sort of terror gripped Upton Sinclair at the thought—the absurd thought—primitive, superstitious!—that the noble Jack London was the victim of an impostor; somehow, he'd been transformed into the brutish, drunken clown in the stained clothes and railway cap, a travesty of his former self; an assassin of the true Jack London; possibly—a demon. . . .

Upton rebuked himself: "Ridiculous! I don't believe in 'demons'— even when I was a Christian, I did not believe in 'demons.' There are only men—human beings—individuals not so very different from myself, though behaving in ways I find difficult to understand."

Now the table and the semicircle of admirers, which had grown to include as many as thirty individuals of both sexes in diverse stages of festive drunkenness, erupted in another sort of laughter, as the

114

berouged and bejeweled Miss Charmian told hilarious anecdotes of her Nordic lover. It might interest them all to know—indeed, Miss Charmian had told *The New York Post* in an exclusive interview—that it was true, Jack London had a Korean valet who called him "God"—and she, Miss Charmian, had indeed trained him. What was so very charming was that the valet, a sinister but "devilishly hand-some" boy named "Manyoungi," was very willing to call London God—"'For 'tis like God my master behaves,' the little heathen says," Miss Charmian laughed. Also, at a recent party in San Francisco hosted by her Jack, at which hashish and opium were distributed to the guests, along with all the liquor they could hold, her Jack had been so wicked as to play one of his famed practical jokes on his guests: He had barbecued a diamondback rattler and served it to them, with hollandaise sauce, under the pretense it was Pacific salmon and, when he revealed what he'd done, a number of the guests became nauseated, and several were sick to their stomachs—Miss Charmian erupted in high-pitched giggles. "Oh, the Sea Wolf is *cruel*—but he is *very funny* also. And Jack never does unto others what he would not happily do unto himself—for diamondback rattler is one of his favorite meats, barbecued or rare."

Hearing his mistress speak so warmly of him, as if he were on dis-play, London grinned, and set his railway cap backward on his head, and, conspicuously, reached over to pinch her plump rouged cheek, leaving a red imprint in the somewhat flaccid flesh.

The tale of the diamondback rattler had left Upton somewhat nauseated as well. He was wondering if he might leave London's company soon—as soon as possible—for London had ceased to no-tice him, and the hour was late. But when Upton rose to leave the table, immediately London swung to him, glaring and grinning, bar-ing "wolf" canines, and gripped him by the arm. "Comrade Sinc'ler! You have been very quiet—you are looking very pale. You have not been eating your 'cannibal sandwich,' I see—which is why you have the complexion of a corpse. Here—a toast, at least—" London forced a glass of champagne into Upton's limp fingers, and lifted a shot glass of bourbon for himself: "Up'on Sinc'ler—salt of the earth! Up'on Sinc'ler—great hope of the Revolution! Kingdom of Heav'n! Meek shall enter—last! Suffer little children—etcetera." All at the table lifted their glasses in a toast except for Upton himself who sat quiet-ly, weakly smiling, yet stubborn, and resistant.

"What? You refuse to drink? And why is that, comrade?—are you fearful of 'demon rum' possessing your papery soul?"

London laughed abusively. Again Upton tried to stand, and again London forced him back into his seat.

"*You* are one of us—though not a very 'potent' specimen—solid Aryan stock: half the earth our heritage, and all the sea, and in three-score generation *we shall possess the earth.* Would you deny your heritage, comrade?"

Upton tried to protest: He had no idea what London was talking about. And the hour was late, and early next morning he had work to do. . . .

"You would not deny, comrade, that there are 'pure' races and 'mongrel' races—surely? If the Socialist movement was not weakened by certain of its leaders—let us speak frankly, comrade: I mean Jews, like—what is his name—'Leet-hauzer'—our war against cap'lism would proceed swiftly. But a Jew is lily-livered in his soul—it is against the Jew's nature to fight—to the death. You would not deny this, comrade? Would you?"

In dismay, Upton said *yes.* He would deny this.

"The Socialist vision is *class war*—to the death! History has shown that the natural man—the natural warrior—may be born deprived of his heritage—born into an 'inferior' class—this is the stuff of legend, fairy tales—the prince under a curse, as a mere frog—his destiny is to rise up tooth and claw—fang and claw!—to tear out the throats of his persecutors and must rise up against those who exploit him—and drink their *sang impur.*" Uttering the French phrase—which London pronounced in phonetic English, with a strong, nasal "a"—London shoved at Upton's shoulder in a way to provoke.

Upton protested: "But—the Socialist vision is also—brotherhood—"

"'Brotherhood'—yesssss." London drawled the word, frowning. A waiter had brought a platter of raw oysters to the table, which London now began to eat, rapidly, tossing the shells onto the floor after he'd sucked the slithery white thing into his mouth, and swallowed it. As he ate he spoke, shaking a stubby forefinger at Upton Sinclair: "But as with our blood kin, not all are 'brothers'—not all are 'kin.' There is a natural aristocracy—it is useless to prevaricate, comrade. I suppose you would defend the lowlife 'Big Bill' Haywood?—I suppose 'One-Eye Big Bill' is your comrade, too?"

"Why, yes—certainly. Bill Haywood has been a great—brave—leader. . . . He has rallied the immigrant workers in New Jersey and . . ."

"'One-Eye Big Bill!'"—London scoffed in contempt. Miss Charmian tried to placate her lover by feeding him oysters, but London, ever more incensed, was not to be placated. "True, 'Big Bill' has

116

organized the silk-worker slaves of Paterson—but the strike is intended to showcase *him*—he has been threatening the owners, and they have insulted him, and—"

"Wait! Please! You should not be speaking of—a strike. . . . No, no!" Upton was horrified: The possibility of a strike in Paterson, of the silk-worker union, was meant to be confidential, he was sure. How did Jack London even know about this plan? "From what I know, a strike isn't definite—Bill Haywood hasn't yet made a decision."

"Haywood is a shameless debauchee," London said, with a sneer. "The megalomaniac drunkard—blatherer, windbag—never so happy as when he's speechifying before a fawning audience of the lowest mongrel sort. The lowest *mongrel-immigrant* sort."

"Bill Haywood is one of our Socialist heroes—a savior! Jack, I must disagree—"

" 'Jack, I must disagree.' " London rudely parroted Upton's words, in a falsetto voice, which inspired laughter at the table, and a flirtatious rebuke from Miss Charmian, who patted Upton's arm as one might pat a misbehaving puppy. "Rather should you say, 'Jack, I must *agree'*—for in your heart you know that I'm right. Should 'One-Eye Big Bill' be spread-eagled and dispatched by the Pinkertons, it would not be a grievous loss."

This remark was so callous, and obscene, Upton rose to leave. He could not bear remaining a minute longer! And when London tried to clutch at him, he lurched away, as a child might do, escaping the embrace of an adult. Except that Miss Charmian quickly restrained her lover, there would have been a scuffle. London's small red eyes glared: "You are not leaving our party so early! No one turns his back on Jack London's hospitality—no more than you would decline the hospitality of the Eskimo, if the smelly In'jun offers you his nasty 'smoked' fish, and his 'squaw.' I did not journey all the way to New York City from California to be rudely snubbed by the only man in the Socialist movement I halfway respect—though—to be brutally frank—much of *The Jungle* is slovenly work, even for a muckraker, betraying signs of the author's hack origins—and the last section is a comical sort of plagiarism of my speeches—my Oakland campaign speeches—did you think that no one would notice?"

Upton was too shocked to speak. He could not believe that London was turning on him—making such an accusation, before strangers.

"I haven't revealed the plagiarism to the press, just yet," London said, "for we Revolutionaries must stick together—like dogs in a pack. There is a lead dog, yes—but there is the pack. The 'lead dog' requires the 'pack'—even as the 'pack' requires the 'lead dog.' That is a law of nature."

Seeing the expression of shock and hurt in Upton's eyes, London laughingly relinquished him, and leaned back in his chair, teetering precariously on two legs. With forced relish he continued to devour oysters, washing them down with shots of bourbon. A sort of prankish demonism shone in his bloodshot eyes. "My friend, the error of your philosophy—your religion—your bourgeois morality—as your Soc'list morality—is the attempted legislation of impulse. 'One-Eye' doesn't comprehend this basic fact, nor Debs, nor—any of 'em! For the primeval spirit *never checks an impulse*. The free man *never checks an impulse*. The rest is all cant, and humbug, and nursery rhymes, and Bible verses! When Philosophy puffs itself up to instruct the individual soul *YOU MUST*, the individual soul at once rejoins *I WANT*—and does precisely what *IT WANTS*. So much for philosophy, and religion, and morality—the phantasms of eunuchs! For the brave man, the warrior, the Nordic soul, knows only I WANT—and never I MUST. It is the I WANT that spurs the drinker on to drink, in the face of all the mewling and puling teetotalers of the world—it's the glorious I WANT that makes the martyr eagerly cloak himself in his hair shirt, if it is the hair shirt that calls forth I WANT. The countless things I WANT constitute my scale of values, my private ethics—and there it is! Meat, and drink, and the passion of a free woman—the potency of the novelist's pen—the power of the voice, the throat, the mouth—and the vengeful class war of the Soc'list movement. Jack London's acclaimed achievement is FOR MY OWN DELIGHT. Jack London's genius is FOR MY OWN DELIGHT. It isn't 'spiritual'—it's 'organic.' Every fiber of my being thrills with it. The primeval I WANT, the glorious I WANT, the ineluctable I WANT, now and forever! —Eh, what's this? Are you mocking me? Are you sending each other signals?"

London had caught sight of Miss Charmian gazing intently at Upton, with tight-pursed crimson lips, and eyes squeezed near shut, as if she were indeed sending him a secret signal—not flirtatiously but with concern, to discourage Upton from further opposing her lover and provoking him to ferocity. But, like one guiltily found out, Upton blushed to the roots of his hair.

"You dare—to mock *me*?"

"I—don't know what you mean. . . ." Upton swallowed hard, he was incapable of uttering the name *Jack*, even pleadingly. "I'm not mocking—anyone. . . ."

Whether the belligerent London really felt primeval jealousy, or whether prolonged sitting in one place had made him restless and spoiling for a fight, suddenly he erupted into action, with a wolfish cry; he scrambled to grip Upton Sinclair in a wrestling hold, shouting his intention to commit murder.

"Signaling to *my woman!—my mate*! In front of *my eyes*! That is punishable by death."

Trying to wrest Upton from his chair and onto the floor, London lost his balance and fell, pulling Upton onto the floor with him. In the frantic scuffle the chair was overturned, there came a shattering of glass and china; there were shouts, and shrieks; Miss Charmian leapt to her feet, quick and fierce as a wild cat intent upon protecting her young. Upton, on principle and by temperament a pacifist, had no idea how to adequately defend himself, still less to fight aggressively, but blindly struck at the heavier man with his fists even as London, bawling like a maddened beast, seized a bottle from the table, smashed it, and brought the jagged edge against Upton's throat—"Mock Jack London, will you! Mock the *Sea Wolf*, will you! There are insults to be repaid only in blood." London outweighed Upton by more than thirty pounds but he was badly winded, and disoriented; Upton slipped beneath his flailing arms and managed to get a chair between him and London—an inanimate, obdurate object that baffled London as if he had no idea what it was or how to contend with it; for London was very drunk, and his bloodshot eyes had lost their focus, and his fists swung wide of their mark. Upton begged for London to let him go, but London would not; again London savagely lunged at him with the broken bottle, and this time by sheer panicked strength Upton managed to overturn the chair onto London, knocking London to the floor a second time on his back, with such accidental force that London's head struck the floor, hard; you could hear the sickening *thud* of the man's hard skull striking the wooden floor like a hammer blow.

Miss Charmian threw her squat little body at Upton Sinclair, clawing at his exposed skin with red-painted talon nails. "Beast! What have you done! Call the police! He has murdered my darling Jack! Oh—the blood! My darling Jack is bleeding from his scalp! This is outright murder! The great Jack London—oh help!"

Upton tried to push the frenzied little woman away—how like a wild cat she was, hot eyed, hot skinned, baring sharp little teeth, and raking her claws against him however she could; valiantly he was trying to help London to his feet, but the stunned man had little strength in his legs; Miss Charmian continued to scream and to claw at him as Upton turned to her, to try to placate her; for she was nearing a state of hysterics, hyperventilating; her small pug face glowered with an unnatural heat. It was so, Jack London had been injured in the accidental fall; he was bleeding freely from a scalp wound, streams of blood running down his fleshy face that was now drained of color, deathly pale; his lips had gone loose and were pale also, wet with salivalike froth. To the staring throng Upton stammered: "It wasn't my fault—he attacked me—I was only defending myself—I didn't mean—you must have seen, I didn't mean to—harm him. . . ."

Miss Charmian screamed: "Oh—stop him! Murderer! He has killed our prince! The greatest literary genius of our time!"

"But—you are all witnesses. . . ."

Upton fumbled to wrap a napkin around London's head to stanch the bleeding, but his hands shook badly, and the wounded man continued to flail feebly at him, and curse him; Upton let the blood-soaked napkin fall to the floor and backed away from the table, desperate now to escape. As if seeing something terrible in his face, unknown to Upton Sinclair, the others shrank from him; a path opened for him to take out of the crowded restaurant and onto Forty-second Street where the night air was startlingly fresh. In Upton's wake were cries—*Stop him! Call police! Murderer!*—dimly heard, as in a fading dream.

Quickly Upton ducked into an alley beside MacDougal's. From the alley, though he had never been in this terrible place before, and had only the vaguest sense of what he was doing, deftly he made his way to another alley, and so to Forty-first Street, and then Broadway, near deserted at this time of night, where he found himself half running, south, in the direction—he believed it was the direction—of Penn Station. There would be no train at this hour but, in the morning—he would take the first train to New Jersey, in the morning—"Demons! I have entered a region of demons, and narrowly escaped with my life."

The clothes he'd so carefully chosen for this evening's rally—beige flannel trousers, a dark-brown gabardine coat, white cotton shirt— were torn, and smelled shamefully of alcohol; his fair, fawn-colored hair was disheveled, his cheeks were lacerated and bleeding as if clawed by a cat; both his ears smarted and stung and, on the following day, when his wife saw him, and stared at him with startled, amazed eyes, he would discover that part of his left earlobe had been torn or bitten off, the tiny wound encrusted with a black, brackish little blood button.

Sunlight
Michael Coffey

IT WAS A TERRIBLE SATURDAY, the kind of Saturday you have after a Friday night spent explaining to your third wife why you had a hooker in your house and how the condom wrapper she spotted under the couch was not, after all, necessary. I promised said wife I would get some help. To mark my sincerity, I suggested we all go to a bookstore—wife, son, me. I'd start there. This earned her gruff consent.

I considered changing everything about the way I read, but my remorse ran deeper. I considered changing everything about the way I lived, loved, breathed, and ate as well. I was in that not-smoking-not-drinking-resume-going-to-Mass place, maybe learn-a-foreign-language-and-spend-a-decade-reading-Dickens place. I would live forever in family. I was in the poorhouse of want and shame, which dogs often call home. It's where I belonged.

In the poetry section, I picked up an anthology edited by Robert Bly—he couldn't have been more disdainful of the kind of work I had loved; I'd always returned the favor. He wanted "story," "emotion," "power," and "love." He wanted language treated as sacred, not something to be torn, shorn, and laid naked. That's it! That's what I wanted to hear now. Next to Bly was an old favorite—Charles Bernstein, founding Language poet, colleague, friend. On the back of his book, this: "Bernstein's allegiance has not been to any one kind of poetry, but to an 'artificed' writing that refused simple absorption into the society around it." Why would I be interested in that? *Refusing* society? What had that done for me? What was I doing? I took the Bly and dropped Charles back in his slot.

I moved to the self-help section. I stood there in the brightly lit area (it seemed more brightly lit than the poetry section—is that possible?). I found the adoption books, most of them on how to adopt. Or how to search. Being adopted was the source of my problems, I'd grimly announced. My wife approved this line of inquiry. I was on it.

I spotted Betty Jean Lifton's spread of titles on the adoption experience. I opened one of them and found a brief section headed "Literature" toward the back. It dealt solely with the writer Harold

Brodkey—"an adoptee who is not involved in the adoption movement." Adoption movement? I decided to leave that part for another time.

Lifton offered up Brodkey as a victim of what she called the adoption syndrome, and his prose as symptomatic of an adoptee's unwhole self. Brodkey had told her that he "used adoption as a form of freedom—it separates you from the norm."

"Brodkey is all adoptees writ large," she concluded. Adoption, freedom, writing. I leafed inside for more:

Orphans—Oedipus, Moses, Sargon, Romulus, Remus, and Superman . . . pretended to be real persons in everyday relationships and then disappeared on secret exploits that they shared with no one. . . .

Unless caught.

Adoptees, then, live with a dual sense of reality, wanted and unwanted, superchild and monsterchild, immortal and mortal. . . . One part chosen, the other abandoned.

And left on the carpet.

Adoptee fantasies are an attempt to repair one's broken narrative, to dream it along. They enable the child to stay magically connected with the lost birth mother.

Her name was Cinnamon, she said.

I underlined the words "broken narrative" so hard I tore through the page: everything I did not know captured in two words—and now it's the only thing I know.

I took the Lifton book, returned the Bly to his slot, picked up the Bernstein again, put it back again, and read in a chair till the rest of the family had made their choices. I had made mine: Lifton, with a promise to find Brodkey.

"An accidental glory." These three words end the first thing I ever read by Harold Brodkey, a story of his called "His Son, in His Arms, in Light, Aloft," long ago. The story appeared in an issue of the *New American Review*, edited by Ted Solotaroff. "Then" was around 1979 or '80, after *NAR* had become defunct, and its slim teal-colored volumes, each bound like a mass-market paperback, could be found in used-book bins all over the city. They made for bargain reading. I was young and new to New York City and its literary culture. I was making $117 a week as a copy editor for the Institute of Electronic and Electrical Engineers on East Forty-seventh Street.

By the time I arrived at these three words—sitting alone in my fourth-floor walkup on Eighty-first Street—I was in tears, breathing hard. That's what I remembered of Harold Brodkey.

"His Son, in His Arms, in Light, Aloft" is about one thing—a son being carried by a father, into and out of sunlight. That's it. In about seven thousand words, you go from "I am being lifted into the air" to the ending, where the sunlight is so bright in the child's eyes that he turns his head inward, toward the heat of his father's neck, and then notices his father's face, "unprotected from the luminousness all around us . . . caught in that light. In an accidental glory."

That passed for love, in Brodkey. It passed for love with me—a tableau, of some relation, in a wider, alien luminousness, where nothing is fated, nothing is assured; where everything's an accident, but nonetheless glorious.

I was particularly vulnerable to that kind of thing at that time: My little boy, from my first marriage, not yet two years old, and his mother, after trying to live with me, had decamped for Indiana, where she was from and where we had met three years earlier. Together she and I had endured a romantic collision at the end of my senior year of college, gotten married at an outdoor hippie/Chicano civil ceremony that August, complete with roasted pig, Mexican rock band ("Los Impactos"), and plenty of psilocybin; we'd braved a year in Leeds, England, as I worked toward a master's degree; survived my parents' disapproval of our marriage and then enjoyed their blessing when my son was born; but we couldn't handle eighteen months of being poor and unaccomplished and kid burdened, and we came apart. Though one part of me was giddy with the freedom of being single again and not strapped by nightly, suffocating family affairs and grinding domestic chaos, I missed my little boy.

I might have seen Brodkey not long after. I was sitting in my local Irish bar, where I stretched out five dollars nearly every night into eight or nine mugs of draft beer with a dollar's tip, mourning my losses by forgetting them. A man wearing the face I'd seen pictured in a copy of *Esquire*, with the long, solid, beveled head and accus-ing eyes, came through the door, his cashmere coat swinging from his broad shoulders like the cape of a warrior, a garment he seemed to expect someone would relieve him of, so that then he could fire off a few quick combinations like a fighter, or, presto, produce a handkerchief from a sleeve and release a dove. An elegant woman with a cap of short silvery hair followed in his wake, looking bemused. She did not remove his coat and they did not stay for a drink, as I had hoped. Harold bulled his way to the bar and asked—a bit imperiously of Leo the barman, I thought—directions to some place he was clearly not in. Snow melted and winked out on the wool of his topcoat. I thought of saying something about his story or something clever in the literary-gossip category—"What's up with Joseph Heller? I read it. *Nothing* happened!"—but I was in my cups, so I swallowed it. Through the bar's large window I could see the two of them on Second Avenue, looking north. Harold donned a hat I had not seen— a fedora; he snapped the brim as if setting a course, put his arm around his lady, and together they sailed forth.

That was the last I thought of Harold Brodkey for the next sixteen or seventeen years, during which time I built a career in publishing, wrote a few books, married again, and then again; cycled out of New York for brief stints—for a small literary press in Dutchess County, for the editorship of a magazine about small literary presses, in Connecticut—and generally filled my reading with writers who were not Harold Brodkey. I could hardly be faulted for abandoning Harold: During this time, if he was known at all, it was for *not* publishing. Something about a long-promised novel, announced more than once in publisher catalogs, that had continually failed to appear, its nonexistence moving from house to house, looking for a home that would have it, for a house that would wait for its author to finish, pronounce it done. When it did come, the reviews were dismissive: *The Runaway Soul.* I did not read it.

Could I be faulted for abandoning my young son? He was now a teenager; he lived in Indiana. He had two younger half brothers. I saw them all at his mother's funeral—my first wife's funeral. She died brutally of hypothermia, alone, drunk, in a cold January rain. Could I be faulted for having moved on, to other marriages, now my third, with a new son? These questions hadn't vexed me much, but they would. And they turned me back to Harold Brodkey—with an assist from that small tear of condom-wrapper foil, detritus from a drunken night alone in the city when the family was away.

Over the years I had maintained a respect for the Brodkey style that I remembered from the father-son story, not to mention a notion of literary celebrity from that sighting in the bar, even if I'd only imagined it. I knew there weren't other stylists working like that, endlessly circling a subject or a feeling, spending an entire story on one small shaft of sunlight and those it falls upon, pushing people, the same people, in and out of it, and writing about it. There was a rawness of emotion in what I sensed in his work: not coarse, like Harry Crews or Charles Bukowski, but deeply nuanced, like very complicated surgery into emotion's entrails—Henry James–like, but speedy, neurotic, modern. I was wary of it. Still, I was too engaged, during those years, in other projects of reading and coping and not coping, to follow what Brodkey was (not) up to. Then that night and the penitential bookstore visit that followed.

I proceeded to read all of Brodkey—the two slim volumes of stories; the huge story collection (*Stories in an Almost Classical Mode*); the novel *The Runaway Soul*; the Venice novel, *Profane Friendship*; the outtakes from *PF* (*My Venice*); the nonfiction essays and reviews, *Sea Battles on Dry Land*; and the final statement about his coming to his death by AIDS, *This Wild Darkness*—and I decided I had no sympathy for him. Inside the front cover of one of his books, I scribbled, "HB: So incapable of forgiveness himself that his principle project is to so irk the reader as to make the reader unforgiving too. Now we're all guilty."

Brodkey was famously prickly, by most accounts vain and preening. He was a braggart in his books—about his genius, his prick, his luck "in sex, in looks"—and he comes off as simply asinine. He thought he was original and brave and at the end declared himself "tired of defending my work." Tired he may have been, but there is no defending the author of so many confused, contradictory, obnoxious, ill-kempt, and self-important paragraphs that tumor his work. Like this, from *Runaway Soul*:

The thing about the absolute and the artists who made art out of it is that the only structure they have which generates emotion is the structure of the awesomeness of the absolute and then the curiously moving pain and comedy of the mind wandering as it inevitably does in real moments, in the immensities of the real; and I prefer the structures of actual emotion and the reality of moments.

It's a shame that Brodkey's excesses were not reined in, because what he was after—"making conscious language . . . deal with wild variability . . . by telling a story in reference to real time"—is a laudable project, one pursued by only a few major practitioners—Proust, Stein, Kerouac. And it led to some remarkable literary feats—his infamous story "Innocence," about bringing a woman to her first orgasm—a thirty-two-page story, fifteen thousand words, some of them laughable, some of them memorable ("To see her in sunlight was to see Marxism die"), full of Brodkey's obnoxious self-regard, but also a rare ride along, in prose, with someone thinking and feeling and, in this case, fucking. True, it was sensationalist, but in a way it was the perfect Brodkey story arc—a steady state of want/desire accompanied by physicality and talk ending in a climax.

I met Brodkey once, and it was perhaps the boldest thing I have ever done, and one that I may have yet to answer for in some literary afterlife—a wild aesthetic gambit born of desperation. I knew from Lifton, whom I began to see as a therapist, that Brodkey was sick, and then I knew from *The New Yorker* ("I have AIDS. I am surprised that I do.") what he was sick from. I knew from Lifton where he lived, and who his wife was. I was reading all his work, I had many questions, complaints, and compliments to offer, and I decided to call Ellen Schwamm Brodkey, Harold's wife. She answered the phone. Her voice was heavy, as if imitating a man's. If it was playful, it was play with an edge. "Hel-lo—o-o," she said, and dragged it out, near peevish, a note or two—as if to say, "Make this good. Or good-bye."

I said who I was and what I wanted—to talk to her husband about his writing and adoption; that I was adopted—she cut me off with some guttural sound. I assumed it was with purpose. I went silent. She was silent. Then I heard a croaky "What is it?" It was Harold. His syllables crumbled into air like a day-old baguette. Wispy. Again I said who I was and what I wanted; I was an admirer of his work and hoped to talk to him about his writing and—he cut me off, but this was for a cough, a long cough that was going to cost him dearly in precious breath. I could hear a gasping receding from the phone.

"Do you mind hanging on?" said Ellen, back on. I realized then, as I waited, hearing the howling run of Harold's coughing, that these were fucking tough people. "No, no," I said. "Should I call—?" She cut me off again. "He does this. He'll get over it. Honey now . . . ," I could hear her say, love in her voice as his awful hoarse huffing began to subside.

They invited me to come up and visit on the following Sunday. "The newspapers bring him to life, and then he is talkative—aren't you, Harold—especially the *Book Review*," she said, laughing, at his expense, I felt. I heard a squawk from him and wondered what I was in for.

It was going to be a big event for me, and my wife knew it. She had welcomed my efforts at reform as a promising start. She suggested I take some time to myself on Saturday—"Do what you have to do"— to prepare for Sunday's assignation. I took a couple of his books—the early stories and the one just out then, *Profane Friendship*, a novel (his second; all of a sudden—written, I heard, in nine months!)—and some clippings I'd found, and a notebook for notes, and I set off for the New York Public. I got as far as the Lion's Head, about forty blocks short.

I remember sitting in the sunlight that spilled in off Christopher Street. It was late fall, a near winter light, the low southern sun coming through a leafless Sheridan Square. I loved the way the day's first drink hit, and how the thin, kind light brought out the burl in the bar's rounded rail.

I set to work in the bar. No one was there to bother me, the regulars not up yet, not in. I wrote down question after question for Brodkey. I decided to assure him at the outset that this was to be an inquiry into writing style and its connection ("if any") to the experience of adoption. I wrote down what Lifton had quoted him as saying and what she had said of his work ("the experience of every adoptee writ large"). I would bring *Profane Friendship* for him to sign. I was certain he loved this book—because it was a clear embrace of love between men, and here he was, dying of AIDS and being accused of being a publicity bitch even as death made its way toward him, and of floating a fallacious chronology of when he got AIDS (in the 1970s, he wrote). I thought immediately—this is a time frame that squares with something he told his wife, he's lying, and I resolved not to ask him about it. "It's your story to tell," I imagined saying to him.

Was this just a fantasy, meeting Harold Brodkey, in his home, to ask these questions? As I lapped at my fourth or fifth Beck's, I got scared. I might blow it off. I might never go. Usually, an idea like this stays an idea, an imagined conversation, one in which I can ask bold questions, be told clever answers, and never have to actually sit in the humid, live space with another person, in this case an enigmatic stranger who is dying.

I would go there, I decided. I must. I closed my notebook. I moved to the other end of the bar, just as a couple of my mates came in, surprised to find me there, and more surprised that I was already well on my way. A long day into evening it was—college football, Clinton jokes. Frank McCourt walked in; over the din, I tried to impress him with my project for the next day with Brodkey. I tried to tell Frank of the broken narrative of the famine survivors. "You're a little cracked there yourself, Michael," he said. He wouldn't say a word about Brodkey. "I hear it's your birthday, is it," he said, and bought me a drink. And it was.

Their apartment on the Upper West Side was like other Upper West Side apartments I'd been in—sudden, intricate warrens of rooms with unaccountable amounts of sunlight within. This was where and how, I had come to feel, a certain professional class from a certain era lived in Manhattan—Jewish, doctors, theater people; the heart of the city's opera and serious drama market; liberal Democrats; good people, people who read fiction. People who would take me in.

The doorman announced me and I was sent up. The elevator opened onto a hallway with a mirror over a small table with a bowl of flowers. I looked terrible. I looked dark eyed and haunted. No, I didn't. I looked more closely in the wobbly light of the glass—dark eyed, I was; maybe handsome. I looked vulnerable. This is how I wanted to appear to Harold Brodkey.

Ellen answered the door. She was taller than I, her face handsome. She said, Hello, Michael, warmly. She had short white hair, enormous bangle earrings. She was made up. There were hoops upon hoops of a silk blouse around her neck and upper body, capri pants, and slippers. She was lovely.

I made my way in. No Harold.

I was offered coffee or tea. Coffee, black, I said. Harold was to be brought out by a nurse, Ellen informed me. I heard the radio go silent—she'd clicked it off. That awful Isaiah Sheffer introducing the awful William Hurt.

I held my tongue about Sheffer, whose pompous intoning over a tuning orchestra introduced every week an otherwise valuable series of short stories on radio. But my mind was slow with yesterday's drink, heavy as a loaf of vinegar-soaked bread. I feared I smelled as bad. I would need to refer to my notes, which were right at hand. Harold rolled into the room.

He was not grizzled, he was shaven. His head looked enormous and dented, as if his skull had suffered an accident and been acceptably banged out in a body shop with rubber mallets. His hair was so short and gray that it was barely distinguishable from his pale skin. The eyes were another matter, though—bright, somehow sharp edged, as if made of broken glass, and they glittered under eyebrows that were restless. He smiled crookedly and extended his hand from beneath a beautiful tartan blanket.

"Thank God you came. Life's too short to hear Bill Hurt do Hemingway over into a what? A car salesman."

"I can't stand that show," I blurted out, as Ellen handed me coffee in a large French bowl. I needed my two hands to hold it, so I put my books down.

"Let's sit down," Harold said. He cocked his head, amused that, of course, seated he already was.

"So, you're with *Publishers Weekly*, I understand." I hadn't mentioned that. I was an editor there.

"Yes," I admitted.

"You like my book?" he asked, looking at the copy of *Profane Friendship* I had placed on the coffee table.

"I think it is very beautiful. It reminds me of Thomas Mann. It's your *Death in Venice*?" My lip was trembling. I hadn't read Mann's short book, but had seen the Antonioni movie with Dirk Bogarde long ago.

He looked at me and puffed a breath. "I guess you didn't write this then?" He closed his eyes. "And I quote: 'Brodkey's logorrhea is painful to read, endlessly, strenuously yet tentatively straining for effect; never has a severe editor been more needed. There is a considerable talent here, certainly, but buried in self-indulgence.'"

From memory he did this. I was silent.

"*Publishers Weekly*," he said.

"Well . . . ," I began.

"My editor was hurt." His face broke into all kinds of parts of a smile. Tough all right.

I told him I loved self-indulgence. "Who else can we indulge?" I offered, and he looked approvingly at Ellen, who was busy adjusting the blinds.

"*Whom*," he corrected me, with a glance.

"We can only try," Ellen said with feigned weariness, as the blinds ruffled down loudly.

"Stop," he said.

I rushed to reassure him, this sick man. But came up empty.

"Turgid and self-indulgent, that word again," he said, quoting. "*Publishers Weekly, The Runaway Soul.* You've been hard on me, but I deserve it."

I told him that anyone wrestling to make a sentence convey the movement of thought and feeling in the act of thinking and feeling, not in reflection, but in action, is going to find it hard going. Only real writers appreciate the bravery of the struggle. He liked that.

I began to feel doubts about my own problems with Harold's excesses. If I wanted a writer to follow the movements of thought as they are thought, why should I complain that some of it lacks structure, argument, discipline?

I had to go on, though. I decided to brave it: "I don't think you do story very well," I said to him, and hastened to add, "I don't either," as if he gave a shit. "I can't even tell a joke"—my favorite line about this malady.

"Hummph." He made the noise, and I waited. "How to tell a joke." His voice trailed off and his eyes settled on a buttercup of sunlight shimmering on the opposite wall. We both watched it. Ten seconds passed.

"I can't master—and I wonder what you feel about this," I said, pulling out my notebook, "the going from a to b to c; the plot building, the holding back of information in order to build mystery and then delivering it with artful timing."

"That's quite true," he said, and closed his eyes.

Ellen was gone now. The nurse I had seen but for a second was gone as well. The room was silent, the furniture respectfully at ease. I thought he might be falling asleep.

"What do you like—*specifically*—about my work? Tell me." His eyes opened.

"I think 'The River' section of *Runaway Soul* is a brilliant set piece. No one else could have written it."

"It's about jerking off," he said, challengingly, "in a river. Who else *would* have written it?"

I said, "Mr. Brodkey, it is about more than . . . jerking off." My hesitation—was it prudery?—brought a look of interest to his face. I think he might have wanted to talk about jerking off, but was intrigued by having the conversation turn, if now it was, to talking about not talking about jerking off.

"It's about sunlight," I ventured, "and shadow and the pull of a river and birdsong and clouds and being a young child, an adopted boy, entering puberty, entering this river—was it the Missouri?—and being afraid that someone—his adoptive father, right?—was about to die, or had died, I can't . . ."

He cut me off. "Yes, yes, yes. I love that piece. I found such release in it. Do you know," he asked, rolling his chair back a little, "Kafka's story 'The Judgment'?"

Indeed I did! "I do, yes." This was a lucky break. "I know the last line, in fact."

"Really. Well, what is it? I forget."

"'At that moment the traffic was literally frantic.'"

"Yes," he said, closing his eyes again. "Something like that."

There was a long pause before he resumed. I realized he was wait-ing out the crunching sounds of some trash compacting from the street. "Kafka said that he wrote that story in one sitting, through the night. A father humiliates a son, and the son runs to the train trestle, hangs beneath the bridge, and lets himself go, down into the gorge. The end. He said it was like an orgasm when he wrote that last sentence—*literally frantic*."

This had to be the end of the interview. I wanted to run out of there. It was too perfect. But I couldn't. There was nowhere to run to, there were tears in my eyes. I felt vivid.

Without composure, I said, "Is that the perfect story then? One that follows an emotion into some kind of . . . release? Death? Or"— I hazarded it—"ejaculation?"

Harold suddenly seemed tired. His eyes were at half-mast. "Yes, I suppose so. It's the best we can do. But not enough."

Ellen brought some scones out, and offered lemonade. "Fruit only for you, Harold." She placed a bowl of melon cubes in his lap.

I crumbled through a scone while Harold sucked at the melon bits. We recovered, for it seemed we had to.

"What else did you want to ask?" he said, and I felt the shadow of the nurse behind me.

"I wanted to know, sir," adopting for no good reason a jocular tone, "if you felt that not having a complete uninterrupted story to your life, because of the adoption and being raised by, what, a second cousin to your father and her husband in a weird place like Univer-sity City, Missouri, you were unable to write—or was it *uninter-ested* in writing—a conventional narrative, something beyond the template of, say, sexual *coming*. Some of your stories follow the same path."

He thought for a long time. I stopped chewing my scone.

"Uninterested," he said. "Ergo unable."

As I descended in the elevator I realized I had forgotten to have him sign my book. In fact, I had left it there. When the doorman showed me the street, the sunlight was blinding. I had no dark father's face to turn away to, for shade. I stared into the sun's wide glare for the second I could stand it, then dropped my lids. An explosion of reds, sheets of Rubylith and sea life, in a flood—all of this a fantasy, for I have never met Mr. Brodkey, but such is what we do with broken narratives: We try to mend them as we can.

The Kiss

Joshua Furst

1.

WHEN I THINK BACK ON THEM—and I try not to—I see them racing, a pack of wild dogs, across the sloping lawn behind our low-slung ranch of a school. It's recess and spring and the game is French tag. The girls chase in looping arcs after the boys—the same boys who, during the frigid waste of January, stood on the ten-foot-high boulders of frozen snow bulldozed along the parking lot's perimeter daring kids like me to climb up and challenge them. The girls chase these violent, scowling boys, and when they catch them, they do so with great fearless, headlong leaps, take them tumbling down onto the patchy grass where they kiss them and kiss them and kiss them without relent until the siren reels us back into Mrs. Bussmueller's room. I'm on the sidelines, watching from a distance, full of awe and longing.

Sandi Shuete, Jackie Voight, Tina Reitz. Their names still agitate like cattle prods. They were the daughters of dairy farmers and corn farmers, of tough, wiry men who clocked in at seven for their daily shifts at the Green Giant plant out in Cambellsport. On the mornings before school, while I was still dreaming under my Star Wars sheets, the girls in my class were out picking rocks and bailing hay and slopping feed into pig troughs.

My family wasn't from around those parts. We'd moved to the region from a long ways off, from a city on the coast, where the food showed up prepackaged at the supermarket and the closest I'd come to the natural world was throwing a Frisbee in Fort Ward Park and studying the bees at the insect zoo. I was awkward and short and instead of knowing how to maneuver machinery or birth calves like them, I took violin lessons and spent hours practicing how to draw the superheroes in my comic books. What I remember most strongly of that time is the deep shame that metastasized inside me. I ached to be a different sort of boy, a harder boy, one who wasn't scrawny and wasn't drawn to art, one who didn't wear glasses and never had to think twice about how his behavior might be interpreted by the people around him.

To combat this precocious self-consciousness, I found an ever-growing number of ways to play the fool and gain my classmates' attention. I scrubbed the knees of my jeans with rocks until I'd worn holes in them and tromped through puddles on my way to school, hoping that with the right costume I'd suddenly morph into one of the bad kids. I swore, often, and always incorrectly, placing the word in just the right position within the sentence to expose how little I knew of its meaning. I was the kid who ate bugs for a quarter and stuck his finger down his own throat, vomiting on a dare, begging for mockery. I searched my prized sci-fi books for dirty sections to pass around the school bus, as though by thrusting bad literature on the kids in front of me, I'd somehow prove myself wise in the ways of love. I made myself known, and if not liked, at least appreciated, an object to be observed and wondered over, like the wounded raptors at the Horicon Marsh Nature Preserve.

During recess on rainy days, when we were forced to play inside the classroom, one of the girls—Sandi, maybe Tina, but I'm going to say it was Jackie—would sometimes pull her chair up alongside my desk and, a glint in her eye, ask what I was drawing.

"That's Cyclops, from the X-Men. He's married to Jean Grey," I'd say, blurting out the words in a rushing stream of bluster and pride. Or, "It's Uncle Duke! Don't you read *Doonesbury*? I'm working on the whole set of them and then I'm going to send them to Garry Trudeau."

And Jackie would nod, her face void of recognition, eyebrows arched high, mouth dropping open a lurid fraction. "That's so interesting. You're a good drawer," she'd say. Then she'd flit away to giggle with her friends and shoot derisive glances in my direction.

I knew they were mocking me but to admit this would have meant succumbing to my social isolation. Instead, I imagined I was expanding their minds, that they were slowly growing to recognize—or in my more delirious moments, admire—the value in the differences between me and the other boys they knew.

What I'm saying is, I was recklessly lonely. And this is the simplest—though not the only—explanation for the crush I developed on Molly Wiggins and for the things I did as a result.

Molly sat right up front next to the door and from my assigned seat across the room I had a perfect diagonal view of her. She wasn't like the other girls. She was taller, for one thing. Instead of muddy jeans, she came to school in paisley print dresses and dainty black dance shoes. Her long blonde hair was always carefully brushed and she often wore it in a single wide braid, tied with a ribbon near the small of her back. She'd hit puberty early and her breasts bulged against her training bra—there was a softness to her body in general that intimated, at least to me, a concurrent softness to her personality. Like me, she was shy and stuck on the edges of the maelstrom that was our fifth-grade class. Unlike me, she had the sense not to draw attention to these facts.

Her cheeks were splashed with freckles and her family raised horses and with this information, and this information only, I spun a great virginal myth around her. She was Heidi. She was Anne of Green Gables. She was fresh bread and dandelion kisses, a wholesome American innocent, and though I had never spoken to her, though I had no idea *how* to speak to her, or even stand near her in line for the lunchroom, I was convinced that it was my calling to protect her from the scabby-kneed society that I feared might shake and spoil her.

Peering at her through the bunker of my elbow while I rested my head on the chilly laminate desk, I'd imagine us skipping off to a perfumed location where no one could reach us, a mountaintop, the seashore, it didn't matter where, someplace where we could run barefoot and pick berries and sit on the hearth singing gentle folk songs that reinforced our belief in the tranquil peace just over the jagged cusp of adolescence.

Or something like that.

I don't really remember what I imagined. The point is that, for hours each day, through Math and Social Studies and Sustained Silent Reading, I'd gaze at her across the room and dream about the cinematic cliché my life would become if she were to love me as much as I did her.

It was all very sweet. Except that, because of the particularly dramatic tenor of my self-consciousness, I couldn't keep my tender feelings to myself. I feared they might be wrong—I might be experiencing them wrongly, or have the wrong idea of what they were supposed to mean—and the only way I could be sure about them was to try them out.

How the news went public has slipped from my mind, another of the endless embarrassments I've self-protectively rid from my memory, but I can imagine the way the scene played out. Jackie, or one of the other girls, would have been standing over the edge of my desk, her face filled with that mix of bemusement and scorn that I still believed could be tilted toward acceptance if I could just find the right way to impress her. She was maybe complimenting my atrocious play in that morning's gym-class game of kickball, or telling me the difference between Protestants and Catholics (Protestants pick their noses, Catholics pick their butts), searching for a way to rile me, if she could manage it, to make me cry. These girls loved it when they could get me to make a scene.

Eventually, she'd squint and quiz me on myself, already knowing the answers she expected.

"Do you like girls, Jordan?"

"Duh. Yeah."

"Yeah, right. You probably don't even know the difference between boys and girls."

A dumb look, head tipped, eyes rolled into my brow.

"Anyway, you don't act like you like girls. I bet you're a gay."

Here I'd have to bluff, steer clear of the dirty, vaguely understood word. I'd blurt out with too much force, "I *love* girls!"

And her face would prune with skepticism.

"I love Molly Wiggins."

Maybe for a moment Jackie just stared at me. Then she reeled away and inserted herself into the cluster of girls on the other side of the room and all I could do was wait. There it came, that horrid, haunting sound. The gasps and cackles of preadolescent girlhood.

Whatever the circumstance, I recall the effect my disclosure had on my psyche. I knew I'd made a mistake. I'd betrayed myself. I'd thrown my dignity away. From that moment forward, my feelings for Molly Wiggins were no longer mine, they belonged now to everyone, and stripped of their nuance, disingenuous, they were something to be performed rather than felt.

It took a while, maybe fifteen, twenty minutes, for the gossip to spread all the way to Molly, demure in her corner, not paying attention to the buzz circling the room until it plopped directly onto her desk. She looked at me then—I remember this clearly—and the expression on her face conveyed a tentative, not altogether disdainful, air. I think I locked eyes with her—I know I experienced my first turbulent lurch of romantic panic. The blush rose to her cheeks.

I looked away in shame.

*

Like Inspector Clouseau in the Pink Panther movies, I became a cartoon of neurotic furtiveness, waiting for her to choose her seat on the bleachers for the board-of-ed-mandated art assembly, then happening—*oops, it was the last one left*—to land the seat directly behind her. Then as the magician/hypnotist plucked volunteers from the audience, I'd scoot inch by dreadful inch forward on the bench, straining for a whiff of her horsey perfume. Or as I returned the long way from sharpening my pencil, I'd brush my elbow against the gauze of her sleeve and spend the rest of the day tracing the magic spot where our arms had touched. Always, always, in the tedious hours during which I was supposed to be memorizing multiplication tables and learning about Paul Revere's midnight ride, I tracked her movements down to the breath like a lecherous man in a raincoat.

She'd catch me sometimes, her glance soft, so precious, and I'd jolt my eyes away, leap furiously into my schoolwork, or into my new doodle of the Wasp or the Thing.

The girls circled around nearly every day. "Do you still love Molly?" "Do you want to kiss her?" I'd go red and they'd tumble away.

From across the room I'd hear them chanting:

> *Jordan and Molly*
> *sitting in a tree*
> *K-I-S-S-I-N-G*

> *first comes love*
> *then comes marriage*
> *then comes Molly with a baby carriage.*

I puffed with pride. I loved the attention. Searching Molly out in her corner, I'd find her shielding her face with her hand, head tilted toward her desk in embarrassment, shame, bashful glee, I wasn't sure what. Sometimes I imagined I saw her smiling, ever so slightly, a minute hopeful curl at the edges of her pale lips.

One day, not tomorrow or the next day, but one day soon, I'd get up the courage to speak to her. I had no idea what I'd say, but it would be profound, a soliloquy to send her trembling into my arms. She'd kiss me. She'd say those three impossible words.

I'm not sure what I expected to happen in the moments following our declarations of love, but I know I had no conception of what a relationship with a real live girl—not some storybook character, not a doll or a myth—might possibly look like. I was ten years old, a long

137

way from puberty. What I felt for my inamorata Molly Wiggins had as little to do with love as it did with her. I was practicing, pretending to complex emotions and urges that I wouldn't truly understand for years.

But of course, I didn't know that then, and when Jackie Voight sidled up to me during recess two or three days before the last day of school and declared, "Molly says she might be in like with you," I believed these words held life-changing portents for me, that if I placed my faith in the shuttle diplomacy of the girls controlling my fifth-grade world, my past acts of self-sabotage and aggrandizement would be forgiven. I'd finally achieve a détente with my neighbors and be on my way toward peace and prosperity. "She wants to see if you know how to kiss first, though."

"I know how to kiss."

"Really? Have you ever kissed anybody before?"

"Uh-huh. Sure. Lots of people."

"Like who?"

My mother, my sister, my Sunday school teacher. The family dog. I'd never kissed anyone useful, never anybody who counted.

"Like who?" she said, louder, crossing her arms.

To have a kiss that counted, I would have had to have played French tag with them.

"It's private. If I tell you, it won't be special anymore."

Jackie rolled her eyes. "Well, you'll have to prove it if you want Molly to be in like with you." She waited there. I want to say she tapped her foot. "So?" she said. "Will you kiss her, or what?" My face must have broken into twelve shades of panic because Jackie had to bite her lip to keep up the illusion that she found this negotiation tedious. "You have to tell me what you want me to tell her."

After careful consideration of my options, I said, "Tell her I'll kiss her. Anytime, anywhere."

With that romantic message in her palm, Jackie reeled away, carrying my hopes off to the far kingdom.

She came back—the next day? Ten minutes later? I really don't know. The details are blurry. What I have is the scar and the conviction that there's a story behind it—she came back and told me I had a date. At seven forty-five tomorrow morning, fifteen minutes before the bell rang to summon us in for the last day of school, the day we'd leave this pip-squeak building behind and begin our summer of preparing for the dauntingly sophisticated environment of the middle school across town, I was to meet Molly Wiggins in the windowless nook behind the gym, the blind spot in the school yard where French tag was played and where we'd be safe from the vengeance of the recess monitors. She'd be waiting there for my arrival, waiting to kiss me, to be kissed by me.

And she was.

When I arrived, trembling in my best polo shirt, and for once, untorn jeans, at the meeting spot Jackie Voight had negotiated, I found Molly resplendent in a scoop-necked sundress, a pink background crowded with tiny bluebells, made of light cotton that clung without revealing and flowed down to her shockingly white calves. Her hair was done up in two tightly woven braids draped over her freckled shoulders. In her icy blue eyes, I recognized the same emotions that were at that moment spiking through my body—trepidation, as well as the sweet, sweet softness of possibility.

That was all I saw at first, her in a prism of light, but as I got closer I realized those pale shadows wha-whaing around her edges weren't rays of light but people, girls, Sandi, Tina, Jackie, all of them, the whole fearsome, unruly flock. They stood in a loose semicircle, surrounding Molly like she was it and this was dodgeball. A current of hyperactive glee hissed and popped through them. But instead of fleeing their malicious joke, I continued toward them, my gaze fixed on Molly and the kiss I'd been promised.

"Jordan!" Jackie shouted. "You made it! We thought you were going to chicken out."

They swarmed me, yanking at my elbows, walking me into position. They placed me two feet, then one foot from Molly. After a brief debate, they nudged me closer. I was inches away. She'd worn perfume, a scent like lavender. Around her neck draped a fragile gold chain strung with a hollow heart, tragically tilted. Through the open slats of her leather sandals, I saw she'd painted her toenails a bubblegum pink. All this for me, I thought. All this for me.

Standing in front of her, my face near her bosom, waiting for my childish dreams to come true, this is the thing I remember most clearly, this and what happened later that day. Everything else has been fudged just a bit, filled in and made up and tricked into being. But I really did stand in front of Molly, praying that her perfume wouldn't make me sneeze and searching her expression for solidarity, for the possibility that shared humiliation might bind us together. I thought I saw it there. I'd still swear to this.

Meanwhile, disagreement had broken out among our captors. They argued and then one of them repositioned me. Molly was a breath away. If I'd looked down, my forehead would have cracked against her chin.

"She has to be lower."

They unstrapped her sandals and peeled them from her feet. My eyes were even with her lips, the wan smile flickering on and off of them.

"She's still too high. Jordan, stand on your tippy-toes."

They instructed us to hold on to each other's waists and we did as we were told. The surprising firmness of her hipbone, and the way it cradled her spongy abdomen, distracted me for a moment from our audience. Her body tugged at me, teased out my yearning. I nearly lost my balance and took us both falling.

It occurred to me, finally, that she might be distraught, and I tried out of sympathy to match her frightened expression.

The girls linked hands in a circle around us.

"Now, kiss," Jackie said.

My lips puckered and, surprisingly, hers did too. We fumbled toward each other, then we both hesitated, neither exactly sure what we were doing. The geometry of noses was profoundly complex. The language of the body hard to interpret. The reality of the moment difficult to trust. I wasn't sure whether or not to close my eyes. Molly had closed hers, but that might just have been a flinch. Compromising, I held mine half shut, stared through the microscope of my lashes at the downy fuzz along her cheek.

And then we were kissing, actually kissing, Molly Wiggins and I, our lips touching each other as though by accident, then smushed up closer, squashing into each other. It didn't feel like anything, really.

"You guys can do better than that!" Jackie said. "Act like you mean it!"

We swung our heads back and forth, imitating the kisses we'd seen on soap operas.

Our audience erupted in applause. But they didn't release us. They broke into another debate, conspiring in whispers about our future.

Despite the forced circumstances of our intimacy, I wanted to believe I'd fulfilled some yearning in Molly, that the distaste pulling at the corners of her mouth wasn't caused by revulsion, or not by revulsion toward me anyway. It couldn't have been. The girls had been very clear. I was in love with Molly. Now that we'd kissed, she'd be in like with me. The border between these two states was slim, easy to traverse once they'd become known.

"Kiss each other twice now."

"Kiss each other three times."

Another conspiratorial conference.

"Give each other an Eskimo kiss."

An Eskimo kiss sounded dangerous, invasive. I imagined polar bears and cold tongues and snow shoes. "What's that?" I asked.

Hilarity. It seemed I'd proven myself as stupid as they'd thought.

"You rub your noses together. To keep each other warm."

We gave each other Eskimo kisses, flicked the tips of our noses back and forth. Our eyes caught each other and I sensed something I thought might be a promise in hers. A smile broke across her face— a small smile, just a wisp that quickly fluttered away, but enough of a smile to convince me that what we were doing was more real than performance.

"Now tell Molly you love her."

I did.

"Molly, tell Jordan that you love him back."

I waited. I searched her face for that smile, willed her to share the conviction with me that nothing these girls might do could degrade us, that the grand emotion we both were discovering transcended the farce of their childish games. Instead, I saw tears welling in her eyes. I saw her brightly glossed lips beautifully quivering.

"Say it, Molly. The bell's gonna ring. Say it before we're all late for school."

She finally did say it, in a sputtered whisper, smiling through her tears, seeing only me, and stunning the other girls into shamed silence.

But, no, wait, that's not true. I'm a cheat and a liar who believes mightily in his own myths. I can't vouch for any of this. Don't believe me. I've been protecting myself so you'll like me, softening, pretending to naïveté. Or, maybe, I've been deceiving myself in order to hide from my own culpability.

2.

The truth is that, yes, I was young and stupid. I really was as isolated as I've said. But I didn't unknowingly stumble into my foolish behavior. When I swallowed minnows live, I did so because I knew the girls would find it outrageous. When I made myself throw up on the school's front steps, I understood this would earn my classmates' revulsion and that this revulsion was akin to respect.

I knew a lot of things about which the kids playing French tag had only vague notions. I'd seen the movies their parents wouldn't let them watch and I'd read the books the librarians hid out of reach on the high shelves. I knew what a gay was—I sometimes thought I was one—and I knew about intercourse; I'd seen pictures, line drawings, of oral and anal. And because none of this knowledge came from experience, it festered in my imagination. Each night in my room, I rubbed my penis until it bled, hoping it would get hard. In the afternoons, when I was home alone, I'd search the house for implements to stick up my butt. I spent hours late at night when I couldn't sleep, imagining the girls in my class—all of them, any of them, except Molly—gagged and bound tightly with ropes.

What I'm saying is I was a dark little soul. And my interest in Molly—my obsession with Molly—didn't rise from the gauzy visions of romance that I have claimed for myself. The visions were there, maybe, sure, but they were clouded by plumes of infection; I knew even at the bewildered age of ten that it was pointless for me to pursue them. The joy they promised was maybe possible for other people, for people like Molly, but not for me. I was a tainted creature. I craved absolution, and I believed that Molly, in her purity, might be capable of granting it to me.

On that morning, while the girls held us hostage behind the gym, I needed her smile, her kiss, her forgiveness. And thinking I'd been set up just like her, she did smile, briefly, when I first arrived. She did kiss me—a chaste kiss threaded with revulsion. Forgiveness, though, was beyond her ability.

Molly was distraught. Unlike me, she'd been dragged there. She had no volition and she was as afraid of me as of our captors. She shrank into herself. By the time we got to the Eskimo kiss, she was barely there at all.

My possibility for redemption, or forgiveness, or whatever it was I'd thought I might receive had disintegrated. Standing inches away from her, my hands on her hips, I gradually realized that I didn't love Molly. I hardly knew Molly. I'd noticed that she was pretty and shy and didn't have many friends, but beyond that, she was just a cipher around which I'd spun my fantasies.

The girls had clasped hands in order to chain us in. Their expectations jutted like spears out in front of them, prickling at my back, holding me in place.

"Now, do something else, you two," Jackie barked. "Act like you mean it."

Act like you mean it. The connections took a second to sink in.

But then I understood. They were asking me to perform. This moment was no different from any of the others. I'd thought it was. I'd wanted it to transform me, and as long as I was held in thrall by this desire, I'd been susceptible to the girls' mockery. Like Molly, I'd been a hostage to the cruel impossibility of my situation.

Falling back on my talent for extravagant self-humiliation, I gave them what they'd been coming to see:

I kissed Molly's perfumed neck, slid my hands off her waist around to her ass. I squeezed. I pulled her toward me, grinding my groin into hers. Molly recoiled like a slug in salt, but she knew she was trapped, she knew better than to resist. Looking around at the girls, I made googly eyes and flicked my tongue lasciviously in and out of my gaping mouth. They wilted with laughter. When Sandi demanded I tell Molly I loved her, she was so breathless she could hardly get the words out.

The rest of the scene played out just like I've described it, except for the part about my empathy for Molly. Recklessness is power. With a cheer, the girls grabbed my wrists and dragged me like a conquering hero through the school yard, leaving Molly stranded there behind us.

By the time the bell rang, I was inside, and ten minutes later, the whole class knew what had happened. I could tell from their bright stares that I was no longer the pariah I'd been. I'd done something praiseworthy, something extraordinary. I'd gained the admiration I'd been gunning for. All morning I marveled at what I'd accomplished, basked in the glare of the legend I'd become. I barely noticed that Molly had never made it inside.

The word spread at recess that she'd gone home sick. It was the last day of school. The summer would be long and filled with loneliness. I'd never see Molly Wiggins again. When sixth grade began, I'd learn she and her family had moved away, and for a long time, I believed this was my fault. It wasn't, of course; that's not how the world works. But I knew Molly must have been relieved when her parents told her she'd be going to a new school, that she'd have to make new friends and start a new life, and I knew I was right to feel responsible and ashamed.

I wasn't, though. I'm not. I'm at one with my world.

143

The Veranda

Frederic Tuten

—For Jill Bialosky

SHE'S ON A VERANDA fronting a beach cut short by the bandit tide. The sea beyond, its mysteries and waves, she's used to them but then again she never is. Those waves pillaging the shore each day. From time to time, she glances at the single white rose on the table. The same crystal vase as always, a different rose each day, but always from the same garden, hers. A Bach partita—winter light in a faded mirror—flows through the open French doors. She's reading Marcus Aurelius again, and again finds comfort in the obvious: To lessen the pains of living, one must diminish desire for the material world, its promises and illusions.

There is a polite rustle at the door. M, the butler—who else would it be?—with a silver pot of coffee wrapped in a linen napkin. He nods. She smiles for thanks.

M is old. He has seen her through three husbands, two who had married her for her money. The first husband died midsentence at breakfast; a sentence she had no wish for him to complete, in any case, because it concerned his allowance and the need for its substantial increase.

She was young when she first married and still young when her husband left her, the planet, his bespoke suits, handcrafted shoes, and the beige cashmere socks he so cherished and had kept rolled in ten cedar-lined drawers. She had come to dislike him not only because she had gradually understood that he had married her principally for her wealth but because she found his sartorial desires so conventional, like his lovemaking.

The second husband, on understanding that her wealth was not to flow endlessly into the mansion's garages, flooded with his custom-made cars, and who considered Bentleys and Rolls-Royces mere Fords, left her for an older woman who appreciated the elegant way he mixed drinks for her guests at intimate dinner parties, and who was willing to pay for his ever-increasing automotive needs.

The last husband, who was sixty-eight when they married and

144

who made her happy well into her midforties, drowned in the same ocean she was now regarding with tenderness and fear. At breakfast one morning together, as every summer morning, he kissed her, a deep kiss on the mouth and not just a husbandly peck, then he was off for his usual swim. He waved to her from far away in the ocean and then he was gone. He was the love of her life.

He was an artist. Not very famous but not unrecognized. He was appreciated, respected, living modestly on the sale of his paintings, which unabashedly had roots in Poussin and Cézanne. Like them, he searched for the immortal structure beneath and underlying the painting in whatever subject it represented. Like them, his life was a consecration to art and a daily presence to its fulfillment. (He, however, would have been shy about such words as "consecration.") "You cannot know what the work will look like unless you show up for it" was the way he put it. He made no fuss about being dedicated to his art and he did not feel superior to those artists without similar devotion. But he did not spend time in their company either.

He lived decently and did not require much to do so—a small loft that he had bought for a song in the early sixties, in a building now the warren of billionaire condos, was all he needed and wanted for shelter and work. He had no retreat by the sea or elsewhere as had many of his colleagues. I say colleagues because he did not have friends in the full sense of the word, though he believed in the idea of friendship as found in the essays of Montaigne. He liked the idea so much that he did not attempt to injure it through experience.

He stayed in the city through the hottest summers on the deadest weekends when no one but tourists and the homeless roamed the burning streets. In the spring and into the late fall he walked to the park on the lower East River and read on a bench fronting the watery traffic of tugs and barges. A white yacht on its way to Florida or the Caribbean might pass by and someone might wave. In winter he kept in, breakfasted on Irish oatmeal and coffee and then more coffee; he often skipped lunch and ate bread in torn hunks and drank coffee: two sugars, three ounces of milk. At night he dined at an Italian restaurant with so-so food on the corner of his street. It had a green awning in summer and you could sit under it in the rain.

Sometimes one of the young female assistants from his gallery found a pretext to visit him. He was friendly, solicitous, but did not mix business with sex. He imagined the resulting complications, the

145

discomfort of going to his gallery and facing a woman he had slept with a few times but in whom he had no deeper interest. And he did not welcome the discomfort he imagined for her or the awkwardness of his circumspect dealer of fifteen years, who never mixed business with anything if he could help it.

He liked the city, he liked solitude, he liked going and coming when he wished; he liked sleeping and waking in his own bed. He liked women but mostly on a certain basis: that they did not want to live with him, did not want to have children; did not want to call him at any hour they chose to chat; that they did not like or affect to like sports; that they did not buy or urge him to buy new clothes, to get a haircut, a shave, or have his nails trimmed, though he always kept them trimmed and his face shaved and hair cut short. The women he liked did not or needed not to work. This excluded many women, even those women of leisure married to wealth because he considered their marriage a job, a fancy one without regular hours or a visible paycheck but a job nonetheless. In any case, he did not consort with married women, first out of principle—the one that has to do with not hurting people, husbands, in this case—and the other because he was selfish about his time and did not wish to waste it on clandestine arrangements and their inevitable time-consuming and emotional complications.

He liked women who read books he honored: He was snobbish about that but did not care that he might be thought so. The books one read were as telling as the friends one chose. You could be fooled or betrayed by friends but never by books. Plato, for example, always stayed faithful and always gave more than he received. Proust could be relied on for his nature descriptions, especially flowers bordering paths through luxuriant gardens. He loved gardens because of Proust but felt he need not visit any because he had seen and walked through enough of them in the Frenchman's world. He used this as an excuse to get out of visiting friends in Connecticut who prided themselves on their gardens, their endless yards of rose beds, especially.

He liked above all women who loved painting. He did not care for them as much if they liked sculpture because he did not care for sculpture, except for smallish items such as Mycenaean heads and masks from the Côte d'Ivoire, very abstract and synthetic. In short, he liked sculpture the starker and the more minimal the better. He disliked mostly everything else ever deconstructed or assembled and felt antipathy for the grand posture and thus disdained Rodin's figures in particular among the moderns. Everything, in fact, after

146

the time of Pericles he found dreary and dead, the stuff to fill old movie palace lobbies. He once wrote in his notebook that we need not bother to fill empty space with sculpture—any natural rock formation is better than any sculpture, so, too, trees. Deserts do not need sculpture; emptiness is their point and their beauty.

About painting he had no illusions. He did not believe in its social or psychological or spiritual transformative powers. He did not believe that there is progress in art—or in civilization. All great, significant art was timeless and equal in value—in beauty. Beauty was the end and reason for all art, period.

He had few extravagances. But he would travel long distances to revisit paintings he loved and he would make, with great planning, expeditions to places holding paintings he admired. He spent two weeks alone at the Ritz Hotel in Madrid so that he could walk across the road after breakfast and before dinner to look at Velázquez's *Las Meninas*, which he considered the greatest painting ever made after the seventeenth century. His certainty about this annoyed other artists, who saw in it an inflexibility of taste that might be applied to his judging their own work. They were also put off by his unwillingness to consider that no single work of art is the "greatest." Sometimes, for fun, he would seem to concede the point and say: "Well, it is the first greatest among equals."

He once trailed a beautiful woman after seeing her studying with great intensity a painting by Picasso in a hall at the Louvre. He followed her into a room of Poussins and was pleased to see her fixed on one painting, *Echo and Narcissus*, for several full minutes. That she might have seen the affinity between the two artists intrigued him and she increased in stature and thus grew more and more beautiful by the minute. Then she seemed to take a different track altogether when she went into other rooms and gave her attention to a canvas by Perugino and then later focused on a painting by Parmigianino. He was a bit let down. It occurred to him that she was progressing or governed along no aesthetic insight or principle but merely visiting artists whose surnames began with the letter P.

He followed her to the museum's café, where she sat alone by the window facing a vast courtyard and Paris beyond. He sat at the table closest to her and took his time ordering *un grande crème* and a tartine with butter—exactly what she had requested and what finally was brought them both. She spoke to the waiter in a French from an earlier day, when words were sounded in their fullness. She would have made a great actress on the seventeenth-century stage reciting

Racine or Corneille. For all that, he wasn't sure he liked the elevated, rich, overeducated, worldly, superior tone of her voice. But then he liked it—he supposed her to be French and thus she could sound as fancy and superior as she wished or why else be French? He glanced her way, hoping to make eye contact, but she had pulled a book out of her bag—expensive, smooth, trim, no frills, oxblood red, with a narrow strap—and engaged herself in its lines.

He was shy except with women, from whom he would gamble rebuff, even rebuke, to meet. His theory was that the chance of knowing an interesting woman was more important than any rejection, and since his advances were soft spoken and courteous, his politeness was met with the like or at worst with a little coldness born of natural suspicion and wariness.

"Look," he said, taking the chance that she knew English. "I understand your interest in the connection between Poussin and Picasso but I don't see your leap to Parmigianino, a fine artist but irrelevant to what connects the other two."

She gave him a long look. Almost scientific in its disinterestedness. Then in a pleasant but firm voice and in an English more beautiful than her French said: "I'm married. Happily or unhappily is another matter, but married and obedient to all its obligations and injunctions and oaths."

"Lamentably so," he answered, not sure exactly what he meant.

She drank her coffee slowly, looking at the sea, its thick swell and sullen heaviness. It covered the world. It raided its shores, carrying trees and husbands in its teeth. One day the sea would gallop over the dunes and drag her into its watery camp. But if she chose, she would not wait for it to come to carry her away and she would take a long swim from which she would never again step on shore.

She had walked into his gallery cold, looking for a watercolor by Marin and a painting by Hartley she knew were being offered there. It was an old-fashioned gallery she felt comfortable visiting because the owner kept his distance, did not make too much fanfare about his artists or their work.

The gallery specialized in early-to-mid-twentieth-century American art, thus he was in the company of Walt Kuhn, Kuniyoshi, Fairfield Porter, artists he admired although they were too tame for him, never reaching beyond the literal. He was sometimes fearful that that was also true of him, too tame, too literal, and whenever he got sufficiently worried he took the train to the Philadelphia and for a full half hour stood in front of Cézanne's large *Bathers*. He would grab a sandwich in the museum's café and let his mind go nowhere, then he'd return to the painting and start absorbing it again. He would come home feeling purified and try to purge his work of the superfluous without eliminating areas that gave his painting its valuable subtext and life. He strove.

He had been approached by galleries more important and chic than his, ones that had offered him monthly stipends and lavish catalogs written by distinguished critics whose names would give added weight to his reputation, galleries that had juice in the art market and could inject oil into its machinery.

But he liked his gallery, having been invited to join it when he was still unknown; he stayed loyal to the man who had the intelligence to understand his work and to act on it—to put his money where his taste was. He found in the dealer a man not too chummy and not too remote and who quietly and successfully did his job of promoting and selling his few living artists. He liked also that his dealer always wore modest pinstripe suits and bow ties, and that he went to the Oak Room at the Plaza at five thirty every weekday and drank a dry martini and then, in nasty weather, took the Madison Ave. bus uptown to his home and to his wife of thirty years.

She bought the Marin watercolor and, undecided, put a hold on the Hartley. Then the dealer asked if she would be interested in seeing the work of an artist he had long admired and long represented and he took her into his office. He had spoken to her of this artist before but she had not made the effort to see the work. The three paintings in the dealer's office unnerved, then calmed her, as if she at last had found her map home after being lost for years in a faraway country whose language she did not understand and could never learn. Musical they were, these paintings, in melancholic counterpoint with death. By what alchemy did paint become music?

She did not know who he was, had never seen his photograph, as he shunned having his face in the catalogs of his shows—there were none, in any case. His picture had never appeared in any of the art magazines she subscribed to, which, with the exception of the bulletin from the Metropolitan Museum of Art, where she was a trustee, were none.

She bought one painting, asking that she remain anonymous.

149

Then, two weeks later, after the first painting's music had occupied her dreams, she returned and bought another.

Weeks later, she sent the artist an unsigned note of appreciation via his gallery. He answered, through his gallery, with a handkerchief-size drawing—in the mode and friendly parody of Poussin—of a tree on fire and a medieval battlement in the distance also in flames. She withdrew, feeling the heat of his closeness and the threat of disappointment. (Better never to get too close or meet an artist whose work you admire because all artists are inferior to their work.) She wrote back thanking him politely for the drawing—and then, in a rush of feeling, added some heartfelt lines on what she loved about his work. She feared those lines would be misunderstood and open doors better left shut but she also felt that a polite mere thank you would not have expressed the fullness of her, of her emotions. She knew she was equivocating, because her letter might suggest that while her doors were shut they were also unlocked.

He responded a day later. Come, his note said, to his studio and choose a watercolor.

While the principle never to meet the artist remained true, she also wanted to meet him, if nothing else than to confirm the principle—a lie. She wanted to meet him because she wished to like him, to be moved by him, to have him move her. She wanted to believe that the untroubled purity she found in his paintings mirrored his own distinguished soul. These thoughts disturbed her for the disappointment should she ever meet him, and she was pained by her longing for someone perfect or someone whose very imperfections and failures she would find noble.

In short, after some days of indecision, she went to his loft. She had her car and chauffeur wait in the street should she decide on a quick getaway. They smiled both comfortably and uncomfortably. They chitchatted some minutes and, much to her own surprise, she asked if he lived alone.

"Lamentably," he said.

She laughed. "You seem fond of that word."

He nodded. And slyly said, "Regrettably."

"What if I said I'm still married? What would you say to that?"

"That should you leave this room, I would lament you."

"Then perhaps I won't leave."

She gave her driver the day off. He was glad and made his escape across the bridge to Astoria, Queens, where his wife and children watched TV until they went blind. She stayed there in his loft until morning, when they both went to breakfast—the scrambled eggs were cut into white strings, the bacon was undercooked and burnt at the same time, the coffee was tar hauled from a back road in Tennessee—in a dim diner by the Hudson River favored by truckers and taxi drivers and artists of that era.

"And what about God," she asked. "Where are you on that?" She was still young enough to think about and to ask such questions. In any case, she was not asking about God, she was probing to discover his blind spot, and having found none after hours of talking and finally, at 2:38 in the morning, when he said, "It's time," she followed him to his bed.

For the first several months of their years together, they divided themselves between his loft and her apartment, from whose windows they could see Central Park and the Plaza. They shared breakfast at six, after which he vanished in a taxi to his studio downtown and spent the day painting. If by seven that evening he felt not ready to leave his work, he'd phone her and they would or would not meet again for dinner, or they would or would not meet again that night, in which case he'd sleep alone but she would come downtown at six to breakfast with him at the diner with the bad food. The string eggs, burnt bacon, and tar coffee had worked into their history. Or sometimes she would appear with a full breakfast, silver service and all, her chauffeur and maid and herself toting platters and coffee pots up to her husband's loft. Then she might linger a while after they had sipped their last cup of coffee and go to his bed.

He had been painting with a new vigor and insight that his dealer recognized immediately. There was also a certain charity, a kind of generosity lacking earlier but still keeping the work within its usual reserved boundaries. "Love does its wonders," the dealer said dispassionately but with a conviction born from romantic memories of his youth, when he first met his wife.

Everything seemed in balance, so the dealer was upset when he learned that she was building a house in Montauk. "Why go out there in the first place?" the dealer asked her.

"For the calm and the air and the sea," she answered. "He's too old to spend summers broiling in the city. I'll build him a studio he won't want to leave. A place he and every other artist has ever dreamed of."

The dealer had seen artists appear from the mist and then vanish from the scene, he had seen exalted reputations fall into the mud—or, even worse, just melt away slowly into oblivion. And not always because the work had changed for the worse. The moment had changed and the artist was no longer in that moment but suddenly somewhere else, far away, in the land of the forgotten and awaiting the day to be rescued and brought home with honors.

But sometimes, their flame went out because the hungry fuel that had fed it was no longer there, and the rich life took its place. He knew artists who, when they reached the pinnacle of their art and reputation and had earned vast sums, turned out facsimiles of their earlier, hard-earned work and were more concerned with their homes, trips, social calendars, their placement at dinner parties than with anything that might have nourished their art, which coasted on its laurels.

And for that last reason the dealer said to her: "Go slow and keep the life contained, for his sake and yours."

She laughed. "Don't worry, no one will come to our dinner parties, should we ever give them, and we shall not go if ever asked."

"This is not a moralistic issue," he said. "And I'm not against money. You *know* it's not about you. I love you," he said, turning red.

"And I love you for how you were in his life and in his work from the start."

He made an exaggeratedly alarmed face and said, "Were?"

"Were, are, and always will be," she said, then repeated it.

They left on good terms. He apprehensive of what was to become of his artist; she concerned that in trying to make a gracious life for her husband she might be digging their cushioned graves.

Now he was dissolved in the sea, vanished in a soup of bones and brine. And now she was alone until the sea took her away, too, if it were the sea who one day would be her executioner. Until that time, she would remain alone with the butler, who in time would tremble and whose hand would spill the coffee and let the morning rose fall. Then, one day, he would tremble all over and, after the back and forth of hospitals, he would be gone. Then she would sit on the veranda and face the sea and listen to music, maybe some somber cello pieces from Marais or Saint-Colombe or Bach—music on a small scale, where, atomlike, the energy of beauty compresses.

Eventually she would answer the phone and seem delighted that a friend had called to invite her to dinner. An elegant dinner with distinguished guests—an ambassador who had written a memoir, a former editor of a venerable publishing house, a novelist always mentioned for the Nobel Prize, two widows who funded the arts, a young poet who would have preferred not to be there but who understood the draw and use of powerful people—all affable and solicitous of her. The food, a poached wild salmon with sorrel, would be excellent, the wine even better. The conversation would flow with delicacy and nuance, with worldly authority. But not one word said the whole evening would approach her heart.

She would be home by eleven and sit and read in an old leather chair he had loved. The lazy cat would curl about her ankles and fall asleep. She herself would start to doze off—as she got older, fewer and fewer books held her interest. Only Proust still spoke to her, an old, intimate friend with long, twisting sentences whose fineness still absorbed her and kept her feeling grateful for his visit. She left her gardens to the gardeners, who went wild with the freedom, each planting to his own vision. Rose beds rushed against walls of blue hydrangeas, a field of yellow daffodils invaded a stand of black tulips. The grass went from tame to wild without transition. She enjoyed the anarchy and the disorder but it delivered only so much pleasure and then the excitement went flat. People also went stale quickly. The interesting ones, the ones with character and who had struggled to make their place in the world, had died. She was too tired and too far away in time to meet their replacements, if there were any.

He had left her everything. His clothes, of course, a closet full of khakis and pairs of brown loafers worn down to the heels; one pair of black shoes, soles and heels as good as new; one suit, gray pinstripe, hardly worn, made for him in London, where he had once spent a week drunk on museums; three sports jackets, two for winter, a red and green plaid for summer; two dress shirts to be adorned with a tie, the rest just blue cotton button-downs. Apart from the art, and there was little of that, she prized his notebooks, some filled with sketches like the one he had sent her years earlier and some with jottings and notes and quotes from the reading he loved.

He wrote about the *Bathers*, how he loved the awkwardness of the nude figures, the almost childish painting of their forms. As if Cézanne had set out to fail. As if he had sought through that failure a great visual truth at once obvious and occult. He quoted from a letter of Cézanne's in which he spoke about his unfinished paintings—paintings he had deliberately left unfinished, patches here and there of raw canvas as if left to be later painted. Cézanne had found truth in their incompleteness. That the empty spaces invited color, leaving the viewer to imagine that color, leaving the viewer his exciting share in the completing of the visual narrative; blank spaces suggesting also that art, like life, does not contain all the information and that it is a lie when it pretends so.

Silence, except for the churning sea. The sea is high, just some fifty yards from her, black and cold. The house, too vast for one, feeling the sea's chill, gives a shudder. She gives a shudder. Then she makes her way up the stairs to her too-large room and her too-large bed, under a too-high ceiling, and she waits for the sea—having taken from her everything else—to come crawling to her window like a bandit hungry for silver.

Six Poems
Rae Armantrout

THE GIFT

You confuse
the image of a fungus

with the image of a dick
in my poem

(understandably)

and three days later
a strange toadstool

(white shaft, black cap,
five inches tall)

appears
between the flagstones
in our path

We note
the invisible

web
between fence posts

in which dry leaves
are gently rocked.

Rae Armantrout

SUSTAINED

1.

To come to
in the middle

of a vibrato—
an "is"—

that some soprano's

struggling
to sustain.

2.

To be awake
is to discriminate

among birdcalls,
fruits, seeds,

"to work one's way,"
as they say,

"through."

3.

Just now
breaking

into awareness,
falling forward,

hurtling inland
in all innocence

BORDER PERFECTION

1.

The days are shorter, but
the light seems to stretch out,

to hark
from a long way off.

Horizons
snap into focus,

while shadows
are distended, smudged.

It's happening again;
we take

discrepancies
for openings.

2.

The sign
that the guy behind me

in the "border protection" line
is demented

is his impatience,

the way he asks
again and again

what we're waiting for

Rae Armantrout

THE VESICLE

1.

To our amazement,
when fed on fatty acid,

the vesicle
did not simply grow,

it extended itself
into a filament.

Now the king's youngest daughter said,

"I wish I had
something like that"—

and the whole vesicle
transformed

into a slender tube
which was quite delicate.

2.

Monks
mimed one another's
squiggles

carefully
by candlelight

as if they thought
creation trailed something,

as if they knew
creation looked like this

from what is
always

the outside.

EXACT

Quick, before you die,
describe

the exact shade
of this hotel carpet.

What is the meaning
of the irregular, yellow

spheres, some
hollow,

gathered in patches
on this bedspread?

If you love me,
worship

the objects
I have caused

to represent me
in my absence.

*

Over and over
tiers

of houses spill
pleasantly

down that hillside.
It

might be possible
to count occurrences.

Rae Armantrout

WITH

It's well
that things should stir
inconsequentially
around me
like this
patina of shadow,
flicker, whisper,
so that
I can be still.

*

I write things down
to show others
later
or to show myself
that I am not alone with
my experience.

*

"With"
is the word that
comes to mind,
but it's not
the right word here.

The Mannequin in Soldotna
Melinda Moustakis

THE MANNEQUIN

SHE STANDS IN THE LOBBY of the hospital, naked. Flesh flies and hooks cover her body. There are flies made from feathers, fur, hair, beads in bright gloried purples and reds and yellows to catch a trout, a dolly, a red, a king in the Kenai River.

Someone comes in with a hook in a nose or lip or neck or hand. The doctor shakes her head. The hook digs deep and pulls, the barb snagging muscle, and she pushes it through. The patient sighs with relief as the bloodied hook clangs in the metal tray. The blood seeps through cotton and the doctor replaces the gauze. Sometimes there are stitches. Today only tape.

After the patient leaves, the doctor holds the hook under the tap. She dips it in disinfectant. On the way, she passes the nurses' station and says, "I've got another one." The nurses follow in their white padded shoes.

"Guess," she says.

The nurses point to spots of open flesh on the mannequin. There. No there.

The doctor touches the arch of the mannequin's foot. "Here," she says.

There are few spots left.

"Will they ever learn?" she says.

RIVER AND ISLAND

What is the sound of a river? The sound of line breaking the surface? The Kenai is a thick vein of brown and runoff from the thaw flows from the mountains, from Wally's Creek and the lower Killey, and wraps around the island where the doctor has a cabin. The Kenai is a rope, choking off a piece of land with a slow, snaking hold.

Melinda Moustakis

RUN

The salmon swim from river into ocean. They fatten up on shrimp and squid, growing until they are two of themselves. Thousands of miles after, the salmon ache for the milky blue waters of the Kenai. Their bodies quiver and they turn degrees of north, they turn toward home.

HOOK

Two buddies go for rainbows at The Kitchen, where Skilak Lake meets the Kenai River. The morning is early and condensation covers the boat, the tackle box, the seats. They haven't been fishing in a while because one had a bad fall, a bad break in the leg. There's a metal pin in the bone. They drink coffee with Jack-Slack.

The one with the bad leg hooks a bow. The other reels in so he can net, secures his hook.

The bow is a fighter. He flips and jumps and makes a scene. The one strains and puts most of his weight on his good leg. "He's right there," says the one.

But the other misses with the net.

"You going blind?" says the one.

"At least I have two good legs," says the other.

"Just bag him this time."

The other stands poised, net in hand. The bow twists under the water and spits the hook. The line jerks free. The one wobbles and puts a hand on the seat to steady himself. He throws down his rod.

"I'll get the next one," says the other.

The one huffs and punches a fist into the seat. "Sure," he says. He bends down to pick up the rod, but he bends wrong. He slips a little on the deck and falls, his head hitting the other rod sitting in the holder. The other helps him up. There's blood and he's attached to the rod—the top of his ear has caught the hook.

"Pierced straight through," says the other. He cuts the line and goes to cut the barb off the hook.

"Leave it," says the one. "I want a story about me catching a bow with a hook in my ear."

*

162

The mannequin is mapped with flesh flies, rabbit fur and yarn and thread. The doctor jabs the hook into the left side of the head where an ear would be. The man had the hook in the right ear, but that side is full.

RIVER AND ISLAND

What is the sound of a river? Glaciers melting? The echo of air and light? The Kenai is a dull shade of dust. The edges of still water clear; the edges reflect small winks of sun. No one knows where the river ends and the island begins.

RUN

The stars, the sun, and the smell of gravel guide them to the Kenai's mouth. Their skin glimmers like knives and their meat turns red. After a heavy rain, the water rises and they charge the river. They grow hooked snouts and wolves' teeth.

TWO PATCHES

A man and his son are in a bad way. They drift down the Kenai on a raft. Neither wishes to talk. The man brought his son hoping they could find the words. They find neither words nor fish. There are two patches on the raft—dark blue rubber cut into squares. The glue surrounding the squares makes a glossy splotch against the faded sides.

The man steers around a gravel spit. His son prepares to reel in, but the line bobs. He sets the hook and the line pays out. "I got one," he says. And the bow is a beauty—a twenty-two-inch female with a rounded head and nickel silver shine. The son releases her.

"We're allowed one for dinner," says the man.

"Too pretty," says his son. He aims the line. The man walks behind him to put up the net. The hook sails through the air and the man feels a sharp pain in his eye. He covers the eye with his hand.

"Don't touch it," says the son.

The hook prevents the man's eye from closing when he blinks, and when he blinks the pain spikes. His thumb and forefinger pry his eyelid open.

"Drive," says the man.

The son beaches the raft on the bank. He runs up to the cabin door and knocks, looks in the window. Empty. But the next cabin has an answer.

The man stands on the bank. Liquid blurs his vision and there's a slicing pain, but the pain feels good.

The doctor removes the hook from the eye. She doesn't flinch. But standing in front of the mannequin this time, she pauses at the colorful geography—woolly buggers, watermelons, spinners. "I'm sorry," she says and she stabs the mannequin's eye.

RIVER AND ISLAND

What is the sound of a river? Edges dissolving? Vanishing stones? The Kenai is a shade of dust. Underneath the skirts of the island, the river's tides pull through, sweeping, branches and sticks and muck swirl in the boils. Webs of decomposed humpy flesh float down in delicate globs.

RUN

They fight the river, the rocks, hook and line. The salmon do not eat and their stomachs close. Their skin deepens with red, and green hoods their heads.

CLEAN

Two brothers stand on the old dock. One shows the other how to fillet the salmon so that they don't lose meat. The knife is new.

The older steps back and hands the knife to the younger. The younger has the knife perched over the salmon. A rotted plank breaks beneath them.

The younger falls first and the knife gashes the forearm of the older. They stand on the rocks and the splintered wood surrounds their waists. Blood from the gash drips onto the dock.

The father drives them to the hospital for stitches.

The doctor says, "Lucky. A clean cut. No veins or tendons."

The older doesn't blame the younger. The younger blames the wood, the rotting, the dock—but not the knife.

The doctor passes by the mannequin—there weren't any hookings that day. And if there were, where would she put the hook? She is running out of space and soon she'll have to start a new mannequin.

RIVER AND ISLAND

The island's reflection is stretched over the river's surface, wavering on water. Are you coming or going, river? The Kenai, milk tinged with ribbons of green and brown, is raging, is at rest.

RUN

And the river is loaded—salmon full of eggs and milt running in an intoxicated cloud. Coming or going?

LIP

One night a guide heads to the bar after a day on the river and meets a girl. She's a waitress at Suzie's, saving up for college and a ticket out of Alaska. She's got a scholarship for jumping hurdles. He just got out of the navy, was stationed in Texas, but he says Hawaii. She's always wanted to go to Hawaii. So he picks her up at Bing's Landing on a Tuesday, so he can tell her more about the islands and the clear, dazzling water he's only seen in magazines.

She brings food from the diner, chicken and fries and biscuits. He brings an appetite.

They catch two dollies. He keeps one.

"I thought we were letting them go," she says.

"Allowed one a day," he says.

The sun burns the top of her shoulders. He wonders if she'll peel, have lighter patches underneath. They stop to eat at a secluded bank.

"Smile," he says.

She clenches her jaw, but her mouth quivers.

"Smile," he says again.

To spite her, her lips obey.

He smiles back. "Hawaii is beautiful," he says. "You should come with me."

"What island do you live on?" she asks.

He moves closer, circles a fingertip on her pink shoulder. "Does this hurt?"

She shrugs him off. "Let's catch some more fish," she says.

He grabs her arm. "Let's stay here," he says.

She could run. Scream. Pick up a rock. An old hook on the ground. She smiles at him and sits down, places her left hand over the hook. She kisses his mouth and readies the weapon in her left hand. She traces his lips with her fingertip, reaches inside toward his teeth, and exposes the red-jeweled flesh of his bottom lip. She stares straight into his eyes. Then she shoves the hook down through, piercing him. He crumples with the pain and she leaves him on the bank and drives away. He'll have a scar and never forget. She'll never leave home without a hook in her pocket.

The boy arrives alone. His story is vague. His friend hooked him while casting. The doctor notices how his eyes dart up and down her body—she isn't as gentle as she should be when removing the hook from his lip. The point of entry is intimate and the hook is old—it uncovers his lie.

"An accident?" she says.

"I told you," he says.

"Tell your friend to buy some new hooks," she says.

The doctor smiles as she traces the exact spot with her finger and jams the hook into the mannequin's flesh, in the space below lip, above chin.

RIVER AND ISLAND

What is the sound of a river? Babble? Chatter? The Kenai is a green of silt, jade and pearl and debris. The island is sinking, caving in.

RUN

They hurdle rapids and boulders, day after day. They turn a bend and the currents slow. This. Here. Their first tang of river. The gravel where they were born. The female shudders and the eggs drop, loose and translucent. The male follows and dribbles seed over the redd.

BACK

Two buddies backtroll for kings. They've anchored the boat and they're tossing back a few beers, waiting for the big one to hit.

"You seen my green spinner?" says Jay.

"You look in the box?" says D.

"Can't see how it couldn't be there," says Jay. He fidgets with the reel. "Packed drift. Don't know how no one's hooking in."

D settles down into his seat. "Might as well catch what I can—get a little shut-eye."

"You do that," says Jay.

D gets into the groove of sleep, makes a racket with his pawpaw snore.

"Useless," says Jay.

D's line smacks with a bite.

"You've got a live one," says Jay.

D jumps to attention and sets the hook. Jay reels in his line and primes the net.

"That my spinner?" says Jay.

"My yellow one," says D.

"You sure?"

"Just looks green underwater."

Jay bags the king. He holds the mallet over the head. Stops. "That is my spinner."

"No, it's mine," says D.

The king flops on the deck between them.

"You telling me you got the same exact spinner? The one I was missing?"

"Give me the mallet," says D. "Then we'll fix this."

"You're a liar," says Jay. "I get mine made special at Townie's." He moves toward the flailing king. "You don't deserve this fish."

"Don't you dare," says D.

Jay bends down and throws the king overboard. D flies at him in a fury. The two wrestle down to the deck floor. D howls a kicked-dog howl and Jay releases his grip.

"You all right?"

D turns on his side. He's got the spinner, the hook jammed right in the meat of his back.

Jay touches the hook.

D whimpers.

And because D's made that sound and Jay thinks he deserves it, he touches the hook again and waits for D to wince. "Don't move," says Jay. "Don't do nothing."

Jay asks the doctor if he can keep the spinner.

"The big fish here has to decide," says the doctor, pointing at D.

"I don't want it," says D. "And I don't want him to have it neither."

"Fair enough," she says.

"Put it on that voodoo thing in the lobby," says D.

The doctor feels, then, each puncture, each hook, prick her body, a wave starting from her head and cresting down to her feet. And every hook is attached to a line, a fishing rod, and a body holding the rod, and each body is covered in hooks that tear open flaps of flesh, small pockets of bleeding, a web.

Two days later, the doctor walks past the mannequin with three charts in her hand and her eye corners Jay running out of the lobby.

"Stop him," she yells and she charges after him.

A man in a flannel jacket grabs Jay, tackling him to the pavement. The doctor holds out her hand.

"Give it to me," she says.

"No," says Jay.

The man in the flannel jacket pries the green spinner from Jay's fingers.

She's standing over him and shaking her head. "You don't know what you've done," she says.

RIVER AND ISLAND

The Kenai is a vein of turquoise, clear and glass and settled. The river cradles the island in its arms, lullabies the trees. It's not day or night or morning and the doctor is still awake, sitting near an unlit camp-fire, and across the river a fisherman throws his line—cast, drift and follow, cast.

RUN

The days are long and thin. The salmon keep to the shallows near rotting trees. With reaching fingers, the Kenai tugs at their tails, drawing them to the channel. The salmon wrestle the water, tap their last beats of blood, and when the river wins, they drift and fodder downstream. Their bodies are carried, broken, and fed to the currents.

THE NEW MANNEQUIN

A man boats across Skilak Lake at the head of the Kenai. Three boys throw rocks from the shore. When he gets close, he sees their tar-get—a log in the water. But it isn't a log. He tells the boys to get on out of there, to go home. But all they do is walk away and look on from a distance. He'd heard a woman had been missing for a week. A drowned body sinks and bloats up and eventually floats back to the top. She's wearing a green jacket so he grabs the collar with his right hand and drives with his left. Her hair covers her face. He gets to shore and tells the boys to look away but they stare. He's in a couple feet of water so he cuts the engine and jumps out, holds her and the boat and walks them both to land. The boys come and get the boat. He has no choice so he drags her to shore. Because she is out of the water, because she has been missing for a week, her face falls off, and there is a crater in the skull, a bullet wound. He turns his back. The boys have covered their eyes. He struggles with the latch on the box seat. The gulls announce themselves as they fly over, descending in a flock, and he hurries to unfold the tarp and cover her. The wind picks up the tarp and uncovers her face without a face. He gathers rocks to weigh down the corners. The boys throw rocks at the gulls.

The mannequin is full—clothed in deer hair, elk, rabbit, quail feath-ers, wire, hooks, a dress of many colors. And next to her is a new

169

mannequin, a blank landscape. The doctor has heard the news about the girl they found in the river, the bullet wound in the back of the head. The girl's name is Dawn Bakten—she lived with her mother in Sterling, the town next to Soldotna. The doctor looks at the new mannequin, but there's nothing she can do to record this—it's too big. And the doctor has to sit down a while because she's thinking that somewhere in the world there's another one happening as she sits there next to a clumsy table of magazines. She jams a fist into her stomach, and she's there, standing in the river, and her waders fill up with water, weigh down in the current, and then she snags the bottom and she steps back toward the bank, slips, and then she is sliding under, gone, and the current takes her, drags her by the ankles into the swarm. She is melting, liquid and heat, and her limbs fuse to her body, first her feet, her arms, her fingers. She streams metallic, a core of red cooling into the shape of a bullet.

"Only hooks," she says to the blank, new mannequin. "I've got one fight in me."

RIVER AND ISLAND

The doctor sits on the bank. The sun slips from the ledge and dissolves into the mountains. She's thinking of bodies, small hooks of metal, the first tang of river. The first tang and sound—small whisperings at the halo of her neck.

RUN

The doctor knows the new mannequin is waiting for her. But how to mark the mannequin for this story? A man has a comfortable cabin on the Kenai and he lives alone. His days on the river are either too slow or too fast. On the too-fast days he stops his truck at Good Time Charlie's and picks up a girl, her hair parted on the side. The first thing he marks—the white line of scalp. He feels good and he feels rich so he offers her double and her drives her to his cabin. They spend an hour or so together and the girl's laughter fills up his cabin where he lives alone. He cooks a meal. Then he takes the girl on a ride in his small plane; he'd gotten his pilot license so he could scout moose and bears. The girl likes the view of the river and mountains and sips wine from the bottle he's brought along. He lands in a bowled spot somewhere and offers her more money to strip. She makes a show, throws her green jacket at him sitting in the pilot's seat. He smiles as she tosses away her clothes, smiles as she tries not to shiver. She stands before him, naked, and he says, "Take off your jewelry." She undoes her bracelet clasp, slides off her rings, and pulls the hoops out of her ears. He's still smiling, but she doesn't know what else to do. He takes out a shotgun and fires, shooting to her left. "What are you doing?" she yells. He fires again. "Run," he says. She turns and runs. She can see shade up the hillside and she pumps her arms. He shoots close to hear her scream. And then he shoots her in the back. She crawls and aims for the trees. When he walks up to her she moans. To him, it is the same sound that the bears make.

The Pest
Georges-Olivier Châteaureynaud

—Translated from French by Edward Gauvin

I'D KNOWN HIM FOREVER, but I never knew his name. He was neither brother, cousin, nor friend to me, oh no, least of all a friend,
despite the insufferable, nauseating expression of tenderness that lit
up those piggish little eyes whenever his gaze settled on me.

Time and again, he'd ruined my life. I'd even made an attempt on
his, but his filthy little fingers clung tight and fast to his filthy little
life. He got away every time and came back to taunt me with it, with
his repellent potbelly, his teary eyes, his incurable acne, his falsetto,
his grubby rags, his inevitable shopping bag bulging with old oysters
and plastic conchs.

It was his fault I'd become a pariah. Every time a chance had come
up for me, he'd chased it off, or embarrassed me so much I couldn't
seize it, mired as I was in him and his grotesque notions. How many
women had withheld their smiles, how many potential investors
their trust, how many taxi drivers their services in the pouring rain—
and all because of him? Oh, how well I understood them! I would've
done the same: A man who knows, or is known by, someone like
him is obviously disreputable.

Let's be honest: Not everything in my life was that hopeless.
Sometimes he was here one day and gone the next. It so happened
that he'd leave me a few months or even years of respite. Disbeliev-
ing at first, I'd rejoice suspiciously. A day without him was already a
blessing. Two, three—I wouldn't yet dare believe it but bit by bit
regained my confidence, I straightened up, I sneaked peeks at women
passing by: He wasn't there to elbow me and loudly pronounce the
crudest commentary on this or that aspect of their physique. A week
went by, the skies cleared, my smile came back, I whistled, I hummed,
I snapped my fingers, I laughed out loud alone in the street, I began
making plans for the future again!

Now and then I had the chance to get these plans under way and,
more rarely, to see them through. That's how I managed to start
several businesses and two families . . . alas! He always wound up

coming back, unbridled, more monstrous and destructive than ever. In a few days he'd reduced it all to nothing. My wife would chase me out. My business would collapse. The mailman would hurl my mail at me from far off, as though at a plague victim, and if I was so imprudent as to protest, my own dog would take the mailman's side and bark at me. I'd find myself homeless, ruined, and riddled with debt, alone . . . no, not alone, that would've been too good to be true! There he'd be, obnoxiously loyal and loving.

Once I tried to place myself under the protection of the law. Still reeling from an incident more unpleasant than usual, I walked into a precinct and asked to speak to the desk sergeant. A patrolman greeted me. I launched right into my tale: "Officer, I'm the victim of harassment."

"I see. What form does this harassment take? Insults? Infringement of civil liberties? Death threats? Insistent, unwelcome sexual advances?"

"No, no," I replied. "He doesn't lay into *me* so much as people I meet. . . . He annoys them, shocks them, frightens, or disgusts them, and their contempt and disapproval reflect on me."

"But you're not the one harassing them, it's him, right?"

"Absolutely! But you have to understand, he's not really harassing them. He's happy just acting like a lout, while treating me in such a friendly and informal way that my acquaintances can't doubt our closeness. A closeness I formally refute, Officer!"

"Hmm. I see. . . ." The policeman scratched his forehead for a moment, silent.

"Actually I don't," he began again. "To tell the truth, I don't see at all. Could you be a bit clearer, more precise: How is this closeness shown?"

I dropped my gaze. "He . . . he caresses my hands, gazes fondly at me, gives me the most excessive, extravagant compliments!"

". . . and?"

I blushed. "Oh, this is absurd! He says my skin is lily white and soft as a peach, that I'm aglow with health, that my teeth are gleaming—"

I bit my tongue long enough to clear my throat. "He praises my wit, my manners, my diction, my knowledge, my fashion sense, the—the freshness of my breath!"

"And these compliments irritate you?"

"To say the least, sir!"

"So why don't you just slap him in the face?"

173

"I have! I've insulted him, slapped him, half strangled him, smacked him silly, left him for dead again and again—"

"That bad, is it?"

"Yes!" I said, nodding frantically, heedless of the fact that in the policeman's eyes I was changing from victim to victimizer. "I've often thrown him to the ground and trampled him, twisted his ears and nose, broken his fingers, even tried to poke his eyes out!"

"But you never managed?"

"No—well, I thought I did once or twice, but sadly, no!"

"In short: You'd like us to intervene?"

"I want it to stop! I want him to go away! I want him to leave me alone!" I'd raised my voice. The patrolman scowled.

"Calm down now, mister. Mister . . . I'm sorry, I didn't catch your name?"

I stated my name. He noted it.

"And this individual . . . what's his name?"

It was inevitable. We were bound to reach this point sooner or later. I felt sheepish, helpless. "I don't know, Officer."

He frowned. "You don't know?"

"He never said."

"How exactly do you know each other?"

The pointlessness of my approach was suddenly clear to me. How could I have thought my agony might be relieved by an outside party? I was quiet for a moment. But the officer was getting impatient. I had to give him an answer.

"I met him at Buttes-Chaumont. Well . . . I think it was Buttes-Chaumont."

"You're not sure?"

"It's just that it's been more than thirty years since he first showed up in my life, Officer. After all that time, I'm not sure anymore. I could just as well have met him in the little square on the rue de Crimée—I was there a lot too back then—but I'm leaning more toward Buttes-Chaumont, since—"

The patrolman cut me off. "Buttes-Chaumont it is. Well? What happened then?"

"I was playing in the sandbox with a few other kids when he appeared. In the wrong clothes, even back then. Grubby and pimply. His nose was running, and a few big snotty drops had fallen on the half-chewed waffle in his hand. He stepped into the sandbox, walked right up to me, and made a great show of friendship: the first of many! He sang the praises of my sand castles, marveled over the stickers on my little bucket, and grabbed the other kids' rakes and shovels, piling them up at my feet like spoils of war. Then he made mc eat his waffle. I got a cold the next day, lice the day after, and two weeks later came down with chicken pox. My troubles had begun."

My voice broke into a sob. Recounting the first station on my long road to Calvary had moved me to tears. I took a packet of tissues from my pocket and blew my nose loudly. Just above the edge of the tissue, I caught the officer's look. It didn't seem quite as compassionate as I might have expected.

"Of course," I said, folding the tissue back up neatly, "if you've never been through that, you couldn't understand."

The patrolman coughed gently. "I understand."

"You'd have to have been through what I've been through. The sandbox was only the beginning of an endless series of encounters. If only you knew—"

Carried away by the desire to convince the officer it was essential he intervene, I gathered myself to tell him everything in the greatest detail.

He stopped me right away. "Let's skip that for now, OK? Where does this man live?"

I grew flustered, and dropped my gaze again. Bad enough that I didn't know my tormentor's name. But how could an outsider ever accept that I'd put up with him under my own roof? For live together we did, for long periods, against my will, of course. I'd change my locks every week, but he'd get in somehow and impose his awful presence on me. If I moved, he'd find me. Even if I fled to the far ends of the earth, it wouldn't be long before he happened by.

"Usually, you'll find him wherever I am. I mean, at my place, since right now I work at home stuffing envelopes because of him," I said, trying to control my trembling voice.

"At your place? You mean you live together?"

"Not exactly. We don't really live together, strictly speaking. He's just . . . there most of the time, that's all."

The patrolman took a deep breath, then shook his head. "One last question, if I may: Do you have a history of psychiatric illness?"

"Excuse me?"

"Have you ever spent time in an asylum?"

"Never, Officer! I don't think you understand. I'm not insane! In fact, I am in full command of all my faculties. I'd have to be, to put up with what I do without losing my mind."

"We'll see about that."

175

*

When I managed to escape the hospital eight days later, I was worried. The doctors had succeeded in raising my doubts again. Did my tormentor really exist? I hurried back home on foot from the distant suburb where I'd been shipped despite my protestations, mulling the question over seriously. If he didn't exist, I was insane. Moreover, doubting his reality meant doubting my own—I felt my reason waver, unsteady as a child's loose tooth beneath a probing finger. If he did exist, my health but also my misfortune would be confirmed, for everything led me to believe he'd be around as long as I would.

Once more—for the thought had crossed my mind many times before—I was tempted to put an end to myself. Only an abiding uncertainty about the nature of the afterlife—and also, let's face it, a certain natural pusillanimity—had always stayed my hand. I'd suffered enough, and been kept from acting often enough (and therefore from acting wrongly) to go straight to heaven if there was one. But if I got up there only to find him, that groper, that toady, in all his sniveling bonhomie, ready to stick by me for the rest of eternity, well, it wasn't worth it. But that day, my despair almost won out.

Despite myself, my steps led me to the river's edge. Night was falling. The waters seemed to be calling me through the gray mists, promising me a blessed oblivion free of everything, especially that despicable puppet who'd ruined my life.

Drowning isn't usually considered a barrel of laughs, but as I was frail of body and a poor swimmer to boot, I was hoping for an easy death without too much suffering if I went about thirty feet out. Besides, the harsh winter would come to my aid. I stood a good chance of succumbing to sudden pulmonary congestion, or something of the kind, before the water reached my chin.

I'd taken a few steps down a half-submerged stone staircase toward the water when a voice rang out in my ears. I'd have known it anywhere. It'd been the cause of each of my innumerable defeats. It was the voice of bad luck itself.

"Oh, it's you! What a pleasant surprise! I was just taking a stroll, and thinking about you, in fact! What are you doing here?"

In the mist that rose from the river, I was flooded by two contradictory feelings: relief at being able to dispel the doubt the doctors had instilled in me, and rage at finding myself back in a life that horrified me.

My reply rang out in the still air. The sound of his execrable voice had swept aside every last hesitation. "I'm going! I'm leaving you forever, you hellish creature!"

"What? You're not thinking of—you can't be! You don't have the right! A man like you can't let down the hopes he's raised in others!"

I burst out with a cackle and took another step into the icy water.

"You silver-tongued clown! 'A man like me'? 'Hopes I've raised'? Fuck all, I say! Without you, I might've been something . . . I'm not sure what. But at least I would've lived! Too bad! I'm going to drown myself and escape you in death, you pestilent meddler!"

"Stop! You poor man! Think about those who'll grieve for you! Who've loved you, who love you still!"

"That's right, keep talking!"

Still cackling, I took two more steps. An icy hand squeezed my belly. Oh river Seine, make quick work of me! I leaned forward and pushed off with my heels. Terror struck my heart, and my entire body rose up prickling against the vise suddenly tightening around me. But I was sincerely determined to die. From here, it looked painful but brief. All I had to do was take a few strokes from shore and let myself go under.

Not far away, something heavy hit the water with a massive splash. I couldn't believe my ears. It was him! The fool had jumped in!

He surfaced, shook himself like an elephant seal, and reached out his hand.

"Get away from me," I screamed. "I don't want you to save me, you filthy piece of trash!"

He shook his big head. "You're wrong, you—"

"Get away!" I hit him again and again with all my strength. He went under, then resurfaced almost immediately, huffing and spitting. "Get away from me, you bastard!"

"I can't! I can't swim!"

"What? But you jumped in—"

"So you'd save me!"

"Me? Save you? That really takes the cake! Save you?" Beside myself, I began hitting him again. A few of my blows landed. His face was covered in cuts and bruises. His blood flowed freely.

"Save me!" he cried, one last time. "It's the only way to free yourself!"

I don't know what came over me then—what reversal of the soul, what sudden clarity—but I gave up on suicide and saved him.

It wasn't easy. He was a fat slob and didn't lift a finger to help. But

177

we hadn't had time to drift very far from shore. I hauled him onto the steps, and we stayed there for a moment, moaning and shivering, miserable. Finally, we made our way back up the bank, hanging on to each other.

"Real smart," I said. "We're going to get sick now."

"Probably. But if you get better, you'll be free. I give you my word."

He spoke the truth. We ran to the nearest bistro. They undressed us by the stove, rubbed us down, covered us in blankets, served us grog, and even called us a taxi. He let me take it on my own. I've never seen him since.

Energy Fools the Magician
J. W. McCormack

STARKER RIDES A DARK CORRIDOR, even out here, in the park's mois-
tened beeline of raincoats and larval buds. It's not that nothing registers, it's that each entry in spring's parade trips two wires at once.
This spider-motif jungle gym, for example, has its place in the cross-
hairs of the sprinkler system *and* eight legs firmly planted in the
realm of received fictionalization, where it (or a facsimile thereof)
is the site of young Toby Griffin's playground kidnapping in *The
Dance of the Mock Turtle*. The coats that hang suspended from
their tags whilst the business class lunches beneath the elms speak
to Starker of the triple suicide that concludes *Ah, Sunflower*. The
statue of Atatürk a more likely model for *The Alchemist of Emmaus*,
the hovering Mister Softee truck an obvious cover for the peripatetic
demons of *Illusion Street* to concoct their seven flavors, the bench-
slumbering gamine with her cup of quarters a dead ringer for the sub-
titular quarry of *A Hundred Thousand Goodnights: The Story of a
Witch Hunt*. And no initiate into the works of Rhesus Z. Crabtree
could witness the preacher feeding the birds, pushing away squirrels
with his folded umbrella, without wondering if each biscuit contains
the name of a verified sinner à la *The Choir Invisible* (supposedly
the novelist's only volume of nonfiction, though Starker knows every
line for a pernicious lie). *Rhesus Crabtree*, thinks Starker, *leave it to
you to ruin an April shower. Why can't you write anything nice?*

But maybe he's still missing the point, after all these years as a poor
scrivener in the master's shadow. Maybe it's a matter of canvas, and
the writing of books is basically pneumatic. Passing under the criss-
crossed arch of the trees to the park's abrupt departure into waste-
land, where Rhesus Crabtree's apartment is one of the few buildings
still presiding, Starker Arlechino gives it a shot. But alas, this stray
dog picking at a tumbled-down construction sign resists reconfig-
uration as either purebred Yeller or dreadlocked hellhound and the
trio of crocuses wreathing the writer's front door stare petulantly
back, too simply themselves to be placed on any imagined Captain
of Industry's coffin or strewn across the Nordic field that Starker's

mind can barely linger at before wandering back to the synaptic surface of a deep-space satellite, Ceres and the Crab Nebula, the lunar zephyrs and mutant insects that—try as he might to conjure turn-of-the-century romances and prim varsity novels—are his predilection as well as his vocation. "At least we know we are," sighs the author of *Captain Kadmon and the Rings of Phoebus* as he pauses under the window where his mentor labors at his typewriter. "You are the genius of Turkey Park and I am the biggest hack in the whole city."

Judges hand out prizes and committees enrich their reputations with grants for this or that unreadable opus, but the life of objects is even lonelier than that of a reclusive writer and one more academy bulletin or bust of Kleist crowding the building's stairwell can do precious little to dislodge longstanding pandemonium. Rhesus Crabtree will have his disrepair. Starker parks his bicycle between the disembodied legs of a presumptive Venus and follows the trail of decomposing foreign editions and Michaux originals upstairs. There's no need to knock—the slightest disturbance in Rhesus's collection alerts the hermit to the approaching threat of interruption and, besides, Starker has a key—but the slow, faintly unsavory scrape of the old man's canes provides the scribe who once willingly signed his name to *Breakfast with a Side of Tentacles* with plenty of time to finger the flowerpot he's carried under his arm all this way.

"Starker Arlechino," speaks the author of *Brahmagupta's Problem* with goitrous good humor, "is that you struttin' around at this ungodly hour?"

"It's ten minutes after twelve o'clock on the morning of April the 21. Floréal." And, gesturing to the plant, "Look at this. I brought poison."

"Barbaco." Rhesus closes the eye that still works and quotes from memory. "'Boxy Ixmuth swallowed three seeds from the demon flower, just as the old woman had showed him, and felt his death blooming from the inside, little pictures of past cares melting deep within the museum of his guts.'"

"*Ah, Sunflower.*"

"Ah, *shit*! Such filth as you read in the Moleskines of moonlighting sportswriters touring Algiers on a stipend. The entrails of monkfish have cleaner passages, heh heh. And you, Starker, you're an inveterate for seeing I spend my autumn years unforgiven for the failures of my middle period." Crabtree wheezes and lopes across the apartment on his metal staves. "Come the hell in. Put your demon flower on the mantel."

The old feeling of grievous mismatch is overwhelming as ever. Not only is Starker out of place, he's the only thing that is. Chemical angels of compulsion dance on the pyramids of perfectly ordered magazines, alighting over the pale liverwort crust afflicting the tiles, the antique *Finnegans Wake* pinball machine, the rug last vacuumed at the insistence of Emma Lazarus. The tables are awash in pens, pill bottles, and fossilized drafts, unframed Weimar-era posters flaking from the walls, fan letters spewed from the funnel of a Victrola, all of it in adherence to a creepy geometric harmonium, an alphabet whose first letter (as, if memory serves, Brahmagupta tells Gilles de Rais in the prologue) is *Amok.* In any case, Starker can't find the mantel, so he puts the barbaco beside March's sphagnum, a jarful of moths up to their eyespots in cherry laurel from February, the rhizomes of January. He likes to bring gifts, Starker does.

Rhesus has crossed into the kitchen. In the fumbling interval before he returns, rasping from effort, with a bottle of Pernod bulging from the pocket of his velour bathrobe, Starker manages to edge his way against the bookcases and sneak a sideways gander at the page protruding from Crabtree's typewriter. He reads: *The scandalous story of Ichthys Heiden of old Düsseldorf is secret and must not be told at this time. The guilty parties know who they are.* My, that *is* a short story.

"Mu-tu-ally ben-e-ficial! Here we are then, something to sweeten your gullet to the sorry taste of surrender, my fine lad. But I daresay you won't regret it, heh heh," croaketh the shade of that august and inviolate writer whose style Lionel Trilling once characterized as "the palaver of a river god speaking for the gulch." "I knew you couldn't hold out forever. You can only have graced my door crack to consent to my proposition."

"But I haven't consented at all, Rhesus. I'm considering it. Only that."

"Oh I see, of course, yes, you're much too busy to collaborate with old man Crabtree! You've got *The Murk that Came to Monongahela* and *I, Venusian* to prestidigitate over. Pot coddling's a fine occupation for a young man like you. And I imagine when the Valkyries whisk you off to your reward you'll hand them a copy of *Captain Kadmon and the Planet of the Priapods.*"

"That's not fair. I have a following."

"Oh? And where are you leading them?"

The generous publishers of *Stand Up for Bastards and Other Invectives* did their readers the service of substituting a younger photograph over the submitted frontispiece, which was to feature the Rhesus of today—or rather ten years previous, the last time the novelist allowed one of his issue out of doors—masking a grimace with a sneer, all the calligraphy of his face far too articulate in its synopsis of fleshly migration. A single hieroglyph joins the face of the svelte prizewinner of *Me and Miss Manque*'s back flap with the scarecrow of Starker's acquaintance: a beauty mark whose papilla points accusingly toward the apprentice.

"It's not that I object to the manufactured aspect."

"Naturally not."

"Right. It's just—I don't write stuff like what you're talking about. I write crap." Go ahead, thinks Starker, get him to admit that he doesn't want to sully his hands. "Surely you could just as easily tear the shroud from the unbelieving eyeballs of the mucked-up modern world *without* me."

"Ah, but you have your commercial pedigree. Come, lad, it's nothing to be ashamed of. Every courtier has his hands on two bishops and a rook."

"When you put it like that—"

"Not just to get the thing on the shelves, either. Our hero will require an advocate in the world of popular letters. Also a detractor. The bohemian element must contain one or two muckrake dilettantes whose infatuation with the life of the mind does not inure them to pecuniary temptation."

"You're volunteering all costs up front?"

"How's *Penultima Thule* selling these days?"

"Very well, actually."

"That's not a good thing!"

"No, I know. Believe me, that's the whole problem. A great man like you, how can you understand? You pound your typewriter keys in rough phonetic equivalency of your ideas, banking on the possibility that you're the first to devise the onomatopoeia for toilet tanks or to set your crescendo in a dry ice factory, blaming television or the indolence of a generation for your lack of an audience."

"And hacks like you, don't forget that! Oh how I loathe the serviette class."

"Absolutely right, Rhesus. I really feel for you on this one. But thing is, there's a finite number of constellations visible from earth. It's the same with story lines. The least expectation of the bourgeois reader must have its bards and ballad mongers and the system that allows— no, *demands*—mediocrity would crawl over Pynchon, Proust, and

Pindar for one crime-fighting FBI cyborg. And that's just the Ps. Nobody takes it harder than I. Look at my life, I'm like a pod person," sayeth Starker Arlechino, pricklingly aware that, with the whole of classical mythology open to him, he's settled, metaphorwise, for the low road. "But it's this or work. You understand my position. No offense, but what can talent and originality offer me, when it's my professional responsibility to drink your blood?"

Except your secrets, goes that hissing canister first set ajar in a Midwestern boarding school in 1989, when a young Starker stumbled upon *The Alchemist of Emmaus* between Byronic attitudes and the cadaverous content of a certain school of French lyric poetry. He'd known by the first spagyric that Rhesus Crabtree's was the only pen that could reach the sulfuric deposit in his being that all the boy's worst instincts had so far failed to transmute, as though the echo that sometimes vibrated across his bedroom ceiling upon awakening from extremely beautiful dreams of waterfalls and distant crosses had been granted an organ. A pure page from this most dedicated adversary of consensual reality was worth your garden-variety fictioneer's whole career, coequal to all his base scribbles with their inevitable adulteries and dysfunctional suburbanites—and then to actually meet the man! Even now, when the predictable strain of low expectations and calculated vocabular vacancy have brought Starker so far, there's the question (*Would you trade your surname, embossed as it is on the quadrilateral contents of airport bookshelves, for a sobriquet that gave you a mainline to that magic?*) and the answer (*Fucking affirmative, I would*). But it's necessary to bait the genius of Turkey Park for a mite longer. If a swapping of their respective muses is truly in the offing, he may as well pretend he hasn't already made an appointment with Herbert "Flip" Dyrshka, publisher of *All Mimsy Were the Meteorites* and Starker's primary enabler, and prolong a done deal with a rhetorical shadowbox at whatever scheme lurks beneath Crabtree's parlance and promises of glory.

"And not only glory, my boy. Legitimacy. A little substance I daresay. And really, who said anything about originality? The Guignol I propose is only marginally preferable to your spaceman. It's a question of venue, of heartfelt trash versus *pastiche*. Genre is all the rage, provided you convince the reader you're not trying."

"I can do that."

"There, you see? I knew you were my man. They won't know what hit them, heh heh. Naturally, we'll need a beard. A dilettante to face the public and mobilize our pseudonymity. Preferably a Gaul."

183

"Leave that to me. But wait, why? I'm certainly no stranger to ghostwriting and, if you don't mind my saying so, you've never objected to scandal." Starker stops short of reminding the author of his blood feud with the editors of *Bedknob* over the Greek hexameter dactyls or the dueling scar supposedly inflicted by G. K. Chesterton.

"Precisely. It's expected of me. Crabtree the charming old dinosaur, cranky-cuddly Rhesus Crabtree, the Luddite with his doomy pamphlets of human iniquity, one of our finest moralists and other such balderdash," so blows the reedy throat of an antique wit now fallen to phlegm and spite. "They think they've neutralized me with biography, boy, but only *I* know what the literature of a country in decline craves. A villain they can all cheer for, yes, a thief to snag the pearls from their ears, absolve them of their venality, and quench their need to be judged and punished for their complacency. There's an undertow of morbidity at work in us now that not even checkout-line rags can keep in check. You and me, boy. We can be the slime."

But Starker perceives a twinge of the old man's ugly mark and reads a lie, or rather an evasion, since what is really expected of Crabtree these days consists of a misanthropy so overwhelming that it has finally jumped the curb of mere creation and broadened to include make-believe. If a character could survive two pages under Crabtree's care without being suddenly smashed by a piece of scaffolding or inexplicably seized by the hand of God and hurled off the side of a bridge, it was a good writing day for them both. Starker's best guess is that he's being brought on as life insurance, to protect their rogue musketeer from the wrath of his personal Demiurge.

"Well, why didn't you say so, Rhesus? I'm always game for a little artistic terrorism. You provide the poison, I'll provide the pen. Put her there."

"Ah well, thank Apollo for sending me one with a soul left to lose, heh heh. Now then, how shall we call our mountebank? Emmanuel Jackanape? Julian Nonesuch? The Black Lotus?"

But then there's another theory that Starker and his set—Hova, Paz, and Fletcher Poole—have been known to venture in the lofty unfurnished nights when pleasure seeking has turned stationary and the disciples wonder at the silence of their patron saint. They pluck passages from the unpublished works Starker dutifully steals during his visits and, in mining each passage for its real-life reverberation, have arrived at this weird crux: Rhesus Crabtree is in love. And supposing it's so, wonders Starker, which of us is the Cyrano and which the suitor?

"I've got a better idea," says Starker as he pours two glasses and eyes the older writer's jacquard bathrobe. "Say, what a lovely smoking jacket you have."

I want your secrets.

From *The Black Angel's Death Song* by R. Triboulet

Beware, O reader, of this tale that it is our grim duty to relay. We doubt very much that there is any comfort to be had from reliving the spell in which the Fiend with Seven Faces lately embroiled this, our city, making a Pandemonium of its settled Sanctuaries and giving vent to conjectures of the wildest character. Those unwise enough to read on will find that we have resisted, at every corner, the Onus of Embellishment, the better to set down, in sober pen stroke, the deeds of that pitiless avenger who dances upon the knife blade of life and death with the same ataraxy as another handles a wineglass, the Maestro of Malodor—the slaughterer Jacquard!

When newsprint and plaster seal shop windows; when door hinges close on the fingers of children desperate not to be caught in the narrow streets at nightfall; when rain falls straight down from a hyperborean sky and quenches the flames of the street lamps; when the too-close buildings whisper their timorous chitchat and strange boats fly their tattered flags from the harbor; when the shadow of the marauder wrinkles on the marble stairs; when all good men shake the storm water from their hats and the Wolf's Hour beckons, what are we to do but set the stage for their opposite?

It was April, a month the doomed argot of an ancient Revolution had termed Floréal, when the first murders occurred. Danton, Marat, the pussyfooting Robespierre, how those bloody garçons, with their powdered wigs and severed heads, would have smiled upon their heir, as he strolled under the windows of Wall Street in his top hat and cane, merging with the night. Is this our man, of the rakish gait and the flicked cigarillo, whistling "La Marseillaise" as he circles the block? Or is he across the way, wearing the guise of an undertaker, polishing his hearse between funerals? So prevalent has the phantom become in the nightmares of the city fathers that the ambulating Judge and Banker glimpse the saucy rascal—whose name they dare not enunciate without the muffle of a carriage door between them and the truants and transients that are the thief's city feelers—bowing from the balcony windows of opera houses or silhouetted in each jagged sliver of sudden lightning that flashes over the cobblestones.

Having identified each other by the light of a lifted match, content that the Judge's beauty mark is on its proper cheek, a firm tug going to show that Banker's muttonchops are homegrown rather than adhesive, they hustle into the gloomy courthouse and pound out the agreed-upon knock on that sturdy door reading SANGVIS CVRRIT VRBIS. The meeting is in progress. Around the table sit the Vicar, the Constable, the General, Professor Institoris, City Councilman Marburg, and Torque the Industrialist, all assembled to discuss What Is to Be Done.

"The fiend struck again last night," the Constable is saying, "at the home of the Lady S____. You've all heard of her collection of rings, each a memento of some lovestruck swain whose heart she fleeced in due course? Well, it seems those unhappy gigolos have been granted their revenge. They found her fingers tied into a necklace and strung about the neck of a cigar-store Indian at the corner of A____ Street, stripped of their ornamentation."

"Not only that," contributes Torque the Industrialist, "they recovered those same precious stones in the donation box of a soup kitchen."

"There's no denying that he hunts for sport, not profit," mutters the Banker as he takes his seat, "and we, gentlemen, are the quarry."

"They say he has a passion for heiresses," observes Councilman Marburg, "and that he slips the poison into their throats when they are in amours."

"I would that he limited his prey to adulteresses and libertines," sighs the Vicar, "but of my congregation, half a dozen have been dispatched in the last month alone. They recovered the architect R____'s bones from the hollow of an angelic statue once the fountain it overlooked began to gush blood. The curator of the Z____ Gallery was found flayed and stretched across one of his own canvases. And the actor C____"

"Yes, yes," says the Judge. "We all know the story of how our friend strangled the actor at the intermission, stripped the poor fellow of his costume, completed the night's production without missing a line, and escaped during the applause. Our friend is a perpetrator, as well as a patron, of the arts."

"I'm afraid I must take umbrage at the Councilman's suggestion," says the Constable, "that those ladies of honorable standing are unfaithful as well as dead. You see, we have recovered the skins of several husbands from the scene of the crime. They have been . . .

exfoliated. It seems he dons their faces and slips into bed with their unsuspecting wives. We still don't know what he does with their skulls."

"Why, what grotesquerie," thunders the General, "are you suggesting the man has no face of his own?"

"Rather," says the Banker, "any face he chooses. I have heard that he has the pupils of a cat. And that he saves a memento from each of his victims. And keeps them in his lair beneath the city, a veritable Museum of Crime. That's where you'll find your skulls, Constable."

"I'm told," adds Torque the Industrialist, "that he goes nowhere without sending his card first. The fellow is damnably polite in his twisted way."

"I say twaddle," says the Constable, "or rather, I wish I could say twaddle. But there's the matter of the calling card our office received just this morning. Scented with lavender. It was all we could do to keep it from the press, who still insist upon publishing his letters. If you can call them that."

"Actually," whispers Professor Institoris, breaking his long silence, "I find those acrostics and ciphers quite engaging. Why, we at the University have taken to racing each other to the solution each time a new one appears."

"Bah," spits the General, "you academics can tolerate any barbarity given it comes with an appeal to intellectual vanity. I've had enough enumeration of the reprobate's crimes. Constable, let's see that card!"

The Constable reaches into his coat and flips the perfumed square onto the table. The assembled officers and civil servants lurch out of their chairs and nearly bang their scalps together as they lean in to read:

O Celebrated Gentlemen

Your elegant tastes and toils for the commonwealth endear you to the collection of the undersigned.

A reception has been prepared in your honor at the Fulton Customhouse.

Come as you are, for soon you will be no more.

Nocturnally Yours,
Jacquard

"Jacquard! The blight of the Bowery, the menace of Midtown!"

"Jacquard! The diabolic dandy, the gabardine ghastly!"

"Jacquard! And look, there's the scalawag's monogram."

"Jacquard! What in blazes could he mean, the Fulton Customhouse?"

"So Jacquard thinks he'll have us that easy, does he? But, Councilman, you've gone pale as a phantasm."

Indeed, the Councilman had whitened from monocle to chin cleft, as though in terror of some annihilating angel lurking just beyond the spooling curtain threads that divided the moonlight into mercury slivers.

"But don't you see? We've been lured into a trap," and, lifting his arms before him and staggering to the window like a somnambulist, Councilman Marburg pulled at the curtain and yanked the rod off the casing to reveal a heraldic fish scowling down from the molding. "The courthouse *was* a customhouse until it was decommissioned by James Buchanan!"

"James Buchanan? The devil you say!"

As the winds of the revelation blew through the features of each man in turn, sorting their expressions like leaves, Torque the Industrialist, chattering with all the mania of a haberdasher, gripped the tablecloth in both hands and pulled, upending ashtrays and plates until a magnification of the same hateful monogram that had attended Jacquard's signet was revealed elegantly patterned into the wood, framed by a hypnotic whorl of roses and thorns.

"Wonderful," opined the Vicar. "Is there any further contretemps someone would like to uncover?"

"Just one," said Professor Institoris, rejoining the group after a brief exploration. "It seems we have been sealed inside this room. Trapped like bugs in a killing jar, if you'll pardon the simile."

"This is an outrage," shouted the General. "I for one won't stand by and wait for some gimcrack to cut my throat. Let us arm ourselves against this invader."

The General reaches for his pistol but is stopped by the Judge's arm on his shoulder. "No good, General. The knave is already here. One of us is not who he seems. You there, Torque. You're our industrialist, are you not?"

"Why, of course. My industry knows no injunction. If industriousness was a rat and lassitude a cat—"

"That's all very well, but does the course of your duties usually include the brocade of tablecloths?"

"It was just a feeling, I swear," pleads the industrialist. "You don't mean to suggest that I—"

"Indeed I do, Torque, indeed I do. Constable, seize that man!"

"But what of Professor Institoris? Why, he's said barely a word this whole time."

"Merely the aftermath of a case of stomatitis I contracted in Caporetto while researching Lampedusa," answers the Professor. "Nothing sinister, I assure you."

"Even so, we can't afford to take any chances. Seize him as well."

"Now look here, Judge, I say!" scoffs the Constable. "No one's seizing anyone. We'll gain nothing by squabbling amongst ourselves like a trogle of water moccasins! Why, I daresay that's just what Jacquard wants!"

The tableau was momentarily frozen with nearly all of the guests on the verge of fisticuffs, each pair of mitts parked on another man's lapels. Then the chandelier flickered and cut out, wiping stars from the sky and replacing the amber lighting with a calamitous darkness over which a voice of shrill appalling timbre was heard to intone, "Oh classic gentlemen! Do not speak my name lightly, for Jacquard is the loom. Now feel my needle!" A sound not unlike the tearing of cloth split the air into two segments: shrieks and the ghoulish laughter of the Caligula of Crime, the Wight of Washington Square, the Cutpurse of Tin Pan Alley—the archvillain Jacquard! When someone finally managed to light a candle, all eyes turned, mystified, to the General.

"I think I got 'im, by Gum! Show him to—what? Why are you all—" And then the General glances down and finds that he is clutching the Judge's severed head in his fists. He does disservice to his station in the scream that follows and drops that dripping orb to the floor, whereupon the head's mouth chatters open and something is seen to protrude from his blackened tongue.

"Pay heed," shouts the Constable. "It's Barbaco, the demon flower. The mark of Jacquard!"

"And that's not all," says the Banker as he kneels down to graze the ex-Judge's cheek. "Someone has stolen the mole right off this man's face."

"You could fertilize salt flats with this stuff," mutters Starker as he slips R. Triboulet's mendacious maiden voyage into the manila envelope and signs the package with his feet. First draft complete, Starker does the rounds.

First stop is Herbert "Flip" Dyrshka, confronted in the schlock merchant's natural seraglio, the office high rise. Here inside and outside views are artfully reconciled: the Chrysler Building answered with a tower of unsold copies of *Sphinctomancer*, the chromium glare of the cars below neutralized by a laminated movie poster of Smithee's *Breakfast with a Side of Tentacles* and, in place of a statue of Moloch, a life-size and semifunctional rendition of the robot from *Under the Volcanoes of Mars*.

"R. Triboulet, huh?" Exit cigar, pursued by a tongue. Smoke ring, smoke ring, smoke ring, "Where's this cat from?"

"The spawn of a French albino and a Canadian eschatologist, R. Triboulet was abandoned at the age of nine and raised thereafter by a Cajun witch doctor on the banks of the Sabine. He dredged his first reading out of that evil old river, where the books had been hurled by barge owners whose apprehension of literature was not the equal of young Triboulet's. Determined to become a writer or follow in the footsteps of his ancestors by dying of malaria, Triboulet injected himself with a slow-acting culture to which he had to administer the antidote every day, something he only did after writing his customary thirteen pages. Having followed a mysterious birthmark in the shape of a sea urchin across continents and quondam demesnes, he has lived in Calcutta, Greenland, Papua New Guinea, and Sark. He currently resides in Brooklyn. R. Triboulet's articles and short stories have been published in many Québécois separatist newspapers, obscure jazz-funk liner notes, and out-of-print anthologies of writers under thirty-seven. This is his first novel," reciteth the more-or-less miserable author of *Hotel Beelzebub*.

"You don't say," Herbert "Flip" Dyrshka nods, unfurling the manuscript on his desk in a fan.

"It doesn't matter *what* I say, Flip. In five minutes you'll agree to publish. You always do."

"Well, Starky boy, you've brought much cashola to this humble publishing house. Yes, many a ripe franchise has come to my attention by way of your recommendation. To say nothing of your own work."

"Yes, I'd prefer you didn't."

"And I've always liked your jib. Mercifully free of the illusions of artistic beatitude that afflict so many men your age." A passenger plane drifts into the frame behind Herbert "Flip" Dyrshka, gradually entering the portion of cityscape blocked by his enormous head and so appearing to enter through one ear and leave by another. "Verily,

I weep to think of the vampire novels I could've coaxed from the viscous pens of a generation of budding language poets and metafictional Magogs if only I'd bound them to me sooner. Instead, I let them slip into the Rolodexes of those self-ordained Waldensians that infect our universities and book reviews with their monkish disdain of pleasure. They laughed at little Herbie Dyrshka, didn't they? They told me I'd never turn a Wiccan memoir of teenage alcoholism into digestible daytime talk fodder. But, ha ha, who's mad now?" shouts the editor as he waves his cigar at the bookstore blowup of *Blotto de Fé.* "You know, I consider myself something of a priest too. A desert prophet. A pioneer! But do they hand out a Pulitzer for film novelizations? Does the Critics Circle have a category for Most Factual Memoir? Well?"

"Flip, we do this every single time."

"A revival of the old Gallic horror shows, eh?" says Herbert "Flip" Dyrshka, for here is a man who proceeds by jettison, losing first the thread, then his shit. "I suppose we haven't tickled that toe in a while. And artifice is ever in fashion. Title will have to go of course. Too crowded for the cover illustration. I can see the promotions already—we'll buy a museum guard or two and stage an actual art theft, yes? Wait, strike that, we'll pay an actor to go around spoiling soirees and fighting duels with the landed gentry. Create a scandal and accrue a little inversely buoyant trash talk. The idea sounds better the more I hear myself rave about it."

"I read somewhere that the same was true of William Shakespeare."

"On the other hand." And here comes the inevitable throwing of the switch. The sucking of the Claro leaves, the twirling of the handlebar, the olive complexion turning tomato: Starker knows what to look for. "We work for the readers, Starky boy, and we mustn't forget how they suffer for us. Scoffed at by the needful lickspittles and flavors of the moment, Amazon Customer Reviews their only outlet. Can you not hear their woesome threnody? We must honor our contract. Thou shalt not flex thy quirks and foibles at the expense of the delicate mores of the tote bagger, thou shalt confirm and never confound, leaving naught but adverbs in thy wake, thou shalt punish each deviation from the consensual order, for we are that order's sentinels and ministers, Starky boy, and *I will not sit idly by* and see our nondenominational creed sullied by another freebooting verb merchant with a pseudo-academic ax to grind. All we need to know is whodunit? Howcatchem? Howsellem? Wherebuyit? Now then, whose books lean upon the brain of this R. Triboulet?"

"Um. Myles na gCopaleen, Boz, Anti Climacus, Bernando Soares, and, uh, Rhesus Crabtree?"

"*Crap*tree. I should've guessed. That sanctimonious troll has been a malefic influence on your work habits from the beginning. His work's been negligible since *The Choir Invisible* and, anyway, a martyr like that's got no right pushing the wound in his side on you. You think I'm simple, Starky boy?" Squinty and frothy, the publisher goes on. "You think I can't guess what you're at? You'll unload this fella on me cheap, then get all the glory for discovering him. Offer to become his agent and absorb the profits. You dishonor this office with your impertinence! You must learn discipline. And I happen to have a sports autobiography that wants ghostwriting."

"Oh no. Please, Flip, not that."

"Oh *yes*, Starky boy! Or should I say Electra Czoket, titan of the tennis court? For there is a price to be paid for leisure, a tollbooth on the road of abstract thought and I, Herbert 'Flip' Dyrshka, have come to collect," and, rising from his chair to face the skyline sitting cozily at the center of the windowpane: "Do you hear me, you bitch? You hear me, you cocksure corps of nostril pinchers? Wherever a basement-bound longhair yearns for a barbarian to commute his adolescent sentence, I am there. Wherever the twice-divorced pilot of a wood-paneled sedan yearns to know what Don Knotts thought about the hippies, I am there. Wherever a sensitive small-town girl with glasses yearns to populate her high school with demon lovers, I am there too. I am the Mjöllnir of the readily amused, the Excalibur of beachside readers."

Having reached the cumulative phase of his cycle, Herbert "Flip" Dyrshka lifts his hairy fists to the heavens and gyrates slowly, inadvertently triggering the motion detect of the robotic replica into miming the same gesture with its wildly flailing vacuum-tube arms, knocking an avalanche of books from the shelves. Starker catches a copy of *Captain Kadmon Meets Billy the Kid* and, turning the cover to face his youthful photo, is unable to keep from visualizing a patently obvious scene of damnation, the tentacles of some Stygian squid reaching through the amassed colophons of this pabulum he has perpetuated, hellfire briar-and-bristling up from the yellow carpet to consume the cackling and mustachioed majordomo and his homunculus together. Which reminds him—he hasn't given Flip his gift yet.

"What about R. Triboulet?"

"Huh? Oh, he's the genius of our times. I'll write him a contract for five books."

"Great, Flip. Knew I could count on you. Mutually beneficial."

"Don't mention it." Spent, the publisher sags back into his swivel chair. "Oh, and one more thing? Whatever gift you brought this time, spare me. They totally freak me out."

Sighing Starker hates to cause a fuss and thusly slips the chicken's claw back into his trousers.

Next on Starker's list is Paz Lindengarten, freelance philosophix and compensated doodler. Behind beaded curtains and a muscular haze of cirrus choke-smoke, the lady labors at her drafting table, studio decked out with casts of Homo Erectoid skulls and feathered serpents. Starker showers her with gifts (today's special being a basket of wax fruit) that she accepts due to complicated views on the politics of give-and-take gleaned from Meister Eckhart. Few of the city's artisan tribe, at least on this lowly rung of the ladder, labor exclusively under the star of their choosing and Paz earns her justification by happier means than most. Her *New Adventures of Artie Schopenhauer* strip is syndicated in dozens of college papers and trendy digital samizdats. Each installment features the pessimist, incongruously outfitted in the capotain of an English Puritan, shattering obstacles and objections with the Boot of Pure Will. A boulder tumbling into the philosopher's path—BOOT!—a busy signal—BOOT!—a smoking ban—BOOT!—crafty, brick-hurling Hegel—BOOT! Absurdist humor is all the geist, so Paz shruggingly besets her Ubu with whatever happens to be annoying her that day, the loophole being she doesn't actually have to get her own jokes.

"Seriously, Paz, between you and Dyrshka, it'll be a miracle if I don't die of secondhand smoke."

"My smoke is different. My smoke is good for you." Paz sucks in the room's imperfect atmosphere and breathes out purified atoms, expelling a Pandora's box of hexes and imprecations with each drag. Her cigars are all inscribed with the names of vices. Intolerance, Impatience, Pretension, and Onanism lie squashed in the ashtray and she's halfway through Dogmatism.

"It's four thirty p.m. on the first of May—"

"Beltane. Yeah, you told me. What do you want, Starker?"

"A bad review."

"Mm, so." Paz trails a comb through her hair. "Your tie is ugly."

"Very funny. I mean for the mutually beneficial thing I told you about."

"I've got a good memory." Now she's tacking up the day's strips and throwing her feet across her worktable. "Entirely selective. Tell me a story, Starker. Tell me the story of what you want to say. I'm the passenger, you be the driver."

But what Starker wants to say is *Step with me through the bad neon, leave this skipping record to its gravitational doings and anoint this pilgrim with kisses the same splendor as your lip gloss. Show me what words are when they take off their clothing. Let me take your haircut in my hands, oh Paz, oh judicious female, and enact the content of songs and the letters of Peter Abelard.* Instead he tells a lie whose falseness resides not in its content but in the greater truths it sidesteps: a syllogism.

"Crabtree and I are manufacturing a murderer. Strictly paperback. But even so, we're killing a lot of people."

"Rhesus Z. Crabtree," Paz says and thoughtfully folds her ear into its car hole. "I used to write him when I was a little girl. What a sinister tautology. You grow up and get to take the measure of your heroes. And it tends to be an arm's length. I wonder if he kept my letters?"

Starker is thinking of the shooting holidays when he acts as Rhesus's second, lifting the writer's wheelchair up three flights of stairs, launching parcels of fan mail from the apartment roof and watching Crabtree take aim with his rifle, vaporizing precocious love letters and signature requests from his chaise longue. "You wouldn't like him if you knew him like I do, Paz. God love him, he's just an evil, hateful old man with a face like a hairy teacup, out to destroy the world."

"Maybe. I reject all essentialisms." Somehow the ear of Paz remains folded, a fleshy flower refusing to bloom. "Besides, we're all out to destroy the world. Just not all of it at once."

"That's Hova you're thinking of. I'm mostly in it for the money."

"I know you're lying, but I believe you. I just don't think they've ever coined the currency you aspire to. You're in revolt against the clumsy punctuation of a feckless Creator, like Kierkegaard's demoniac man. I think it's charming. Anyway, Hova's a Marxist, so he's spoken for." The ear finally comes back out and Paz opens her sketchbook and begins to draw as she speaks. "See him lately?"

"I'm seeing him and Fletch after. Rhesus wants to stack our deck with the counterculture. You need at least three pillars for a cult hit."

194

"Ah. And haven't you considered that if your book is synthetic from the nursery, you can expect feigned enthusiasms at best?"

"Don't try to confuse me. It's an old-fashioned literary hoax. Our transatlantic moon balloon, our chess-playing automaton." But then the cranial wheels turn and Starker switches tactics. "Wait, what am I saying? Paz, you're perfect. Your humorless disapproval is just what I want. Now if only you could synthesize that into a column. Or, I don't know, have Schopenhauer boot it. People will read out of perverse curiosity. I mean, just think, you could object as a feminist!"

"Oh, Starker, the very idea"—still scribbling in her sketch pad— "as if I would drag *that* emulsified dialectic through the mud when the notion of grown-up children taxing their feeble vocabularies on penny dreadfuls is already offensive beyond belief. Really, you flatter yourself. What gives you the right?"

"This. I have been formally deputized." Starker reaches into his breast pocket and withdraws an object whose Sistine proportions and perfect heft are evident from the ease with which Starker twists the pen through his fingers.

"A canary yellow 1909 Tyndale Jackknife," gasps Paz, "with a crescent ink sac, fourteen-karat nib, and a star clip instead of a diamond! Holy shit, Starker, is that what I think it is?"

In place of an answer, Starker tilts the pen so that the light of Paz's lava lamp saturates with Vulcan tincture the inscription reading QUI IN GURGITEM SPECTAT.

"Desiderius." She's breathless. "They say it was a gift from Farouk I after Lawrence Durrell introduced them. That's the pen he used to create *her*."

"Who?"

Of course, he already knows, but Paz's implacable diction is a delight ("What country is she *from*?" ask initiates upon introduction, to which Starker can never bear to answer, "Calhoun County"). Equally pleasant is the callipygian flipside she turns to Starker as she stubs out her cigar, slips it behind her ear, and climbs the wooden ladder to her bookshelves. She returns with a donkey-eared copy of *Margarita Maybe* and begins to read: "What was she, this soft stream in the storm of lives, more than two breasts borne on a body and a chin that knew enough to nod at the name Margarita Gosselmeier, yes, nod with the bold manner of an acknowledged beauty, tossing curls and curling fingers as though the secret that lulled admirers was not equally closed to her whose self-love was strangely unrequited? Keys might turn the lock, but the door remained. What was she, pale Madonna of frogs and fireflies, but the puzzled incarnation of a girl sometimes sleeping sometimes waking, but always catching herself midstream midlaugh midthought as though in a glass, opening her diary to a random page and finding scrawled there the gloss of a distant contemporary? A gosling on the embrasure might slip into her soul and be just as easily and inadequately clothed as Margarita Gosselmeier, the width of an eyelid all that kept her from merging with the cosmos. The only defense against eternity was to close her eyes."

"So we're back to this. You think that's why he hasn't published in ten years. He's in love with a person who doesn't exist."

"Saudade, love of the purely noumenal. The ruiner of my gender. But it's sweet when a man does it." Having set aside her cigar and still incorrigible with regard to her desire for chemicals, Paz flips opens a globe—though its continents are apparently arranged according to Ptolemy—and, browsing the liquor selection therein, decides on a glass of whisky and milk. "Want one?"

"No thanks, I'm lactose intolerant."

"Pity you're so compliant in your other aspects." She may lack Herbert "Flip" Dyrshka's hairy chevron, but now Paz can at least boast a milk mustache. "You've read the book?"

"What, *Margarita Maybe*? About a million times. Sometimes, when Margarita goes to sleep, she wakes up one hundred years in the past, in someone else's body. Eventually, she learns how to balance one side of the century with the other. But her soul gets lost at the end of the book."

"Exactly. It's all very basic Jungian shadow play. His anima is loose and he's waiting for her to come back. Then he thinks he'll be cured," Thoughtfully, Paz chooses a cigar marked Indolence and lights it before returning to her sketchbook. "He'll be able to write again. Write something beautiful."

"In the meantime he's settled for crudity, violence, and pretension. He's settled for me. So you agree to rally your sisters against Jacquard? You agree to hate my book?"

"Why, Starker, I hate it already. Free of charge. Here, I made you something." The philosophix tears the page from her tablet and hands her guest a mess of cubic triangles and smooth wrinkles that gradually resolve themselves into a preemptive aging of Starker's features, fusing the author of *M Is for Megapsychomachiamania* with that of *Margarita Maybe* and *Three Cheers for Mr. Leopard*.

"Creepy."

"No, uncanny. *Unheimliche.*" Puff puff. "Anything else I can do for you today?"

"How about a date? We could go to a lecture on the death of the author. Or an execution."

"Charmed, I'm sure, but if I've never let you take me out when you were merely a mediocre science fiction writer, why would I now that you're in the prime of your highest low?"

"It's a Hegelian synthesis"—staring bleakly into the cartoon buckle on Schopenhauer's hat. "You'll love me by and by."

FROM *Sister Midnight* BY R. TRIBOULET

The oar stoked the smoky waters and the underground river obliged, parting at this bend or that foul deposit to reveal the skeleton of some unfortunate stumbler on the secret kingdom whence the Lady S____ found herself so unhappily ferried. Her captor, with white gloves perched atop the wand that stirred all this stygian soup, gave a loathsome chuckle to see the lady start from her posture at the ship's bow, from some gastric rumble had coaxed her attentions toward the crepuscular depths.

"Fear not, gentle creature," spoke that man who lately had been the Marquis of A____, but whose handsome countenance seemed to shift under his cowl. "You hear only my pet squid, Unheimliche, welcoming his master home."

At this, a single green tentacle emerged from out the watery netherworld around them. Reaching into his gentleman's purse, the oarsman passed his nimble claws over rolled and priceless paintings filched from the abodes of certain heads of state, gold-plated cigars plucked from the mouths of tycoons, the rings and jewel-entrusted eyeteeth of visiting dignitaries, before settling on the body of a chicken and flinging the fowl into Unheimliche's flailing appendage. The tentacle retreated back into the brine with its prize, granting the lady some scant and enervated seconds of wonder before all this decorous underworld: the rocks that drew back to reveal gilded portraits of kings and conquerors all defaced to wear the likeness of the Marquis, the insidious isle even now materializing out of the sewer's subterranean haze, before the swimming monster gave a belch that rustled the chimes that hung along the exposed piping and ejected from the frothy muck two curved and blackened claws.

"You see? No harm will come to you," said the oarsman and threw back his hood as they arrived at the island's crude port, so that there could be little doubt that the draughtswoman was in the company of the very basilisk that held all the city in his paralyzing gaze, the villain Jacquard. "At least," said he, as he helped the lady from her boat, "not without my express wish. All that is here corresponds to my desire. Welcome to the Museum of Crime!"

They were standing beneath an architectural marvel, a pillared chantry in the heart of the Malebolgean cove. An arch inscribed QUI IN GURGITEM SPECTAT fairly shadowed a torch-lit stairway, around which there grew a nocturnal garden, an orchid of nightshade, mandrake root, and the famous barbaco, a couple of copses ornamented with oddly translucent fruit. Bowing before the lady, Jacquard reached and plucked one of these pale vegetative eyes and handed it to his guest, placing it in the hand that was not clutched to her quaking bosom. She took a bite, then grimaced and made to spit before thinking with horror what might repay refusal of her captor's generosity.

"But," trembled the beauty, "this fruit is made of wax!"

"Of course, milady. For my house is the trough that sits inversely to the upper world, where art suffers and tyranny prospers. Here grow ingenuity, imitation, and forgery. Only such things as please Jacquard."

"Can it be? You mean, the Marquis is in actuality—"

"That boorish Swabian is merely a mask, my dear, one of the seven," grins the thief. "Or did you think it was by mistake that, upon the unholy night of Beltane, you accompanied your foolish sow of a husband R____ to the suburb of Z____ to attend the séance of Madame C____? Imagine that fat robber baron's shock when the lights were restored and he found you vanished, lured from the fields of Demeter to pay tribute to your Hadean admirer! But, lest you think I impugn the talents of that spiritualist or you take the Madame to be a charlatan in my employ, know that she did her work only too well. For worse than any shade out of perdition, she conjured me, who speaks for Dis and Sodom, for horn, ivory, and the Lords of Panic."

They stood at the Museum's marmoreal gates, where a carved chimera held in its hideous talons a tome of anthropodermic binding. "I lament that I remain the slave of custom," said Jacquard, "albeit none but my own. I must insist you sign my guest book before our tour continues!" And so saying, the wicked libertine produced a quill and jabbed it sharply into the lady's artery. So stricken, she allowed the pen to soak the sanguinary fluid from her bloodstream and with that elixir committed her nomenclature to a census of missing persons, of mislaid women of easy leisure and milk-carton cover girls (these she recognizes not, as Madame is a lactose-intolerant).

"My first exhibit," said Jacquard, steering his houseguest by her arm, "the statue garden. Though all art opposes itself to God, I insist on applying my criticism directly to the original," says Jacquard and, indeed, beneath each Olympian brow sits a pair of watery eyes, helpless but to follow their path through circles of stiff-corseted nymphs opening onto a tennis court whose imprisoned athletes stand poised in the fashion of a Grecian discus thrower. "You recognize her, I suppose, the so-called Titan of the tennis court. When she agreed to model before the Marquis, she was primed to surpass her previous record. Unfortunately, she came down with a case of stiff joints before the game."

The tour continued through Jacquard's parlor of vices—a necrotic tromp l'oeil where postured skeletons enacted indolence and onanism—and his gallery of disguises, but when they reached the library, where a jewel-encrusted tortoise loped diffidently between the columns, the lady gasped to see her own letters cured of their hasty creases, reconstructed from the pieces into which she had shamefully torn them and lovingly preserved behind cherrywood frames. "That's right, Madame. I know of your passion for the Don Juan of thieves. No doubt you thought to hide your love letters from your husband by flushing them down the commode. But Madame forgot that Jacquard dwells in the country of secrets, the necropolis in the earth's crust where buried desires wash ashore and dead letters obtain resurrection.

"I was moved by your words, my lady, for evil is no easy infatuation. How you must have trembled in your sleep to feel my caress." Jacquard flips open a globe—though its continents are apparently arranged according to Ptolemy—and, browsing the liquor selection therein, decides on two glasses of bloodred wine. "And since you have worn your heart so nakedly with me, I would unclasp my own cloak." The baleful glare of the chandelier caught the fiend's cuff links as his gloves trailed the length of a tie (whose poor taste was the exception to the ensemble's ghoulish elegance) and ended at the candles of his eyes, two pupils he suddenly unpeeled to reveal golden sickles. "And now for my dagger."

But the horrid sight of the lady's emaciated reflection incarcerated inside those feline orbs was finally too much. Overwhelmed, she fled from the library and jogged the length of a hallway lined with blowsy curtains. Each drape did the bidding of her demonic suitor, catching on a succession of underthings and pulling free skirt, slip, and brassiere, until she was stripped to the rose and alabaster. When she came to the last curtain, this one draped over a forbidding portico, it caught about her neck and dragged her into its open embrasure.

When she managed at length to untangle herself, the lady was huddled before a massive credenza. Scrambled and battered by the cruel granting of her heart's perverse desire, her mind was now attacked by wistful recollections of the house of her youth, of Calhoun County where she spent her girlhood dressing in skirts chosen from a locker whose design matched this selfsame box of doors, minus its forbiddingly bone-like handles. She pulled the doors open, thinking vainly of hiding herself before the ectomorphic ogre whose converging footfalls sounded notes of reveille. But escape is a thought all too many have had before, for the cabinet is stocked with skulls that spill upon the ground, pooling about her soft toes and mocking her screams with jaws that clatter through the air and crash upon the ground. The dandy's hands emerge from under her long hair's cascades, scooping up in one palm a skull from which the flesh has not quite fallen and gripping the lady's chin in the other. She recognizes the same features, exactly, that she'd discerned in the archvillain's eyes.

"Until now," comes the dulcet whisper of her clean-shaven Bluebeard, "you loved a vapor, you commended your affections to a phantom made of newsprint and rumor. Now that we are here as man and woman before all eternity, tell me. Do you tremble for me now?"

Starker sets out for Fletcher Poole's. The state of the translator's apartment, like the chip-chop hairdo Fletch likes to call Continental but which looks more like an ill-starred groundhog had followed its shadow into a wood chipper, testifies to how rarely he leaves the comfort of his brownstone. It isn't a question of being too rich (most of his translations were performed freelance on behalf of warning label companies, though he still managed the odd Boris Vian limited edition or anthology of Icelandic free verse) or too lazy (Fletch had been so incensed at not being asked to contribute to a collection of lesser-known Proust that he had stayed high for a whole July during which he pounded out a seven-volume laundry list that effectively told the history of every single item in his apartment called *In Search of Lost Keys*) but rather that his faculty with languages, the serpentine tongue tracings of the Babellian key slot, had long ago abrogated his appalling hygiene and lured to his lizard-festooned nest an international cast of nubile refugees, from chain-smoking Finnish grad students to Parisian *belles dames sans merci*, who repay his protection from Immigration by seeing that his every errand in the outside world is accounted for. In fact, Fletcher Poole hasn't been positively ID'd for weeks and Starker's first thought, upon finding the door propped with an Amharic thesaurus, was that somewhere, amid the copies of Musil buried in Müeslix, the typewritten towers of possible translations for obscure varieties of nostalgia and vague dreamy sensations foreign to the Anglo-Saxon register, somewhere under the needlepoint Halldór Laxness throw pillows or beyond the bottle-lined bedroom where an eerily warped Noam Chomsky recording kept going *Vuelvo a ser yo, I return to be, je retourne pour être, I return to be* while a Brasileira played Fletcher's PlayStation and a red-haired lass in a Morrissey shirt lectured an iguana in the Hibernian tongue, he would find the Bacchae-chewed remains of his chum. Instead, he finds Fletcher Poole in his bathtub, crouched inside a paper castle, wearing a paper hat, circling malconjugated verbiage with a red pen, apparently deaf to an argument between two of his harem, presumably over bathroom arrangements, being conducted over a shag-covered toilet seat while a third translates.

"All right, ladies, this is a raid." Starker raps a paramilitary beat on the bathroom door. "Now let's see those green cards."

"Forgive Monsieur *Plus Rigide*," says Fletcher Poole without looking up. "His sensibility is not every man's. *En tous chemins, en tous lieux, il ne parle que du bon Dieu, il ne parle que du bon Dieu.*"

"Fletcher Poole, I thought you were dead."

"Dead on May 5, the same day as Sherlock Holmes? Aha." Fletcher chucks a bar of soap at Starker. "Beat you to it, didn't I?"

"Custom is hard-won in such a dissolute age." It's not that Starker's too conceited to say hello to Svetlana and Roselina, but that the soil has not yet hardened over the memory of an international incident he touched off by shooting the thumbs-up at a native of Barataria. He remains unaware that (a) thumbs-up in Barataria is suggestive of the anus, (b) Barataria is not a place, and (c) this was all a joke at Starker Arlechino's expense on the part of Fletcher's girlfriends, who call him "Artichoke" behind his back.

"Honestly, Starker, you must have such a thoroughly annotated little calendar. Say, I have an idea." Fletcher Poole slouches to his feet in the tub and carefully folds a few moist pages of manuscript over the towel rack. "A Borgesian almanac that presupposes the protraction of the Napoleonic Empire into the modern world. The best part would be the illustrations of you and me—"

"—with our fingers inside our jackets, I get it," Starker says and crowns himself with the translator's paper hat.

"Ah well, alternate history is the only time frame in which you and I can be considered successful." On his way out of the bathroom, Fletcher snags a towel and swathes it around his head, even though he doesn't appear to have showered since Paz and Hova forcibly hosed him down at their last New Year's. "Force of habit. What did you bring me?"

"An ice sculpture Ganesh. But it melted. All that is left is the trunk." Actually, Starker stopped bringing gifts to Fletcher when it became obvious that every headdress, carapace, and Lady's Slipper was being systematically regifted from Fletch to one of his queen bees, from the queen bee to some diplomat parent and from the diplomat parent to some distant head of state. The camel straw had come when he discerned a homemade velvet painting of Pogo the Possum in the background of a photograph of the Georgian prime minister. "What is all this rumpus?"

"My latest commission, an anthology of emerging voices from the Third World. Here we have a Horatio Alger yarn from Burkina Faso. This is a tale from Chad. It's called "A Tale of Chad." Then I've got a Hercule Poirot mystery from Laos that's actually a subtle indictment of the Politburo—I don't mean to spoil it for you, but it turns out the famous detective has a split personality and actually has to arrest himself. Several Malian Flarf poets. A bit of romantic PC revisionism from Uzbekistan's resident Danielle Steele proxy and a Swaziland story that posits *Starry, Starry Night* was a code foretelling the rise of radical Sikhism. What a sovereignty of independent states!"

"Jeez. I guess it is nice to know landlocked nations are receiving all our exports."

"Actually, shhh." Fletcher puts a finger to his lips. "They're all me. It's a lot less work than actually translating the stuff. Who'll know the difference? My job is to see that expectations are regularly met. Caring is not reading and vice versa. Just shove the grant money in my slot and let's go on dancing our global-village ghost dance, that's what I say. Anthology is a nightmare from which I am trying to awaken."

"You're a piece of work, Fletch. Imperial propagandists must've creamed their blue jeans dreaming that the colonial youth of today would be so singularly diffident." Starker hears his kettle calling. "Like we don't have enough ethical violations in the rest of the world."

"The rest of the world! Do you hear yourself, Starker?" Fletcher Poole need merely hold out his hand and one of the displaced persons from the bathroom fills it with a blond ale. "Your problem is that you still believe in that putative fantasy *the rest of the world. Entres vie*, old buddy! It's just a marketing ploy hatched by the mother tongue, a fable perpetuated on all the baby tongues so that you'd have a flimsy Eurasian dartboard for all your inbred feelings of ethnological inadequacy and huffy self-consciously centrist superiority. But get this! The money you send to starvlings in East Timor all goes to Reebok. Chinese food is just rice and pork doused with fermented soybeans. When I was speaking"—here he hands the beer to Starker so his hands are free to make quotation marks—"'Italian' at the car dealership that time we got marooned in Ithaca, we were talking make-believe moon language. The WTO is just a mailbox in Spokane, Tetris was dreamed up at MIT, news reports from the Middle East are all filmed inside Universal Studios, and Winston Churchill's speeches are slowed-down tapes of Alvin and the Chipmunks. Why, even Klavdiya here is as American as the death penalty. It's all part of your indoctrination, Starker Arlechino. It's all part of the plan."

"This is an astounding revelation, Fletcher, and I thank you for it. And all this time I wondered why you'd never offered to translate any of my books."

The translator coughs to cover a laugh, chokes, and goes into a paroxysm. When he recovers, he mutters, "Think of all those Basques deprived of *Hotel Beelzebub, mais non*?" And then, spotting Starker's quietude, "Oh no, sahib, don't do it. Don't get all what-happened-to-us. So we are shams, this is true. Sham is a star. Svetlana, fetch this moper a phosphate!"

"No, look." Starker answers a mean look from Svetlana by lifting a portrait of Pushkin from the nail where it hangs, turning it to face the wall, and sticking out his tongue. "That's why I came to see you today. I've got a morally decrepit venture on the barbie. Your kind of thing. Just answer me this. How would you like to be a cult hero?" Starker proceeds to lay out, in detail, a pitch calculated to put the pseudonymous spring in R. Triboulet's step. "Mutually beneficial. Think of it as translation in reverse. And the best part is, other than affecting a Marcel Marceau accent and acting famous, you don't even have to do anything. Of course, there will be author photos, interviews, public readings. And parties, loads of parties."

"You mean," says the translator, a trickle of a teardrop coming into focus between his eyelashes, "a reason to leave? A reason to leave the house? To walk down the street? Oh, Starker, you mean— I could be free from conjugation? I could *live* again?"

Though their morphologies never lapse into any tongue that should alert the attendant harem girls to their conspiracy, when Fletcher tears the pinned-up rug from the window, unleashing an eye-blast of sunlight that sends lizards scampering and makes to stride outdoors, his flock of dependents sense their captive's newfound agency and leap upon his ankles, protesting in a chorus that reaches Starker, sans subtitles, as the chirping of half a dozen feathered pterodactyls, strapped to a mounting meteorite. Thusly encumbered, Fletcher drags a line of squirming belles and señoritas across the kitchen floor. "By God, I'll do it! I'll be your fall guy. Look at me"—catching his up-turned reflection in a faucet—"look at my hair! Why, Starker, I look awful. I can't face the public like this."

"That's all right, Fletch." He fishes some of Rhesus Crabtree's cash from his pockets. "You get your normal fee. Soon you'll be as presentable as a department-store Santa."

"Money!" Fletcher flings it overhead, sprinkling the still-writhing gaggle of harpies spitting vulgarities worthy of a Venetian gondolier. "I *love* money. *Quel courage, voulez-vous*, Monte Cristo, the great big blimp and the glorious bean curd—the words, they are mingled in my throat! Someone else to be!"

And someone else for me to be too, thinks Starker, *Mephistoph-eles. Desperate wordsmiths from here to the hinterlands, get me behind you.*

Last stop, the one Starker has been avoiding. Coating the spoons of born sellouts is one thing, but in asking Hova García-Terrycloth to fix the critical prizefight, the industrious and anonymous author of Senator Kip Kimbal's memoirs of recursive homosexuality fears he has his hands full. He rehearses the whole drummed-up routine three times before a stuffed pineapple, a prospectus one part populism and two parts Society of the Spectacle. When he actually arrives at the Marxist's virtual "country cottage," the emerald-painted office Hova rents under the campus clock tower, the door closes so fast over Starker's wrist that the plush fruit he'd come bearing plummets to the floor.

"Oh no you don't, Starker!" comes the disembodied voice so often heard to holler over the crowded halls of community centers and organized protests. "Not a chance. You can just turn around, mister."

"Oh, shit," pronounces the hack with his hand infringed by the deadbolt, "Paz warned you?"

"You better *believe* Paz warned me."

"Wait, give me back my hand. There. Watch this." Clapping together his reddened appendage and the other, Starker triggers the pineapple's automated dance, blaring "Tutti Frutti" from the other side of the door. "Isn't that great? Now just hear me out, Hova. We're talking mutually beneficial."

The door slides open an eye width and Hova puts his peepers to the crack. "You came to convince me to perjure myself in print with a vibrating pineapple?"

"Perjure? Oh, Hova, you and your principles." Awopbopaloobop Alopbamboom. "What's a paragraph praising the politics of a new line of pulp novels? An appreciative blog entry identifying the Brechtian subtext of a bit of Old World phantasmagoria? All I'm asking for is a little spin. I need a fashion plate, old boy. A cult hit. Surely you could afford to yank the coattails of your Young Turk buddies a little bit."

"I might as well ask you to put your Captain Kadmon into the service of Monsanto."

"Captain Kadmon is a pirate on the sea of fate. His ethic is informed by the flux of Mercury. Captain Kadmon's got a more durable model of ideals than Max Weber."

"I'm sorry, Starker, you're on your own. I know you too well," Hova goes on, quoting selectively from his zine *Spartacus Smartacus.* "It's only natural that the petit bourgeois, whose advancement depends on a deadlocked status quo, should feel threatened by any pedigree that's halfway to highbrow, while ironically elevating the low. A cultural dumbwaiter, that's what you are. Commodification, appropriation, neutralization—you dream of bringing everything down to your level and what you can't kill, you corrupt. You may have fooled Fletcher and Paz, but I will *not* go down this road with you!"

"If it was just my ass on the line, I could understand, Hova." Starker's stomach longs for the room, where he can smell the legumes and miso that are his friend's macrobiotic talismans. "But it's Rhesus Crabtree we're talking about. He's practically a Cossack and, besides, it's all a big smoke screen for his latest—his latest—for his big—"

For the first time since he's begun co-writing the Jacquard books, it occurs to the tongue-tied architect behind *Mason Dixie Meets the Moonbillies* that he still doesn't know what his mentor is up to. Who is Jacquard *really* and, all propaganda and theories of intertextual reincarnation aside, what *does* he want? There's no way for a fictional fool-killer to harm a real person, is there? Because if there were—but these are silly thoughts to have in the middle of the bloody Dewey Commission. Hova interjects: "Rhesus was with the Party at one time, yes. But at his age, if you haven't served every cause in some capacity, it's because you've been doing two Julians for buggery and, besides, his late canon is filthy with aristocratic nihilism. You two are the very model of late-stage phone-off-the-hook capitalist overdubbing. You're dummy to a sinister ventriloquist, Starker, the monkey of an agenda whose abuses you cannot even imagine, peddling petty amusement and losing a little more of your voice every time you type *hyperborean* or *crepuscular*. But The Man's been speaking through you your whole life; what's one more act of gracious submission, eh? I can no more support you than I can vote for a two-party system that not only divides, it *slices and dices*. When the revolution comes—"

"OK, OK. That'll do, Hova."

Hova's eye twitches suspiciously behind the green door. "Yeah?"

"Yes." Starker takes a step backward and Hova cautiously opens the door, a ponderous potato-fed, inversely Americanized biracial sporting long curls, the peerless George-Orwell-beard-plus-pipe combo and homemade specs with chopstick frames. "You don't want to write a review, no one's going to make you. In fact, I respect your consistency. It's fine. I'll just have to succeed or fail based on my own merits. It's new, I admit, but I'll try to be open minded. Like you're always saying."

"Yeah? We're friends again?"

They clasp hands as the clock chimes six. "Oh yeah. We're thick as thieves."

FROM *From Safety to Where . . . ?* BY R. TRIBOULET

The ancient gears turned like the unbelieving eyes of an apostate on Judgment Day and the clock's antique lever swiveled ever closer to the sinful sixth digit. The razor-sharp hour hand was said to be embossed with characters whose cuneiform apologetics had been chiseled by the indigenous tribes of Chad or, according to another of the stories the city's chief chronologist had spread to justify the enormous price of reassembly, a relic of Napoleon's occupation of Burkina Faso. But for all the clock tower's architectural beauty and eschatological forewarning, Professor Tova Rodriguez-Corduroy had not one jot of a Julien to spare on its inspection, pendulous as his situation was, spread-eagle and upside-down high above the streets, his neck stretched across the clock tower's groove.

"What's the matter, Professor? Perhaps you'd like a cherry-flavored phosphate?"

"Jacquard! Is that you?" The soon-to-be-punctured professor opened his yap and out tumbled his pipe. Tova's captor made his entrance, strolling along the tower's edge, arm in arm with the mechanical bell maid: Jacquard, whose midnight rounds along the S____ Gallery had left many a gilded frame stripped of its masterpiece, Jacquard, the calico-coated boogeyman said to eat the eyeballs of the slumbering children of the Orphanage A____ and who held the fearful hearts of coquettes and diplomats in his velvet grasp.

"You were expecting perhaps Alexander Pushkin?" With all the air of an esteemed maître d', he removed his satin-lined greatcoat with a flourish, draped it around the automaton, and pulled tight its clasps before recovering from its pocket a pair of tropical refugees: a pineapple and a small lizard, the second of which he placed on the supine professor's chest while carving the second with his penknife.

"Jacquard, please!" The blood rushing to the prisoner's curly head gave it the appearance of an artichoke in bloom. "Man, can't you see we're on the same side? We both long to overthrow those blasted dumbwaiters that run city hall, we're both champions of the common man and we are both hated by the hell-bound bourgeois. I am your fondest advocate, don't you know how I applaud your escapades in my column? You're a great hero to the Party! Just think what we could do together—I with my pen, you with your dagger."

"Oh, poor Professor Tova. I see I'm going to have to teach you a lesson." The dandy forced a sliver of pineapple down the throat of this poor excuse for a Spartacus. "I am a Cossack in the service of no cause but Bedlam, nurse no philosophy but Discord, know no mistress but Mania."

Professor Tova, mouth filled with pineapple, lizard squirming under his collar, jerked hard on his manacles, only to tear from the clock's face the numeral nine to which his left leg had been tethered. The street below was suddenly littered with delicious females wearing expressions of the most profane ecstasy—the long smears of lipstick that trailed across their cheeks, their torn gowns, and the wild hair streaked with the leaves and moss of many a graveyard coupling marked them as Jacquard's harpies, his devoted church of immoral women. Some of the succubae the haplessly dangling provocateur recognized: the bewitched ex–first lady of Georgia, Madame R_____, said to have poisoned her husband for love of Jacquard; the artist's model Z_____, whose white body provoked the ruin of many a Post-Impressionist; Baroness C_____, matronly proprietress of *The Plus Rigide*; all assembled sisters *sans merci* lifting their arms in ravenous anticipation of the professor's plummet. "You see? I can no more abandon my flock for the materialist ravings of a Kris Kringle–whiskered Prussian than you can surrender your precious macrobiotic diet to the tastes of the moment. Speaking of which, chew your *pamplemousse*."

The clock twitched another fateful minute closer to Tova's foreshortening. Now that the ticking-tocking scythe was at an arm's length, he dragged the chain, gradually turning his right wrist blue across the razor edge, and lurched into a sitting position as his bond severed. Then there came a bleating, an angry forcing of a blocked-up blowhole such as might herald a herd of wildebeests across the Serengeti or uproot angry hunters from a Swaziland stakeout, but which seemed grotesque and most out of place stifled inside the clock tower. And yet the disembodied trunk that came surging out of the open window and pinned Tova hard against the clock face left little doubt that his life was being threatened by a mammoth.

"Allow me to introduce the latest member of my menagerie, Professor. I liberated him from the local zoo after a night of routine carcass disposal. It seems Monsanto here has a sweet tusk for bone marrow." Five fifty-nine, the moment of truth. The women howl below and citric acid rains from Tova's nostrils as the *mystificateur* Jacquard pinches one of his captive's earlobes and whispers, "It's just as you said, Professor. What I cannot kill, I corrupt."

"Hova? It is Starker. About 11:05 on the first day of the summer solstice. I just saw your piece in *The Ejaculator*—"

"It's not a recording, you blackguard, it's me. I thought you never read book reviews."

"I make exceptions for my friends and archrivals. Besides, Flip insisted. He wants R. Triboulet for ten more books with you doing the cover blurbs and I figured I'd better act before he changes his mind."

"Then you'll honor the terms we agreed on?"

"Tell me the truth, Hova. Do you *really* think Jacquard speaks for all whose creative energies are fundamentally destructive or do you just want me to take Desiderius out of your heart and let you down from that tower with your earlobes intact?"

"It's easy to gloat when nobody's almost had you eaten by a blood-thirsty elephant. It's not simply self-preservation, you understand. I believe it would hurt my readers to see a scholar of my stature infringed upon."

"Perfectly understandable. So you're not the least bit curious to see what will happen next?"

"I already know what will happen next, Starker Arlechino. American society will crumble."

"And the masses?"

"They will all be reading Jacquard."

When Herbert "Flip" Dyrshka throws a party at the Center for the New Netherland, felicity compels attendance on the part of the four-eyes concern, cramping the marmoreal doorjambs with a surfeit of blazers and a generalized paisley aura that, had the Walloons and Knickerbockers of the Dutch colony come stumbling through the sconce light of four centuries to behold Starker Arlechino schmoozing with the staff of *The Ejaculator*, would have flipped many a wig. Jacquard's sales are such that Dyrshka's reliably herky-jerky mood is still swinging high despite the live band's last-minute replacement by a Moog synthesizer, and the publisher is seen boogying opposite one of the center's caryatids to a sonic-carousel version of "The Firebird." But the man to watch is R. Triboulet, greeting his public in a cravat and a trim Vandyke (both presumably nods to the hero whose rise is concomitant with the writer's own), answering Flip's toasts in scrupulously fractured English, autographing copies of *The Black Angel's Death Song* with a flourish and generally diminishing the memory of Fletcher Poole a little more with each fastidious firing of the cuffs. Hova shows up halfway through the reading, dutifully disruptive despite his recent escape from Jacquard's clutches, ruffling dilettantes in the bad company of his usual entourage of rabble-rousers—there's a Revolutionary Communist who speedily sloganeers the bathroom stalls, a beat-boxing Fenian, and a discredited, semi-certifiable primatologist who periodically howls, "I am a BEAST!" and upends a tray of martini glasses in evolutionary solidarity with the apes, something that causes Starker to visibly cringe every time it happens. The real guest of honor, however, is Rhesus Crabtree, making a rare public appearance in a motorized La-Z-Boy and attended by sycophants who obediently corner all who dare to approach the master without explicit introduction.

"Rhesus, glad you could make it," says Starker, sliding between an amanuensis with halitosis and, if he's not mistaken, the unlucky second banana charged with incinerating Crabtree's unpublished poems one irregular antistrophe at a time, "but are you crazy? You and me get spotted here together and we're basically one blog entry away from blowing the whole imbroglio."

"I'm so fuckin' sorry I taught you that word." Rhesus hits a lever on his chair, propelling the reclined maestro through the crowd and forcing Starker to stroll discreetly along, feigning interest in hors d'oeuvres. "Would you deprive an old man the pleasure of seein' his bouncing baby contrivances into awkward adolescence? 'Sides, looks like our ringer is doing fine." As a matter of fact, Fletcher Poole is at that very moment regaling a ring of R. Triboulet's fan base with tales of his youth as a witch doctor, waving his hand dismissively every time some woozy damsel observes, "You should *write* about that," and saying, "Ah, but the Loa are very, very shy, *ma chère*, and besides, I am under a curse," pressing her hand to his lips. "I am *très modeste* and in love with beauty."

"Yeah he's a regular Roger Tichborne, until someone asks him what the R stands for."

"D'ya doubt that Jacquard will do what it takes to get himself written? It's beyond you and me, boy."

"Well that's great, Dr. Frankenstein, but I'd like to keep collecting the filthy lucre, if that's OK with you. I've adjusted to the decadent lifestyle. Now can you please get back *behind* the throne instead of driving it?"

"You're overlooking your lesson, boy, and time'll be you won't have me to point these things out to you. Ideas are a plague spread by a scabby bird called the world. It sucks where it sees a hole."

Just then, Paz, probably the lone critical holdout against the Jaco bean craze, makes her entrance wearing a suit and tie like it's the nineteenth century and she expects the sight of a trousered female to shock the acrimonious guardians of gendered *politesse* and inspire all self-respecting lady novelists to change their name to George. It falls to Starker to shepherd her out of Flip's earshot before she can denounce the commercialization of lady killing and soon she is provided with an introduction to her literary hero that, had he been Ben Jonson instead of Rhesus Crabtree, would have turned the most stiffly corseted courtier protozoic with embarrassment. Instead, she spits in her fist, holds it under the master's quivering taupe-colored lips, and says, "Blow."

To the great writer's inquisitive glance, Starker mutters, "She thinks you're God."

"Hmm. Who says I'm not?"

Before Starker can defuse the flirtation in progress, Herbert "Flip" Dyrshka, without so much as flaunting a fin in the water, jerks him by the collar and drags the author of *Loch Ness Impostor* before a person of offensively youthful countenance.

"Starky boy, meet your opposite number, Idris Peach. The newest recruit to our glorious cause. Wait till you see this guy write. You'll be sharing your ghostwriting with him from now on."

"It's a pleasure, Mr. Arlechino. I loved *Penultima Thule*. I think it's a very good time to work the Reichean leitmotif into the existing cyberpunk logos."

"Oh really?" He raised his voice over the synths playing "Toccata & Fugue." "Did you think the prose purely instrumental or did you read into the metacritique of U.S. pragmatism?"

"I beg your pardon?" Idris Peach has the cheekbones of a teen model, or possibly a developmentally stunted cyborg, and has no idea what to make of Starker, who figures this here *opposite number* probably committed the scholastic sin of stopping halfway through. "Was that a real question or are we talking shit?"

"So, like, what's your angle, Idris Peach?" With Flip having left to glad-slap a pair of poorly camouflaged movie people, Starker is free to sound out this latest lost soul. "I guess you always dreamed of writing the autobiographies of disgraced senators. Visions of crack pipes and airport bathroom stalls dancing in your head—"

"Actually, I thought it would be a good way to learn the trade. Of course I can keep my own work as a hobby. Mr. Dyrshka even says he'll look at one of my novels once I finish the Electra Czoket autobiography."

"I thought I was writing that one."

"Two volumes, sir. The franchise has expanded."

"Along with my expendability, apparently. Christ. Where did Flip dig you up again?"

"Metropolitan Writing Workshop. I'm not afraid of losing my voice. I think it's good for a writer to be able to subsume himself in earthly dross once in a while. I mean, we're not trying to impress anybody, right?"

"Excuse me." Brushing by Flip, Starker mutters, "You are a murderer," and makes a beeline for the punch bowl before the editor can undergo his trademark werewolf transformation from gregarious blowhard into shouty cheese eater. A perusal of the prosciutto entrails leaking from bloody melon-carved bawds and shrimp arranged to pick a plate of mushroom pockets ends with the conclusion that whoever prepared this Gentleman Criminal–themed spread has not actually read the books. Starker spoons a sliver of counterfeit-diamond-motif cheesecake into his bowl just seconds before the primatologist plunges a light stand into the whole gooey zirconia ("I am a BEAST!"), which is all the cue the author of *Kiss Me Scaly* needs to lift the tablecloth and resume his munchings under the buffet. Hova García-Terrycloth has beat him to it.

"This seat taken?"

"What a collision of diverse realities." Hova appears to be exercising the right of all true Morlocks by monitoring the affairs of surface dwellers from a translucency worn into the linen. "I just want to see how this is all going to play out."

"Smart money says tomorrow your buddy Darwin turns up in the Hudson with three hundred unsold copies of *Blotto de Fé* tied to his Chucks."

"Tell me something, Starker. Is this how you pictured literary celebrity?" Hova, ever the censor of his own stomach, actually eats around a Fig Newton, returning the uneaten cream to his plate with his knife. "I mean, it must kill you not to be able to tell all these people that they're here because of you. To see Fletcher surrounded by a new batch of barely legals, the toast of a town momentarily distracted from its nascent collapse by a villain that *you* created, preorder breadlines centipeding from bookstores in *your* name, the movie people buzzing his beehive instead of yours."

"Oh golly. I think it's good for a writer to be able to subsume himself in earthly dross once in a while."

"Is that a caustic note of ironically detached proletarian yawp I hear?"

"If only. What was that you said about movie buzz?"

"Mere scuttlebutt. One of those Beverly Hills jobs backed me into a corner. I figured he'd think a cultural critic was a writer for *TV Guide* so I said I played the cad on a Mexican sitcom called *Si Señor Vergüenza*." Hova adjusts his spy hole to frame Rhesus and Paz noticeably reveling under a portrait of Henry Hudson. "Well, here's a rhino and an oxpecker if ever I did see. Wait, he's whispering something in her ear . . . wow, she's laughing. And he's examining her hands. Starker, this looks serious. I think you better—"

But he's already there, sidling up to Paz with a palm resting flat on Rhesus's wheelchair, wondering whether, given a push, he could bowl over the wire-rimmed, sweater-vested thought police blocking the front door and make a break for it with his in-and-out amorata snugly tethered to his waist.

"I say, what's all the jubilation over here?"

"He told me his middle name," Paz elaborates, positioning her lips over Starker's ear. "Oh, Starker, he's positively *delightful*. Not at all like you described. Why didn't you introduce me sooner?"

"Ah, no need for that," rasps Crabtree, who worked summers at Coney Island as a lip-reader, "we've met before. Under Oceanus, on the surface of Sirius, in the castle of Lord Shiva, drinking kvass from vine leaves. We met in a dream, heh heh. And this is a *dreamy* party!"

Rhesus, who by some pigmentary fluke can't seem to drink wine without turning eggplant, claps his hands and hauls himself out of the La-Z-Boy, causing its seat to give a vile wheeze and the writer's dinner jacket to sag like wings over the rag and bone of him, and staggers past an abruptly silent, slo-mo tableau of slapstick solipsism that includes sweating, showboating Fletcher Poole, Flip going full tilt on Hova's rounded-up culture rustlers, and the desperately polite Idris Peach suckered into reciting "Jabberwocky" by a few of *The Ejaculator*'s more sadistic editors. Every idle figment falls away, but only for the couple clinks it takes Rhesus to cross the room. The center's doors open wide and the sound-complemented sight of a fountain spitting its stream over the drunken head of "one of our finest moralists" lends the momentarily suspended ruckus a bread-crumb rubato with which to find its way back to a Moogified "Jesu, Joy of Man's Desiring" and another midsummer spent indoors.

FROM *Lady Grinning Soul* BY R. TRIBOULET

This house has nothing to hide from Jacquard. Beyond the courtyard that rings the manor, the masked coachman steps from the shadow of a caryatid, where just scant moments ago he seemed a statue, to survey windows lit by chandeliers that grow dim under his kaleidoscopic gaze, listen to the "Toccata & Fugue" (reflecting that, in a different humor, it would have amused him to slip the ivory keys into his pocket faster than the pianist could strike them), and to dwell in the warm laughter that strays from the party whenever the door swings open. Oh, that sound will dawn no more, not where Jacquard strides, sweeping his cape over silver spoons as he takes his feathered cap in hand and bows before costumed debutantes the pallor of china dolls and holds their unsuspecting stares inside the mirrors that shine from inside his mask, a hand-carved Death's Head. For what Jacquard, uninvited specter and grim guest of honor, seeks inside the governor's "dream party" is more precious than any diamond he has filched so far, rarer than crystal and the teeth of firebirds.

The Dutch paintings that line the walls no longer interest him and the aria that enchants the other guests stirs him not, though the melody is a record of his past deeds and the showboating tenor is dressed as that pale caricature who populates the weeklies and amuses those lucky innocents so far spared the song of Jacquard, whose leitmotif is blood, whose highest notes are squeezed from the throats of women. Nor does he feel obligated to tolerate the grotesque harlequins and legislators clad in the beaks of plague birds, all of whom will drink from the punch over which this newly arrived Nephilim briefly alights and sprinkles with poison. Exotic idols line the hallway where Torque the industrialist and Professor Institoris, dressed as dauphins and grown bold following Jacquard's temporary mercy, are heard to wager on the odds of a gate crash on the part of Jacquard, plainly unaware of just who is hanging his coat on one of Shiva's outstretched arms as they speak.

He is not alone here. There is an unholy order of oxpeckers who, having forsaken the heavenly elect for sempiternal darkness, live to groom their master's hide and profit by his wrongdoings. Here is Fenian, that razor-wielding Irishman deported from the isle of his birth to rack up John and Jane Does along the Bowery, nodding beneath a beastly ape mask; this Jabberwock leering over the balustrade is none other than Harry Hudson, great-great-grandson of the famous Henry and avenger of his drowned namesake. The black skull that conceals Jacquard nods three times to acknowledge the rest of his accursed brotherhood as they take their places among the ungulates: the body snatcher known as Baron Samedi of the Loa and that insidious cad of a Spaniard, Señor Vergüenza. "The grand masque is over, comrades. Now is the time," declares Jacquard before his gallery of villains, "to dance the 'Danse Macabre.'"

The poison has already taken a hold in a ballroom gone berserk with dancers who've ended their tarantella with a most definitive pirouette. Señor Vergüenza and Fenian opt to help St. Vitus on his way by torching the curtains, while Harry Hudson and Samedi upend a tremendous ice sculpture of Oceanus. All is screams and flaming cloth, but for one person who sips kvass from a vine leaf, unmoved by the spectacle. One star shines brighter than Sirius at the center of all the scattered corpses, whose death rattles only serve to coax a smile from her lips. Jacquard extends his glove and she lifts a pale painted fist and bids him blow. Her mask marks her as a bird of paradise, but the peacock feathers that flutter over her eyes disguise neither her beauty nor the gaping hole in her moral compass. And Jacquard is one to suck where he sees a hole.

"Forgive all this dross, lady. These seven faces are only the masks I had to wear to find you."

"I've been waiting such a long time. I knew you would come for me, my love. I wondered if you would recognize me when you did."

He lifts the mask from her face and takes her in his arms. As they begin to dance, more bodies fall around them, flashing scarlet underskirts as their legs scissor the air, but these two lovers pay heed neither to the wailings of the slaughtered nor the laughter of the upstarts, and a tune like the trickle of a music box springs up mysteriously from the air, as though conjured from another time and place. Jacquard lifts the horrible mask off his head, but, oddly, doesn't stop at his face, all caked with powder and carefully applied eyebrows, instead reaching just under the skin and pulling gently until it too slips off.

"I would know you anywhere, Margarita. I've prepared a place for us, my love. Our coach awaits. Now open your fist. And come into my world."

Starker freezes midedit, with Desiderius suspended above the galley proofs.

"Wait, I didn't write this." Furious, he sweeps the proofs from his desk and reiterates, "I didn't write this! I did not even *approve* this!" But there's no one to listen to him, so he dials up Rhesus and is greeted by nothing so much as a message to preface the impalpable beep to which he wails: "Rhesus, it's Starker. Look, either we have a deal or we don't and you told me I'd get final edit of any changes you made on the draft. Now I've got a galley and there's a whole section I never saw and that I *know* I did not write. I mean, look, we are too far along for this *meta*shit. Ugh. And what's up with the present tense all of a sudden? OK, maybe it's not too late to fix. Just let me know when you get this. Oh and happy Tomatina."

Arlechino hangs up, says fuck, and hops on his bike, unable to keep himself from riding to Turkey Park for a little unscheduled face time with *The Alchemist of Emmaus*.

"Rhesus? Are you home? I brought tomatoes," calls Starker on the curiously swept stairs, the contents of the basket dangling from his elbow, a little worse for the bumps and swerves of city driving. "Rhesus? Have your hired a maid service or—"

But the room is empty. The walls are hastily repainted, all the accumulated clutter of Rhesus's hermitage miraculously vanished, leaving the redolent odor of a sealed tomb. Worse than the shock of a true-life plot twist is the dodgy déjà vu that comes of reading too many sci-fi novels. And in this case—Starker realizes after some internal rooting—he's not only read it, he's written it. The conclusion of *Hotel Beelzebub* featured the same hideous no-place, but Rhesus's redux, as usual, does Starker's crass melodrama one better: There's not even an outline in dust to testify to the disappeared writer's residency, no demonic letter of explanation, nothing. Well, maybe one thing. Leaning against the far wall is a tiny key and no door and no notch, only the light streaming through the window to snare its metal in tinny glare. Starker, for no reason he knows of, looks out onto Turkey Park and witnesses a scene even stranger for having no precedent in the work of either author, though Starker knows immediately he'll spend the rest of his life trying to capture the stochastic symmetry of the carriage, driven through the trees past the ruined fences and wild dogs below.

Hoofbeats match perfectly with the passage of the horse, which is lucky since what waits in the box is so out of place as to throw the whole fresco out of sync. Even at a distance, Starker recognizes from antique book flaps the handsome chin, unfurrowed beauty-marked cheeks, and somewhat preening expression of the boy genius behind *Three Cheers for Mr. Leopard* and *Ah, Sunflower*. And who should be seated next to this phantom but Paz Lindengarten—he's sure of it, even garbed in a chintz dress, her hair actually brushed and braided for once. Her mute eyes do not flinch from the road ahead and one arm limply encircles the cloak of her companion, who aims an inscrutable expression at Starker's aerie and blinks twice. And then they are gone.

The ghostwriter handles his hysteria admirably, confining his compulsions to an innovation in home decoration, repainting the walls tomato. He smears what's left across his face and trundles numbly outdoors to face joggers and stray children who cannot be more frightened of Starker than he is of himself.

"Let me get this straight." Fletcher Poole is absently stacking dominoes on the hotel bureau before heading off to R. Triboulet's latest speaking engagement. "You think Paz ran off with Rhesus Crabtree?"

"It is not her anymore. It is Margarita Gosselmeier." Starker has had time to wash his face, but there are stains soap and water won't scour. "He used Jacquard to find her. He must have been searching for her the whole time, but she wasn't there. Not with the heiresses or soubrettes, not in the Museum of Crime. She was here, with Paz, someone who'd taken the story into her. And now it's taken her inside it."

"I dunno, paleface. I read every page you write and *I* don't remember any reincarnation subplot."

"It's not necessarily a subplot. Could be a supporting character, a tossed-off background detail, even some kind of anagogical spy inside the sentences, like an acrostic or a mixed metaphor. They could be hiding anywhere. Look at this." Starker opens the latest issue of *The Ejaculator* to the funny pages. "They've replaced *The New Adventures of Artie Schopenhauer* with something called *Jumping Beans*."

"All those electoral politics and bailouts going unbooted."

"And it's the same online. Her apartment looks like a poltergeist hit it and her phone doesn't ring when I call."

"Perchance she knows it's you." Fletcher applies another handful of powder to the wig he's set aside for tonight. "*Rappelez-vous*, Starker, you've been working harder on this project than anything since Captain Kadmon. Take it from me, this kind of thing happens to real writers all the time. Guy de Maupassant used to hallucinate himself stretched out on the sofa and they say Antoine de Saint-Exupéry saw the Little Prince crouched on his wing like the thing from *The Twilight Zone*. Do you not think that this, er, mental mome rath you're experiencing might be the price one pays for dealing intimately with monsters?"

"That's pretty much *exactly* what I think. I can't believe I fell for that fine art of fraudulence stuff. 'You and me are gonna change the world, Starker, heh heh.' Mutually beneficial, my ass. Who knows when or how, but somewhere along the line, Crabtree must've found the door to the other side"—he brandishes the key from Rhesus's apartment, strung through a shoelace—"and left without bothering to share it with anybody else. He's there now. What's even scarier is, with Margarita back, he can write again. Have you seen the clouds lately, Fletch? Have you noticed how strange they look? I would know his handwriting anywhere. I can feel his energy leaking from every skinny letter."

"Far be it from me to put the yardstick to a young man's dementia." Fletcher Poole's trail of dominoes complete, he makes the crucial tap and smiles as the bone snake flattens its modular length from bureau to footstool, before tumbling into one of the platform boots that account for the three inches between Fletcher Poole and R. Triboulet. "But just what do you intend to do?"

"Why do you think I'm here? I'm pulling the plug. No more Jacquard. No more R. Triboulet."

Fletcher's newly plucked eyebrows flinch at the suggestion. "You want me to step down?"

"C'mon, Fletch. It's not a game anymore. And it might be the only way to stop him."

"I can't do it, pal." For all his practiced histrionics and ease with impersonations, the translator looks genuinely pained and not just from the snuff practically dripping from his nostrils.

"Why not?"

"I just *can't.*"

Starker nods at his hands for a few minutes, growing completely motionless where he sits embraced by a Swedish, undoubtedly umlauted, chair, then leaps to his feet as though at some triboelectric shock. Lifting a finger to keep the translator's nascent apology inside his lips, he speaks. "It's all right, Fletch. I understand. One life is not enough," and, turning to go, he adds, "Maybe it's not too late to learn some energy of my own."

FROM *Energy Fools the Magician* BY R. TRIBOULET

"What do you make of it, Plonquin?"

The detective kneels over the body bearing the customary signet and powdered wig of Councilman Marburg, now reduced to a cadaver stretched out on the hotel sofa. "It's the work of Jacquard, all right. I daresay I would know his handwriting anywhere." Plonquin dips his finger into the scarlet pool trailing from the dead man's temples and dabs a little on his tongue. "Feel free to chime in any time, my dear Constable."

But the Constable has doubled over at the sight of Detective Plonquin's apparent vampirism. "Sorry, Plonquin. It's just—all this blood."

"Oh, it's not blood," says the detective cheerily, holding out some for the Constable to taste. "It's ketchup. Jacquard is taunting me and quite charmingly, I might add. He knows I'm close. But not as close as your man here was."

"Beg pardon?"

"Really, Constable, you might've told me you had another agent on the case. Were you afraid I'd be jealous?" Detective Plonquin strikes a pose. Pink albino eyes, the purple raincoat dabbing the detective's aura with the pigment that is his skin's deficiency, and the polished moonstone of his head, in which many a reprobate has read his guilt, combine to mark Plonquin as a man you do not meet every day. "Jacquard must have known that sooner or later we'd discover that he had merely returned your spy in the Councilman's clothes, so there must be another clue. Constable, fetch me this fellow's file and a yardstick."

"You are astonishing as always, Plonquin. Tell me, how did you know he was ours?"

"Why, he told me himself. The same snuff with which your cadets routinely court Karkinos is practically dripping from his nostrils." Accepting the ruler proffered him, Plonquin takes the young man's measure and reports, "Just as I suspected. He's been stretched three whole inches. Look, the bones hardly connect."

The Constable shakes his head at the pain his agent must have endured at the hands of Jacquard, that unbeatable bête noire, but it is considered common knowledge that Plonquin's regard for life only extends insofar as it can provide him with grommets through which to thread the shoestring of his intellect. "Bones! That's it. Councilman Marburg is an impassioned player of the bones, is he not?"

"Whatever are you on about, Plonquin?"

"A reader of the stones? A Goldbergian? A biscuit doffer?" The detective slips on a pair of gloves and stacks a nearby footstool on top of an overturned chair, the better to reach the heating vent overhead. "Dominoes, man!"

"Why yes! He holds the title in six precincts and was to be the guest of honor at the tournament this Sunday! I say, Plonquin, does this mean he could still be alive?"

"One thing is certain," says the detective, rapping the grate so that it plummets to the floor below, "neither he nor our friend died here."

"Then who do you propose is responsible for this donnybrook?" questions the Constable, gesturing at the crashed lamps and overturned bureaus that litter the hotel room. "A poltergeist?"

Staring into the opened vent, Plonquin mutters back, "Jacquard wrecked the hotel well in advance. Note that the air is not disturbed, but rather retains the pleasant aroma of Swedish furniture. He slipped this man through the slot. Which means that his bones were broken for convenience, after he was dead. Which takes our inquest back to aught."

Plonquin jumps to his knees and, turning his back to the Constable, takes something out of his coat pocket and begins to peer at the contents of his palm. So, thinks the Constable, it's true what they say. And indeed, of all Plonquin's mental mome raths, all the constabulary wags whisper that this is by far the oddest: Before any big decision, the translucent detective consults with his magic jumping beans. Even now, he can be heard saying, "Ah hah," "But of course!" and "Yes, I see your point." His interview seemingly at an end, Plonquin pours the beans back into his pocket and returns to the stiff.

"My beans have spoken. Now here's where we see if your fellow earned his stripes." So saying, the detective pounds hard on the body's stomach until he seems satisfied at the state of his God-rested guts, then pries open the dead man's mouth. The tips of Plonquin's gloves disappear into his gullet and emerge clutching a key.

"Constable, give this man's widow a promotion."

"And I suppose you know where the lock is, Plonquin?"

"Not a bit of it. But"—he aims his primrose oculi down the distantly ringing tunnel—"I will, my dear Constable. Am I not Plonquin? I want you to post your best men at that tournament. When Jacquard slips through your fingers, as we both know he will, it'll be for wherever this key leads. And that's where I'll be waiting."

As he continues to speak, Detective Plonquin turns to the window. Thin gossamer clouds have begun to shower, spraying the city's hairlines and the pelts of stray dogs, washing petals down storm drains and sounding diaphones that mean nothing to Plonquin, for here is a man who is his own fog. "We have danced too long, he and I. They say Jacquard is an artist, but to abide in a vacuum is to fall short of the muse, even if that muse is murder. All those letters and riddles he sent to the papers, all those masks and desperate clues. How he must have longed for an adversary. Very well. Let the bones fall as they may, this time he shall not elude me."

By what duplicitous verbatim is life to be extended and does the model from which books and tales take their cue deserve to be protected from its progeniture? You can span the solar calendar enumerating alien landscapes and dressing up the close-to-home in an increasingly far-fetched set of skins and plots, but artifice merely twists the blanket in its dream of better things. It takes a magician to find the way through and, in the meantime, reality retracts its favors; frame stories and allegories are base perversions of a Whatness whose trap doors and sliding bookcases' best defense against narrative consists of simply refusing to open before the pretender who approaches without a key. Starker, on the other hand, lacks a lock and hardly a day passes without his catching sight of she whom this world has written out, as though swallowed by a crack in the margins even Desiderius has so far failed to widen: Paz looking up through the well of a public water fountain, Paz briefly winking in the stock footage of a late-night infomercial, Paz melding with a midtown crowd as Starker's bus rolls past on his way to see Flip. The appointment drags on with Dyrshka assuming both sides of whichever argument he's having this time (something about foreign distribution and imprint downsizing), leaving Starker free to let his eyes wander to the office high-rise across the way, where he's certain he can make out Paz, riding a windowed elevator in and out of sun glares. Only after he's lost sight of her inside the shadowed seahorse of a passing cloud does it dawn on him that he's just been fired.

Yes, with the impending big-screen adaptation of *The Black Angel's Death Song* (and optioning of *Sister Midnight* and *Lady Grinning Soul*) reforging Herbert "Flip" Dyrshka's priorities along the lines of hastily outsourced manga knockoffs and a stake in sales of the video game, the money previously allotted to the ghostwriting beat is now gone to fund Jacquard's transition from franchise to synecdoche. From a mélange of industry gossip sites and his contacts at *The Ejaculator*, Starker catches the rumor's gist and harks to the lesson: The crisis of id he'd read into Fletcher's refusal to shed his alter ego turns out to have had a decidedly less existential slant. It seems

R. Triboulet has ransomed the rights to the Jacquard books for a record-breaking figure, proving that there are bat-winged behemoths to be found in Tinseltown's Cocytus, Geryons with the faces of honest men with which a mere Mephistophelian like Starker, with his tawdry literary temptations, cannot compete. Suffice to say Starker Arlechino is too angry to take on Fletcher face to face. And, the digital age being what it is, he doesn't have to:

CapKadmon1023: Say there, Machiavelli. Nice double cross.

CapKadmon1023: I didn't even know you *spoke* douchebag.

GreenIdeasSleepFuriously: Eh, you know. Money's the easiest language to speak in the world. It only has one word.

GreenIdeasSleepFuriously: Actually, it's not even a word.

GreenIdeasSleepFuriously: More of an *S* with a line through it.

GreenIdeasSleepFuriously: Alternately, a pyramid with an eye.

CapKadmon1023: Let's play a game of anagrams.

CapKadmon1023: I'll go first.

CapKadmon1023: Brown's coy velour.

GreenIdeasSleepFuriously: Boy's cowl overrun?

CapKadmon1023: Your cover's blown.

GreenIdeasSleepFuriously: Cowboy lover runs.

GreenIdeasSleepFuriously: . . .

GreenIdeasSleepFuriously: Oh, I get it.

GreenIdeasSleepFuriously: Actually, my cover's *un mauve-foncé* with a harlequin on the spine. You can't blow what's inverted.

GreenIdeasSleepFuriously: And my name is motherfucking *embossed*.

CapKadmon1023: That does not make sense.

CapKadmon1023: And it is not your name.

GreenIdeasSleepFuriously: Nor yours.

GreenIdeasSleepFuriously: Nor, as you point out, mine.

CapKadmon1023: Fletcher, pardon the Anglo-Saxon recourse, but

CapKadmon1023: WTF, mate? Why couldn't we just have sold the rights and split the money?

CapKadmon1023: Even Jacquard cuts in his church of decadent sinners.

GreenIdeasSleepFuriously: Blame the new Dark Age.

GreenIdeasSleepFuriously: Believe it or not, even we translators are not recession proof. *Quem irá colocar uma dinamite na cabeça do século*, as the poet says. Anyway, it's out of my hands now. I pulled the pin.

GreenIdeasSleepFuriously: It's out of my hands.

GreenIdeasSleepFuriously: Whoops. Already said that.

CapKadmon1023: How is being beneficiary of an empire of immediate gratification "pulling the pin"?

GreenIdeasSleepFuriously: I sold R. Triboulet to Herbert Dyrshka.

CapKadmon1023: I thought you sold R. Triboulet to the movie people.

GreenIdeasSleepFuriously: No, I sold Jacquard to the movie people. I sold R. Triboulet to Herbert Dyrshka. Or at least he's legally guaranteed the right to keep bringing out books under that name while I fuck off to Dubai. Or Addis Ababa, I haven't decided yet.

CapKadmon1023: What in the world would you go and do a thing like that for?

GreenIdeasSleepFuriously: Tired of writing the books. Didn't want to have to live up to a new audience.

CapKadmon1023: But you *never* wrote the books.

GreenIdeasSleepFuriously: Well, then, tired of acting like I did. It was nice at first, but everywhere I went . . . you don't know what it's like dealing with all these high expectations all the time.

CapKadmon1023: Can't argue with you there.

CapKadmon1023: So, wait, who's writing the Jacquard books now?

GreenIdeasSleepFuriously: Flip's got his new guy on it. I forget his name.

CapKadmon1023: . . .

CapKadmon1023: Does it rhyme with *Star-Bellied Sneech*?

GreenIdeasSleepFuriously: Hmmm. Guess I'm not as good with rhymes as I am with anagrams.

CapKadmon1023: I have to go. I'll deal with you later.

CapKadmon1023: And let me know if you see Paz anywhere strange, will you?

GreenIdeasSleepFuriously: Are you still on that? I thought you said the new book would fix everything.

CapKadmon1023: Waiting for the proofs. But it *will* fix everything.

GreenIdeasSleepFuriously: Bye, Starker. Sorry about before.

GreenIdeasSleepFuriously: You ever get tired of the old button push, you're always welcome to the spare harem in my supersonic love mansion.

For the writer who has embraced inconsequence, nothing offers more consolation than a story come full circle. Just when the knife is about to fall upon the son, given up as a sacrificial offering in good faith, just as that agitator who sought to unsettle the wisdom that comes in threes stands poised to mate the miller's daughters with hideous dwarves or call upon the fates to endorse the underworld's arbitrary laws, the neutralizing afflatus comes upon us and delivers a bow-tied world reconciled to the paradox of middles and the affinity of beginning for ends. As he stands to see Idris Peach to the door, Starker wonders whether he hasn't at least grazed the secret that animated *Illusion Street* and *The Choir Invisible*—perhaps the storybook dominion with which Rhesus Crabtree thinned the skin of circumstance until he could actually pass through it was only ever a knack for seducing inevitabilities in their youth, before the daily decline of possibilities winnowed them down to certainties. If you equalized yourself to every outcome and guessed the plot from the syncretic pillow talk of sentences, what could poor planetary substance do but lay down arms against dreams and yield up its spirits to Desiderius?

Starker can feel the pen humming in his pocket as he says, or rather hears himself say, "Think it over and get back to me. It's an offer I am only prepared to make once, and, frankly, I think you'd be a bit of a dunce to walk away from a chance like this. Just imagine, you'd be able to focus on your own work while collecting on the most vital and profitable narrative of our times. Mutually beneficial."

"So you said." Idris Peach plays desultory, but is guilty of at least three of the five classic tells, from the wobbly eye to the Jolly Roger arms. Was Starker ever so young? "And I *will* consider it, Arlechino. Only that."

"We both know what the literature of a country in decline craves. A hero detective pale as our faith in institution, prone to a bean-speaking spontaneity that catches logic in the bathroom and entreats God to play dice, a candy-coated gamesman playing on the side of the angels, but no stranger to the rough-and-tumble methods of the cretin. A silver lining in an age of deceit and the perfect foil to Jacquard, a fellow gambler to keep him in check."

"But Starker, man, look," the amateur hesitates before the open door, "who ever heard of a book with two heroes? I can already see Flip saying that the reader won't know which to root for."

"And I am more than certain that you'll think of some way to placate him. That's your job now, and one, I might add, you'll be nicely compensated for. Take as long as you need. You *are* my man."

Idris Peach is half out the door when he spins around on his heel and produces a copy of *Captain Kadmon and the Planet of the Priapods*. "Nearly forgot." He hands Starker a pen. "Can a fan score an autograph?"

Breathing a real-time specimen of that idiomatic standby, the sigh of relief at the eventual departure of his so-called opposite number, Starker wonders whether he actually signed *To one with a soul left to lose* or if he only thought it. Either way, for once, the writer feels no particular fear of rejection and, though he tells himself that finding Paz is his first concern, he's looking forward to the free reign to conduct his investigations that anonymity will award him and isn't surprised when the doorbell rings a second later, presumably because Idris Peach wasn't able to outpace ambition (or a deficiency thereof) even so far as the end of the block.

But Starker's visitor is no person at all but a book sitting square on the welcome mat, wrapped in its plain white review copy cover, pages freshly cut. It's *Energy Fools the Magician* all right, but who's fooling whom? Even at a glance, the author of numerous instances of peripeteia sees his plot twists straightened, holes in his logic unaccountably filled in with an expert hand, red herrings turned into genuine clues and vice versa, all done with a minimum of tampering. A clause inserted seamlessly into a sentence so that the reader never gets farther than the detective, a smoking pistol so that the villain's motivation never begins to look like the writer's convenience, all these edits in the same style, the Crabtree style, all serving to widen the gulf so that Plonquin arrives two lines too late to stop the Butcher of Broad Street from pitching his hostage off the side of a terra-cotta high-rise or discovering that the phony diamond Plonquin planted at the Daniel's Gallery has been left well enough alone, while Jacquard has somehow nicked the real McCoy from its locker in the precinct evidence room.

Here, from the other side, is an outstretched hand rustling words to lift his player king out of checkmate. The author is dead, long live the author, but as Rhesus Crabtree can no longer be called upon to account for his code, Starker can only take the genius of Turkey Park at his word, for that is all either of them has left. Ignoring the feeling that Paz is calling out from some distant room, Starker Arlechino shuts the blinds and begins to read.

J. W. McCormack

FROM *Energy Fools the Magician* BY R. TRIBOULET

"Well played, Plonquin," hisses Jacquard from where the detective, still wearing the gold paint and Roman helm of the ship's figurehead, has handcuffed his foe to the mast. "You knew I would find theft of the *Lindengarten* irresistible. Or was it your accursed beans that gave my scheme away?"

"From the egg to the apples, old boy. But the beans only told me you would sail this fair and antique vessel from the harbor to your cavern. You did a bloody good job of giving the rest away yourself. Why else would you steal all that glass and crystal?" From the bow, Plonquin looks up into the distorting surface of the enormous bottle in which they are encased. Beyond it, everything—the Museum of Crime, the sewer tubes, even the Stygian squid Unheimliche with his suckers puckered at the bottle's punt—is elongated and thin, stretched to the limit.

"You are well matched with your legend, Detective. It's a damned pity that we should be cast as urge and demiurge when we'd be so much stronger under a single inclination. However, you forgot one thing," and so saying, the mastermind behind the *Lindengarten*'s one-man mutiny jerks free of his cuffs and makes to scamper up the mast just as Detective Plonquin recalls that when Councilman Marburg's body was finally recovered, it was *with the hands cut off*!

Plonquin grips his cane by its hilt and unsheathes the blade secreted in its length. But, seeing that his enemy is unarmed in at least two regards, he lifts an antique saber from the galley door and tosses it into the damask gloves that sprout from Jacquard's cuffs just in time to catch the weapon in their bloodied grip and reverse its position so that the inscribed edge, reading A QUOTATION IS NOT AN EXCERPT, A QUOTATION IS A CICADA, is pointed straight at Plonquin. Very well. If it is to be a duel, let it be a battle between gentlemen.

The detective follows the flapping of Jacquard's coattails up to the crow's nest, where he parries the first blow and puts the point of his sword through the archdandy's top hat. Nimble as two flames dancing atop a match, the stark white detective and his nemesis encircle the foremast. Jacquard cuts a figure eight through the air, but Plonquin inscribes a seven in reverse, guiding his fencing partner's sword into the wooden post. Seeing his chance, the albino levels his sword cane at Jacquard's cravat and calls for the swash's surrender. Jacquard lifts his hands toward the ceiling his larger-than-life bottle has improvised over their heads, making a microcosm of their skirmish—

226

only to jerk one gold-buckled leather boot straight up, the last-minute ploy of a cornered scapegrace and one watched over by a dark star indeed, for steel connects with steel toe and as the flashing sword goes hurtling overboard, Jacquard follows up with a rakish right hook that sends its pink-eyed owner tumbling after.

Plonquin plummets toward his reflection. He locks eyes with his widening double in the bottle's glass-blown fluting, only to swivel in midair, having heard some lady's voice cry out his name. Instead of the siren he expects, he finds Jacquard, reaching out from a slashed piece of rigging to catch his bone white flesh in his hand.

"Gotcha! Easy does it, my friend. That end is far too ignominious for you," speaks Jacquard as he lowers the vanquished detective down the bottle's slope, so that he skates harmlessly into the *Lindengarten*'s hull. From his perch upon the rails of the deck above, Plonquin's implacable enemy sings out, "You are indeed a worthy adversary, Detective. I'm in no hurry to end with treachery what was begun as shadow play, not when you've learned to inhabit your shadow so well. They go loose without us. We'll meet again, Plonquin. You've no idea how long I've been waiting for another illusionist whose lessons have washed his hands of illusion. Now that you know what's real, come and step lightly. Come and get me. We'll be waiting. But for now—"

And so saying, the venial magician called Jacquard makes good on his getaway, slashing the last of the rigging and causing the sail to flutter airily before it falls, draping the proscenium inside a huge blank page.

So it goes and so it *will* go. Success is ill measured by book sales when somewhere there's a woman only pen marks can set free, but the volume of orders that fills shelves with copies of *Energy Fools the Magician* means that R. Triboulet (a manikin in the service of Idris Peach, who is himself a marionette) can follow Plonquin and Jacquard's ongoing itch-and-scratch in *Kick in the Eye* with *Shot by Both Sides* and, after that, *Sons of the Silent Age*. Each deadline brings another manuscript to Starker's door, always the evildoer gliding out of the best-laid plots and prisoners' dilemmas. He'll not stray from his search for Paz, though it means digging upward through print and overturning the text to salvage a meaning that so far achieves its fullest expression too late, Detective Plonquin beaten by a mimetic technicality, a depth-charged subplot, or, sometimes, the brute force of better writing. Clearly, the only way out of either world is through and Starker's too caught up in the widening gyre to miss Captain Kadmon and cult heroics of science fiction convention meet-and-greets.

Nor is he alone in his newfound vocation. Fletcher Poole funds a prize in translation from his Abu Dhabi stronghold, Idris Peach toils on under the Triboulet mantle with the occasional piece in *Bedknob* or *The Ejaculator*, and Herbert "Flip" Dyrshka collects on the copyrights of an empire. And Hova García-Terrycloth, despite the potential blowback to his reputation as a Marxist, faithfully reviews each volume. Met in the back row of a reading by Starker, who happens to be on his monthly sojourn out-of-doors, he slaps a dog-eared copy of *Metal Guru* and fans a small wind from the flipping of pages that Starker can see are reticulate with red ink.

"Ah ha. Fresh off the presses, as it were. How'd I do this time?"

"Starker, I mean really." Hova takes off his glasses, maybe for emphasis, maybe because he's got something stuck in his eye. "It's your best."

"Really? You mean, you actually think it's good?" Frankly, this possibility had not occurred to the lapsed author of any number of out-of-print space operas. "Something *I* wrote is good?"

But Hova stammers in place of a straight answer, replaces his glasses (it *was* something in his eye, after all), and says again, "Your best, that's all. Take it or leave it."

And why should he not, when he has known the best already, crossed swords with the best, worn its aegis and watched it disappear to a secret place? As long as he remembers that his concerns are mystical, what need has Starker for the stiff-backed binding of *respectable* letters? Letters are letters and he's overfed. If settling for less is the most Starker can get, he'll take it. So he does. Starker Arlechino takes it.

Available Light
Arthur Sze

1.

Sandalwood-scented flames engulf a corpse—
further down the ghat, a man carries fire
in his right hand to a shaved body placed
faceup on logs. He circles five times, ignites
the pyre: The dead man's mouth opens.
Moored offshore, we rock in a creaking skiff,
stiffen at these fires which engulf lifetimes.
A fine soot hangs in the air; in a hotel room,
a woman infected with typhoid writhes,
"Do not let me die," and a doctor's assistant
injects her with antibiotics. Today, no one
comprehends how dark energy and dark
matter enlace this world; no one gazes
at the heart-shaped leaves of spring
and infers we are ensnared by our illusions.
After the barbed wire across the arroyo
is cut, three-wheelers slash ruts into slopes.

2.

Huddled by roadside fires—

teens ditch school and ransack mailboxes—

cracking a skull with a hammer—

"In the end, we're dust streamers ionized by ultraviolet radiation"—

a yield sign riddled with bullet holes—

along the dark street, an elephant lumbers—

gazing in each other's eyes,
they flow and overflow—

a one-legged girl at a car window.

3.

Along a sculptured sandstone wall, a dancer
raises a right foot to fasten ankle bells;

a naked woman arches and scrubs her back;
a flute player wets his lips and blows.

We try to sleep, but a rat scavenges
on the floor; at dawn, pulling a curtain,

you find a showerhead wrapped in plastic,
crank the faucet: red-brown water gurgles out.

Theriomorphic gods pass through the mind,
but an egret may be an egret. Pausing

at a bomb alert on a glass door, I scan cars
jammed into the square; you hand alms

to a one-eyed woman, whiff red chiles
in burlap sacks. Soldiers cordon off a gate,

set rifles with inverted-v mounts on sandbags.
At dusk, someone on a motorcycle throws

acid at two women and grabs a purse.
A woman wraps a leg around her lover;

dressed only in gold foil, a man gesticulates—
we wipe soot off the backs of our necks.

4.

By the acequia headgate, a rib cage—

smoking in a wheelchair,
she exhales and forms a rafflesia flower—

pit bull on a leash—

he set his laundromat ablaze—

the rising spires resembling Himalayan peaks—

green parrots squawking in the branches of an ashoka tree—

heat death—

when is recollection liberation?

5.

Streamers around a bodhi tree, the elongated
leaf tips; under a porch, the hexagonal shapes
in a wasp nest. In a wheelbarrow, someone
hauls mixed clay and sand to men along a wall.
Once I tilted hawk and trowel, plastered cement
on walls, ran metal lath across the setting coat.
"Their gold teeth and rings burn with their bodies,"
says the boatman. Our love cries vanish into air,
yet my tongue running along your clavicle
releases spring light in the room. Our fingertips
floodgate open: death, no, ardor will be violet
flare to our nights, and the knots of existence
dissolve when we no longer try to grasp them.
The net of the past dissolves when the mixer
stops mixing: Cranes stalk fish in shallow ponds;
a woman aligns basil plants in terra-cotta pots;
out of nowhere, a fly bangs against a windowpane.

6.

At a rink, you step onto ice and mark the lines
already cut, but they are not your lines;
the mind pools what will happen with
what has happened. Moving out and
cutting an arc, you find the locus of creation
is here. You do not need to draw "nine"
and "four" in ashes to end your attachment
to the dead; you hunger to live as a river
fans out in a delta. A man tosses a pot
of water behind his shoulder and releases
the dark energy of attachment; fires recede
into darkness and become candlelights
bobbing downstream. In this hourglass place,
ants lift grains of sand above brickwork,
creating a series of circular dunes;
two baby robins sleep behind wisteria leaves;
in an attosecond, *here* and *there* dissolve.

7.

Lifting off a cottonwood, a red-tailed hawk—
in a carved sandstone wall, a woman applies

henna to her right hand. By the papaya tree,
we climb to a rooftop, gaze down at wheat

spread out on another roof—pink and madder
clothes pinned to a line in a backyard.

A bull with a swishing tail lumbers past
the flashlight store; and what is complex

is most simple. In a doorway, a girl leaning
into sunlight writes on the stone floor.

We sip chai in a courtyard, inhale the aroma
of neem leaves laced with diesel exhaust.

I hose new grass by the kitchen, guess
to be liberated from the past is to be

freed from the future; and, as sunlight
inclines, making the bougainvillea leaves

by the window translucent, I catch our
fugitive, living tracks as we make our way.

Respecting the Daedal Anonym
Paul West

IDEALLY, ANYTHING WRITTEN about Shakespeare's plays should have a subtractive quality. It should draw attention to the plays at the same time as rendering unnecessary some portion of the critical comment that has gone before. I cannot pretend to have realized this ideal, but I offer these ruminations in the hope of encouraging the reader and viewer of Shakespeare to fend for himself and be to some extent unprofessional.

In one sense I am suggesting an anticritical critique. I want to open some questions that might seem to have been officially closed, and I want to argue for a relativism where the critical canon has appeared to set things straight once and for all. My argument is threefold. First, I must explain that I have borrowed two terms, *entropy* and *atropy*, from peculiar regions: the first from thermodynamics, which I understand very little still, despite the patient instruction of expert friends; the other from Greek mythology. Entropy, to me is *transformability*, and I shall use the term more for convenience and contrast than in the hope of applying the theory of thermodynamics to Shakespeare. Atropy, which I have risked coining, means *untransformability* and comes from the name of the most inflexible of the Fates, Atropos. I intend these terms as complementary opposites, as useful terms to steer by, but not in any sense as a new cant.

My first contention is that all the plays present some version of the inevitable: the things, the facts, we cannot steer round, such as birth, copulation, disease, physiognomy, excretion, death, and so on. These, as teachers and insurance salesmen say, are the facts of the human condition. They do not vary. Neither does Nature, of which Man is a part but against which he is a combatant. About these matters Shakespeare is insistent.

Second, I contend that, because he is so keenly aware of these matters, Shakespeare is only too ready to celebrate free, human vitality. Therefore, by creating a poetic and not just an episodic or expository drama, he gives our own imaginations a certain amount of free rein, and we are justified in getting from the plays whatever we do get. This I call the entropy of the plays: their transformable contents as distinguished and distinguishable from the atropy of their nontransformable contents.

I pause here to expand two points. In the first place, the atropy covers both what is unchangeable in life and our common agreement about Shakespeare's presentation of it. These facts of our condition, he seems to state, are immutable, and there is little dispute about his having presented them as such. In other words, what is steady is two-fold: the facts of life and the general agreement that Shakespeare knew them. So there is little critical dispute about what he presents. In the second place, the entropy covers not only the reader's or auditor's free imagining when prompted by the text, but also the transformations made by actors, producers, interpretive critics, and, of course, by changes in the English language itself. (The death of a connotation is the birth of many a high-sounding modern imbecility.) All these factors help to ensure that there can be no objective, canonical interpretation of any of the plays. I mean that we can usually fix on the atropy but we can never freeze the entropy. The plays are part stable, part volatile, and to read or see them is to participate in a deliberate rehearsal of what it means to be "human." At the same time as we acknowledge our degree of imprisonment we exercise as fully as we can what privileges of liberty remain to us. The radish and the gooseberry are fixed, but what each of us finds in such a statement as "Ripeness is all" is not.

My third point takes us full circle. Because the plays assist us to counter the inevitable by imagining freely in metaphysical defiance, as it were, Shakespeare ties us (and himself) down to the concrete. He presents atropy through plot and action, permits an entropy in character and texture, and then through the use of such things as radishes and gooseberries implants atropy in the texture itself. Our imagining is therefore constantly interrupted by the down-to-earth. So while the plays are not, like Greek tragedy, unquestionable expositions of atropy, neither are they freewheeling extravaganzas. Shakespeare balances things, and to be constantly aware of this as we read is to intensify in our own private terms our knowledge of the human position. His wisdom is that he rarely overdoes the one at the expense of the other and the risk he takes is of provoking the critical delusion ("critical" in both senses of being the critics' own and also rather dangerous) that tries to achieve an atropy of interpretation, as if to say: Because Shakespeare dealt in the inevitable, and because he achieved an effect of inevitability in his phrasing—being a master wordsman—we ourselves should strive to fix the "meaning" of each play. These critics forget that although there is an undisputed account of part of life, there is no undisputed account of all of it. Shakespeare was as definite as he felt he could be; the rest he left to individuals to fill in for themselves.

Most of this is, of course, pretty obvious stuff. Shakespeare is not the Witch of Endor or of Cumae, not the Delphic Oracle, not Nostradamus or the keeper of all the keys; not even the one realist whose realism is perfect, and not even the one fantasist whose fantasy is wholly actual. He was a great manipulator of words; in fact, he was much manipulated by words. He knew what they could and what they could not do. It is time we stopped asking the impossible of him to attend to the enormous possibilities he does bestow. And if, in the end, I am taken as pleading for his sheer vitality, then I shall be content. He celebrates it in three main ways. First, there is life itself: self-renewing and abundant, requiring here and there only a few seeds to float, a carcass to decay, or a bit of careless contraception on Saturday night. This is the atropy of life's force. Second, there is the vitality of imagination, and he celebrates this like a nympholept. And, third, he relishes chaos: not only the chaos out of which human life continues to emerge, but also the chaos that human imaginations and human minds make through their private endeavors or in print.

We are faced with two facts: Shakespeare was a person who has become an extraordinary phenomenon. For every attempt to get at the man through the writings there has been an attempt to prove their impregnable impersonality. Yet the accounts given by neither attempt will do, not if we are sensible. The plays are highly, almost obtusely personal; yet it is impossible to say exactly what Shakespeare thought. We know what he thought *about*, we know what obsessed him, and he can be quoted for almost any occasion in self-contradiction. The problem (and there has never yet been a Shakespeare who was not a problem) is to respond fully to the personal nature of all he does without pressing too hard for something we might call, if we are silly, his "philosophy of life." And the completest response will be that which notices the intense individuality of the plays and yet accepts the impersonality behind which he so often disappears through seeming to have too many opinions or no opinion at all. Such a response may strike us as pointlessly dual: We feel that we should be able to apprehend writing as something organic and unified in which a man memorably tells us what he thinks about the world. And we can do this fairly well with many authors, from Dante and Goethe to Shelley and Balzac. Or so we think until we go a little deeper, for to say this is to ignore the sheer impersonality that makes Dante so lucid, so unexcitingly transparent; it is to forget that the definite-sounding Goethe was also a *Schwindelkopf*— a man with a spinning head who is all opinions and no constant view, and it is also to miss the shining muddle Shelley could not help creating and the untheoretical amassing method at which Balzac is best. Yet, somehow, as soon as we have modified our position and admitted that these authors never speak out so clearly, so consistently as we suppose, we go back on ourselves. For we *can* justly identify them with certain views on matters both trivial and considerable. And Milton, say, or Wordsworth, is surely as explicit as we could wish.

The point is this. We must train ourselves in self-consciousness; we must learn to stand outside our comfortable attitudes to authors and ask: Is this honest of us? Away for the time being with disparity between an author's intention and what he does; between what he means and what we get; between what we get and what others insist is there. Imaginative writing is never that clear anyway. The truly difficult thing is not to find inconsistencies or to lose a rough general accuracy in pedantic exegesis. It is to train ourselves out of simplicity and, through reminding ourselves of art's true nature, to let art be what it is. Differently put, this is to say that Shakespeare is one of those writers who leave us guessing. It is no doubt an intelligent activity to seek out his doctrine of nature or of statecraft, and students taking examinations find the resulting treatises less bewildering than the actual plays. But it is far from intelligent, and less than human, to fix Shakespeare as a doctrinaire playwright when in fact he occupies himself with one particular license conferred by the nature of art. In other words, he expresses his temperament and imagination with immense power and little restraint, but he expresses his ratiocinative side more by shuffling ideas about his principal obsessions than by coming out and declaring himself. One of the main contributing factors to his greatness is his ability to combine intense personal flavor with a dramatic witness of his inclination to be disinclined. It is that impartial position or that tentative plight that he, more than any Racine or Corneille, imposes on himself and us. The agony is that of making up one's mind and the pleasure is that of reviewing all the possibilities. It is also a good way of appealing to many sections of a heterogeneous audience without disappointing anyone. In this, Shakespeare's mental habits coincided well with his career as a dramatist. I am not saying that he held no views: only that if we say he did we must realize our presumption and live with it right through, or we must be willing to define clearly the views he did *not* hold. And that would only lead us to define him as a compassionate human being. I am trying here to amplify that definition by looking at the variety of his heart.

II.

The constants of his world do not differ essentially from those of our own. There was death, birth, disease, and so on; matters cosmic, chemical, and emotional were just as baffling and daunting then as now. Twentieth-century man has merely had made available to him analyses and explanations that confer a feeling of immense knowledge. Never has there been so much "information"; never have there been so many cults of data. Yet our fundamental questions remain unanswered: We have only acquired more complicated ways of expressing our ignorance, and the complication only intensifies the original darkness. When we set alchemy, the doctrine of humors, the Chain of Being, and Elizabethan superstitions alongside, say, nuclear physics, genetics, cybernetics, and twentieth-century psychology, we find many intermediate zones fully explored and named in detail. But the zone *is* intermediate: between teleology and everyday assumptions. We are better informed, but we are probably not wiser and we are certainly no nearer to solving life's main mysteries. Dust still closes the eye of a Helen and kings, though too few too late perhaps still go a-progress through the guts of a beggar. So when we approach Shakespeare's plays we do not need as much background information as we do in matters of Elizabethan *mores*, language, and politics. Our so-called knowledge is mere superstructure, and it does conceal Shakespeare from us.

We are just as much in the dark as any Elizabethan was. Certain phenomena appeared everywhere and yet for all their frequency remained mysterious. Shakespeare had to present them in their human aspect, in all their varied repercussions upon the lives of all sorts and conditions of men, and approach the mysterious through imagination. What we find in the plays is a feat of double imagination, making the repetitious fascinating and the inexplicable not entirely beyond the scope of the average playgoer's apprehension. What Shakespeare knows, he portrays with incredible variety; what he does not know and what tantalizes him, he implants in the mind of the soliloquizing Hamlet or of the young Claudio awaiting execution in *Measure for Measure.*

The trouble is, of course, that mundanity always defeats imagination because it is more complex than anything imagination can produce, and imagination ends up not explaining or solving but inventing new mysteries of its own. And these facts, as Shakespeare found, made the composition of accurate and exciting plays almost impossible. At his best he always gives us a sense of interpretation; at his worst he allows the mundane to take over and appears to be setting entropy to work only to relieve the boredom of all that atropy. But imagination is more than sugar for a pill; it is the best pill of all.

A great portion of man's life is natural: Involuntarily man has a great deal in common with nonhuman forms of being. No wonder, then, that Shakespeare delighted in emphasizing those parts of mankind that affiliated it upward to the king's divinity, angels, archangels, and God. I mean that a thinking person such as Shakespeare soon tired of man's animal aspect and evolved an almost impetuous compensatory humanism that eventually tended to place man too high for his own good. Shakespeare, anxious to write plays about all kinds of men, found himself having to reconcile within those plays the animal nature that man and other creatures held in common and a spirituality by no means equal in men. He therefore had to choose between being demotic and being snobbish when, really, he wanted to be both. The problem, as for any intelligent Renaissance man, was to be honest about humanity without losing sight of man's variable spirituality and at the same time to exalt that spirituality without exaggerating.

Shakespeare's performance in this dilemma is far from perfect, but, considering how little was known in his time of the nature of the physical universe and how fierce religious dispute had become, it is very much better than any of his contemporaries might have expected. After all, the majority of people, no matter how interesting the details of their behavior, speech, and dress, are not highly imaginative, and a Shakespeare, anxious to communicate life's full variety, including the power and the feats of imagination, has to rely largely on himself. It is not a matter of making shallow people deep, but of relating them to mental and creative experiences that few of them have. The problem is to do full justice to life's pageant, to use multitudinous detail in order to state life's atropy with as much variety as possible, but also to incorporate into the statement the rarer experiences. Thus we get Hamlet the intellectual alongside Hamlet the soldier and alongside other soldiers; the philosophizing, haunted Macbeth alongside men of unimaginative honor and diligent militarists. Richard II broods and moons, Richard III releases his twisted mind in twisted rhetoric, Lear is half a visionary, and Prospero is a potent seer. These are special men, and Shakespeare needs them. Through them he can express the subtlest, least commonplace aspects of life, and this consorts nicely with the presuppositions of tragedy at least. Otherwise he has to equip ordinary characters with astounding powers of rhetoric and unlikely vocabularies, not to mention improbable powers of imagination.

It might be objected here that since Shakespeare was concocting plays—making art—"likeness to life" would not matter much one way or another. In life, special men are much rarer than they are in Shakespeare's plays and much less communicative. Again, in life, ordinary people are by no means as racy and deft in speech as in these plays. But since the plays are metaphors and emblems limited to a few hours on a stage, the distortions are permissible. Shakespeare wishes to echo life's actual texture while summing it up: His quest is both descriptive and inductive. He tends to intensify and epitomize, treating individual lives as a vast superstructure built on a few unvarying principles. He gives the variety and epitomizes it, thus being fairly accurate and at the same time avoiding the boredom of rehearsing the commonplace. It is small wonder that he made the most of both life's and art's limits, pushing each as far as possible because he knew that all descriptions distort anyway and that art can never *become* something else: There can never be a description so precise as to be indistinguishable from what it describes or a work of art so loose as to lapse from art into being life. Whatever happened, the thing in hand was always itself, and the hackneyed assertions of our own times— "Just like life; it's not like reading a novel at all" or "It's so unrealistic and far-fetched"—have no meaning. Shakespeare pushes his precisions until his account of life is a long way from what the average person can discern, and he gives his imagination so loose a rein that some Procrustean critics deny him the rank of craftsman at all. We have only to look at the plays. All is in the illusion, however guilty we might feel about responding to fiction as if it is life:

> Is it not monstrous that this player here,
> But in a fiction, in a dream of passion,
> Could force his soul so to his own conceit
> that from her working all his visage wann'd. . . .

The word, we notice, is "monstrous." The truth is that we can be taken in and sometimes wish to be. On the other hand, Hermione in *The Winter's Tale* seems a statue and deceives the watchers. They cannot help themselves any more than Romeo can in assuming the drugged Juliet is dead. Eventually we are forced to admit that our only defense against the iron facts is our imagination in "fiction" or "dream."

The atropy of life's facts includes the essential artificiality of art, and as far as both are concerned we can be Shakespeare's contemporaries without labor, whereas his language and the Elizabethan assumptions he subscribed to require considerable homework on our part. The plays demonstrate time and again the relentless, boring victory of pattern or process over the individual. The orchestra swamps the soloist eventually. The Roman plays were also English history plays, with the same concepts dramatized at a safe remove from the Elizabethan present. In the histories, both English and Roman, and the comedies, we are shown man-made rebellion, in itself a virtuous or pernicious result of natural vitality, running into trouble with the established order. Granted the notion of a hierarchy (king, duke, father, uncle, etc.), the eventual correction of offenders is a human process supervised by human agency. In the tragedies, on the other hand, we go beyond the social and the civic into a study of human nature itself as evidenced in exceptional men who wish to go beyond social and even cosmic restraints. Tragedy has to do with apostasy and heresy, and it is the disordered mind rather than the disordered state or family that attracts Shakespeare and thus gives him a chance to release his full imagination. He illustrates the range of human possibilities, documenting the full relativism of action, idea, and imagination. Eventually the whole drama becomes that of a disordered mind reviewing all possibilities and finding nothing to hold to except the possibility of order's emerging from chaos. The atropy of man's cosmic place triumphs always over the entropy of human initiative.

It is not a theme to have complicated ideas about; it is there, like the sky, and all the playwright can do is go on showing in varied ways how the same end recurs. The image of the tamperer takes us from Bolingbroke, who *has* Richard II murdered, and repents publicly and calculatingly at the play's end, to Brutus, who justifies in civic terms the murder he commits with his own hand. Brutus, unlike Bolingbroke, studies the drama in his own mind:

> Between the acting of a dreadful thing
> And the first motion, all the interim is
> Like a phantasma, or a hideous dream.

So does Macbeth, but he can find no justification for his act: It is gratuitous butchery. Tragedy arrives here through a privately arrived-at lust that will not be curbed and thus supplies Shakespeare with a context in which anything can be done, thought, or imagined. The discriminations implicit in a state of order go, and all we learn is that chaos defeats the chaos maker.

III.

The most noteworthy technical feature of the tragedies is Shakespeare's avoidance of straightforward exposition and merely helpful monologues. He resorts to complex metaphor in order to convey various forms of mental turbulence and deliberately compresses utterance until the dark of ambiguity becomes more revealing than the light of explanation. Nothing in these plays is as definite or as unequivocal as the comedies and histories are: Instead, Shakespeare seems bent on reflecting mental confusion. The sense of control weakens, and many speeches are thick with impacted connotations. It is as if multiplicity has become the keynote along with despair at understanding anything at all. Othello, Macbeth, Hamlet, and Lear sustain gigantic conceptions of themselves, of their own enormity, and also of the forces they serve or fight. All wish the world destroyed. Antony says, "Let Rome in Tiber melt, and the wide arch of the ranged empire fall!" and Cleopatra matches him:

> O sun,
> Burn the great sphere thou movest in! darkling stand
> The varying shore o' the world.

The tragic heroes are continually stressing their closeness to vast cosmic forces, to the planets and the elements. Despairing of satisfaction on earth, in human society, they affront the universe and appeal to or revile it. As Wolfgang Clemen has observed, the tragedies are richly instinct with "nature-atmosphere": beasts, vegetation, and things mineral serve to remind us of man's place in nature and also counterpoint his hurtling ambition to go beyond both humanity and nature.

As often as not, the method is one of indirection: Shakespeare wants to communicate a baffling agglomeration in which clear distinctions have gone and the only certainty is sheer force of will. Half statements ("Macbeth is ripe for shaking") consort with elliptical profundities ("Ripeness is all"), and the dramatic impetus hurries us onward as if there is no time to explain, unwind, or underline. The result is a mimicry of chaos, a chaos that the heroes seem to will upon themselves out of obstinate grandiosity. All the balances are finely set—too finely to endure for long. Wonder at man's magnificence adjoins disgust with his pettiness. Evil is everywhere but so is a perverse belief in resurgent good. The theme is cosmic yet all calamity is made reducible to psychology. Pity, which is everywhere, emerges as the most horrendous, destructive emotion of all. Life is revered but death is longed for. In fact much of the tragedy is in the uncertainty and indecision. The agony of never being sure finds its perfect reflection in the contorted, often ambiguous imagery, so much so that the final effect is musical: There is a wealth of emotion that we can label approximately, but it is more powerful and captivating than it is minutely explicit. The exhilaration of living close to death and destruction imbues the tragedies with an astonishing feeling for the magic of being alive. The best energy seems to begin when the holocaust is at hand and, quite clearly, Shakespeare finds vitality and energy more absorbing than any simplified problem of good *versus* evil.

Coleridge, a romantic critic who delighted to find opposites fruitfully interacting, says laconically in one of his notes for a lecture on Shakespeare, "Signal adherence to the great law of nature that opposites tend to attract and temper each other. Passion in Shakespeare displays, libertinism involves, morality." Thus in the tragedies the hero is ambitious enough to will his own destruction; yet his very destruction releases new springs of life, and the hero vaguely knows this. Self-sacrifice is the under motif of the grandiose lust for power. And, in a way similar, Shakespeare's own imagination is self-consuming in the tragedies: Hardly has an idea, an image, flashed up at us than it is gone and something else has caught our attention. There is almost a shorthand manner to the speeches; the mind is fed, crammed, and made to leap about almost as if Shakespeare were conducting a race with time. The action forges ahead toward destruction and the images lean forward, anticipating, warning, and getting in one another's way. The final effect is of struggle: not just the struggle between adversaries, but as if a section of the forming universe had been isolated to show the forces of nature working through upheaval into final creation of a world. In such plays the hero must have formidable stature if he is not to seem puny compared with both the cosmic forces surrounding him and the imagination informing him. When chaos and evil actually bring forth order and virtue, the performance has to be in the grand manner. It is not enough to say, as many do, that the camaraderie among soldiers at the front or among civilians during heavy bombarding is superior to anything evolved during peace (save, of course, the quasi-peace of such totalitarian hives as Spain and Hungary). True, the presence of death at every moment is a violent stimulus, but Shakespeare's tragedies go beyond this into the special witness of special men who are probing death itself in order to surpass their human stature. Admittedly they begin by semi-accident: Macbeth has an ambitious wife who eggs him on, Othello murders because he cannot sift or ignore spiteful blather, Lear is a daft old heresiarch who divides his kingdom unwisely and gets bitten, Hamlet is caught up in a revenant situation he had done nothing to create. And then, suddenly, something takes over: The hero feels his powers and, paradoxically, in exercising them ruins himself. The recklessness that would abolish the world also abolishes the destructive impulse. These tragedies do not so much versify or dramatize such facts as display them in jarring commotion. The process is revealed in all its rawness and untidiness. Things are not worked out according to some preestablished philosophy; they work themselves out haphazardly as if there were no conclusion or doctrine in Shakespeare's mind.

It is this quality of seeming unrehearsed that is of capital interest. The tragedies give us not the careful regulations of the comedies or the inspection of the kingship idea we find in the histories; instead, they catch turbulence on the move and rarely offer ideas commensurate with the energy on show. In other words, I am proposing the tragedies as the least doctrinaire of the plays. They demonstrate a *process*, not a doctrine. There is not a meaning *behind* the action; the action *is* the meaning; the hero is not separable from his context any more than his context is something called the "indifferent universe." Perhaps these tragedies are not as explicit or as orderly as we would like them if we wish to compare with Racine or Socrates, with St. Augustine and St. Thomas. The point is that Shakespeare hit on a way of presenting an action without seeming to supervise the action's progress, and what we finally have is a species of uncontrolled chemical reaction in which accident is as important as design, in which results are not predictable except that there is bound to be death. Each tragedy is different; each has its own way of discarding and refusing formulas, of tripping the message finders and bewildering the factorizer. Each is an image of how difficult it is to understand the world we live in. Ross's comment in *Macbeth* that "good men's lives / Expire before the flowers in their caps" expresses the general situation and also reminds us that this play is full of images of fertility—maternal and agricultural, and that these images always occur to the speakers when destruction threatens its worst.

There is a tendency to make the tragedies, even *King Lear*, "nicer," or more homiletic than they really are. John Vyvyan, for example, in *The Shakespearean Ethic*, becomes soundingly vague:

> Descent may be, and perhaps must be, a preliminary to ascent; and from Shakespeare's hell there is an open but not easy path to heaven. Essentially it is love's path. Truth to one's Self, fidelity to Love, and creative mercy are inseparable. . . . Shakespeare traces the soul's journey from the pit of chaos, to a point where it seems about to unfold celestial wings. . . .

This is wholesome stuff indeed, but it has little to do with Shakespeare's plays. It is the sort of medieval personification we find in *King John* or in the literary pages of small religious magazines. Shakespeare in fact had long since discarded the straight allegory, and his manner of representing metaphysical powers had, by *Lear*, become concrete and flagrantly original. The imagery in this play is not illustrative at all, but direct, self-contained perception. Lear himself *talks* imagery all of the time and, in so doing, reviews a universe. We should all try to be like Lear: that is, stay with the images themselves without trying to distill from them some "scheme of values." The tragedies immerse us in experience and what we gain is the sense of having been in a process, a process that approximates to repeated creation and repeated destruction. "Meaning" occasionally suggests itself but only generically, for no one meaning comprehends the process before the process enters into some new phase. At its sublimest and most harrowing, the process works through violence, as in *Lear*; the storm is at once both mind and universe, microcosm and macrocosm. But its meaning? What meaning have the successive stages of the phenomenon we call lightning? None: Lightning just happens, adding to the world's sum of liveliness. And so too in the plays: Madness, viciousness, brutality, overweening ambition, and unmeasured lust all contribute in their respective ways to the vitality of Shakespeare's offered dream; they energize it, and, like it or not, Shakespeare has to present them alongside what he finds noble or decent, both of which can be found in the tragedies as lacking vitality. (There is no need here to pursue human analogies; the vital are often foul, the decent not vital.) In the long run this presupposes suspension of moral criteria and produces what we get: the nondidactic presentation of phenomena and possibilities. Shakespeare is torn, but not in half: His moral sense remembers itself and his appetite for vitality lures him away from it. He knows what goes to make up the world and he is bound to acknowledge the principle of fruitful collision. In other words, the tragedies do not moralize to us but review the types of evidence available as well as the types of availability evidence can embody. Thus his supreme awareness develops into a supreme mode of impersonality and we have to recognize this fact if we are to gain any personal satisfaction, any increase in awareness, from the most ambitious of his plays. The paradox is that his awareness is imaginative and his imaginativeness involves him constantly in mental building and mental destruction. His imaginative method gibes exactly with his approach to the tragic. No wonder that anxious moderns, upset by too much psychology, want to lock him into systems; anything, it seems, is safer than that eye rolling in its fine frenzy and that vocabulary coping indefatigably (but wildly) with the mercury in his head.

Misapprehensions
A Mobile in Ten Parts
Miranda Mellis

STUFFED ANIMAL

THE ORIGINAL "STUFFED ANIMAL" referred to an animal post taxidermy, killed, skinned, stuffed with cotton and rags and sewn back up in a wooden frame, a phantasm with a pair of glass eyes. Sometimes a taxidermied animal is set in a fictional habitat that, were it to come back to life, it would not recognize as its own. (Like deaths in amusement parks, this occurs more often than you might think.) The educational diorama then blurs into curiosity cabinet. The animals become, in death, misrepresentations of themselves. "Let's put the dead thing in context," someone suggests. But what is context for the dead thing?

REPET

If your pet has passed on to the "Rainbow Bridge," one company suggests, you may want to consider freeze-drying its inanimate body, to keep it near you in effigy. Or, for $150,000 you can now have your pet cloned. For those who are not comfortable with the impermanence of forms, this is a step up from taxidermy. Does one still grieve the original pet? Or, in the age of biomechanical reproduction and infinitely reproducible sameness, is the original pet to be viewed merely as a prototype, and do we instead grieve the obsolescence of our future commodities? What is the difference between nature and commodity when it comes to love and pleasure? What is the difference between impermanence and obsolescence?

WIND EYES

The word "window" refers to openings, prior to the invention of glass, which allowed a building to breathe. They were called wind eyes. Have you ever looked through a grimy glass wind eye so opaque it barely filtered the light? And did you perchance think you saw, as into a dirty television, action figures? Perhaps they wore fatigues. Within moments you thought you heard them running through the building, their shouts of war echoing in the halls. Or (more fortunately) perhaps you thought you could make out shapes resembling animals, leaves, baby faces, carnivals, nebulae, salutary geometries, embrous filigree bonbons, or stencil birdlike intimations? As with auguries derived from cracks in mud paths, tea leaves, and the firmament, ambiguous surfaces resemble the mind that is looking (as Kurt Schwitters says of collages and their makers).

FIRST PERSON

First-person narration is an armature of subjectivity that unifies all the variegated elements of story. Through that singular voice—an artifice, to be sure—is transmitted the vapor of reality. Similarly, the installation artist mobilizes a first-person point of view to unify the variegated elements of installation. We might view its organizational patterns as continuous with the artist's subjectivity, the more or less masked, more or less reflexive *ur*-context. We are made aware that we are contacting the worker via the work. When the artist wields *subjectivity as his or her subject*, in order to reflect upon another scene of (more or less masked, more or less reflexive) subjectivity (for example, science) and to argue for a reckoning with the ramifications of that subjectivity (the scientist's) with respect to the subject, then the "first-person" function itself is richly emptied out; it becomes a rhetorical figure.

TEMPORALITY

As we enter the contested site of superimposition (overlapping the ethical subject of installation with the instrumental object of laboratory), we see planes of continuity (temporal, associative, ideological, disciplinary) where they were not obvious; ruptures and

power where they were concealed; the undoing of archaic raciona-
tions, and even auras (of the polis? the earth? our condition?). The
objects before us have become metonyms for whatever has forced
them into social consciousness in a new guise: if flag for nation and
crown for king, then polar bear for climate change and T-shirt for
sweatshop. And thus may semantic figures, in their immanent
recognizability, show (by comparison) the staggered relays, botched
negotiations, and time lags—the slow stitch, the shadow fight—between perfect insight and broken infrastructure.

PREPOSITION

Suppose identity is prepositional: *You live outside/inside of a prison;*
outside/inside of a national border; outside/inside of a battlefield;
outside/inside of educational, health-care, or economic systems;
under/over the table; beyond/within reach of help. Recall Julia
Kristeva's articulation of the crucial role of abjection: Whoever is
not abject is negatively defined by whoever is. When am I me only
because I am not you? Self is an unstable infrastructure and a muta-
ble currency. Syntax describes cultural values. Syntax is a social
arrangement.

FAMILIAR STRANGER

Ostranenie, Viktor Shklovsky's term for the method of defamiliar-
izing ("estranging") what had become obscure through overfamiliar-
ity, makes the commonplace shocking and therefore newly luminous, re/cognizable. But what if one works in reverse and, *beginning*
with the illegible artifact, one endeavors to find for it a context in
which it might become familiar, legible? For example, one places the
vivid nonesuch (a headdress of bird skulls, an albino rhino) in an art
museum where it is framed, named, located, and elevated to the
highest cultural stature, swimming in the same current as ready-
mades, wrapped islands, and the Dutch Masters of Light: *inside.*
Thus are the human arts a commons. (The question of animal arts,
such as the architectural flourishes of bowerbirds, is usefully mobi-
lized by the question of animal rights, the intelligent artfulness of
animals being one argument for their rights.) And so, at the museum,
where we are supposed to go to contemplate the sublime, we find

that everything is ordinary; anything is within reach of a domesticating framework. The world is not imaginary but we must imagine it; we must light and relight our eyes.

FACTUAL ANIMAL

Representation gives us the feeling that what is happening *right now* is also happening (or has happened, or might happen) elsewhere in a different (more vivid) way. Representation alters our sensations of time and its motions, as well as objects and their history. The placing of an object into an alien context, in which it is framed nonetheless as more *factual* than ever, is how scientists make art. The placing of an object into an alien context, in which it is framed as fully *imaginary*, is how artists exceed science in speculative range. Our curiosity is as aroused by the "scientific" or "artistic" object as such as it is by the representational processes of appropriation, framing, and displacement that occur under the signs of science and art, disciplines that, however differently valued (culturally speaking) themselves, value similarly the play between aporia and gnosis, light and shadow. The installation can function as an experimental laboratory; the laboratory might become the site of political intervention/be made meaningfully unproductive. (The sign of production, in any case, casts a shadow.)

TO SHADOW

On YouTube there is a video of a three-year-old afraid of her own shadow. She stands with the sun behind her in the glare of a playground. When she moves, her shadow moves, and she weeps with fear. Every time she notices her shadow, she cries. Every time she cries, the audience laughs. Haplessly framed, voided, simulated, and reproduced, she tries to escape. But she can find no refuge from her evil twin or from the unseen audience. Trees' wayward shadows lace crookedly, weaving disorder through the system of the playground. A nearby building's shadow makes a large swathe whose edges demarcate a seeming interiority, a provisional indoor quality: It is colder just inside the wall of that shadow than it is just outside. The shadow of a small bird making its way over to a swing set is a film, a moving slant rhyme. A mimic, the shadow moves as the sparrow moves. Though the outline of the shadow, taken by itself, would not necessarily convey that it is cast by a bird (it could be a scrap of paper, or a teacup, or a hand), its movements are birdlike. The shadow is anamorphic, seemingly alive even.

WUNDERKAMMER/INSTALLATION

An antecedent of the artist's installation (alongside the bowerbird) is the *wunderkammer*, the cabinet of marvels, whose startling beauty cannot be separated from the (colonizing, ecocidal) violence of empire building (that is to say, private property, commodity, profit, and acquisition). The *wunderkammer* brings the *monstrare* down to scale, redistributing and containing the uncanny marvels of creation (alternately considered works of divine punishment, wonder, and design) for both aesthetic and moral purposes. The installation, also invested in aesthetics and morality, operates material forms as social, conceptual forces. *Things* are repurposed, defined not by their intended uses (whether sacred or banal) but rather by their shaping, sensous contact with the turning world: the world-historical, the world sensorium. The installation describes a view of history, a politics of recollection, and an aesthetic (the etymology of "aesthetic" describes sense making in both senses of the sensible: cognizable and sensorial). A thought experiment suggests itself: Imagine that all things are continuous with one another, that your subjectivity is not located inside you, but rather distributed, permeating. To take up this thought experiment would mean to willingly switch places, to imagine ourselves as others, and to meet the world with the very care we desire for ourselves.

Glitter
Mei-mei Berssenbrugge

1.

A wood violet has bloomed, when I come back from my walk in early spring.

I stop to welcome it, cooing, walking around it, not as if I were floating, but the surface of the world circled unfurling petals.

My song is really a manifestation without beginning or end of trance, sleep becoming sound.

Person and violet with so little in common my voice reveals as a resonance of unmanifest identity.

The violet looking back, loses objectivity, and enters the expansion of recognized things.

I could say our identities reach out to encompass the forest environment, like telepathy: A moment opens space by rendering it transparent in intensified consciousness.

Others embrace weather and wild land as means to the suprasensible, in violets an emotional desire for spring light: glitter, the mirror.

Connection, often the form emotion takes, appears to me as a visual image.

2.

Thoughts are sent out by one rock informing other rocks as to
the nature of its changing environment, the angle of sun and
temperatures cooling as night falls, and even its (loosely called)
emotional tone changes, the appearance of a person walking, who's
not appropriately empathic.

Thoughts meet and merge with other thoughts sent out, say, from
foliage and other entities.

I tell you, your own thoughts and words can appear to inhabitants
of other systems like stars and planets to us.

Intensities of thought, light and shadow between us, contain
memories coiled, one within the other, through which I travel to
you, and yet are beautifully undetermined.

For what you say to me is not finished within my thought or
memory, but you grow within my memory and change, the way a
shadow extends as light passes over it in Akashic emptiness.

You grow through what I have to say to you, as a tree grows up
through space, then what I have to say changes.

That's why we need the identity of our physical forms.

Here, we don't know what's behind physical stars and planets.

3.

The tree encompasses its changing form, while ego, my self of
physical experience, looks in the past for something to recognize.

Flexibility would be the key word to another, since the experience
is plastic, and carries a larger identity.

When he looks into my eyes, she said, I see adoration that makes
me feel wonderful.

Mei-mei Berssenbrugge

Then, I can do things.

Here we mean sun, alteration, myself are actions, the culture of Tibet disappearing, a thousand hopes of David Foster Wallace.

Imbalance between identity's attempt to maintain and intrinsic drives results in an exquisite by-product, consciousness of self, so richly creating reality, which seems plastic, but continues like a light beam, an endless series of beams.

Creativity breaks through identity, and my awareness flows through transparency as spontaneous synchronous phenomena experienced with others today.

Its changing light and weather spectacles are fantastically aesthetic.

4.

The moment it sees me, the violet grows more deeply purple and luminous to me.

Its looking collapses violet frequency into a violet in the world, cohering attention and feeling.

What I perceive as a flower in woods may be the shadow of a flower-being's action in fairyland, a transcendent domain of potentia.

The transparency I imagine moving through is being through, not actually seen or touched, not the buzzing of a million invisible bees.

What you call feeling, like connective tissue or vibrating lines between us, represents this vitality, and I prefer the term vitality to time.

In fairyland, all violets are simultaneous.

Fission

Susan Daitch

J. ROBERT OPPENHEIMER SEEMED nervous when Chevalier, a French teacher at Berkeley, asked him if he would like to get in touch with a man who could pass scientific information on to the Soviets. They're at a party, they are all drinking what I imagine are martinis and highballs. Later Oppenheimer refuses to give Chevalier's name to General Groves, and then he does. During the moment of betrayal it's Christmas in Los Alamos, carols are sung in the background, and the patriotic General Groves looks very pleased and beefier than usual. It's Christmas and even the general's family doesn't know where he is, it's that secret. He asks Oppenheimer if he celebrates Christmas. Groves acknowledges that he knows Oppenheimer is Jewish as if that, too, were some kind of secret. He tells Groves they give presents to their children, and the television general looks relieved. During a commercial I called my mother. No, my mother answered, he couldn't have been at Los Alamos. She thought he did some theoretical work, maybe checked some math for the Manhattan Project, but he was in New Haven at the time, not Los Alamos. I asked my mother to call me back when the show was over, and we both returned to the television, several hundred miles apart. Edward Teller complains to Oppenheimer. He refuses to work with Niedermeyer. He wants to work alone. The last time I saw my father alive I had been reading about the McCarthy hearings and had asked him about them, but I didn't ask him how he knew Teller. Perhaps I thought I'd ask him another time or on the next visit, not knowing this was to be the last one. After he died I found a letter Teller had written him in 1952 inviting him to Livermore Laboratories in California to work on some kind of computer. In my father's short reply, he turned the job down, writing that he was no longer interested in doing classified work. In the unflattering television scene, Teller is angry at Oppenheimer. He wants his own laboratory. He insists that he must work alone to the extent it's possible.

At eleven o' clock my mother called me back. Her voice sounded hollow, and I assumed it was because the program reminded her of my father, but the answer wasn't as simple as that. He rarely discussed what he did. *The names are all familiar, but I can't remember details.* In 1945 my father was twenty years old, and they hadn't even met yet. You weren't supposed to talk about what you did, so it remained a mystery, but the names were all familiar to my mother.

Before she met my father, she had gone out with a man who'd been to school in Germany with Klaus Fuchs, the spy. *It seemed romantic and dangerous even though we hardly knew what Fuchs had done.* Many exiles came to live in New Haven, but my mother's family were Russian-Yiddish speakers, working class, the kind of *ostjuden* the Germans barely recognized. She remembered the physicists were all eccentric in different ways, not just because many had been refugees, but they were just odd. After the war, in movies, in comics, scientists had German accents, flyaway hair, wore funny clothes, and were absentminded, like Peter Sellers as Dr. Strangelove, or Professor Barnhardt in *The Day the Earth Stood Still*. Strangers in the American house who had turned the world upside down, they were easy targets, and, without their knowledge, they provided a subject of parody, an image that has far outlasted their early years in America.

Oppenheimer, tall and elegant, presented a very different image, but some of the physicists my mother remembered were uncomfortable, awkward, sometimes went a bit mad. There was one who thought people were sending messages about him coded in taps produced by radiators; another, a good friend of my father's, had seen the explosions on Bikini Atoll and ended up making potholders in Connecticut sanatoriums. I played with his children. There was a man who fit the Barnhardt model who visited my parents in the midsixties and would only eat kosher food. My mother didn't have any so he would eat only a banana and a glass of milk. Hearing this story on the telephone over twenty years after the visit I imagined a man in a wrinkled suit and gray hat kept on indoors, sitting silently in my mother's upstate New York kitchen, a fire going in the fireplace whose stones had fossils etched in them, far from anything familiar to him.

> There were names like Fermi, Wigner, and Teller, Rabi, another queer name, Szilard or something like that—but I have the impression they came over here, and probably imbued with a certain anti-Nazi fervor that tended to stimulate thinking, and it is that type of mind we certainly needed then.
> —John J. McCloy, chairman of the board of the Chase National Bank. Assistant Secretary of War to Henry L. Stimson. 1946.

He didn't talk about it and that's what was upsetting to my mother, more than the names that jar our memory. This was a part of his life, before he met her, long before I was born, about which we knew very little.

We were sitting in the kitchen talking as if he might walk in any minute. Two days after he died, when my sisters were asleep, my mother told me that she was not his first wife. The woman of whom I'd had no clue whatsoever until that moment had met him while they were both still in school, and it had been a brief marriage that ended badly. She was said to be a *mieskeyt*, which means frankly ugly, a sourpuss, but from a rich family, and she had gone to graduate school, something that wasn't possible for my mother. According to the story, she didn't want to accompany him to Paris in 1947, where he went to work with Louis de Broglie, so they were divorced. Who wouldn't want to go to Paris? When they first met one another, my mother's family knew no one who got divorced, and my grandmother had said, *Zolle eir gane vyhter*, let him take his business elsewhere.

He had died so suddenly, the telephone rang and he was gone, that I didn't believe it was quite true. Death was a rumor, a mistake, somebody got it wrong. Disbelief about his death was translated into shock about a previous marriage, secret and never discussed.

The television physics lab props look archaic yet vaguely reminiscent of childhood memories. Instruments appear almost primitive, made of wood and glass rather than plastic or metal. There are slide rulers lying around, but no pocket calculators, no computers as they're usually represented in movies. The red line tracking a graph has the aura of a scientific antique.

The FBI takes pictures of Leo Szilard as he meets Oppenheimer, and as he meets another refugee, a woman. An agent leans out of his car and snaps the pictures. On the television the eight-by-ten black-and-white pictures follow one after another as they are slapped on top of General Groves's desk.

When I opened his file J. Edgar Hoover's signature blared like a car alarm on a quiet street. It seemed to say, you can float along humming all kinds of vague possible interpretations of a person's life and motivation, and then one name says it's all serious business, unpleasant business, prying, perhaps making life impossible.

> You are instructed to conduct an immediate, thorough, dis-
> creet investigation concerning the character, associations,
> and loyalty of the above-named individual in accordance with
> the Atomic Energy Act of 1946. Conduct Full Investigation.

It was as if he were brought back in some perverse way through his file, which turned into a sort of federal Aspern Papers, an impossible mystery to solve. A form letter enclosed in the envelope stated that there was one part of the file that was not being sent to me. It was not in Washington and contained accusations that could not be proved. I have no idea where this other file is, or how I might be able to get it. I'm not even sure I want to know what the unproven or un-provable accusations might be. During the Clinton years, a friend told me he had no intention of writing for his file. He had heard that parts or entire files are made up so it seemed to him that there was no point in digging up what, in his opinion, would certainly contain little more than fabrication. If I can believe him, then I'm back where I started. I don't know what is apocryphal and what is authentic. The papers I received contained a skeletal photocopied map of my father's life: jobs, addresses, schools attended. I discovered the name of his first wife. Her family, the report said, was from New York. I looked up the name in the Manhattan telephone book. There were five of them scattered around the borough, one with her initial, but I would never call.

> ███████████ stated that P. had married a girl in Providence,
> Rhode Island, sometime after the war, but that it turned out
> to be an unhappy marriage and the couple is now divorced.
> He stated that he had never heard exactly what the grounds
> of divorce were, but that he felt it was not P.'s fault since it
> seemed to him as though the girl forced herself on P.
> Both persons were studying for the doctor of philosophy
> degrees; and to ███████████'s knowledge, she had agreed to
> accompany P. to Paris to complete his studies. After their
> marriage she changed her mind and refused to go to France
> with P. After only three or four months of married life P. sued
> her for divorce because of her refusal to remain with him.
> ███████████ stated that he believed P. to be of fine character,
> brilliant, loyal, and entirely reputable. He concluded that the
> above marriage was "just an unfortunate affair" and would
> recommend P. for any position of trust and confidence.

The FBI report said he was a serious smoker, but then, everybody was.

To see another woman referred to as my father's wife seemed like a mistake. It isn't really unusual, people get divorced all the time, but this was strikingly foreign to me, as if I were reading about a stranger, then I got used to it. According to the file, she remarried right away. Years later when I visited the Stasi Archives in the former East Berlin, where a great deal is accessible and easily found, I wondered again about the identity of those who informed, whose names were redacted in the only file I was able to obtain.

The United States Strategic
Bombing Survey

The Effects of Atomic
Bombs on Hiroshima and
Nagasaki

Chairman's Office 30 June 1946

I took a thin blue book out of the library. The concept of ground zero was the first idea that came to mind as I looked through the pictures. There was only one of a human being, a man whose cap shielded his head from radiation burns. On the right, cap on; on the left, cap off, before and after. The rest of the photographs were of buildings and landscapes. There are times I've walked around New York and wondered what the island looked like when there was nothing on it. Empty leveled fields where Fourteenth Street runs from Fifth Avenue to Avenue D, a few grassy knolls extending from Grand Central up Park Avenue, pine groves and stretches of sand extending from West Forty-second Street to what would later be called the Hudson River. It's a benign emptiness with trees and animals. The pictures in the blue book show a pancaked, devastated landscape. Some of the pictures are familiar and have passed into photographic history the way pictures of the Vietnam War and African famines have. Others are new to me.

All kinds of annotators were sent to observe and record the aftermath: architects, engineers, photographers, all engaged in a de-irradiated reproduction of the event, an eerie simulacrum. A vast flatness, full of broken objects, building parts, impossible to identify. Impossible to say: That's a column, that was a doorjamb. What had been streets was filled with tile, brick, stone, corrugated iron, machinery, plaster, and stucco. The pictures seem similar to garbage-strewn lots in the middle of an active city, the kind littered with used, useless, smashed things emblematic of cultural endings, deliberate junk heap, deliberate contaminated marginalization. The caption read, *Like a graveyard with not a tombstone standing.* . . . Hiroshima was a city of six islands joined by eighty-one bridges. To read that sentence is to imagine a beautiful city even if it was in fact industrial and militant.

The catalog of before and after continued. The state of rails, electrical works, sewer systems was all documented. Two hundred and ten thousand out-of-town newspapers were brought in to "brace morale." Who read them? According to the report, the effect of radiation on living tissue was not yet understood, but minute data on physical problems, septic bronchopneumonia, blood count, skin problems, numbers of pierced eardrums were detailed. The photographs reveal more than listings and tables.

. . . *scarring and peeling of granitic rock, almost one mile from ground zero.* A shadow of a hand valve appeared on a wall at Hiroshima. Radiant heat instantly burned away paint except where heat rays hadn't been accidentally blocked. Funny shadows were marked on the concrete walls that remained. The skeletal remains of the Mitsubishi Steel and Arms Works looked like a series of collapsed Ferris wheels or roller-coaster tracks. The report seemed to come to the conclusion that reinforced concrete (they were not yet called fallout shelters) would protect people if far enough from ground zero, *although against a full and sustained attack they would be ineffectual palliatives.*

A book by Chevalier on a nearby shelf contradicts, in some ways, the television depiction of Oppenheimer's betrayal. My father is getting lost in this. The mystery is leading to other mysteries, yet they all lead back to the question what did he think of the people involved with this? Had he never worked on another defense project or had he never worked on one to begin with? I knew him so well, or thought that I did, how could I not know this? For months, the dog sniffed around my father's chair looking for him, and in this trying to remember, I'm not sure I'm doing much better. Thinking, like the dog, that he still might be around somewhere, and in trying to remember, coming up with fragments discussed over black coffee at Dunkin' Donuts or an image of piles of change at the library photocopying machine while he helped me photocopy a French biography of Delacroix.

*

Home movies: the Physics Department picnic. I would guess it is 1963 or '64. The women, the wives, stand on one side in plaid shorts and cat-eye sunglasses, the men, the physicists, stand apart, talking among themselves, a few children run around. When Lawrence won the Nobel Prize in physics, the first thing he did was to buy his wife a washing machine. My mother hated department picnics. Other home movies, my mother pushes my youngest sister down a slide. She's about three, in a snowsuit with a pointed hood that makes her look like a small red star, like a Crockett Johnson character. My father catches her at the end of the slide. The expression I love you to pieces lingers. No one in my family would have interpreted this expression literally, but the idea slips a little; for a physicist those words come so close to having only a literal meaning that there may be some irony embedded in the phrase, even if it's only an unconscious irony. Victor Navasky wrote, "The collective memory is often preserved in tales passed on from one generation to the next." He was discussing what screenwriters, blacklisted after refusing to testify before the House Un-American Activities Committee, decided to tell or, in many cases, to withhold from their children. What was it that we weren't told, or was there nothing to tell in the first place?

In 1945, in Boston, a friend of my father's noticed an ad in the paper for movie extras. The film *13 Rue Madeleine* with James Cagney was being shot in Boston; men in United States Navy uniforms were needed, and they had all the qualifications, so they went down to the set. One man was needed who could speak French and operate some sort of radio the prop department had set up for sending signals to the resistance. Since my father could do both, he got the part. Occasionally various members of my family have gone to revival houses or stayed up late to watch *13 Rue Madeleine* on television, but no one has ever seen him perform. The story is not apocryphal; my grandfather has said he ended up on the cutting-room floor, the boys really did go down to the set, and my father really was used as an extra. If he was in the navy, only twenty years old, in Boston performing in a James Cagney movie, then he couldn't have been in Los Alamos discussing implosion with Hans Niedermeyer.

My father didn't like to be called doctor; he thought the title made him sound like a fake. He didn't like awards, he didn't like to speak in public. He wouldn't have said he was involved in something he had no part of whether it was the first nuclear explosion or a James Cagney movie. It was only his back that they shot anyway, my grandfather said, but from what I can remember, it's only a shadow that taps out the code.

The Validity of the Born-Oppenheimer Approximation. High Energy Nucleon-Deuteron Scattering. Semiclassical Approximation to Coulomb Excitation Integrals. Reprints of pieces he wrote for *The Physical Review* from 1951 to 1956, clipped together with rusty paper clips, were in a drawer with letters including the one from Teller. His thinking life was so different from the thinking life of anyone I know or anything I can imagine. In the drawer was also a piece written by Helen Bailey, an Australian friend involved in nuclear disarmament. She had written shortly after his death, *Finally I came, through being pushed somewhat by Paul, to realize that the greatest threat to our health, welfare, and happiness was the threat of nuclear war if not nuclear war itself.* It seemed like the kind of argument he would make; the economics of the thing are nearly as damaging as the thing itself. My blind spots weren't so much the articles he wrote that I couldn't read as the unreliability of my own memory. The contradictory evidence and false trails may have been of my own devising. A few days after his death a distant cousin I'd never seen before came to the house. She had barely sat down before she began to talk about her work, and when she finished she left with her parents as if a gust of nuclear winter had come, establishing an example of how funerals, shiva, whatever, aren't only sites of mourning but a platform for people to advertise themselves, perhaps because they don't know quite what else to do. She was working on Star Wars because, *if the technology is available, I think the United States should have it.*

"Often," Helen said, "no one wants to work on these projects. It's the only work women physicists can get."

What did it mean to become a theoretical physicist in the early 1940s, before there was any notion that isotopes might be split? To decide to do this kind of work at school, to know that this was what you planned to do, even in 1939, even at the age of eighteen, was to decide to go someplace your family couldn't follow you. Few knew the language itself. How is splitting an atom like furthering divisions in a fractious family? Bits of stories: Abe Borenstein's hot seat. One night a week my grandfather used to play poker with various male relatives. There was a cousin he didn't like, one who complained about never having any money. It was the Depression, but my grandfather, who was incapable of sympathizing with anyone, did not have much sympathy for this cousin in particular. My father, about eight or nine at the time, was experimenting with electricity, building a Jacob's ladder and wiring things. The evening before the game he rigged Borenstein's poker chair, the one he always sat in, running wires under the rug, then at the appropriate time crouched on the floor around the corner. The game was in progress, the cousin was in his chair, my father threw the switch. Nothing happened. Puzzled, he left the room. Later my father's older brother walked by and innocently flipped the switch without really knowing where it led or what it was for. Poor Abe Borenstein received a mild electric shock. My grandfather told the story with glee for many years, long after all the participants were dead. He was the last survivor of all those poker games.

My father spent a lot of time with his grandfather, an inventor of mechanical gadgets. Of his thirty grandchildren he was the favorite because, it was said, he and Paul spoke the same language. He had a license in almost everything, was very dashing, looked like a kind of Omar Sharif of Roxbury, and was also known for "giving the ladies a lot of service." Among his inventions was a cap to fit over a single gas flame that would reconfigure the fire into a circle rather than a single jet. A group of men came from New York to help him sell the thing, but apparently stole the idea, and he never saw any money from it. "He wasn't interested in making a living. His children supported him." My grandfather often repeated this statement, emphasizing that his father-in-law was a man who didn't care about money and never had any. Through his inventions he met Oliver Wendell Holmes, and when my grandfather was studying anatomy insisted he borrow a skull from Dr. Holmes. My grandfather remembered going to fetch the skull in Boston, and he kept it for decades, but it has since disappeared.

I want to ask him about my father's first wife, but I can't bring myself to do it. He doesn't know that I know, and it's easier to talk about Abe Borenstein's hot seat and the lost spare skull of Oliver Wendell Holmes.

263

Susan Daitch

When I was in college I became interested in the three daughters of Karl Marx. Eleanor, the youngest, described Marx as a brilliant, formidable father who loved his children, although they grew up to have unhappy marriages and difficult affairs with men. Ten years later I reread a description of Eleanor Marx's discovery that Freddy Demuth, working-class son of their housekeeper, was actually her half brother. It had always been assumed that Engels was his father. Engels was dying of throat cancer. He could barely speak. Near the end, when she was finally alone with him, Engels wrote the name of Freddy's father on a piece of slate. In the years remaining before Eleanor committed suicide, they became very close. A Freddy Demuth, a lost relative who can fill in all kinds of answers, who wouldn't want to meet your own private long-lost mystery relation?

The superbomb debate from 1946 to 1949 was acrimonious. Oppenheimer opposed its construction. His analogy of the United States and the Soviet Union as two scorpions in a bottle became well known. Teller seems to have been bomb crazy. During the summer of 1952 Lawrence Livermore became the second American nuclear laboratory. Teller, Lawrence, and Alvarez wanted to respond to the Soviet A-bomb. The superbomb was exploded in September 1952 in the Eniwetok Atoll. One book on the debate written by a physicist who chose to go to Livermore Laboratory said he was seduced by the idea of working for the "heroes" and "legends" of twentieth-century big science. He knew what he was getting into and twenty years later expressed regrets. My father turned Lawrence Livermore down. By choosing not to work on the "super," my father missed the giants, the big guns of the moment and their history, but he had his reasons. During this period he worked on a project that would use the heat given off by a nuclear reactor to desalinate ocean water. The plan was to be first implemented in southern California and later in India. There were trips to La Jolla and San Francisco, and we would meet him at the airport with enormous anticipation. It didn't matter when his suitcase was lost, or he picked up the wrong one by mistake. One spring there was a fatal crash in San Diego. We were afraid his flight had been involved, and my grandmother, who was visiting us that weekend, locked herself in her room. She wouldn't speak to anyone until he called, as if the crash had been entirely our fault. My youngest sister was a few months old, and my mother held her while we listened to the radio. Finally he called; he hadn't been on the plane. My grandmother came out of her room dressed in red and black. She wouldn't speak to any of us, but got into her Kaiser (the only thing wrong with it was the name) with a rolled-up Tabriz carpet she'd given to us (well, not really) and drove back to Boston in the middle of the night.

The desalination project proved too expensive and was never completed. A few years later he abandoned physics, turning to biomedical engineering. The last project he worked on involved constructing computer models based on certain disease and acquaintance networks. It was still the early days of computers when discs were the size of dinner plates and screens were entirely black, chalky letters and symbols blinked out of the monitors' depths. One might not know anyone who had a case of cancer X, but one might know someone who knew someone who did. There was a little bit of finding the man who shook the hand of the man who shook the hand of Napoleon in it, but patterns did emerge. His group at the Centers for Disease Control in Atlanta decided to study venereal diseases, and one day a pile of information arrived from a health center in Stockholm. Among the computer printouts were fliers given to patients that explained prevention and treatment of sexually transmitted diseases, and among these pamphlets, which had no connection to the epidemiology project, was a mobile in the shape of a bumblebee. One of my sisters pulled it out from among the papers left on the table, hung the cardboard bee from a ceiling light, and went outside to play. The bee was penis shaped, its wings were testicles, and its black stripes were Swedish words that translated into a warning about being stung. We learned this because a Swedish woman happened to visit my mother that afternoon. My sister had long since bicycled off on her paper route, when my mother and her friend walked into the kitchen, greeted by the minatory bee, smiling and twirling in the breeze.

The scientists of *E.T.*: large teams of smiling men sitting before bluish computers, benign and cooperative, a few have trouble unpacking a globe and it rolls into the hall. This is friendly science, although it will become ruthless. In *The Fly* and *Altered States*, they are turned inward, though diabolical, they experiment on themselves. In the early eighties this was the image of the scientist, no longer quite Strangelove or Barnhardt.

"Peter Kapitza, a Russian physicist, built a laboratory outside

Moscow to do research involving high magnetic fields and extremely low temperatures." General Groves is trying to make a point. I find this impossible to visualize, and although I know these experiments don't exist in a vacuum and are based on historical precedents, I can't help but think literally and stupidly of horseshoe magnets and snow. On television General Groves persuaded Truman to drop the bomb; our boys, he seemed to say over and over, our boys, our boys.

The house was built in 1961, the year the Thresher, a nuclear-powered submarine, sank in the Atlantic. One of my most vivid early memories of that house was watching a huge wreath thrown onto the ocean on *The Today Show*. They showed pictures of all the sailors who had been trapped in the submarine, and I ran to catch the school bus with a sense of what claustrophobia might be. There was half a fallout shelter in the cellar that had only two cinder-block walls, no door, and was entirely useless. It contained no canned food, only chemicals for printing photographic negatives and a single electric light. My father used it as a darkroom. He began to print color film, which was more complicated, and made a tape of my youngest sister's voice describing each step of the process in the dark; agitate for three minutes, her voice said, and she was followed by three minutes of music. An enlarger sat on a table with a single drawer. The drawer was filled with photographic paper that has since been eaten by mice. After he died I found three half dollars under the paper, each minted the year each of us was born. The chemicals have turned into brown syrup, and my mother, a formidable cleaner who doesn't believe in shrines, declared or otherwise, wants us to clean the place out. Still none of us go into the dark, cold chamber, and the half dollars remain under puffballs of paper chewed by mice.

Thirty years later while waiting at the San Francisco airport I saw three little girls greet their father, running down the hall as he dropped his bags to hug them all at once. He had a mustache and wore a tie and jacket. They spoke Farsi, but I watched them as if they were simultaneously ghosts of my own and enviable strangers.

The New Year
Michael J. *Lee*

EARLY ONE MORNING, a long time ago, I was bathing in the Okeh River, near downtown Hernville, gently scrubbing the most neglected parts of my body with an old bandanna I had recently acquired. And though I was alone, and the water was cold, I kept myself warm by remembering all the memories I had made the night before, when I was out on the town, ringing in the new year in style. And when I had finished replaying all those memories, and each, in its own way, had brought me a small flicker of warmth, I found that I still had more of myself to cleanse, so I changed the direction of my thinking, from memories to more tangible items, and began listing all the things I was thankful for in my life:

1. The recent return of my health.
2. The range of my mobility.
3. The fact that there was always someone listening to my prayers.
4. The fact that I had not been murdered at any time the past year.
5. My couch.

And once I had finished listing these things, I found that I still had a few more crevices that needed attention, so I continued scrubbing, working the bandanna over myself, as quickly but as industriously as I could, even as I felt my arms and legs losing feeling. And finally, realizing that I really was fighting a downhill battle, knowing that in order to save my precious life I would have to emerge from the water before I got myself to a level of cleanliness I could live with, I tried, in one last push, to distract myself again, and began formulating some resolutions for the new year, hoping they might grant me that last bit of warmth I needed to finish, but before I could even begin to envision the year ahead, and all that I might accomplish in it, I heard a voice call down to me from way up on the bridge.

"Hey," it said. "I know what you're doing."

"I'm just taking my bath for the day," I said. "No big deal."

"Didn't look like bathing to me."

"Oh, don't pretend to know anything about my morning routine."

"Looked like frolicking," he said. "And my name is Moany."

"Well," I said, "if you were down here, you'd be able to see clearly," and while I wholeheartedly agreed with what I was saying, I instantly regretted saying it; I didn't really feel like engaging with Moany, or anyone at all, for that matter, especially after having such a social time the night before.

"I still say you were frolicking," Moany insisted, as he—a little recklessly, I thought—stepped sideways down the steep embankment to meet me. Once he reached the riverbank, I looked at him closely to make sure he was safe to associate with. Much to my relief, Moany was thin and little. I would really like to pay him more tribute in my description of him, because of how nice a person he was, but he was quite ugly. His only possession, beyond his clothes, was a little jar full of clear liquid that he kept under his arm.

"What made you think I was frolicking?" I said.

"You were waving your hands around."

"I was cleansing myself," I said, feeling my muscles beginning to spasm. "It's too cold to be frolicking." I told him then that I would talk a lot more candidly if he would give me a moment to put on my outfit: my jeans and my jacket. Moany was silent, though he seemed to understand my needs, politely turning away as I emerged from the river.

After I was dressed, I invited Moany to join me on my couch. When I'd first moved under the bridge, there was plenty of unoccupied space for the taking, but at the same time, there wasn't any real cozy spot I could call my own—a place where I could sleep, eat, and get some thinking done, while not constantly having to readjust my position due to the sharp stones on the riverbank. So I really was overjoyed, and at the same time very humbled, when, one day, on the bridge above me, a head-on collision occurred between a furniture truck and a truck carrying combustibles, and as a result of the tragic accident, a smoky but brand-new leather couch tumbled down the embankment, end over end, until it came to rest, right side up, at my feet.

"Say you were frolicking," said Moany. "What would you have been frolicking for?"

"I don't know," I said. "Maybe I would have been frolicking at the fact that we have a new year upon us."

"And why would that be cause for frolicking?" said Moany.

"I'm not sure," I said.

He offered me a drink from his jar, which was full of tepid tap or perhaps river water. I drank one sip, and then told him that I would be fine for a while. I was particular about my drinking water.

"I had a pretty good time last night," I said.

"I'm not sure I like sitting here," Moany said. "You better hurry up and tell me about your New Year's Eve."

He really wasn't the kindest of listeners, but it was rare that I had one at all, so I kept going. "I was downtown for the festivities," I said. "Usually, I stay here under the bridge during holidays, because they tend to get me a little down, and I don't like having to put on a public face when I'm having trouble wearing my private one. But last night, though I was feeling just about as down as ever, and though I tried to sleep it off, all the exploding fireworks kept snapping me awake, and I decided that if I was going to get through the night I needed to be around some kind—any kind—of life, so I went down to Big Square. I also decided that I wasn't going to let my mood spoil anyone else's that night: As I walked, I put on a smile, and held it there, and if ever I felt it slipping a little, I would do my best to raise it back up for the benefit of those around me. There were crowds of people there, in Big Square, all dressed in costumes and acting out of character in a fun way, and with my wide smile I think I fit right in. The strange thing was, at some point—right around the time a complete stranger gave me a paper bag with a party hat, a noisemaker, and a warm bottle of beer inside—I realized that the public face I was wearing was equal to my private one, that the smile I was smiling was actually genuine, and that I was having a good time without even trying. And after that, I found that my legs were more limber than I was used to them being, and felt myself starting to dance, first just by myself, but then with anyone nearby, until, gradually, as my moves became more inventive, I could sense that every eye was on me and every smile directed toward me, and I watched as those nearby formed a circle around me."

Moany's face began to darken when I described the dancing—out of jealousy, I supposed. I started to think twice about continuing with my story. He was in pretty bad shape.

"Go on," he said. "It's fun for me to live through your fun."

As long as he was willing to hear it, I really was more than happy to tell it. "Well, by the end of the night, I was up on people's shoulders, and they were telling me that they were going to make me their king, and all sorts of other friendly promises that I never really expected that they would make good on. And then the hour grew really late, and I found that my only company left in Big Square was the garbage that people had left behind, and I came back to the bridge, still smiling wide even though I was alone."

Moany didn't make any real effort to hide his frown. "That sounds like a good time," he said. "Have you ever had a girlfriend?"

"I don't know," I said. "There was an old woman who used to lean over the bridge and show me her breast every day for a while, but I'm not sure if you would count that."

"I wouldn't count that," said Moany.

I sensed a sad story coming on, and shifted my hips a little lower into the couch to get more comfortable.

"While you were out dancing with the crowds," Moany said, "my girlfriend and I were roaming the streets, dancing for money."

"I've always wanted to dance professionally," I said. That I haven't really is one of the major regrets of my life.

"It was just a dance," he said bitterly. "I would lie on the concrete, my girlfriend would press play on the boom box, then she would climb on my back and sway. When I couldn't take her weight anymore, I would tap her ankle and we would switch."

"Moany," I said, "I am not a dancing authority, but it seems like this dance was very simple."

"We tried the more elaborate stuff before," Moany said, "but no one donated. So we settled on the dance I just told you about. Ugliness is in anyway. And we did well last night, until the boom box broke. After that, we started to head for home."

"Where do you live?" I said. I wanted to make sure he still knew that I was interested in him and his story.

"My girlfriend and I live in Balltank, not far from here. We live under a bridge, pretty much the same as this one. Last night, my girlfriend and I were walking home after making a good amount of money, and we passed by a shop, where we saw the most magnificent dog in the window. I asked my girlfriend several times how much she thought the dog cost, but she assumed I wanted to buy the dog, and told me that we needed a new boom box before we went ahead and got a pet. But that wasn't what I wanted at all. I just wanted to know the price of the damn dog, just to get an idea. She told me if I went into the shop, she was going to leave for the electronics store without me and start shopping for a new boom box. I didn't believe her, and went in the shop, and I found the manager in the back. He had more dogs around him, but none were as good as the one in the window. I asked him how much the dog was, and he kind of sniffed at me and told me I couldn't afford it. I told him I didn't want to buy it, but that I wanted to know the damn price. He told me fourteen dollars. I was satisfied, for the moment. When I left the store, the streets were empty, and I found my girlfriend at the electronics store a couple blocks away. She was talking to a clerk and choosing between two boom boxes. She asked me for my opinion, but I didn't want to give it. I was just thinking about the dog. I told her that even though the manager at the shop sniffed disdainfully at me at first, he quoted me a price of fourteen dollars. She still thought I wanted the damn dog, even though I told her again that I didn't. Then she held up two boom boxes and told me to pick, and I told her I'd rather get the money we made that night and take it back to the shop and just show the manager that we could afford the damn dog. She told me that if I went back to the shop with the money that she would leave me, and I could find my own way home. Like a fool, I ripped the money out of her hands and ran back to the shop, which the manager had closed, and was locking up. I showed him the money and proved that my girlfriend and I could afford it, but he told me to put my money away because he'd just sold the damn dog to a loving owner, and when I asked him if he could see that I could have afforded the damn dog in the window, he told me that he didn't give a damn. He made me very upset."

"Some people really don't want to get to heaven," I said, though I felt bad about casting judgment on a person who was only real to me as a character in Moany's story.

"You're right about that," said Moany. "But it gets worse. When I got back to the electronics store, my girlfriend was gone, and so was the clerk, and by the time I made it back to the bridge in Balltank, they were already done making love, and were talking sweet to one another. I knew I had no say, and the whole thing was my fault, so I gave the money to my girlfriend and started walking. I made the Hernville county line just as the sun was peeking up, and then I saw you frolicking as I was crossing the bridge."

"What did the dog look like?" I said. "I was not frolicking."

"The dog in the window was beautiful and proud," he said. "I'd seen others that good in my life, but not for a long time."

"Moany," I said, "tell me the truth. Did you really want to buy that dog in the window?"

"No."

"It's OK if you did. Sometimes I want things that I shouldn't have, like a big brass bed, for example, instead of this couch. I think that's pretty normal."

"I didn't," Moany said, "and what made me leave my girlfriend was I realized that no matter what, no matter how long we stayed together or how many people we entertained over the years, I knew I'd never be able to convince her that I didn't want that damn dog. Now, if someone had given me the damn dog for free, I certainly would have cared for him, but I just couldn't justify spending money on him, beautiful as he was."

"What do you do now?" I said.

"I don't know," said Moany. "I don't know, and I don't really care what happens."

"You're depressed, aren't you?"

"I guess so."

"The doctors at the clinic will give you free trial packs of medicines," I said.

"What clinic?"

"The one in Big Square."

"I like medicines," Moany said, "when I can get them."

"They don't always tell you what the medicines do, so you have to be careful, but I'm sure they could give you a couple of trial packs to experiment with until you find the one you like."

"How many medicines are in a trial pack?"

"Two or three tops," I said. I was happy to have gotten him off the subject of the dog. "And when they run out you can go back to the clinic, and if they have any more trial packs, they'll give them to you, no problem."

"What if they don't have any more of the medicines that I like?"

"Well, doctors and drug companies are always working hard to develop new medicines, so they'll have something comparable, I bet."

"What do you take?" said Moany.

"Oh, I don't take anything at the moment. I pray."

"You sure know a lot about medicines."

"When I get really down, financially speaking, and when my prayers take a bit longer to get answered than I had originally expected, the clinic lets me take out their garbage and restock the paper-towel dispenser for a little change. The doctors try and push those trial packs on me, but I always tell them that trial packs don't put hot meals in my stomach."

"So are you saying I should pray or go to the clinic for medicines instead?"

He had me in a tough spot. I had been given a lot of medicines from doctors before, and they did work pretty well, until the clinic had to shut down for a while and I had to learn to live without them. It was hard, but I made it through, thanks to prayer. When the clinic re-opened I didn't need the medicines at all, just the money they would give me for my janitorial work.

"I guess either some praying or some medicines or a combination of both would be good for you," I said. I wished I could have been more helpful to him, but at the end of the day, people just have this sad private pain that is impossible for anyone else to access. That's exactly why I get so excited about heaven and its promises.

"The more I think about it," said Moany, "the more I realize how much I wanted that damn dog in the window. I don't know why I couldn't be honest with myself."

I wanted to respond, but thought there was a good chance that my words would not have been kind ones, so I started looking at the river again, just watching the trash swirl around. When I turned back to look at Moany again, I was surprised to see that he'd taken a knife out of his pants. I thought there was only about a fifty percent chance that he was going to use it to murder me, given how little I had, but I didn't want to offend him, so I got up from the couch and casually pretended that an insect had bitten me under my jeans. But then Moany just kind of dragged the knife across his own throat until he bled so much that he lost his balance and fell off the couch and onto the rocky bank. It was all over quickly. I really hope that was the most nonsensational way to tell you about the death of Moany. It was a surprising moment for me, and I wanted to make you feel my surprise, but not to the point that you thought I enjoyed talking about it. It was a terrible thing to see.

I buried Moany and the knife behind some shrubs that were grow-ing along the bank. I really didn't know what to think. I had just met this man about an hour before, and we had had a nice conversation and now here I was throwing the last of the topsoil over his bald head because his bandanna had come off in the fall. I began a prayer over his grave, a long and sweet one, because I thought that Moany, espe-cially because he was able to admit his desire for the dog, deserved to get to heaven. About three-quarters of the way through the prayer, though, I got this spooky feeling, and decided to stop, because the last thing I wanted to happen was for Moany to wake up one fine morning in a place that he never wanted to go in the first place. Some people are scared of heaven, and you have to respect that.

I tried to go about my day as I normally would: I cooked a modest breakfast, replayed all the positive memories from my life, and continued to list everything I was thankful for. I considered another bath in the river, but didn't feel like disrobing again, and besides, the morning had only grown colder since Moany's demise, so I settled for just rinsing the blood off my hands. After I dried them on my bandanna, I got back on the couch and tried to take my mind off the image of Moany's empty eyes just staring at the dirt over him. I knew his brain was not getting oxygen anymore, but for some reason, I really believed that his eyes could still see. Before falling asleep for an afternoon nap, I was finally able to formulate my new year's resolutions. They were:

1. Bathe more frequently.
2. Establish better relationships with people.
3. Spend less time on the couch.

I don't want you to think that Moany had a negative effect on my life. And I don't want you to think that it was significant that Moany's death happened on New Year's Day. Actually, looking at it one way, although the relationship hadn't been given time to develop, I had already made a good start on keeping my second resolution. Really, all I mean to say is that Moany's death was certainly sad, but I was sure it didn't have any symbolic meaning or anything terrible like that. To the living, death doesn't bring symbols when it comes, it just brings death. But I also don't want to suggest that his death was meaningless, as some might argue. It might have been meaningless, in the grand scheme of things, but even now I find it hard to refer to Moany's sudden death that way. I'll say it this way: The meaning of Moany's death has yet to become clear to me, but I know one day it will.

When I woke up from my nap, I heard a man calling to me from the bridge.

"I love you," he said.

"I love you too," I said. During all the years I lived under the bridge, I found that it was never a bad idea to respond in this way.

"I am the mayor and I want to speak with you," he said.

It isn't every day that you get to meet a mayor, so I climbed up the embankment and met him on the bridge. He wore a suit and tie but had covered his face with a bandanna—on account of the dust, he said—and spoke to me from behind it. Next to him sat a magnificent dog, and I immediately thought of the dog in the window. It might have been how well behaved this dog was or it might have been the fact that Moany's death was still fresh in my mind. It would have been an incredible coincidence if the dog Moany had seen in the window was not only now owned by the mayor, but was also standing before me, in all its glory, so soon after Moany's death.

After I introduced myself, I asked about the dog. "That is a beautiful dog," I said. "I wonder how long you've had him."

"Several years," the mayor said.

"Oh," I said. That just about settled it. It wasn't the same dog, unless the mayor was a liar, and I don't think that he was, given how upstanding he appeared. But even if the mayor was a liar, I realized that it still might not have been the same dog. You might call this some sort of epiphany on my part.

"Are you a citizen of this country?" asked the mayor.

I nodded yes.

"Are you a resident of this state?"

Again I nodded yes, but was less sure.

"And you live full-time in this county?"

I nodded again.

"Are you happy with the life you lead in this city?"

I shrugged. "I had fun downtown on New Year's Eve."

"Do you know I'm running for reelection in the spring?"

I nodded no.

"Do you know why I think you should vote for me?"

Again I nodded no.

"Prepare for my stump speech," he said.

"I have a couch down there," I said. "I don't own it, but I think of it as mine, and I would be a lot more comfortable listening to you if I could sit on it."

He agreed, and we walked down the embankment together. I held on to his arm out of politeness, because he was pretty old, and because, as I've said, the decline was surprisingly steep. When I was good and settled on the couch, I told him I was ready. He gave me his stump speech. It was like a prayer, a prayer better than any one I could have dreamed up, even if I had been given all the time in the world. I pledged my vote to him then and there. As repayment for listening to his speech, the mayor agreed to help me unbury Moany, just to see if his dog had any reaction to his corpse. But after all our digging, we found Moany's grave empty, and I realized with joy that he'd been called home to heaven. Then, wouldn't you know it, right there under the Okeh River Bridge, the mayor gave me a job in his reelection campaign, where I was paid to stand behind him at his rallies, smiling a wide, mostly genuine smile and representing a hopeful, new kind of voter. After he was reelected, I had his ear for the first part of his new term, and made sure that the New Year's cele-bration that year was even more elaborate than the one before it. I want to end this positively, on my uplifting time with the mayor, because I know that these kinds of moments are the only things peo-ple remember from the stories they hear. I want to leave you feeling good. But however you feel, good or bad, for some reason, right now, I feel the need to tell you that, selfish as it might seem, the most important reason I am telling this is because I want you to remem-ber me.

Surf a Tide of Weirdness
Anne Waldman

SHE WAS AND IS ALWAYS mentioned by someone or other I love or made love with as someone I resembled and as I took this to account in my technology of inscription, as I had questions, many questions, questions of her life, her life-in-mind and her life as one-who-played-so-many-others, as if in entropy of a death-drive one might say she kept the roles coming, so many to keep up with, so many others of myself as I resembled her. So many troubled others. "I" as phantom or "function," I as "factotum" or I as poet in my anterior subversive poet-structured activity, and many possible ulterior roles inspired by hers. Think of them. Count them, many to keep track of. Conglomerations of seductive tendencies, dangerous tendencies, where paper, cardboard, and ribbon is not your game. Rage. Heartbreak. Edgy. A sob sister not your game. A heartbreaker might be. A gun, a dagger, three furious volcanoes inside. A confused Nazi inside. Emanating a specter of myself that fills her show, fills her screen, fills her shoe I ask what size is she. That was my first question. Eight, eight and a half, narrow I'd guess. They look—those bodies and parts of bodies we project so much upon—larger on screen than they naturally are. And it's interesting to guess when you see a body in a doorway, when you see a body in a street, when you see the body walk across a room and sit down or open a door, hand on the brass doorknob what is the measurement of the rest of the architecture to that hand to that body to that face not to mention the dimensions of the room itself. Angles of relational strife. Someone figuring it all out behind the lens. Or stand-ins. They have to be similar in size. Especially in bed or naked, slaughtered on a floor. They might be creating smaller furniture for this very purpose. False props. Simulacra. They might ask the leading man to stand on a box to lift his height to proffer a kiss. And of her dress size I wonder. Not a twelve, which I have been now and then and sometimes eight, but tall and thin, an eight I'd say, an eight but tall eight. Or six, definitely a six. A narrow bust. Yes, six. Walking down a sandy beach, narrow hips, and she over sixty, that's what I like I was confessing just now, sexy over sixty. Another question was were there any Mongolian epicanthic folds in her genetic history.

All my life ones I love as I was saying comparing me to her and just last week one saying again when I had been in public space and done something publicly, oh you look so much like her do you know that? Your eyes and neck. And he had seen me in private space, and said that before, some years back, like her, like her. Your back, that was it, backing up now. A tattered tux crying, a uniform, an Italian wife of another Nazi, a young wife. Acting them out, sometimes with her neck in my mind. Rotten to the Core, a girl with a George in her title, a girl with Oz in her title. Boyish. Someone impish, someone testing you, provoking you to do some damage, or you might be someone (this is a difficult role now) who is with someone who just walks away. Disappears. Why? He had said, another he-I-loved-once had said—you resemble her neck or perhaps I wasn't hearing it right, or "What a neck, so much like hers—like C's," as if he knew her. Perhaps he did, he who too had acted many roles and loved many actresses, that's what we called them in our early years, tresses. And then he married one, a real one. There was a role now in memory to absorb and as I sat there thrilled, I was her neck, I was her hair, her slanted eyes, I was the color of her hair. I was not alone, a woman-alone-dreaming-of stardom because I had stardom, her acting the roles for me because he said, "You don't follow the money," was he implying that she did? A different klieg light and a pace, a voice, the way she lights the cigarette. I close my eyes now and visualize her. I know her. She does not follow the money.

Another question has to do with sex, the story of her real-in-life *ménage à trois*. I'll back off here again. I've never exactly lived in a *ménage à trois*, although there was a very close friendship with two men at once and one had a crush on the other the one who was with me and maybe I had been with this one before I was with the one I stayed with many years. We were what you might say carefree. We lived in the country where new mountains jut up from primal matter. Where tundra was ocean once, you may collect shards of seashells fourteen thousand miles above the sea. We drove together in an old truck. We all took peyote in the woods in an act of sympathetic magic ritual for a friend in coma and then because of that more psychic inscription and I am still wired after all these years, he's dead now that one that one I have mourned most of all my dead ones. I was discreet wanting not to know much about her private life, and I didn't or it would spoil the illusion of her as other, as double I might get my psyche in trouble. Simulacrum. I might retaliate on myself some injury accorded by an act of shame or frivolity. I don't want her to be frivolous. I want my simulacrum to read deep in literature and she plays that writer maybe my favorite role of hers the one who . . . yes, I've already hinted the plot. A writer of novels. Page 1: What did she type that very first take of the scene? That was another question. The circular aspect of what she was writing, was straight enough, but how did the character the writer behind the movie decide or did she as actor decide and had the leeway to type whatever she wanted, or with pen. Please don't say poetess. I don't mind actress. Not right now. Because one has that freedom of tresses, of abandon. The movies I have acted in are few. In *The Edge* I play an introspective but ignorant woman who walks by the beach and whose husband is an activist, maybe even qualifies as a terrorist, part of a plot to assassinate a president. This character does not know what is going on. I never take my clothes off—shy?—when we go to bed in the scene in our little home by the ocean in Deal, New Jersey. There was taking my shirt off my breasts are naked in *Brand X* opposite you, the one I played this scene with who was one who early said I resembled her. But I don't think you had met her yet. Then. Had you? That was another question. Then you went away and eventually married another one who plays roles, one of her best being one, a glamorous one, who cracks up, it's a biopic. Once she the true one my familiar, my other who lovers say resembles me, she the object of my obsession and she the object of their obsession and their attraction to me-as-her obsession (and I have to ask do they visualize her when they are with me?) who I address here, the one on whom I focus my attention to eyes and neck and back who ramps up the tension in real life or movie life said, "To discover what is normal, you need to surf a tide of weirdness."

Sitting here in a quiet house far away from a city. I do this too occasionally, get away to write. Like a lady novelist. Border line of prim cover and seething sex underneath. Was it all three of them, she the duchess, and one a model and one a . . . what was she? I digress. Many identities blur in celluloid. Many others also had questions of her. I only wondered because we were close in age and of that time. Her father was a NATO commander, that interested me. Fathers-in-war, daughters-of-the-long-ago-heroic-war. And then I was in the ladies-of-the-night scene in another movie filmed in Quebec with its red silk wallpaper and brothel vibe and playing it in red bra, a feather boa, and my line—I made it up—unscripted as it were—was "I'd rather be home reading a good book," and something about my red Tibetan Buddhist protection cord. "What does it protect you from?" "One's own ego" . . . did I say that? And later that same time when we were alone he said it too—"What does it protect you from?"—he another I loved—and also he said *You look so much like her.* I was sure he had met her by then. He lived near Hollywood and was one of the most famous people in the world.

Clone Poems
Jaime Robles

A girl enters an elevator to find another girl
within. The elevator floats above silence,
following gravity's urge, forming a bubble in time.
She faces east, she faces south:
She blinks, or perhaps that was only you, the watcher.
Seconds pass.
                          Doors open,
escalators carry figures down and down:
Song takes place elsewhere—in the corridor between opposites.

A woman sits facing elsewhere, only the light flickers:
she confesses that there are long landscapes,
narrow spaces between immense ceilings and floors stretching out,
reflecting silhouettes—both floor and ceiling red,
etched with mystical figures, multiple angel wings—
where no one moves.

*

(the imagination of free will + memory) equals self
divided from others but not minus matter . . .

self slithers across thought . . .

And mother equals zero, which is indivisible
from the self, which is one, and the other, which is 2.
Or any other number because n = n + 0 as
a = a

Or minus A equals A times—the opposite
of divided by (but in this case the results
are the same)—minus one.

Which is to say A times minus one equals A divided
by minus one,

as surely as mother = 0

*

Is this the danger of replication:
that the loved one never dies?
These many copies are not the same, although you may not see it,
mackled at the edges, color sliding thick over surfaces,
between collections of tangible or isolated objects,
lacking the definition of the original;
each copy degraded some undefined percent.
Or is it that the lover is left suspended,
knowing that some unutterable quality is gone:
That the mind, or was it the soul, has gone
elsewhere, if anywhere, and that waiting
is all that remains to the lover, waiting
until the body embrangled with memory
finally crumbles beyond recognition?

*

Jaime Robles

MIRRORS

Claimed not an instrument of enlightenment but illusion—
    light skittering across the surface or sinking
    into the silver backing, which
    echoes the body, tracing its substance in distant matte fields
    that are smooth and near featureless. Through space they reflect,

    lose form, cleaving three dimensions into two,
    snuggling gradations of shadow into line
    until all that's left is movement: a man walking through space

    slowly, seeing the same event over and over:
    the bird flying above becomes an oddly formed airplane,
    mechanical, a headless angel, a feathered gull—he subsumes
    flesh into thought and memory
    reflects that the body's beauty aligns itself with mirrors
    and shiny surfaces, pools formed by rain

*

On the other side of the one-way
mirror a man has lost his memory,
replaced with another's:

tears sparkle through the darkened glass

As she watches, her body:

        reflects in the looking glass

        in windows

283

Jaime Robles

up from rain-sheen'd streets

surface of the river under which she dives—

her body lifting finally toward its burnished image

Across the night-dark city
many-limbed doppel-
gängers multiply, whitely
proliferate: become human—
vanish

*

Unravel the window—
Beginning with the gleam of sunlight there
in the corner
near the wood frame

Pull a single thread of light

The clear barrier thickens. Air from
outside falters

unfolds like a letter,

falls in a heap

as a necklace of beads;

her hand curls shut, closed like a loose fist

*

. . . pulled into recurrence, gesture drowns itself deep into the brain, flesh and tissue's memory—love goes under. Repetition dividing mitochondrial from chaos, from terrors of the unpredictable—
What is the point of having a body, presenting open terrain and suggesting occult passageways? For you the observer, something perhaps edible, for him the artist, a reverie, erotic and subliminal. But for her? A past, a ticket to the park of humanity. She stepped out of it as easily as clothing, dropped splotches of her skin and frame, discarded fluids to sink into the earth's hard surface.

*

He wraps her naked shoulders in clothing, his clothing, which doesn't fit her but somehow shrinks to enfold the surfaces that are her body at the moment. Like the eye that only sees what it is focused on, that is to say the mind's eye, because the lens has no focus, is only a partition, curtained by a shutter, a fringed eyelid. The eye in order to see divides itself, discarding myriad simultaneous events—masked children standing in an urban alley, congested orange storm heads in fast flight across the sky, careening flocks of birds—enchains itself to the solitary, the composed field, the intersection.

Larghetto Intimacy
Catherine Imbriglio

I.

Though she has not been formally diagnosed, she suspects she may
exhibit traits associated with a childhood anxiety disorder
known as selective mutism.

In social settings, she can talk easily one on one but has difficulty
when three or more are in the room.

Signs of selective mutism include a consistent failure to speak in
gatherings where there is a generally agreed-upon expectation
for speaking.

Afflicted children often present in their first year of schooling
while continuing to speak normally at home.

In one traced population 58 percent refused to speak to the teacher
and 20 percent spoke to no one at school.

SM is usually distinguished from extreme shyness though both are
likely to be comorbid with other socialization difficulties.

Girls play with dolls, they don't swaddle favorite red metal shovels
and take them to bed.

One might attribute SM behaviors to an oppositional nature,
though some clinicians have found anxious and oppositional
behaviors in the same child.

Phrases such as "let's not get carried away " or "that isn't
happening" shouldn't be endlessly practiced for just the right
vocal entrance.

Catherine Imbriglio

Rumor has it one student used his fist to break a classroom window a few days after an ill-informed teacher tried to force him to read aloud.

Often in conversation with acquaintances, she stumbles over names and ordinary small talk like "Hi, Harry, how's it going?"

Is her continued fascination with repetitive musical behaviors opportunistic or a purposeful engagement with the inhumanity of the linguistic code.

A father and a mother may be ill-advised if they think their daughter will grow out of it.

You shouldn't bring a book to a party or family gathering and spend hours reading by yourself as a safety mechanism.

Daisy, Daisy, give me your answer, do.

A common denominator may be a neurodevelopmental immaturity that makes afflicted children react badly to sensory overload.

For example, how do you say what a mess in a teasing tone.

For a Carthusian monk, the absence of spoken language impresses on him the singularity of each moment.

Five will get you ten he will not tell you of his God cart, glowing.

Even days later, you could still see the knuckle cuts on the young man's hands.

II.

Though she was often mute, she found herself preoccupied with internal word bursts.

Spider glass, spider glass, spider in the glass, alas, alas.

At night she really did hear her clock ticking ten times more loudly than ordinary, an auditory hallucination not unlike Poe's.

Unlike children with other conduct disorders, often mute children are not seen as a bother.

This one conjures up a giantess for acting out hairyscary disagreements with nearby "higher-ups."

There has been little research about the course of the disorder into adulthood, so the eventual removal of symptoms may not necessarily be indicative of a successful turnabout.

Whose boundaries are confused.

However, one could argue it is the very fact that a person does not speak that makes her more noticeable.

Impressed upon her is anything that rests on a silence, so as to install weighty moments, lengthening ear reach, wool after the carcass has decomposed.

The worst carnage came north of Baghdad at a Shiite funeral.

Implosive findings suggest a familial resemblance between speech avoidance and nonaccountable spectatorship.

She could sit with the father for hours in what she thought was a comfortable silence.

Silence! Silenzio!

Still, she thinks she might manipulate her environment by being silent, a refusal not unlike Job's.

Or that silence can help you with forming neural intimacies, unlike coming to your subjects already predisposed.

Brain be nimble, brain be quick.

The president says his decisions were based solely on conditions on the ground.

Catherine Imbriglio

She reverts to about-face maneuverings, forms for speaking when
there are no expectations for speaking, broken ear nests,
deathbeds on paper, an aluminum skull.

Lotus seeds 1,200 years old have been sprouted in China.

For the monk, death may be simply "my death," an alter ego, a
winnowing.

NOTE. Approximately one-quarter of the language on selective mutism has been
taken, some verbatim, some with varying degrees of modification, from "The Quiet
Child: A Literature Review of Selective Mutism," by Sally Standart and Ann Le Cou-
teur in *Child and Adolescent Mental Health* 8.4: 2003. "Inhumanity of the linguistic code" is from Mutlu Blasing's *Lyric Poetry*. "Nonaccountable spectatorship"
reworks a phrase from Eve Kosofsky Sedgwick's *Epistemology of the Closet*.

The Resurrection Bake-Off
Jacob M. Appel

WORD CAME OF THE third resurrection while Amber's mother was serving tea. We were relaxing on Zelda's mahogany deck in Laurendale, soaking in the balmy spring morning and the scent of the blossoming peonies. My mother-in-law's kitchen radio was tuned to a Mozart marathon—and the festive strains of the *Haffner Serenade* drifted through the open window. Then Virginia Public Radio broke in on the recording to announce that a factory worker, recently decapitated by a metal press, had reappeared outside the gates of his Dayton, Ohio, plant with his head intact. Zelda nodded knowingly, as though she'd foreseen this development all along.

"Well, Doctor?" she said. "Riddle me that."

This I could not do. My wife's mother teaches folklore and comparative eschatology at the state university, and the previous week, after an oil rigger from Louisiana "woke up" at the morgue, Zelda was burning to anoint him a modern-day Lazarus. Sixteen years as a neurologist had rendered me somewhat more skeptical. *Death and taxes*, as they say. I was similarly doubtful when a teenager from Vermont disrupted her own funeral by pounding on the inside of her coffin lid. After all, we live in an age of hoaxes and swindles. Also, every profession—including medicine—boasts its share of incompetents, and, even in this era of technological wonders, patients are sometimes pronounced dead prematurely. In contrast, as I reminded my mother-in-law, there were *no* reported resurrections in the scientific literature. *None.*

"*I* can't explain it," I replied. "But *someone* will. Soon enough. And when they do, a lot of people will be sadly disappointed."

My mother-in-law frowned. "You're so sure of yourself, aren't you?"

"I don't make the rules, Zelda. I just play by them."

"And hope? And imagination? How do they fit into your rules?"

We'd had this conversation many times before, of course, in various guises, but it had acquired a sharper urgency now that Amber's cancer had returned and Rust Belt laborers were rising from the dead.

291

What Zelda Marcus really meant was: *Miracles* do *happen. If my daughter is going to die, so be it, as long as she comes back to us in better shape than before.* I could confirm the first part. After six years of remission, Amber's disease had crawled from her liver into her spine and lungs. She *was* going to die. I have nothing against hope, you understand. *False* hope is what I object to.

"It must be so hard for that poor man," observed Amber. "And for his family."

"What's that?" asked Zelda.

"Psychologically speaking, I mean," my wife explained. She worked as a crisis counselor for the county, although she was on extended leave. "Grief is designed to be a one-way process. Undoing it might prove highly traumatic."

"Not to mention the practical considerations," I added. "What if his children have already squandered their inheritance? Or if his wife is dating again?"

Zelda dried the base of her teacup with her paper napkin. "Well, it's a trauma that I could live with," she declared. "If Amber's daddy strolls through those doors tomorrow morning, you won't hear me complaining."

My wife's father had drowned when she was eleven—and it struck me that Zelda's life had not changed much in the intervening three decades. She had no skeletons to hide, no replacement lover to conceal beneath her mattress. Nor did I suspect that Jack Marcus, a trusts-and-estates attorney of impeccable reputation, would have divulged any of the secrets that he'd previously carried to the grave.

"Trust me, Zelda," I said. "At the end of the day, this decapitated guy will turn out to have had a twin brother, or something like that."

"We'll see, Doctor." Zelda only used the title *doctor* ironically. "Maybe there are more things in heaven and earth than are dreamt of in your philosophy."

As she so often does after claiming the final word, my mother-in-law conveniently excused herself to go to the restroom. That left me alone on the deck with my wife, the embers of death rekindled in the gentle spring air. On the great lap of lawn beyond Zelda's rose garden, the resident robins and starlings mingled with a flock of migratory geese. Behind the privet hedge, Zelda's neighbors tossed a football around. Sprinklers pulsed in the opposite yard. Virginia Public Radio had returned to the *menuetto galante* of the *Haffner Serenade*.

"I'm going to miss you and Mother arguing," said Amber. "I never thought I'd say that, but I really will."

She wouldn't miss anything, of course. Because she'd be dead. But we both understood exactly what she meant.

I circled behind Amber's chair and rested my palms on her frail shoulders. The bones were palpable beneath her flesh, like the frame inside a well-used sofa.

"Would you *want* to be resurrected?" I asked. "If it were possible. . . ."

A long pause followed—so long that I grew concerned Amber had lost the thread of the question, when she finally said, "I suppose it would depend how much time has gone by . . . and upon what *you* wanted. You and Mother. . . ." She turned and pressed her tiny fingers to my lips. "Please don't say anything more, Charles. What you believe you want today, and what you will actually want, in years to come, are two very different things. . . ."

So I said nothing. Because I knew she was right. As usual.

I was thinking about another woman, a folk musician named Rochelle Logan, whose resurrection I'd once longed for—and now feared more acutely than death itself.

My affair with Rochelle is not an episode I am proud of, nor is it something I can explain—not in any meaningful and satisfactory way. The facts speak for themselves: Six years ago, shortly after her diagnosis, my wife started two months of experimental, in-patient chemotherapy at Methodist General in Petersburg, and in the course of visiting her, I struck up a liaison with a single mother who worked at the hospital gift shop. Deplorable, but true. My lover was one-quarter Cherokee with deep, tragic eyes and jet-black hair cascading to her waist. Rochelle had ambitions as a singer-songwriter, but they'd grown vaguer once she'd passed thirty. She was also a widow—her husband had succumbed to a glioblastoma on the same floor where my wife received her daily poison—and she listened well. I suppose that if Amber had died then, as was widely expected, I'd have married Rochelle Logan. Instead, the oncologists beat my wife's disease into remission, while Rochelle and her daughter asphyxiated in an electrical fire.

I pleaded with God for months to restore my lover. I bargained. I shouted. But I conducted all of my grieving privately. In public—at Methodist General, on Zelda's porch—I was ever the devoted spouse. What never crossed my mind was owning up, or pleading for forgiveness, at least not until that teenager from Vermont revived during the Twenty-third Psalm and accused her uncle of strangling her. (Before that, the authorities had pinned the crime on a drifter who'd done odd jobs at her father's dairy farm.) The next morning, I heard on the news that an elderly Norfolk woman had admitted to poisoning her late husband, fearful that he might return from the grave for revenge. My thoughts drifted to my own gnawing secret. So when the factory worker in Ohio reemerged with his head on his shoulders, I was already far less confident in my skepticism than I'd made out to Zelda. By the time the first World War II vet materialized on the beachhead at Normandy, and that murdered prostitute incriminated those Reno councilmen, I was already contemplating a preemptive confession to Amber. Why wait for Rochelle Logan to appear upon our doorstep strumming her guitar?

I learned of the Nevada call girl's charges on the drive home from a racquetball match—not my regular Thursday night game, but a Tuesday evening stand-in for a surgeon who'd ruptured his Achilles tendon—and I determined to unburden myself to Amber without delay. My wife was slaving away in the kitchen when I arrived home, as I'd expected, her forearms caked with flour, a dab of batter atop the bridge of her nose.

In January, she'd joined a support group, and the leader, a social worker who'd lost a leg to chondrosarcoma as a teenager, had asked each participant to identify one goal that she hoped to meet before passing. Amber responded that she wanted to win the baking competition at our state fair. Honestly, if she'd announced a plan to take up mud wrestling or cockfighting, I couldn't have been more shocked. In our twenty years together, my wife's culinary endeavors had never extended beyond scrambling an egg or ordering a pizza. Now she revealed to me a distant memory of accompanying her paternal grandmother to the bake-off, and how, for her, cobblers and tarts represented *the path not taken*, a yearning so secret that she'd suppressed its very existence since her adolescence. "Or it's a baby substitute," she'd said—offhandedly, though not casually enough to mask her regrets.

The next morning, Amber circled the final Sunday of September on her calendar and purchased enough nonstick bakeware to lodge a battalion of Pillsbury Doughboys. And I give her credit. Even as her appetite declined through the spring, she wouldn't let a day pass without a foray into rhubarb or banoffee or meringue.

Amber greeted me with a broad smile and a slice of pie. Our evening ritual. I loosened my necktie, set my attaché case on a kitchen chair, and kissed the prow of her forehead. She pressed a fork into my hand, desperate for a verdict.

"Taste," she ordered.

One of the ironies of Amber's quest was that her cancer had killed not only her appetite, but also her taste buds. So she spent all day baking, then waited for my tongue to judge her output. Like a deaf Beethoven, asking his beloved Therese, *"Ist es nicht schön?"*

"Fantastic," I declared. "What is it?"

"Well, your favorites were the pineapple pecan and the strawberry coconut," Amber explained, beaming. "So I merged them. You're sampling a gastronomic first: pineapple-pecan-strawberry-coconut-buttermilk pie." She wiped her hands on her apron, clouding the air with flour, and drew up a chair beside mine. "So it's decided? That's my recipe?"

"I can already see the trophy on our mantelpiece."

Amber hugged my arm. I reached forward and gently wiped the batter from her face, then licked my fingers clean. The idea of a confession, which had seemed so promising on the expressway, now churned my guts uncomfortably.

"I heard there was another one today," I ventured. "In Nevada."

She already knew. "Do you think they're real?" she asked.

As real as anything else, I wanted to say—which meant, I had no idea. Rochelle Logan no longer seemed real to me. Our stolen moments together in the gift-shop stockroom seemed as much a fantasy as a cure for cancer. "My mind says no," I answered, "but the evidence increasingly seems to shout yes."

"Mother called. Do you remember how, last weekend, you said that factory worker's wife might have started dating again . . . ?"

"Vaguely."

"Well, *she* does. She's convinced herself that my father is going to show up for breakfast one of these days, and she's afraid he'll be displeased that she went out with some veterinarian from Newport News twenty-five years ago." Amber rose abruptly and carried the pie dish to the sink. "She was *genuinely* upset, Charles. They went out on something like *three* dates when I was in college—and now she's all worked up about whether or not she should tell my father. She's getting impossible." Amber sighed and turned on the faucet. "Have you heard anything about if the returnees know what happened while they were gone?"

I acknowledged that I hadn't. "But I'm sure your dad will forgive her."

"She is too," said Amber, over the running water. "That's not the issue. The question is whether or not he'd want to know about the dates."

"Would you?"

"I'd trust your judgment either way," she replied. "It's not like they were still married, after all. Father had been dead for *eight years*. How could he possibly expect her to plan her life around the remote possibility that he'd come back?"

Amber shut off the tap and dried her arms on a dishtowel. The fluorescent ceiling bulb limned her face a gloomy violet, and her fragile body looked nearly diaphanous—not strong enough to carry a secret. Outside, the neighbor's dachshund barked for its supper. I crossed the kitchen and wrapped my arms around my wife, but said nothing. I was willing to risk allowing her one more night of peace.

One night drifted into a second, then a third. By the end of June, the authorities had confirmed two hundred seventy-four resurrections, while another thirty or so claims remained under investigation. In May, these incidents had bumped earthquakes and tornadoes from the headlines; now the media reported them reluctantly, as a thankless and time-frittering duty, after the names of the war dead overseas. None of the countless government epidemiologists and freelance parapsychologists probing the phenomenon had made any headway in explaining who came back, or why, nor did demographic patterns emerge—except that the majority of the resurrected had been dead fewer than fifty years, with the most remote born only during the Fillmore administration. Nor did there appear to be any reason why some returned as senior citizens, and others in the prime of life, or why one Kansas housewife, who'd died at eighty-seven, reappeared in her nine-year-old body. The resurrected, incidentally, had no clue what had happened while they'd been gone. As a dyed-in-the-wool Washington Senators fan told his local newspaper: "Last thing I remember, it was June 3, 1919, and Walter Johnson had a 2-0 count on the Browns' George Sisler—and then I had trouble breathing."

Here in central Virginia, the first returnee was Mabel Steinhoff, a German-born domestic who'd once worked for Amber's grandaunt. Zelda insisted that we drive out to Hydesville to pay the old woman a visit.

We made the trip on a Sunday morning. My mother-in-law had phoned ahead to arrange the meeting with the resurrected woman's grandson—a seventy-two-year-old ex-boxer—and we found the pair of them playing checkers on a splintered picnic table outside a mobile home. Mrs. Steinhoff, a rotund, chinless creature, who looked as though she'd passed the afterlife gorging on jelly doughnuts, smiled at us vacantly.

The grandson, Hiram Jenks, remembered my mother-in-law from grammar school—and the pair embraced like kissing cousins. Then he offered me a meaty handshake. Amber presented him with a freshly baked raspberry cheesecake.

"Much obliged, ma'am," he said. "What a strange world, isn't it? Who ever thought I'd be playing checkers with my own grandmama?"

My mother-in-law settled down alongside Mrs. Steinhoff.

"Mabel?" said my mother-in-law. "It's me. Zelda. Alice Larue's daughter."

"I'm afraid to say Grandmama's memory isn't what it ought to be," explained Jenks. "She had a couple of strokes before she passed last time. When it comes to anything that happened before her return, she's pretty much hit or miss."

Zelda ignored this warning. She clasped the elderly domestic's hand between both of her own, and asked, "Have you seen Jackson Marcus?"

Mrs. Steinhoff blinked vigorously—as though waking from a nap. "I really couldn't say," she replied. "Hiram? Have we seen Jack's son?" Then she turned to my mother-in-law and inquired, "I'm sorry, but what did you say his son's name was?"

"Please, Mabel. *Think.* Jack's son. *Jackson.* Jackson Marcus. A tall, frightfully handsome man smoking a corncob pipe." Chords of desperation rose in Zelda's voice. *"Please* think. Did you run into him while you were gone?"

"Gone where?" asked Mrs. Steinhoff.

"When you were *dead*," snapped Zelda. "I want to know whether you crossed paths with my husband while you were dead."

"Please, Mother," interjected Amber.

"It's all right," said Jenks—who displayed the crooked nose and dashed teeth of a fighter, but angelic blue eyes fit for a choirboy. He lit a cigarette off a lighter shaped like a pistol. "If I were in your shoes, I'd be asking the same questions."

"Jackson Marcus," pressed Zelda. "He wears a tweed jacket with elbow patches."

My mother-in-law had been fixated on her late husband's return for weeks. She'd cleaned out her spare room, so that he'd have an office, and she'd taken to preparing his favorite meals, on the off chance that he arrived hungry. On Tuesday, she'd dragged Amber to the Gentleman's Depot in Hanover Crossing to pick out collared shirts. Zelda had as much confidence in her husband's eventual return as I did that the sun would rise in the east. Meanwhile, I had my own set of inquiries for the demented lady—questions that I dared not ask. Had she encountered a thirty-two-year-old dimpled beauty who played "Blowing in the Wind" and "Lemon Tree" on a steel-string acoustic guitar? Did the musician have an olive-skinned toddler in tow? Could she tell me if this woman had found peace? Or was Rochelle biding her time, waiting to emerge from the hereafter and avenge herself ruthlessly upon my own happiness? Mabel Steinhoff couldn't answer these questions, of course. Her memory of the years since her departure was as blank as the expression on her plump, docile face.

I suddenly realized that my eyes were misting up, and I dabbed them with my handkerchief. Amber noticed too. She wrapped herself around my elbow. She thought I was crying because our time together loomed so short, not because I had used it so poorly. "I adore you," she whispered.

Although I'd seen more than enough of Mabel Steinhoff to know that I was ready to return home, Hiram Jenks asked us to join him for a glass of "homemade lemonade," and Zelda graciously accepted.

The beverage Jenks served tasted like a Tom Collins, but packed the punch of Kentucky bourbon. My mother-in-law polished off two glasses while listening to our host describe his grandfather's attempt at rabbit farming, and the bout he'd *almost* fought against Rocky Marciano, and myriad other irrelevancies. Every so often, Zelda broke off listening to ask Mabel if she'd recalled Amber's dad. By the time we departed Hydesville, thunderclouds had steamrolled over the afternoon sun.

"She's holding out on us," declared Zelda. "Maybe not *intentionally*. But somewhere in that addled mind of hers, she knows where Jack is."

"Would it matter?" I asked.

"Of course, it would matter," snapped my mother-in-law. "How can you even ask that? Any news is better than nothing."

I wasn't so sure. *What if Amber's father doesn't want to come back?* I couldn't help wondering. *What if the departed have a choice whether to return—and your dead husband and my dead mistress have both declined?* All I said was, "I'm sure if she does remember anything, Hiram Jenks will phone you."

We dropped Zelda off in Laurendale and then inched north on the interstate, surrounded by inbound traffic from the beaches and the Civil War battlefields. On the radio, CBS news was reporting that one of the original Ziegfeld Girls had shown up for work at the Jardin de Paris. I flipped to an oldies station.

"Thank you," said Amber.

"For what?"

"For loving me so much."

I responded by reaching across the gearshift and squeezing her wrist. A moment later, we pulled up in front of our home in Culpepper Heights—and an olive-skinned toddler in a diaper came charging along the flagstone path toward our sedan. My soul went cold. Then the girl's mother called after her—our neighbor, a sharp-featured, heavyset Cuban attorney who looked *nothing* like Rochelle—and the child stumbled.

Amber sprang to the child's rescue, gently cradling the sobbing girl until her mother stepped in. I was reminded of the many times that I'd watched Rochelle kiss a scraped knee, or tape a Band-Aid over an imaginary wound, and of the great injustice that my Amber would never raise a daughter of her own.

That week witnessed the first wave of mass resurrections. Now the numbers were too large to process, like corporate layoffs or deaths from Pacific typhoons. Many of the returnees had no surviving kin and had to be housed in school gymnasiums and FEMA trailers. Not a day passed without sightings of deceased celebrities. Although many of these reports ultimately proved false, the mere possibility of running into Elvis or John Lennon while running errands had sixty-year-old divorcées flashing cleavage at the laundromat and the post office. Widows across the county joined Zelda in preparing the favorite meals of their late husbands—a logistical challenge for those who had married more than once—and, with each passing day, more of these women found their efforts rewarded. At the same time, the returnees brought with them century-old grudges and long-buried resentments. In one case, a resurrected pharmacist discovered his wife *in flagrante delicto* with her second husband, who happened to be the pharmacist's younger brother, and stabbed his replacement with a fireplace poker.

I did not expect any physical violence if Rochelle returned—just emotional fireworks. Yet I realized that might prove enough to shatter Amber's tenacity for living. My every encounter with a returnee served as a reminder that my own days of tranquillity were numbered. When my third-grade teacher, whose funeral I'd attended, accosted me in the Quick-Mart to tell me how proud she was of my accomplishments, I knew that I had to act.

That evening was one of the warmest nights of the summer. I waited until Amber had gone upstairs to bed, then slipped onto the patio in my bathrobe and wrote out an uncensored confession in longhand. I measured each phrase like a potentially lethal elixir before committing the words to paper. It felt as though I was composing a suicide note. Somewhere in the distant darkness, revelers ignited volleys of illicit firecrackers. Fruit bats swept low in the yard. Moths circled the patio lamps. As I recorded the details of my affair with Rochelle—making no effort to mitigate my responsibility—I found myself reviling my late mistress. Why had she chosen me, of all her gift-shop customers, to invite into the stockroom? What right had she to shower me with such affection at a time when all seemed so hopeless?

My thoughts drifted and my pen fell to the page. The shadow of the Angel of Death suddenly shook me from my reverie, a long black scythe in the night. Seconds later, I registered that it was Amber herself who had stepped silently into the beam of the lamps.

"You OK?" she asked.

"Not really," I answered honestly. "Are you?"

Amber shook her head. "Two valiums didn't even help," she said. "You're going to laugh at me when I tell you what's keeping me awake."

"I'd never laugh at you."

She allowed her wraithlike body to sink into the chair beside me. I slid my elbow over my confession.

"Have you ever heard of Theodora Smafield?" she asked.

"Never," I replied. "Do I want to?"

"Theodora Smafield was the world's foremost pie baker during the golden age of pie baking. When pies mattered," explained Amber. "She won the Pillsbury Bake-Off in 1949, the Great American Recipe Competition in 1950, and practically every blue ribbon awarded for piestry over the next two decades . . . and I heard on the radio this afternoon that she reappeared in her niece's kitchen last weekend and has been baking up a storm ever since." My wife took a deep, tremulous breath, and added, "Her niece lives in Richmond."

"And you're afraid she'll enter the state fair?"

"Of course, she will."

"Good," I declared. "That will make your victory all the sweeter."

Amber searched my face for conviction. "You really think I can beat her?"

"I'm sure of it," I said. "Your pies are like ambrosia. Anyway, she may not turn out to be all that she's cracked up to be. People had simpler tastes back then. Lower expectations."

This was precisely what Amber needed to hear. A gleam of delight spread upward from her smile to her sharp, deep-set eyes. "You always know exactly what to say," she said.

That was when I knew that I would *never* show her the confession. My best hope, from that moment forward, lay in Rochelle Logan's ongoing absence. Maybe she had reunited with her first husband in the hereafter and wanted no part of me. Or, if Rochelle did return, maybe I could persuade her to keep our secret—as I had done, tryst after tryst, during the months when we both thought Amber's death was imminent. I'll confess that a third option also flickered across my mind. Murder. Not that I would actually silence Rochelle in that way—although I'm sure one could rationalize the killing of a returnee—but, for the first time, I understood how a man could kill his mistress to protect his wife. I also despised myself for wishing ill on a generous young woman who had never shown me anything but kindness.

"You're worried about me, aren't you?" asked Amber. "You're thinking I might not even make it to September. . . ."

"Don't talk like that," I said. "Human beings aren't statistics. Nobody can predict with any certainty whether you have five years or fifty years. Got it?"

"You're the doctor," agreed Amber. "And even if I only have five days, maybe I'll get lucky and come back again before the autumn."

My wife stood up, bracing herself against the table, and kissed the back of my head. Then she dragged her body across the patio to the kitchen door.

"Don't stay up too late, all right?" she warned—and she was gone.

I waited until I saw the lights switched on in our bedroom window, and then switched off again, before I ripped apart my letter. Then I offered my bargain to the Unknown: *Please don't let her come back while Amber is alive, and I'll never ask to return again either.* My sacrifice carried unanswered across the darkness.

*

Three weeks later, my wife collapsed in the produce aisle at Gwench's. That's technically in the Petersburg catchment area, so the ambulance transported her to Methodist General—even though Jefferson & Madison is probably closer. By the time I arrived, nearly two hours later, she was moored to an IV in the intensive care unit. Her admitting diagnosis read: *altered mental status*. The underlying reality was that she'd had a seizure. Her cancer, after months encamped within her spine, had launched a stealth assault against her brain.

I hadn't been inside an ICU in several months. My neurology practice focuses on movement disorders—Parkinson's disease, multiple sclerosis—and I encourage my patients to pursue hospice care in their final days, so few end up on ventilators. I wasn't prepared for the degree to which a summer of resurrections had transformed end-of-life care, changes summed up in a maxim markered across the dry-erase board behind the nurses' station: "The sooner they're gone, the sooner they can come back."

Amber's hospitalization occurred at the height of the second great wave of reappearances, the "August Maximum" that followed the "Midsummer Minimum." For several weeks in late July, resurrections had slowed to a trickle. A pair of economists at MIT had linked this decline to changes in the sunspot cycle. They predicted that resurrections would end entirely—"a return to the permanent mortality status quo"—by August 1. Instead, after a brief lull, the number of returnees soared into the millions. This brought joy to an untold number of families and exacerbated the housing crisis. For those still waiting, like Zelda Marcus, every waking moment was charged with anticipation.

My wife sat propped on a bower of pillows. What amazed me was how strong Amber seemed for a woman with cancer cells nibbling through her gray matter. She looked frail, yes—but not as though she might soon cease existing. That was the nasty thing about brain metastases: They lulled you into unwarranted optimism.

"I thought I might run into you here," she said.

Her voice betrayed her condition: strained, distant, breathless.

"Next time you're going to collapse in the supermarket, can't you at least give me some warning?" I asked. "How about eighty years?"

"You wouldn't want me to be so predictable, would you?" she asked, forcing a smile. "You'd get tired of me rather quickly."

I locked my fingers around hers, relieved that my wife's personality appeared intact. That's not always the case with seizures in advanced cancer patients. Sometimes the humanity evaporates, leaving behind only a fleshy shell.

Amber laughed unexpectedly—a sharp, hoarse burst of laughter that at first I mistook for choking. "So Theodora Smafield is going to win her blue ribbon after all," she said. "All that baking suddenly seems so silly . . . so frivolous. . . ."

"Don't think that way," I shot back. "To hell with Theodora Smafield."

We sat together for another hour, talking for the sake of hearing each other's voices, until the transport crew arrived to convey Amber to her MRI. As soon as she'd gone, a senior attending approached me: a tall, drooping spirit with a hangdog white mustache. He'd clearly been waiting for an opportunity to speak with me alone.

"Mr. Windham?" he asked.

"Dr. Windham," I answered, shaking his hand. "I'm a neurologist."

My revelation caught him off guard and he paused to recalibrate. Then he introduced himself as Dr. Todd Sewell, the head of the critical care unit. "I'd let you view the CT scan, but honestly, I'm not sure I'd want to see it," he explained. "I'm sorry."

"Me too," I answered.

"For what it's worth," said Sewell, "I had another case like this about a month ago . . . a woman in her early twenties with kidney mets everywhere . . . no prognosis, really . . . and the patient came back in under a month. At the beginning of that first wave of returnees. Now she's in school again, as happy as ever." The elderly physician patted my shoulder. "It's a different world these days, Dr. Windham. There's always hope."

Sewell filled me in on the results of Amber's lab tests. He sounded far more confident relating potassium levels and white blood-cell counts than he did while speaking of the Unknown. I'm afraid that I'm the same way with my own patients. When Sewell excused himself with a second pat on my shoulder, I was grateful for his departure.

I hurried down the service stairs to the ground floor. They'd renovated the main lobby since my affair with Rochelle, so the gift shop now occupied a free-standing hexagonal kiosk opposite the cafeteria. Our treasured stockroom had been replaced by a public alcove packed with ATMs and vending machines. While grieving, six years is a long time. In hospital planning, six years is an eternity. But what

303

better choice did I have? My departed mistress had been cremated, her ashes spread by plane over the Blue Ridge. The cluttered aisles of Today's Treasures offered the closest proximity to Rochelle that I could imagine in this lifetime.

I fell to my knees between the plush animals and the knit goods, indifferent to the stares of the other customers, and I prayed. "Please, Rochelle. Don't come back. . . ." I took a deep breath and added, "All I'm asking for is a few more weeks."

Amber's condition declined in fits and starts, like a ball bouncing down a corridor of ramps and stairs. Zelda and I spent our days at her bedside, trying to keep up her spirits. I no longer challenged my mother-in-law's prophesies of miraculous recovery, her predictions of bake-off victories to come. But I knew Amber wasn't fooled. My wife merely smiled and nodded politely, as though humoring a child or a lunatic. By the end of the first week in the hospital, she could no longer raise her head off the bed. I was so immersed in her care—and in absorbing those precious, evaporating moments—that I lost track of events in the outside world. Days passed before I learned the dramatic news: The resurrections had stopped.

As with any pandemic, the realization did not occur suddenly. Word of resurrections continued to trickle in from remote locations—so it wasn't until midweek that the media reported the abrupt cutoff. By the weekend, every television station in America was broadcasting snippets of an interview with a sharecropper's daughter, Ida Barnswallow, who claimed to be the very last of the returnees to return. Everybody wanted to know her secret, as though she'd lived to an unheard-of age. "Dumb luck," she explained, aglow with recaptured youth. "Never opened a Bible after I got married and certainly never ate no yogurt nor whatnot. Just minded my own damn business and tried to have as much fun as possible."

I discussed these developments with my mother-in-law while Amber dozed under the sway of exhaustion and morphine.

"So what now?" asked Zelda. "It all seems so hopeless."

"Maybe they'll start again," I offered. "We have no way of knowing."

Zelda sighed. "I can't help thinking that Jack *was* going to come back—that his return was part of the cosmic design—and that something happened, something unexpected, that threw the plans of the universe off course."

"It may still happen yet," I replied—wanting to believe.

I sat beside Amber through the remaining twilight, already missing my wife's love, but also reflecting upon Rochelle Logan and how much I had dreaded her resurrection. Slowly, incrementally, my fear was replaced by yearning: the desperate, helpless longing for the departed that overcomes us, once we recognize they will never return.

Waterfalls

Jess Row

THE PAST

SO I WAS A COUNSELOR at a summer camp.

Not the kind of camp you see in the movies. It was on an island; stranger still, an island smack in the middle of Boston Harbor. In the nineteenth century it had been an orphanage. There was a quadrangle of old brick buildings, athletic fields, patches of woods, tidal swamp. There was a ropes course and a nature trail and a campfire circle and even a dock with sailboats and canoes. Though no swimming. You can't have kids swimming in Boston. The summer I worked there three corpses washed up on the beach: one whole, one decapitated, one just a human torso, headless, armless, an oblong chunk of flesh.

It was a charity camp, of the Fresh Air Fund variety: Our kids came from the joyless telephone-wire blocks, the broken-glass street corners, the squalling asphalt parks of Roxbury, Dorchester, Quincy, Bunker Hill. They rode the ferry carrying corner-deli subs in wax paper and Super Fizz Cherry Blast, Golden Krust meat patties and Champagne Cola; they brought boom boxes and yesterday's tabloids with photographs of drive-by victims they'd known from around the way, and teddy bears, and Super Soakers, and asthma inhalers. Monday mornings they descended from the camp ferry and swept across the island in a cacophonous wave, like Vikings; we trailed behind with first-aid kits, tubs of sunblock, bottles of DEET, picking up debris, nursing the trampled and maimed. Every so often we came across a pistol, its serial number filed away, tossed in the bushes or drowned in a toilet tank.

These children—because they were still children, at twelve, thirteen, even fourteen, with children's faces staring out of startlingly long-limbed bodies—drew you in, so that you lived among them, sharing their rituals, their taboos, the sweet oppressive stink of young bodies shoved together, and then expelled you, a pathetic interloper, with wry disgust. You could see it in the faces of the replacement

306

counselors, who came nearly every week: beatific joy, as the game proceeded, the shrieks of laughter, the hollers, the pretend-back-of-the-hand kisses and slaps on the ass, and then, at dinnertime, red-eyed, thin-lipped rage, as they sat deserted at the far end of the cafeteria table, bewildered, insulted, spiritually mauled. As often as not they'd be on the special Tuesday midnight ferry that hauled our worst offenders back to Juvenile Justice and summer school. There was no shame in leaving; really it was a matter of luck. Who among us could have withstood the pyromaniac lighting up his bunkmate's sleeping bag three nights in a row, the cabal who spray painted 187 ALL COPS across the front of the gym, the eleven-year-old suicide case who rubbed poison ivy across her bleeding wrists and ankles? At night we huddled in our cells and ate through our stashes of chocolate and Xanax, waiting for the scream, the explosion, the shattering windowpanes, that would indicate our clocks had run out, and it was time to flee: back to our parents' lazy sprinklers, their decomposing patio furniture and six o'clock rations of Chardonnay.

No one worked there because they needed the money. We could have gone to Maine, New Hampshire, the Poconos—Ramapo, Katahdin, Bide-a-Wee—and made three or four thousand a summer, plus tips. The staff ran high in Ivy League degrees, plus a sprinkling of Oberlin, Amherst, Haverford, and Bates. Millions of dollars, collectively, had funded our upbringings, our delicate educations; we tended toward battered L. L. Bean backpacks and Teva sandals, thrift store T-shirts and ratty cutoffs, nose rings and pretend dreadlocks. We were a renewable resource, like bamboo: There were always more where we came from.

MISSION STATEMENT

We weren't saints; we were unknowing children, too; trying to locate ourselves in the shifting sands of theory and guilt, and we thought what better place to start than with pain, someone else's pain, the pain of the dispossessed? It was a black thing and we wouldn't understand, but we were optimists, weaned on *Eyes on the Prize*; we were used to obstacles miraculously dissolving in telegenic time: an hour-long documentary, a two-page application essay. Was it guilt, naked ambition, an excess of good intentions? No, it was an excess of love. Love pooled under our tongues and collected like calcium deposits beneath our fingernails. Overestimated, overvalued, overresourced, we sensed the deficit, and offered up our bodies as collateral.

Who was I, in particular? I have a vague memory of my father sailing in the 1984 Solomons Island regatta, his bare, tanned back turned away from me, the sun riffling his bleached hair. I loved "Sunday Bloody Sunday" but never bought another album after *The Joshua Tree*. My parents' house in Sagoponack had an acre of lawn that sloped down to the water. I lost my virginity to Adele Saperstein at Model UN camp in 1988.

Or was that me, or was that a dream I had? I sometimes wonder if I dreamed my entire slot-fitting childhood. Does it matter to *you*, one way or another? Would an answer make it hurt any less?

OBLIGATORY QUALIFICATION

Nelson Quang-Torres—he was there too, bright as a flare in a basement full of old newspapers. He was from Lexington by way of J.P; he'd done a few years of community college, and had once danced with Madonna, he claimed, at a nightclub in New York, and she'd offered him a backup spot on the Vogue tour, but he was fifteen, in the city without his parents' permission, and had to turn it down.

Fuck *me*, he had a habit of saying, at the least provocation. In front of the kids, in front of Melissa, the camp director. It didn't matter. He was possessed of what he himself called the *inherent inner fabulous*; all of a piece with the immaculate Nikes and the matching headband coiled around a mop of tight, shiny curls like a planter, the lisp and the flick-of-the-wrist model wave, the falsetto RuPaul imitation. *It's your birthday, go crazy, go crazy.* He directed the talent show at the end of each three-week term: a wild affair, with colored lights, deafening sound, and a catwalk, where girls barely in their teens strutted in dresses made of feathers, tape, and heavy-duty tinfoil.

In those days I hadn't realized I would never overcome my revulsion to smoking long enough to develop a habit. Even toward the end of the week I always had a nearly full pack of Parliaments and a lighter that worked. They weren't menthols, he always complained, but he was too broke to care. In the evenings, the sunset softening the sky over Boston to a child's smeared pastels, we were allowed a fifteen-minute break on the beach between dinner and Evening Activities, while the overnight kids returned to their cabins to smoke their own cigarettes, and devise new forms, and venues, of havoc.

We *got* to get out of here, he was saying, that particular Thursday. Saturday was our day off, and we could leave the island Friday early evening, if we wanted to. But no one ever did. Friday night we had encounter sessions; we sorted through our biases and agonized over our problem campers. It was team building, tearful, motivational, not required but required. He hated it. But he couldn't leave the island by himself.

Troyer, he said, Troyer gave me the keys to his car. He's away for the week. Grandmother's funeral.

So?

So tomorrow's Friday, baby. Time to make something happen. My moms sent me a hundred bucks for my birthday. I've been sitting on that cash for weeks. We ought to go down to J.P., have some decent food, go to a club. Score some weed. Not that skunky homegrown shit Julia brought down from Vermont. I'm talking *hydroponic*.

He lit a new cigarette from the tip of the last and stood up, shucking his shoes. Check it out, he said, clasping his palms together above his head, tucking his right foot against his left thigh. Tree pose. He stood there for a full minute, his cigarette flaring at the corner of his mouth.

Nelson, I said, if Troyer finds out you borrowed his car—

Shit, if he cared so much, why'd he give me the keys?

I considered.

Whatever, he said, staring straight ahead. Come with me or don't. You white people give me the creeps.

THE FUTURE

What I do in life, what I did in life, is sit at a desk in an office building and watch numbers flickering across an enormous flat monitor and talk on the telephone. I am, I was, director of capital projects for a midsize medical equipment company. A company you would never hear of in ordinary circumstances. We make, that is to say we paid others to make, components of artificial joints: hips, knees, elbows. We have squadrons of materials specialists and quality-control engineers all over the world. And in retrospect we should have known that the price was too low, that a silicate molding manufactured in a town no one could find on a map in Shandong Province couldn't possibly stand the weight of two titanium joints rotating over and over, over years, in an artificial hip, though all the tests came out fine.

309

They were rigged, those tests. Someone in the Chinese company paid off someone in Singapore who paid off someone in Hyderabad who filled out the paperwork from the testing company, and now we're on the front page of every business section in the world, and my former boss, my CEO, has been photographed walking into federal court, shielding his face with an umbrella I bought for him as a joke on a business trip to Montreal. *Merde! Il pleut*, it says. He doesn't speak French.

In the office, all around me, people are packing cartons, throwing out reams of unused stationery, and using the mail carts to carry off potted plants and flat-screen monitors and expensive recessed lighting components. I hear the maintenance staff are being paid fifty bucks a pop to look the other way if you want to take your ergonomic office chair as a souvenir. I'm the only one still working at my cubicle, noise-reduction headphones clamped over my ears, typing this. My severance check sits next to me on my desk. If I don't cash it in the next hour or two, it may bounce.

THE SOURCE OF ALL PATHOS

There was the girl who cracked her gum as she spoke, as a kind of punctuation; the boy who turned and sprinted away whenever he saw me, a flash of knobby knees and a Pistons jersey ballooning away from his skinny frame. The girls who spent all their time on the dormitory steps, braiding and rebraiding one another's hair; the boys clustered under the ancient oak tree at the far end of the soccer field, trading contraband copies of *Hustler* smuggled in their sleeping bags. The ones who cried for their mothers at three thirty in the morning.

Call her Tanya, she whose real name has been excised from my memory, who stood a head above the rest, who was so matchstick thin her body seemed to bend light around it. She was always sucking on the tiny wooden spoons that came attached to the paper cups of ice cream in the dining hall. And she never spoke to any of the counselors or the staff. No one was sure what cabin she belonged to. At every activity—capture-the-flag, kickball, pottery, scavenger hunt—she stood on the sidelines and watched, a silent referee, an oracle.

In those days, before liability insurance forbade it, we did trust falls: forcing them to stand, blindfolded, on the edge of a picnic table, and fall backward, arms folded King Tut style, into the waiting arms of their cabinmates. Even the short, fat boys, not even five feet tall, who had the gravitational density of cannonballs: We called in the cooks from the cafeteria, six footers, former nightclub bouncers, as reinforcements. Everyone fell, everyone got caught. It was the Thompson Island rule. When it was my turn I nearly choked from fear, seeing stars beneath the bandanna, and passed out on the way down, and came to on my side, breathing into a paper bag. And I was seized with the belief that my upbringing fell away from me, inadequate, incommensurate with this world.

You all right? Tanya asked. You OK?

I squinted up at her, in silhouette, against the fluorescent glare of an overcast summer sky. With the little spoon jutting away from her mouth she looked like some kind of icon, like a returning warrior, toothpick in gritted teeth. I wondered if she might kick me in the stomach to get me back upright. *Walk it off.*

I guess I was just too heavy, I said. Should've gotten backup.

No, they caught you, she said. You just had your eyes closed and didn't *believe* it. F'you don't believe you're gonna get caught nobody can't do nothing for you. You counselors, you're supposed to know that shit.

Don't say *shit*, I said automatically.

Yeah. Exactly.

With great delicacy she removed the spoon, flicked it into the bushes, and walked away.

THE PRESENT

This ferry is crossing the churning, oily waters of Boston Harbor, speckled with black ducks, who float with only their long necks and slender needle-like heads above the surface, and it is crossing, too, out of the luminous confines of our good intentions, back into history, to the pier where T. J. Hales's restaurant sells fried clams and onion rings to the pimply, close-cropped, creamy white-skinned teenagers of South Boston, whose parents—perhaps grandparents, the generations here are short and swift—fought pitched battles to keep the children of Dorchester and Roxbury from being bused to their schools. That our summer camp has its designated pier and private ferry here is a matter of geographic necessity, involving a generous yearly donation for the upkeep for the Donal O'Reilly Memorial, Donal O'Reilly being the very same state assemblyman who vowed to lie down across the path of any schoolbus crossing L Street in 1971. Needless to say, we rope our charges tightly together going to and from the boat, in midday, with police cruisers nearby, and we don't often come or go at night, not even ourselves, myself, I who have sandy brown hair and a few dark freckles on the bridge of my nose, and could pass for Irish until I open my mouth. When we finally reach the pier it's 7:45, the sunset dissolving to a sickly pinkish twilight, and the story has shifted firmly into the present tense, to indicate a change in mood as well as history, judging from the stone-faced stares of the boys clustered around Hales's window as we walk up the ramp and onto the sidewalk, looking for Troyer's old Volvo.

Fucking European cars, Nelson says. You know how to drive one of these things?

I tell him no. My family, my supposed family, drives Subarus till the undercarriages rust out. It's a point of pride. Or at least we ought to. We should have some distinguishing memorable detail.

Nelson and I slide into our seats, he on the driver's side, reluctantly. It can't be *that* difficult, he says, gripping the stick shift, which refuses to move into reverse. One, two, three, four, five: He tests them all. The radio wails the third chorus of "Brown Eyed Girl"; I shut it off, to help him concentrate. The pier, strangely quiet, smells of strawberry lip gloss, briny harbor air, and spilled Velveeta. For a moment, apropos of nothing, I think, *I love America.*

Hey, a voice says, speaking through the open window on my side. See that little grip underneath? Pull up on that thing.

There are four or five of them, surrounding us, on both sides of the car; we see them at waist level: the elastic bands of their Notre Dame basketball shorts, their ruddy hands with the tiny four-leaf clovers tattooed between thumb and forefinger. The one leaning in has a Caesar-style haircut, a gold tooth on the left side, and a friendly, skeptical grin.

Hey, Jimmy, one of his friends calls out, how come you know so much about Jap cars?

I don't. But I guess I know more than this spick does.

Nelson laughs. I don't see his face; I couldn't look at him in the face. But he laughs as if at the entire world's expense. Man, he says, can't you do better than that? Spanish Person in Charge?

Get the fuck out of here, faggot, he says. And take your faggot friend with you. We don't like your kind in Southie.

Oh yeah? Nelson says. What kind *do* you like?

THE PRESENT PERFECT

They are chasing us out of South Boston, on Farragut and roaring down Broadway and out Summer Street past the piers and the Harpoon brewery and the convention center, in a Jeep and another car behind that, eight of them or ten, bottles bouncing off the roof, chunks of concrete and boomerangs of rebar punching holes in the rear window. They have baseball bats and broken malt liquor bottles and who knows what else, a gun or two, a can of gasoline and a lighter, a roll of duct tape? Keep your fucking head down, Nelson screams, and guns through one red light after another. The roads are strangely deserted: not a cop, not a passerby. It's a Friday night in Boston, and no one there to see. Now you know what my life is like every goddamned day, Nelson is shouting. Even now he's still shouting. And they are still chasing us. My sphincter seized into a fist, my hands scrabbling at the dashboard for something to hold on to. It's still happening, it's not allowed to be over. To allow it to be over, to end the suspense, to enter the unbearable future, to forget it, to blot it out of memory again: Isn't there another way? Every story doesn't need an ending. They are chasing us out of South Boston, left on Farragut, left on Broadway, right on Summer, acting out their part in an ancient ritual, the chasing of The Faggot and The Faggot's Friend. Every story needs a victim, every story needs a sacrifice, and here we are.

SUPPLEMENTARY MATERIALS

We lost them by the time we passed South Street Station, but, just to be sure, Nelson swung three sharp rights in a row. A circle, he said, through clenched teeth, that's how you throw anyone off, get back on the main road when they least expect it. Satisfied, finally, he turned onto the Mass Pike ramp, and took us flying through downtown, headed west, the office blocks and convention hotels suddenly as enormous and bizarre to me as illustrations from a comic book. The seat belt had dug itself into my left armpit; I pulled it away gently. Slowly sensation returned to my hands and feet.

Should we call the cops?

He turned and skidded across two lanes of traffic to make the Tremont exit.

Where are we going?

Home, he said.

We turned onto a street of white clapboard rowhouses, turned a sallow yellow beneath the street lamps. Here and there a crumbling brick apartment building, a school building behind caged windows and a cyclone fence. Boys in long white T-shirts turning lazy circles on freestyle bicycles, the handlebars of welded shiny chain. *Lechonera, Pastelleria, Muebles, Comida China, Check Cashing.* My eyeballs were dry and sandy around the edges; I was aware of them rotating in their sockets, newly fashioned orbs, as if I'd been issued a replacement pair.

Nelson fiddled with the radio knob until he found an R&B station. *Don't. Go. Chasing waterfalls,* he sang under his breath, *please stick to the rivers and the lakes that you're used to.* All right, he said, that song's *over* already. He switched to a college station, and the car filled with a long, low, stretched note on the bass, and Lou Reed intoning, solemnly, *Jackie is just speeding away, thought she was James Dean for a day. Then I guess she had to crash. Valium would have helped that bash. I said, Hey, babe—*

I reached over and switched it off.

Viejo J.P., he said. Egleston Square. You never been down here? The island bus does pickups over at Hennigan. Look, that's the playground where I used to hang out. My *abuela* owned a house down that corner till my dad died and she had to sell it. You should be taking notes, man. His hands danced a beat against the steering wheel. The autobiography of a genuine colored person.

In the center of it all, at the corner of Columbus and Washington, he parked outside a bodega and returned with a pint of Captain Morgan's in a brown paper bag. We passed it back and forth in silence.

I got a friend from here who lives in Omaha, Nebraska, he said, finally.

Yeah?

He says, just learn to speak like they do, all polite and *whiny,* you know what I mean, kind of uptight? And they just treat you like they've known you all their lives. Gays too. It's so boring they're desperate for whoever they can get. I'm going to move out there in September. There's one club in the whole town and they need a DJ.

Good for you, I said. At least you have a plan.

What could I have been thinking about at this moment other than my own future? And how is it possible, you may ask, for a character such as I, pastless wonder? How is it that I could have been wishing my own death instead?

On the East Coast shit's just too *old*. Isn't that what they say about all those people out on Martha's Vineyard and Nantucket? It's like they get *transparent*. Like they been bleached or something. All going to the same schools, same clubs, same parties, same people, for like, *four hundred years*? Swear to God, it happens to everybody eventually. Dominicans too. My mother, my *tíos*. They've all been here since the fifties, practically. They get to looking kind of inbred, you know what I mean? Everyone's all wrapped up in everyone else's drama. It's the Hatfields and the McCoys all over again. Used to be I knew everybody that walked down this block. Thing was, I went to college, and all this shit happened had nothing to do with me. My homeboy Augustín got a married girl pregnant and her husband came after him with a machete. Old-school shit. I came back and people looked at me like I was a ghost, man. It's like, you don't stick around, you're not even *alive* anymore. Know what I'm saying?

He turned and looked at me.

Hey, what's up with you, anyway? I don't even know nothing about where you're from.

It's like you said. I swigged from the bottle and belched out the sugary-fiery taste of the rum. I've been bleaching so long, I turned invisible. I don't even remember.

He pursed his lips, as if he was about to laugh, and pounded a fist on the steering wheel, shaking his head.

You really think you can get away with that? You think you're the only one who wishes it were that easy?

What do you mean?

What I mean is, he said, yo, if you really want to disappear, genealogically speaking, you should get yourself a girlfriend who looks like me. Chinese and Jamaican, Korean and Brazilian, some shit like that. That way one of you will fit in almost anywhere. And your kids, man, they'll just look like the *future*. Like that golf guy, what's his name, Tiger Woods?

Maybe you're right, I said. But that's not what I meant.

No, he said, I understand what you *meant*.

I know he did. Wherever he is, he still does. We both do.

WE PAUSE FOR A COMMERCIAL INTERRUPTION

Around this time—'95, '96, the milky haze of my postadolescence, substanceless as the foam of a skinny cappuccino—Volkswagen had a commercial for its New Beetle: *If you sold your soul in the eighties, here's your chance to buy it back.* We sneered, of course, as our parents reached out for them, slack faced, drop jawed, like children clutching balloon animals at the circus. *The commodification of dissent,* we called it. What was there to worry about, once you understood the world was only the play of signifiers? It was a matter of moving the frame slightly to one side: a hundred-dollar laptop and a little venture capital for the impoverished cotton farmers in Mali. Change is just a by-product of making money, someone said. It doesn't have to be such a *struggle* anymore.

Were we, as the magazines said, fundamentally slack, allergic to seriousness? Or were we seduced by our own metaphors: the never-ending network, the flat world, God forgive us, the tipping point, the killer app? It doesn't matter now. By the time we saw ourselves whole we had useless graduate degrees, fortunes on paper, closets full of embarrassing wedding presents. Money was the by-product of making money, and the world was the size of a two-bedroom, one-and-a-half-bath apartment, PK VWS, EIK.

The hush that descends on the offices of a bankrupt company—the hum of one last vacuum cleaner, the screech of a razor blade chiseling a logo into little white shavings—is not the silence of the stage strewn with bodies at the end of *Hamlet*: not the screams of catharsis, but the gray noise of an imploded abstraction. Not life, but an interrupted, half-tumescent masturbatory fantasy of life; the abrupt ending to a bourgeois dream time. Who feels sorry for the pasty office worker, trudging back to his car with his carton of dusty photo frames and stained coffee mugs? Who *should* feel sorry? And what is a confession that goes on too long other than an act of self-annihilation, a way of making forgiveness impossible?

THE END

That we did make it across the bridge:

That we slammed into a concrete piling, did a header into the Inner Harbor;

That the Southie boys caught up with us, left us shit-kicked, concussed, bleeding from the mouths and ears;

Who's to say I never wished for these things to happen?

But of course that's the way with us: All our losses are imaginary. It was Nelson, not me, who was fired, when Troyer returned, and refused to believe the car had been vandalized where it sat; Nelson who forgot and refilled the tank with unleaded instead of diesel, so that it backfired and stalled, and gave him away, and then sat silently, refusing to tell the story, refusing to let *me* tell the story.

Every story has a scapegoat. And every story has a martyr. And because this is an American story, as we all know, they are always, always, one and the same.

MISSION STATEMENT (FINAL DRAFT)

We weren't saints; we were children, too; trying to locate ourselves in the shifting sands of theory and guilt, and we thought what better place to start than pain, someone else's pain, the pain of the dispossessed, but the truth was that all that was a distraction, a youthful dalliance, and the serious business was already ticking in our throats. We were children of the clock and of the deadline. Even the wealthiest, the most blue-blooded and trust-funded among us understood those rules. You could tattoo your face, declare yourself transgendered, become an anarchist or a Zapatista, get arrested with a truckful of cocaine, spend a year meditating in a locked room in Bhutan, sleep with prostitutes in Ciudad Juárez, and still, at the magic hour, at twenty-two or twenty-five or at the outermost limit, thirty, your life would resume as if it had never been interrupted. Money flew upward, and caught us in its traps.

I was dissolved, but only for a time; I was dissolved and reconstituted, like Kool-Aid, in a more concentrated form.

I FRIEND YOU

There's a Thompson Island counselor alumni group on Facebook now, of course. We have among us scores of advanced degrees and fashionably scruffy toddlers. We live in Mountainview and Cambridge and Tokyo and Carroll Gardens. We teach at prep schools, we are endocrinologists, we are partners at Debevoise, we own organic farms outside Woodstock, we are married to partners at Debevoise

and sit on the board of the Juvenile Diabetes Foundation.
Isn't it amazing!!! How much time has passed!!!

A CONFESSION

I think, again, of the children, of my charges on that unfortunate
island. I think of their knee-length T-shirts stained with Kool-Aid
and mayonnaise. I think of their glowing skin in all its glorious
shades, of their pudgy hands raised to catch me when I turned my
back, crossed my arms over my chest, and toppled over. I don't remember their names. It's too long now, and there were too many of
them. Why is it that we can never answer, truly, for the sources of our
pain? I hope they survived. Who's to say I didn't wish they could
bring me back to life, to bring blood back into my veins? I've said
enough. I've said enough. I've said enough. I hope they forgive me for
loving them.

The Isle of Youth
Laura van den Berg

I.

I ARRIVED AT MY SISTER'S APARTMENT just before the hurricane. My plane had been one of the last to land before the Miami Airport closed. From the taxi, I saw banks of black clouds settling on the horizon and palm trees bent from the wind. Bushes flapped like invisible hands were shaking them. The roads into downtown were empty. On the radio, a reporter said the hurricane would skim the western coast before spinning into the Gulf of Mexico, that it would all be over by morning. I didn't believe him. The sky looked frightening. I'd never been to Florida. My sister, Sylvia, and I were identical twins. I had not seen her in over a year.

"Does the hurricane have a name?" I asked the driver as we rolled down Sixth Street, scanning apartment buildings for the address I'd given.

"They're always named after women," he said.

He parked in front of my sister's building. It was tall and made of tangerine-colored stucco. I paid the driver and got out, pulling my carry-on toward the door. In the front lobby and in the elevator, the lights buzzed and flickered.

When Sylvia opened the door, I didn't enter right away. She looked like me and she didn't look like me. She had the same dainty nose and rounded chin, but she was thinner and had better posture. She had a ring in her lip and carefully styled bangs. Sweatpants, a sheer white tank top, pink socks. Chipped black polish on her nails. I had no idea what my sister was doing for work. I was a forensic accountant, employed by a divorce lawyer in Connecticut. My suits were poly blend, and I hadn't been to a hair salon in over a year. When my sister asked me to come, I had not considered our many differences. She said it was an emergency and I told her that I had vacation days saved. I didn't tell her that my husband and I were on the brink, and I'd been looking for something to take a chance on.

"Sylvia," I said. "How are you?"

319

"Looks like you brought the weather with you." She opened the door wider.

Inside, unlit candles sat on every possible surface, on top of the coffee table and the stereo, on the ledges of bookcases. I squeezed my suitcase handle, taking in everything: the sectional sofa and flat-screen TV to my left, the kitchen to my right, the balcony with slid-ing glass doors straight ahead, legions of candles. Even with the lights on, the apartment was dim, the storm having brought on a prema-ture night.

"Is that safe?" I pointed to the bookcases. "To have candles so close to all that paper?"

She shut the door. "You'll thank me when the electricity goes out."

I asked my sister what I should do with my luggage. She pointed to a hallway past the kitchen. The room was empty, save for a futon bed, and had been converted into a storage space for musical equip-ment: a guitar, amps, stacks of records. I had to clear away cords and a plastic box of guitar picks to find the mattress. I put my suitcase on the bed and opened it. I stared at the folded slacks and shirts and my plastic toiletries case. I closed the bag and walked out of the room.

Sylvia was on the balcony, the sliding doors open. I stood beside her and looked out at the empty streets and the windblown palm trees and the distant gray stretch of ocean.

If someone were to ask about my sister, I would tell them she was a dangerous person. The signs started showing in junior high, when she sent a neighborhood boy, who was in love with her, into a cata-strophic depression by taking his virginity and then sleeping with his two best friends. At thirty-four, she had been through three fiancés, countless jobs and cities and hair colors, bankruptcy, names. *Call me Lisa Anne*, she said one time. *Call me Suzette*, she said another. It wasn't just that my sister behaved badly—she was a shape-shifter, someone who bounced from one life to the next like a drug-resistant virus changing hosts. The longer I went without seeing her, the more comfortable I had become with the idea that she simply didn't exist, that I had no other half, no shadow self. But, after all those years, there she was, there she undeniably was, reaching for me at a time when I already felt like throwing myself under the rails.

"What's with all the music stuff in the bedroom?"

"I used to be in a band," she said. "But you wouldn't know about that."

"No," I said.

"We'll have to board these up soon," she said, pointing at the sliding doors behind us. "In case the glass breaks."

"Is this going to be a bad one?"

"A Category Two," she said. "Small potatoes around here."

I crossed my arms on top of the railing. "What's this hurricane named?"

"I've named her Marie Antoinette," she said. "The weather people call it something else."

"Marie Antoinette? As in let them eat cake?"

"More like off with their heads."

Nine o'clock was when the power went out. We had already boarded the sliding doors; I'd held small sheets of plywood across the glass while my sister pounded nails into her stucco walls. When the apartment went dark, Sylvia started lighting the candles. She did it effortlessly, as though she had practiced walking around her apartment blindfolded. Soon the living room was washed in a warm orange glow.

"That's it," she said. "Not much to do now but wait it out."

I sat on the couch, facing the bookcase filled with blazing candles. Rain and wind lashed the building. My sister stood in front of me, swaying from side to side. The ring in her lip glowed.

"Will you need to call Mark?" she asked. "Sometimes the reception is spotty during a bad storm."

"It doesn't matter," I said.

"I take it things aren't so good at home?"

I looked up at her. "How would you know?"

"I've called a few times in the last month," she said. "You weren't around, so Mark brought me up to speed."

I took one of the decorative pillows and tossed it across the room. It grazed Sylvia's knee before hitting the floor with a nearly inaudible thump. The last time my sister visited, she and Mark had gone out together one night, while I was working late. They came home drunk and vicious. They sought me out in the kitchen, where I was going through documents with a highlighter, and mocked me about everything from my thick-heeled pumps (Like a witch's shoes!) to my habit of grinding coffee every night before going to bed (Look who's so organized! So grown-up!). Even after I threw down my papers and left the room, my sister showed no mercy. She knew how to turn people, how to get someone to abandon loyalties, to change sides. She should have gone into espionage.

"And what did Mark say?"

"He said the marriage counselor suggested you take a vacation together."

"He told you we were seeing a counselor?"

"He said she has this really annoying habit of saying 'you see' before making a point. Like 'You see, you're misdirecting your anger again,' or 'You see, now is a time for compassion.'" Sylvia sat on the floor, pulling her legs underneath her. "Where do you think you'll go for this vacation?"

"We don't know." I couldn't help but feel, through these secret conversations with my husband, that my sister had gained a kind of power over me. "Did Mark sound like he wanted to go away with me?"

"He said he was on the fence."

"We're on the fence about a lot of things."

She asked if I wanted to hear a song she'd recorded with her old band. I nodded, trying to imagine my husband standing somewhere in our house and listening to my sister's voice on the other end of the line. What might she have said to him? What might he have confessed to her?

Sylvia slipped a CD into the battery-operated stereo. When the song came on, I recognized it as the one we had danced to many years ago, when we were college students, and felt an awful pang.

"Sylvia," I said. "That's David Bowie."

"Wrong track," she said. "It's a mix." She pressed a button and turned up the volume. A woman's voice overwhelmed the room. It was hollow, stretched thin, the words so elongated I couldn't understand the lyrics. An electric guitar kicked in, then drums. Sylvia tapped her fingers against her thighs, bobbed her head. The woman's voice grew shrill. I heard tambourines, another electric guitar. The song ended with the crash of cymbals.

"Which part were you?" I asked.

"The singer," she said.

"I see." The woman singing had sounded nothing like my sister.

"You don't believe me?"

"I didn't say that."

"Fine," she said. "I'll play you another one."

The next song opened with rapid-fire guitar and drums, breathless lyrics. I put my hands over my eyes and listened hard. *I haven't seen her in years*, I told myself. *How would I know what her singing voice is like?* But the more I listened the more I knew it wasn't her.

I uncovered my eyes. Sylvia was dancing, in her sweatpants and socked feet and transparent shirt. The candles cast strange shadows onto her face; I could see the outline of her breasts. She raised her arms, and I caught the glint of a belly-button ring. She opened her mouth wide and words came out, her voice clashing with the singer on the stereo. Was this me in another life, me in an alternate ending? I'd heard stories about twins having secret languages and dreaming the same dreams, but I had no idea if my sister was happy or sad or terrified. She turned the volume even higher. The candles flickered. The apartment was hot.

"Sylvia," I shouted over the noise, but she didn't seem to hear me. I tried again and again. Finally I got up and put my face close to her face and called her name.

"What?" she screamed back.

"Why am I here?"

What my sister wanted was to change identities. I wouldn't have to do much, just show up for her job at the Bortaga, a club on Miami Beach, and hang around the apartment for a few days. Sylvia explained this to me after she'd turned off the music and sat down on the floor. I was still on the couch, studying her face as she spoke. There was a man. He was married. She'd been having an affair with him for the last year. His wife, suspicious, had hired a private detective, who had taken photographs. Once the wife knew what Sylvia looked like and where she lived, she'd started following her. Sylvia would leave her building and see this woman sitting in her car, look over her shoulder while on the sidewalk and see the woman behind her. She had followed Sylvia to work, the grocery, the park, the post office, the beach, the hardware store, the hair salon. My sister and the married man had decided to end things, but they wanted one last fling. He wanted to take her to this place called the Isle of Youth, an island off the coast of Cuba, Isla de la Juventud in Spanish. There were stories about the isle being a sacred area, a place that hurricanes always missed, a place that was always on the right side of luck.

"But you can't leave because you have this woman following you," I said. "And if you and her husband are gone at the same time, she'll never believe that he's away on business or whatever he plans to say."

"Bingo," Sylvia said.

"I didn't see anyone loitering outside your building," I said. "I didn't see any suspicious cars."

"She's learned to blend in well," my sister said. "And I hope she's not deranged enough to stalk me during a hurricane."

"When were you planning to leave for this Isle of Youth?"

"Tomorrow night, if I can get you on board."

"Will the airport even be open by then?"

"It'll be open before noon," she said. "This city knows how to recover quickly."

There was a loud crash outside. I rubbed my fingertips against my nose. A candle on the coffee table went out. The wind and rain were unrelenting.

"You won't be able to wear the clothes you brought," Sylvia said. "You'll have to take things from my closet while I'm gone."

"What are you doing for work?"

"Stamping hands at a nightclub. It's one of those 'in the meantime' things."

I stood and walked over to the boarded doors. "There's no way I could pass for you in a nightclub."

"A comprehensive makeover is in order," Sylvia said. "Hair, makeup, clothes. The way I'll send you home will do more for your marriage than any romantic getaway."

"Speaking of Mark, what am I supposed to tell him?"

"That you've decided to extend your stay. That we're helping the city of Miami with hurricane cleanup. That I'm teaching you to snorkel. It doesn't matter."

All of a sudden my sister was behind me. I knew she was there, felt her heat, without turning around. "I think Mark and I have lied to each other enough," I said.

"Deception is necessary. In marriage, in life. Otherwise the world will just sandblast us away. You have to keep something for yourself."

"There's not one good reason why I should do this for you."

"Well, for one thing, you don't like where you are right now. You've been wanting a change, an escape, for a while." She put her chin on my shoulder. She touched my hair. "Here's another one: You've always wanted to know what it would be like to be me."

The makeover began at midnight. I sat on a stool in the kitchen. Sylvia placed a makeup bag, comb, hair spray, scissors, and a glass of water on the counter. She propped a flashlight on top of the microwave, so it shone in my face. She dipped the comb in the water and picked at my hair until it hung straight. She took a few inches off my bangs and then used a makeup sponge to apply foundation, a big brush for the powder and blush, little brushes for the eye shadow. She tweezed my brows, pulled at the skin beneath my eyes as she smudged on black liner, laced mascara through my lashes. She used her thumb to smudge red lipstick onto my mouth, another little brush for the gloss. She swept my bangs to the side with the comb and dusted them with hairspray. Through all this, we were silent, serious. By the time she finished, the candles were melting into wax stumps and the wind was still howling.

"You've got quite a collection of beauty products," I said.

"I used to work at a salon, before the band," Sylvia said. "But you wouldn't know about that either." She held a mirror in front of me. In the half-lit kitchen, it was like looking at myself in a carnival mirror; my face was slimmer, my cheekbones higher, my lips swollen with color, my bangs stiff with hairspray and curving over my left eye. My sister crouched beside me, squeezing her face into the frame. We looked identical. I brought my fingers to my mouth; Sylvia batted my hand away, saying I would mess up my lipstick.

She put down the mirror and kneeled in front of me. She ran her fingertips over my bangs, almost tenderly. "The hair's easy," she said. "Just brush your bangs to the side while you're blow-drying in the morning, then spray, spray, spray."

"There's no way I'll be able to do this on my own," I said.

"I thought of that already," she said. "I wrote out instructions for you. We'll go over all of it tomorrow." She told me there was an envelope that had everything I would need to know, from instructions on hair and makeup to directions to the club and the names of her co-workers to the description of the woman who had been following her to lists of what she usually bought at the grocery.

"You're being very organized about this."

"I love a good scheme," Sylvia said. "I would have been a great criminal mastermind."

"What about when I'm at your job? What if I forget someone's name or make some kind of dumb mistake?"

"People are used to me making plenty of dumb mistakes," Sylvia said. "That's the last thing that would make anyone think you're not me."

At two in the morning, the electricity came back on. We blew out the candles and turned on the lights. The apartment was a mess—wax drippings, newspaper pinned beneath the stool in the kitchen, brushes and compacts and tubes on the counter, boarded windows.

Sylvia said we would worry about cleaning in the morning. She put on cotton pajamas with martini glasses printed on them and tossed me a pair with flamingos. I had brought my own things to sleep in, but didn't protest; her pajamas were soft and smelled like perfume.

I followed Sylvia around the apartment as she bolted the front door and clicked off the lights. I still heard the low roar of the storm outside. We went into her room and sat on her bed. A Sex Pistols poster was pinned to the wall, the head of a woman colored purple and white with gray text blocking out her mouth and eyes.

From the bedside-table drawer, Sylvia took a damp pad from a jar and wiped off the makeup. I closed my eyes. The pads were cool. When she was done, she asked if I wanted to sleep in her room, like we sometimes did when we were young, when our parents were shouting at each other and we were afraid. I said OK. She kneeled on the floor, cleared away a mound of clothes, and yanked out a trundle bed.

"This is where I would make my boyfriends sleep when I was mad at them," she said.

We got into our beds. Sylvia turned off the light. In the darkness, the white outline of the poster glowed. It was hotter in the bedroom, and I pushed the sheets down to my waist. I heard tree branches slapping the building and a terrible, tearing wind.

"When the weather's nice, I have drinks on the balcony," Sylvia said. "There's vodka in the freezer. You can do that too, if you want."

"OK," I said. "I'll think about it."

We were quiet for a while. I couldn't relax, couldn't even think about sleep. There was an electricity in my body that was unlike anything I had felt in a long time.

"I jumped off that balcony once," Sylvia said. "About a year ago. I landed in the bushes. I broke my arm and two fingers. I got a concussion. I had to spend the night in the hospital."

I rolled toward her. I saw the silhouette of her raised arm, her fanned fingers. "Why didn't someone from the hospital call me?"

"I told them I didn't have any family," she said.

"I would have helped," I said. "If you'd called me, I would have helped."

"I couldn't be sure," she said. "Since you told me to disappear the last time we talked."

She was referring to the time she phoned to say she was in love with Mark, and that she was going to tell him so, and that she thought there was a chance he was in love with her too. I'd told her she was a sickness and I was cutting her out. After the call, I asked Mark if he was having an affair with Sylvia. He said "no" then and he said "no" years later, in the office of our marriage counselor. But I still just had this feeling. Maybe it was my imagination, or maybe I wanted someone to blame. I was willing to entertain those possibilities. What I couldn't understand was why I didn't seem able to do anything more than stand around in pain.

"You told me to stay away," she said. "So I did."

A week after the balcony, Sylvia tried to hang herself in the bathroom, but the shower rod broke. She said that she didn't even go to the hospital that time. All she had to show for her efforts was a ring of bruises around her neck.

"I have the worst luck sometimes," she said.

"Some people would say you were lucky."

We were quiet for a while, though something about my sister's breathing told me she wanted to keep talking.

"I'm glad you're here," she finally said.

I'd heard that line before, always when I was doing whatever it was that Sylvia wanted.

"It's good that you called," I said. "Thanks for the trip to beauty school."

"Maybe you'll like my life so much, you won't want to give it back."

II.

My first day as Sylvia began at dusk. From the balcony, I watched my sister slip into a taxi. All afternoon we had been looking for the woman's car, but the coast had seemed clear. After Sylvia confirmed the airport was open and her rendezvous was on, a hushed phone call taken in her bedroom, we went over everything in the envelope, spreading lists of names and work schedules and addresses across the kitchen counter. She had even gotten a fake lip ring for me. It was shaped like a comma and came in a tiny plastic Baggie. She picked out an outfit for my shift at the Bortaga, a black minidress and red heels, and did my hair and makeup once more. When it was time for her to leave, we stood in the apartment doorway. I wished her luck. She put her arms around my neck and kissed the side of my face. And then she was gone.

After her taxi had disappeared down the street, I went into the bathroom and stood at the mirror. My face was bruised with makeup.

327

My bangs drooped over my left eye. I wedged the lip ring on. The metal felt strange inside my mouth. I couldn't stop running my tongue over the thin silver curve. I studied the photo of Sylvia leaning against a palm tree that hung on the bathroom wall, wondering who had taken it. An old lover, a friend? This man she was meeting? I stared at her wide smile, her narrowed eyes. I tried out the same expression in the mirror. I looked just like her.

In the kitchen, I poured a vodka on the rocks. I stood on the balcony and watched the sun drop. There was sand on the concrete floor, the grains rough against my bare feet. The air was wet and heavy. I saw palm trees that were nothing but brown stalks, sagging power lines. Everywhere there was paper and glass and spears of wood, like the aftermath of a concert or a riot. Sylvia's building had made it through the storm without any damage, but others in her neighborhood, we'd heard on the news, had broken windows and leaks. I heard a rumbling and saw a street-cleaning machine inching down Sixth Street. I finished the drink. The sun was halfway below the horizon, a watery orange orb. It seemed much bigger than the sun in Connecticut, the heat radiating across the tops of buildings and into me.

I woke the next morning feeling groggy, as though I'd been asleep for days. I rose and showered, using Sylvia's gardenia-scented soap on my skin, her pink pumice stone on my feet. Afterward I put on a silk bathrobe and poked around in the medicine cabinet: a nail file, red polish, an eyelash curler, makeup sponges, pills. I examined the label on the bottle—Lorazepam, the same thing, incidentally, a psychiatrist I once saw had given me for nerves. I would take one and be immune to anything my husband said, any argument. I opened the bottle; there were all kinds in there: tiny blue ones, round red ones, rectangular pink ones. I pushed them around with my index finger and took the one that looked the most familiar, placing an oblong white pill in my mouth. I closed the medicine cabinet and watched in the mirror as the pill dissolved, bleeding white on the reddish flesh of my tongue.

I wrapped my hair in a towel, took the bottle of red polish from the cabinet, and painted my toenails on the balcony. The streets were a little cleaner. It was hotter than before. The sky looked like a wet canvas someone had smudged with their fingers. I couldn't remember the last time I had so many open days in front of me, since Sylvia only worked three nights a week at the Bortaga. Her next shift was tomorrow. Today was training.

In the bathroom, I moved a hair dryer over my toes until the polish hardened. Then I found some jeans, low-rises with holes in the knees, and a purple tank top in the bedroom. I studied myself in Sylvia's full-length mirror. My stomach wasn't as flat and my arms were paler. I taped my sister's beauty instructions, complete with a diagram of a face drawn in blue pen, to the bathroom mirror and did my hair and makeup. After I wedged the lip ring on, I looked myself over. The eyeliner was too thick, the lipstick a little smudged, but not bad. A decent imitation Sylvia.

Before leaving the apartment, I picked up the grocery list and the car keys. My sister had an old Mazda convertible. I looked forward to putting the top down. In the lobby, I opened my sister's mailbox with the tiny key she'd given me. It was empty. Outside, the car I'd been warned about was the first thing I saw: a beige Lincoln town car parked next to Sylvia's Mazda. As I passed, I saw a woman with shoulder-length hair and sunglasses staring through the windshield. I started the Mazda and rolled down the top. I was a little drowsy from the pill and the sun hurt my eyes. I found rhinestone-studded sunglasses in the glove compartment and put them on. I headed to the grocery on Creston Avenue. The beige Lincoln followed.

At the grocery, I parked and rolled up the convertible top. I pushed a cart toward the entrance. The woman trailed behind me, picking up a small basket inside. She kept her sunglasses on. She followed me up and down the aisles, never more than a few feet away. In the frozen foods section, I kept an eye on the woman by looking at the reflections in the freezer cases, like I once saw a character do in a detective movie. Her basket stayed empty. She dragged one of her ankles slightly. I went about my business and by the time I'd checked out, she was nowhere to be found.

After the grocery, I stopped at Coco's, a café on Miami Avenue. I wanted to keep practicing being Sylvia in public. The café had red walls and a dusty black floor. A window was covered with plywood, and a sign that read COCO VS. FLORA was taped to the planks. I peered into a glass pastry case, trying to decide between a chocolate cupcake and a poppyseed muffin. I went with the cupcake and a coffee because I thought that was what Sylvia would want.

"So the hurricane was named Flora?" I asked the woman behind the register. She had drawn-on eyebrows and cropped hair.

"That's what they call it on the news," she said. "I call it something else."

"What's that?"

"Magdalena," she said. "After my mother."

I took a table facing the entrance. I scraped the icing off the cupcake with a plastic knife and ate it, just like Sylvia did when we were kids. The ceiling fan moved in lazy circles. I was finishing my coffee when the woman who had been trailing me came in and sat down. When I first saw her, I almost let the mug slip from my hands. In the grocery, she'd kept her distance. I expected her to wait on the sidewalk or in her car, ready to follow whenever I was on the move again. I didn't think she'd come so close.

She took the booth by the boarded window, facing me. She didn't order anything and kept her sunglasses on. She folded her hands on top of the table. I took my time finishing my coffee; the last few sips were bitter and thick. I waited for this woman to say or do something, to shout or throw something at me. But she just sat there, square shouldered, her big black sunglasses covering half her face.

After the coffee was gone, I put my own sunglasses back on. I was worried the woman might detect a difference in my eyes. Then I went and sat across from her. Her brown hair was streaked with blonde, her skin freckled and tan. She smelled like coconut oil. She wore a white T-shirt and jeans and a thick gold watch. I wondered if my sister had even gotten this close to the woman before. I liked the idea of being braver than Sylvia.

"What's your name?" I said.

"My husband never told you?"

"Never."

"I've been following you for a month and you've never said a word to me." She crossed her arms, holding onto her elbows. "Why today?"

"I want to know why you're following me."

"You know plenty."

"I want to know when you'll stop."

"I could hurt you. Right now. I really could." She pressed her fingernails, done in a French manicure, against her forehead. "I don't know when I'll be able to stop."

"I'm going to the video store next, just to give you a heads-up," I said. "It feels like a Hitchcock kind of night to me."

I left her sitting in the booth. I wasn't sure she'd followed until I walked out of the video store, where I'd used my sister's card to rent *Vertigo*, and saw the Lincoln in the parking lot, just a few spaces away from the Mazda. I waved to the woman before driving away.

That evening, as I watched the movie on Sylvia's TV, the phone rang. I ignored it, as I imagined Sylvia would. When I heard my sister's voice on the machine, I paused the film and sat up. She was calling to give me the number of her hotel on the Isle of Youth. She said the island was split into two sections, the north and the south, and that a large swamp ran through the center, reaching from coast to coast. She said it was even hotter than Miami, that there were green iguanas on the rocks and black coral in the ocean and that if you dove at Los Barcos Hundidos, you could see the remnants of sunken ships. She said it felt good to be someplace else, to see different things. *Thank you,* Sylvia said. She paused. I thought I heard bells in the background. *I owe you big.*

For my first night at the Bortaga, I put on the outfit Sylvia had given me and prepared my hair and makeup with extra care, following the diagram on the wall. After the sun went down, I drank a vodka on the balcony. The Miami skyline was a wall of white and pink light. Before leaving, I took a pill. In the car, I practiced saying my name was Sylvia.

On the road, it was too dark to see if the Lincoln was following. I put the top down and let the wind roar through my hair. The bridge that led to Miami Beach was lit gold. I saw dark water below, heard music coming from party boats. My husband always said Sylvia was more fun, more freewheeling. I wondered what he would think if he was riding beside me, if he would be frightened when I hit the gas and screamed around a corner, if he would be surprised, if he would know who I was.

I took a wrong turn on Espanola Way and got to the club late. I touched up my lipstick in the rearview, then gave the valet my car. I walked past the line outside and the black-shirted bouncers, trying not to wobble in my heels. When I entered the club, I was hit with sharp, cold air. A stainless-steel bar stretched down one side of the room; on the other, a staircase spiraled into the darkness upstairs. In the back, DJs stood on a stage and people danced beneath streams of flashing light. The lights made the dancing bodies look fragmented and strange.

I walked up to the woman sitting on a black stool and stamping the hands of people entering. She was pixieish and scowling. Her silver dress showed the dragon tattooed on the tops of her breasts. Her name was Lydia, according to my sister's notes.

"Sorry I'm late," I said.

"You're always late." She jammed the ink pad and stamp into my hands, then drifted over to the bar, where she sat for a minute before disappearing into the dark mass on the dance floor.

My sister was right about one thing. Her job was easy. The people knew to stick out their hands, palms down; all I had to do was press on the phosphorescent stamp. I zoned out. I listened to the music. I thought about Sylvia on the Isle of Youth, with the black coral and the iguanas. I imagined my husband watching the news in our living room. He liked to turn all the lights off when he watched TV. He felt so far from me, now that I had slipped into this other dimension, this crack in the earth. All the questions that had plagued me on the flight to Miami—Does he want me to go? Want me to stay?—felt so remote, like background noise.

I'd been stamping hands for an hour when I spotted the woman who had been following me. She wore a dress with a scoop neck and long sleeves, which looked out of place in the sea of naked bellies and thighs. When she reached me, she looked straight ahead and stuck out her hand. I rolled on the stamp.

"Won't your husband wonder where you are?" I whispered.

"He could care less."

She went to the bar. The bartender brought her a drink without being asked. She didn't seem to be watching me very closely, which I took to mean she'd been to the Bortaga enough times to know what my sister did.

I was watching the woman when I felt a hand on my shoulder. A man in a gray suit stood over me. His rich black hair fell to his chin and his eyes were different colors, one of them blue, the other hazel. He leaned down and pressed his lips against my ear.

"Meet me upstairs in five," he said.

He went up the spiral staircase, vanishing into the darkness above. I was gazing upward when a bouncer called my sister's name and pointed at the small group waiting for me to stamp their hands. Only a few minutes passed before Lydia came back. She looked paler; sweat had beaded on her temples and forehead.

"I'll cover you," she said. "You're needed upstairs."

I handed her the ink pad and stamp, then got off the stool and went to the stairs. I put my hand on the cool steel railing and started to climb. What had my sister failed to tell me? It could be anything. That I knew.

At the top of the stairs, there was a dark hallway with doors on each end. I could tell from the flat sheets of light coming through the bottoms. The growl of heavy metal came from behind one of the doors. The man in the gray suit was waiting in shadows, leaning against the wall. I stood next to him. My palms were damp. I felt on the verge of being exposed. Up close, would I sound like my sister, smell like my sister? I was grateful for the darkness.

He stood in front of me and put his hands on my shoulders. He asked me if I had it.

"It?"

"What we discussed."

"Yes," I said. "I mean, I will."

"Sylvia." He moved his hand over my face, closing my eyes. Then his hand went down my stomach and between my thighs. He kept it inside my legs, his fingers barely touching my skin. I leaned into the wall. I wasn't sure if I was supposed to be terrified or enjoying this.

He said my sister's name again. I asked what he wanted. I kept my eyes closed.

"I need to know that you'll be there," he said.

"There?"

He pulled his hand away. "Don't act dumb. It doesn't become you."

"OK," I said. "I'll be there."

"With what we discussed?"

"Right. With what we discussed."

He stepped back. "I don't want to see anything happen to you, Sylvia."

"I know," I said. "Of course not."

He touched the base of my neck before walking down the hall and disappearing behind a door. When I went downstairs, into the blistering light, the ceiling was raining silver confetti.

When I returned to Sylvia's apartment, I took the cordless phone onto the balcony and called her hotel. The front desk transferred me to her room and when she didn't answer, I left a message. I told her about the gray-suited man, that she was supposed to have something for him, that some kind of meeting had been arranged. I said she had to tell me what was going on, that this wasn't the kind of thing I could pretend my way through. I said she was wrong about what she'd told me earlier, that I hadn't agreed to this because I wanted to know what it was like to be her. *Couldn't you see*, I said, *that I just wanted to get out of my life?*

The sky was black, the horizon electric. I heard the distant whoosh of the ocean. Even at night, the heat was crushing. I leaned over the railing and stared at the sidewalk below. Cars lined the street; people drifted up and down the sidewalks. I tried to imagine Sylvia flinging herself over the iron barrier and dropping through the air like a meteor. Her apartment was only on the fourth floor. Thick hedges bordered the sidewalk; the lawn was green and soft. It was certainly possible for someone to jump off this balcony and survive. I imagined what those first waking moments, on the grass or in hedges, might have been like for Sylvia. The realization that she had failed, that she was still alive. I wondered, as I lived my own unhappy life fourteen hundred miles away, if any of those sudden, inexplicable pains—the ache in the belly, the cramp in the knee—could be attributed to some primitive part of my brain registering that my other half was in peril.

I went into the living room and dialed my husband's number. I hadn't called him since I phoned to say I was extending my stay in Miami. But, I realized as the phone rang, I didn't have to be the person calling him now.

"Mark," I said when he answered, adopting my sister's slightly higher pitch. "It's Sylvia."

"How's the weather?" he asked. "The storm?"

"It's passed."

"And my wife?"

"She's fine," I said. "A bit difficult at times."

He paused. I thought I heard a door close. "Sylvia would never say 'a bit difficult.' She would say 'she's a pain in the ass' or 'she's fucked in the head.' She wouldn't be delicate about it."

"You got me." I relaxed my throat and my voice slipped back into its regular tone. I lay on the floor, my legs stretching underneath the coffee table.

"Why would you pretend to be Sylvia?" he asked. "After all you've been through with her?"

"You mean after all *we've* been through with her."

"When are you coming home?"

I nestled the phone between my chin and shoulder. "Soon," I said. "When Sylvia is done needing me."

"Since when do you care about Sylvia needing you?" he said. "I don't understand why you went down there in the first place, let alone why you're staying."

"Since when do you have conversations with my sister without telling me?"

"It's not what you think."

"How would you know what I think?"

He was quiet for a moment. "Let's not let this go the way it always goes."

I picked at the wax that had dripped onto the carpet and dried. "When I get back, are we going to take that trip or what?"

"Yes," he said. "We'll do it."

"You really want to?"

"Yes," he said. "I really do."

"Sylvia said you weren't sure."

"Sometimes we get frustrated. Sometimes we say things we don't mean." He sighed. "I don't know what else to tell you."

"So much," I said. "There's so much more you could tell me."

"I've decided I want to go away with you," he said. "Can't we just leave it at that?"

"That's been our whole problem," I said. "Deciding to leave things at that."

"You're making it impossible to talk."

"Fine," I said. "Where will we go? Tell me."

He sighed again and then fell silent. I listened to his breath on the line.

"One summer, when I was in college, I visited a Tibetan monastery," he said. "It was just outside Lhasa. I sat in silence with the monks for three days. We could do something like that, something spiritual."

I already knew about this trip. He'd taken it in the company of his former girlfriend, who he'd come close to marrying, but I didn't bring that up. His voice reminded me of who I really was, of the deepness of my—our—unhappiness. When you're married, our counselor had told us, happiness is like a joint banking account; it becomes full or depleted in tandem.

"I was thinking an island might be nice," I said.

"I hate to swim," he said. "You know that about me."

I rested the phone against my chest. My husband started talking about practical things—how long we could afford to stay away, whether or not we should use a travel agent. His voice passed over me like wind.

335

III.

The next morning, when I went into the kitchen to make coffee, I found two men sitting on the living-room sofa. They stood and introduced themselves as A2 and B2. They were broad shouldered and bald. They both had fleshy lips and soft chins, though A's face was longer, his forehead higher and ruddier, while B's was rounder, his eyes a little squinty. They wore black T-shirts and black slacks and boots. They told me my name was no longer Sylvia Collins. To them, I was only the mark: C2.

I hadn't done my makeup or hair or put on the lip ring. I was naked underneath my sister's silk bathrobe. I crossed my arms over my chest.

"What's with the names?" I said.

"It's the Pythagorean theorem," A said. "We used to be mathematicians."

"You missed your meeting this morning," B said, stepping closer to me. "You told Andre you'd be there and you weren't. So we've been sent to keep an eye on you, to make sure you're getting things in order, like you've told people you would."

"And to make sure you don't split," A said.

I sat on the floor. My bathrobe gaped open. The whole picture was coming into focus, a blur in my periphery gradually taking shape, like when your sight starts recovering after getting eyedrops at the doctor's office. I pressed my legs together. I felt like I was sinking into the floor.

"This is a complicated situation," I said.

"Everyone tells us that," A said.

"Sylvia isn't here right now. I mean, I'm not actually Sylvia."

"Everyone tells us that too," B said.

I asked about making a call. The men shrugged. I dialed my sister's hotel room. I got the machine again. I told her that two men were in her apartment and that she needed to take the next flight home. After hanging up, I turned to A and B and raised my arms. They seemed unimpressed.

"Listen," A said. "Nothing is going to happen to you. Not yet. It's too soon for that sort of thing, we've been told."

"Just do what you've promised to do," B said.

"I didn't promise anything," I told them. "I'm not Sylvia."

"Whatever," they said.

I made coffee and got dressed, taking the first thing I saw in the drawer: jean shorts and a red tank top. In the bathroom, I styled my bangs and did the makeup basics—lipstick, mascara, blush—and put on the lip ring. When I came back into the kitchen, A and B had emptied the coffee pot. They took up too much space in the apartment. I needed to get out. I drove to Coco's, A and B in the backseat. Before leaving, I took one of Sylvia's pills and when they realized what I was up to in the bathroom, they demanded a dose of their own. These kinds of jobs have their perks, A had said, knocking his back without any water. In the car, they squabbled over radio stations.

"Are all people in your profession like this?" I asked.

"Like what?" they said.

We passed high-rises and surf shops, snow cone vendors and hot dog stands. There was little sign of the storm by then, just the occasional ripped billboard or bald palm tree. In the rearview, I noticed the Lincoln behind us. At a red light, I rolled down the window and waved.

"Who are you waving to?" A wanted to know.

"No one," I said.

"Is this a convertible?" B asked.

"Yeah," I said.

"Put down the top," he said.

"I don't feel like it."

A leaned over the console. I smelled cologne that reminded me of what my father used to wear. He had a tiny silver stud in his ear. When he spoke, I felt his breath on my neck.

"Who gives a fuck what you feel like?" he said.

I put the top down. Wind raked through my hair. The breeze felt good. At another red light, I took my hands off the wheel and thrust my arms into the open air.

At Coco's, A and B took a table in the corner and waited. The window was still boarded. The boy behind the counter had a black eye. I noticed ants crawling beneath the plastic dome of a cake plate holding half a lemon meringue pie. While I was in line, the woman came in and took the same booth. She wore her big sunglasses and had a little orange scarf tied around her neck. I got my coffee and joined her. This time, I kept my sunglasses off.

I touched the boards covering the window. "I wonder how much longer these will be here," I said.

"Who knows," she said. "We're used to seeing the mark of storms."

"Don't you want something to eat?" I asked. "Something to drink?"

She shook her head. I asked what she knew about the Isle of Youth.

"Many years ago, I went there with my husband," she said. "It was full of marshes and huge insects. The houses and hotels were all falling in. It was anything but a paradise."

"What's your name?"

"I find it hard to believe my husband never told you. He isn't very discreet."

"I don't know your husband," I said. "But he isn't on a business trip, like he said."

She took off her sunglasses. Her eyes were an odd shade of gray. "What are you talking about?"

I looked past the woman, at A and B, who were huddled together at their table, watching. "I'm not sure how to explain this," I began, and then I told her everything. That it was my sister, Sylvia, and not me, her twin, who had been having the affair with her husband, that I was just filling in while they had one last hurrah. And now, thanks to my sister's involvement in God-knows-what, I was being followed by two men who wouldn't believe me when I said I wasn't her.

The woman cupped a hand over her eyes. "My husband hasn't left town for business since April."

"What?"

"He lost his job," she said. "I thought you knew all about that."

"When did you see him last?"

"This morning," she said. "I watched him do a crossword puzzle. He kept asking if I knew a synonym for flummoxed."

"You mean he's home?" I asked. "Right now?"

"Yes," she said. "Right now."

I propped my elbows on the table and pressed my face into my hands. On the radio, I caught the end of one of the songs Sylvia had played for me and claimed as her own. My feet tingled. I leaned back in the booth and dropped my hands into my lap.

"Why do you even believe me?" I asked. "I mean, how do you know I'm not Sylvia?"

"You walk like you're not sure where you want to go. You're more nervous, more tense. You sister acts like she has nothing but ice inside her."

I felt relieved that there might be a way to tell us apart after all.

"Why would you do this for someone?" the woman asked. "Why would you agree to take over their life?"

338

I considered telling her that I had wanted to help my sister, that I had wanted us to reconnect, even though that wasn't it at all. I had always thought of Sylvia as being free—of responsibility, of decency, of career and home, of building the things you're supposed to build, the things that everyone says are so important, but just turn out to be window dressing.

"I wanted to feel free," I said.

"Who doesn't?"

"I'm sorry for all that's happened to you. My marriage isn't in the greatest shape either."

"I don't know why I've done what I've done." She sighed. "Why I didn't just leave."

"I could say the same thing about myself."

"Where are these men?" She leaned toward me. "The ones who are following you."

"Sitting behind you," I said.

She nodded, but didn't look over her shoulder. I admired her restraint.

"What are you going to do about them?" she asked. "Should you call the police?"

"I don't think it quite works that way." I stood up. I had the number for Sylvia's hotel in my purse. I looked down at the woman, then over at A and B. The only time my husband ever followed me was on our second wedding anniversary. He waited outside my office and followed me to the park where I usually ate lunch. I was unwrapping a tuna-fish sandwich when he jumped out from behind a tree, holding a little white box with a cake inside. Flash forward five years, and he'd stopped chasing after me when I stormed out of the house during our fights. As I looked at the three faces of my followers, I was hit with something that felt almost like desire.

I headed for the door. The men followed. The woman did not.

I went to a pay phone down the street, A and B in pursuit. I fished some quarters from my purse and dialed Sylvia's number. She answered after one ring.

"Hello," I said. "It's me." The sky was bright. I put on the sunglasses.

"Oh," she said. "I thought you were going to be someone else."

"So here's what I know: Your lover is home, in Miami, and you're in deep shit. Two men have been sent to keep an eye on you because you missed some kind of meeting." I looked over my shoulder at A and B. One of them leaned against a telephone poll, the other rolled a little gray rock around on the sidewalk with the toe of his boot.

"I needed you." She was quiet for a moment. "You wouldn't have agreed to fill in for me if you'd known what I was really doing."

"Which is?"

"Correcting a supply problem."

"You cannot be serious."

"A and B are harmless. They're never sent to do the really dirty work."

"This is more than I can handle," I said. "This is more than I agreed to."

"You can handle a lot."

"I handle more than I should," I said. "Are you even on the Isle of Youth?"

"That part's true," she said. "But it's not what I thought it would be like. It's hot and dirty and run-down."

"This trip hasn't been what I thought it would be like either," I said. "Not even close."

"I'm still coming back when I promised," she said. "I'll meet you at the apartment tomorrow night. Everything will get straightened out then."

"As soon as you walk through the door, I'm gone."

"You don't care about what happens to me?"

"You said everything would be straightened out."

"Wouldn't you want to be sure?"

"I don't think I can afford to."

My sister sighed. "So what's my life like these days?"

"Lonely," I said. "Very lonely."

"Tomorrow night," she said. "I'll be there." She inhaled sharply, as though she was about to say something else, and then hung up the phone.

"See?" I said, turning to the men. "I'm not Sylvia. I'm her sister. I was just talking to Sylvia on the phone."

"Bravo," A said.

"Nice show," B said, applauding.

"You two should have stuck with mathematics," I said as we all walked back to the car.

*

I drove around downtown Miami in a daze. The sky was clear; it was hard to believe a hurricane had blown through only a few days before. We kept the top down. A and B were bickering over the radio again. They finally agreed on NPR.

"We like *The Infinite Mind*," B told me. This week's program featured a woman who, after brain surgery, woke up believing she was a nineteenth-century monk. Formerly a fifth-grade English teacher, the woman now recited details of her ascent through monasticism and her life in the monastery, all of which checked out with religious scholars. Soon her speech and motor skills began to decline, and the last word she spoke was *Megaloschemos*, Greek for Schema, a term used for a monk who had reached the highest level of spiritual enlightenment.

After the program ended, B said the story illustrated how speech is an unauthentic form of communication.

"Think about it," he said. "She reached, symbolically speaking, the highest level of enlightenment just before she stopped talking."

A countered that it was a commentary on inborn knowledge, on how we hold inside ourselves ideas and experiences that exist on a plane far above our conscious minds.

"For example," he said, "the first time someone asked me to take a gun apart and put it back together, I did it automatically, even though I'd never been taught how. I'd been holding this knowledge inside me without knowing it."

"Maybe it's a commentary on how badly this woman's surgeon fucked up," I said.

"That's just cynicism," A said. "That's too easy, too shallow."

"To look away from mystery is to look away from life itself," B added.

"Jesus Christ," I said. "Why are you talking like that?"

"It's what distinguishes us in our profession," B said. "Our thoughtfulness."

We passed kids riding low-slung bicycles and a bus full of nuns. I wondered what kind of inborn knowledge I might have inside me; I imagined a silver spiral sitting in my chest, waiting to be utilized. I had just turned onto Eleventh Street when the men began to criticize my driving.

"You're just driving around the same blocks," B said. "You're way past deadline. You should be getting it together, sorting things out."

"I don't know where to go," I said. "I don't know what to do."

341

"Figure something out," A said. "We're getting bored back here."

I considered our options while stopped at a light, tapping my fingers against the wheel. "I've got it," I said, turning the car toward the one place I knew my sister stayed away from.

Sylvia had never liked water. Once, when we were twelve, our parents took us on a seaside trip to Carmel. At night, in our resort room with dolphin-printed wallpaper, my sister was kept awake by nightmares about being swallowed by a tidal wave and swept out to sea. I had enjoyed the trip because it was one of the few times I was better at something; I swam with abandon, ducking underwater and holding my breath until I felt my lungs would burst.

After parking the Mazda on the edge of Miami Beach, I took off my sandals. A and B lumbered along behind me. The beach was a great sweep of cerulean water and white sand; when I looked into the distance, I saw nothing but the peaks of boats. Striped umbrellas jutted from the ground; lifeguard towers painted pale yellow and lavender dotted the shore. Girls lay facedown in the sand, their bronzed backs and legs gleaming. Since leaving Coco's, there had been no sign of the woman and her beige Lincoln.

I left my sandals in the sand and went in up to my ankles. The water was warm. I continued until the water reached the ragged hem of my shorts. I looked back at A and B. They were standing on the beach, in the shade of a palm tree, their arms crossed. I only needed to go a little farther to feel the bottom disappear, to feel nothing but water beneath me, but I liked the firm boundary under my feet. I liked feeling there was one thing I could count on. I stood thigh-deep in the water and dragged my fingers across the surface, staring at whatever it was that lay beyond: blueness, escape, certain death. It felt strange to know that behind me stood such an immense and troubled city.

I remembered once trying to convince my husband and Sylvia to spend a weekend at the beach, but he said he didn't like the ocean and Sylvia looked at him and smiled and then commented on how alike they were. I had been grating carrots for a salad. I put down the grater, confused. My husband and I had gone to the Jersey Shore all the time during our first year of marriage. I'd never known that he didn't like the sea. *Since when*, I'd wanted to ask him. *What changed?* It seemed clear to me that my sister's fear had infected him.

I went back to that fear, to that seaside trip with our parents, which revealed a side of Sylvia I had never seen before: shivering, small, vulnerable. She always looked so unhappy when she emerged from the water, with her slicked-down hair and blue lips, like a cat that had been sprayed with a hose. On our last afternoon, Sylvia suggested we play a game where we held each other's heads underwater, to see who could stay down the longest. Her only condition was that we didn't go out past our waists. I agreed, certain I could win. Sylvia lasted twenty seconds before she pinched my leg, the signal to let go. I still remembered how slim and pale her limbs looked underneath the water, and the silken feeling of her wet hair between my fingers. When it was my turn, I made it forty seconds before running out of air, but when I pinched Sylvia's leg, nothing happened. Her hands bore down against the back of my head. I swung my arms and legs, dug my fingernails into her knee. By the time she released me, I was gasping, open mouthed, like fish do when stranded on land. *You didn't follow the rules*, I shouted, but she just went back to shore and ran down the beach, the shallow water spraying around her ankles, her power restored.

Clouds had started banking along the horizon and the boats had disappeared from sight. The ocean looked choppier, its color more gray. I pressed my hands against my face and bent over. I wanted a jolt, something that would snap me back into a world I recognized. I dunked my head into the water. The salt stung my eyes.

When the sky began to darken, I trudged out of the water and drove home. In the lobby, I checked the mailbox. There was a postcard of the Isle of Youth: a photo of a turquoise sea and a white sailboat. The back of the card had gotten wet and the ink had bled. I held it up to A and B.

"Sylvia sent me this card," I said. "She sent it from the Isle of Youth."

"I can't read the message on the back," A said.

"You could have sent that card to yourself," B added.

I put the postcard back into the mailbox, then turned to the men and asked why they weren't making me do whatever work Sylvia was supposed to be doing.

"That'll be someone else's job," A said. "We're just supposed to watch you."

In the apartment, the men asked if there was any pizza, so I ordered one. Later we ate and watched *Die Hard* on TV. After the movie, I didn't wrap the extra pizza in tinfoil and put it in the fridge, like I would have at home; I left the box on the kitchen counter, our glasses and plates and crumpled paper napkins on the coffee table.

I slipped into the bedroom, where I changed into a pair of Sylvia's pajamas and called my husband.

"It's me," I said when he answered.

"I know," he said. "You don't have to tell me."

I lay on the bed, facing the wall. I touched the smooth edge of the poster, looking up at the woman's covered mouth and eyes. "I'm in a situation."

"A situation?"

"This is going to sound like a lot to ask," I said. "But I want you to come down to Florida tomorrow night. I want you to meet me at Sylvia's apartment and bring me home."

"I'm sure you're capable of doing that on your own," he said. "You've never had much trouble coming and going."

"You don't know what I've been through."

"Then explain it to me."

"I'm being followed by three people," I said, but my mind was already moving in a different direction entirely. I thought back to certain times with my husband, when the fights were just starting to get dangerous, when every night, it seemed, we found ourselves on the brink of losing irretrievable ground. There were things people could say to each other that brought about a kind of death, in that you never got over it; you apologized and sought counseling, you told people your marriage was "recovering," but really you were just presiding over a dead thing. Of course, I didn't have such ideas back then, when we still had a chance. I thought we were like rubber; I thought everything would just bounce off.

"Who are these people who are following you?" my husband asked.

"Well, actually, now I think it's down to two."

"Did your sister get you stoned?"

"I haven't seen Sylvia in days." I rubbed my eyes. "She went to the Isle of Youth, an island off the coast of Cuba. It has black coral and iguanas."

Someone knocked on the bedroom door. I heard A's voice. He wanted to know whom I was talking to.

"I have to go," I said. "Please think about what I asked you to do."

"What's that noise?"

344

"I can't go into it right now."

"If you think I'm going to drop everything and fly to Florida, you're nuts."

"Do you think speech is inhibiting our spiritual enlightenment?"

"What?" He huffed into the phone. "What, what, what?"

The door opened. I hung up. A stood in the doorway, B behind him. They demanded to know whom I had been talking to.

"That wasn't an authorized call," A said. "I sincerely hope you weren't calling the cops."

"I didn't know I needed permission," I said. "Anyway, I was just talking to my husband."

"They told us you weren't married," B said.

"They wouldn't know." I put on a pink bathrobe and pushed past them, toward the balcony. They followed. I leaned against the railing, my hips digging into the metal. The skyline was brilliant with light.

I recalled what Sylvia said that first night in her apartment, about my wanting to know what her life was like. I turned my head from side to side, looking at the men standing next to me. "Now I know how it feels to never be alone, but in absolutely the wrong kind of way," I said.

"We're probably no better or worse than any other company you keep," B said.

"You might be right about that," I said.

I leaned over the edge of the balcony. The ground below looked dark and smooth, like the surface of another planet. I wanted to touch it, to feel the grass against my cheek. I kept leaning and leaning until I was weightless. As I went, I felt something—fingertips?—graze the bottom of my foot. I hit the lawn hard. My legs were tangled in the bushes, my arms sprawled across the grass, as though I were trying to crawl away from the scene. I wondered if this was where Sylvia had landed when she went over the edge. I pictured a chalk outline and my body filling the shape.

My lip was bleeding. I was sweating underneath my pajamas and bathrobe. The back of my head ached. I pressed my face into the grass, not looking up when I heard footsteps or voices. I imagined A and B trying to explain this to their boss: She was there and then she wasn't.

"There is something very wrong with you," A said.

"If you wanted to really hurt yourself, you should have gone to a higher floor," B said.

"How could I have gotten to a higher floor with you two around?" I muttered into the grass.

"What?" they both said.

Their voices sounded like they were coming from outer space. I rolled onto my back. Blood had pooled below my bottom lip. I swallowed a mouthful of metallic liquid and grit. The sky had that smudged look again. If my husband knew I'd gone over a balcony, would he come for me then?

A car passed with the stereo turned up so high, it made my entire body vibrate. B kneeled next to me. He pressed two fingers against my throat, checking my pulse.

"The good news is that you're going to live," he said.

"What's the bad news?"

He said they were going to have to take me back upstairs. I nodded.

"We have to keep you safe," B said. "No one will be able to make you do anything if all your bones are broken."

I nodded a second time.

"Why did you do this?" he asked.

"I had to do something."

A kneeled on my other side. He pressed his palm against my forehead. "What hurts?"

In the apartment, A and B helped me down the hall, my arms hooked around their necks, and into bed. They put a pillow underneath my left ankle, which was already swelling. They cleaned the dirt and grass from my face and hands and the bottoms of my feet with a warm washcloth. Using a Q-tip, A swabbed blood from my bottom lip, then peered down at my mouth.

"It's just a cut." He held out a coffee mug and I spit blood into the white bottom. "You don't need any stitches."

"I feel like I've been shot," I said.

"No, you don't," B said, picking leaves from my hair.

They wrapped my ankle in an Ace bandage, then brought me two pills from Sylvia's supply and a glass of water. I took the pills and gulped the water like it was the last thing I would ever drink. They turned out the lights. They told me that tomorrow was a new day.

The door opened. I knew they were about to leave. I asked them to wait.

"Why did you drop out of graduate school?" I asked. "Why didn't you become mathematicians?"

"What do you care?" they asked.

"I want to know something about you."

The room was dark. I tried to find their silhouettes, but the looking made my eye sockets hurt. I rested a hand over my face and listened for their voices.

"It's not a very interesting story," A said, and then the door clicked shut.

I woke in the middle of the night with a violent energy inside me. I was on my back, a thin blanket over my legs. I had to get out of my sister's room. I limped down the hall and locked myself in the bathroom. I padded the tub with towels and eased myself in. I pulled the shower curtain closed. I uncapped my sister's gels and shampoos and sniffed the liquids. Everything smelled like a bad imitation of something else. I pushed up a bathrobe sleeve and examined my arm. My elbow was bruised. My cut lip throbbed. The back of my head still hurt. I wondered if my brain was bleeding. I heard A and B snoring in the living room, where they'd taken up residence for the night.

I fell asleep in the bathtub. In the morning, I woke to the sound of A and B shouting. Finding my room empty, they thought I had slipped out of the apartment. I got up, using the tile walls for support, and splashed water on my face. There was a greenish bruise on my cheekbone and dried blood around my mouth. I imagined the previous day repeating itself over and over and that sick feeling returned. When I opened the door and hobbled into the living room, the men stopped yelling and stared.

"I was in the bathroom," I said.

"The bathroom?" A said. "What were you doing in there?"

"Who cares," B said. "She was just in the bathroom. We didn't lose her after all."

They looked at each other and laughed until they were red faced and doubled over. They shook their heads and rubbed their eyes. I sat on the floor and leaned against the wall. I felt a strange pressure in my cheekbones.

"How are you feeling?" they finally asked.

"My sister is coming home tonight," I said.

"I'll put on some coffee," A said. "Looks like you could use it."

I told them I wanted to make a call. They glanced at each other, then handed me the phone. I lay down on my side and dialed my husband's number. I thought of the stories I'd heard about crises bringing couples back together. When the machine came on, I repeated his name until the tape ran out.

After the sun had been swallowed by a phosphorescent night, I waited on the balcony for Sylvia, a vodka sweating in my hand. My ankle was still wrapped and I couldn't put weight on it, so I stood with my foot slightly raised, like a wounded flamingo. A and B stood with me, of course, complaining about the heat and the mosquitoes and how much trouble I had caused them.

"Who are we waiting for again?" A asked.

"My sister," I said. "The person you're really supposed to be following."

"Lady," B said, slapping at a bug on his forearm, "has anyone ever told you that you have a reality perception problem?"

I watched the street. A car that resembled the Lincoln was parked in the shadows, but it was too dark to know for sure. I thought of the last fight I had had with my husband. It had started in the kitchen and then progressed to the bedroom. In a fury, I'd climbed out the bedroom window and onto the roof. My husband had stuck his head outside and called to me. I'd ignored him. A little while later, he'd walked down the driveway and gotten in his car. He left and didn't return until morning. I stayed on the rooftop for hours, watching the dead black sky. Every now and then, a plane passed over me. I wanted badly to be on one and a few weeks later I was, bound for Miami. And even with all that had happened, with everything that had gone wrong, there was still a part of myself saying, *Please don't send me back to where I came from.*

Before my sister appeared, a little black briefcase in hand, there were several false alarms—women who had the same slim silhouette, who walked with the same kind of swagger. It was startling to see how many people I mistook for my sister, stopping just short of leaning over the balcony and shouting her name; it was even more startling to realize that to mistake someone for Sylvia was to mistake them for myself, that there were so many women out there who could pass for me. And so when the real Sylvia got out of a taxi and moved like a shadow across the street, I didn't call to her, I didn't wave. Instead I remembered watching her run down that beach in Carmel, looking radiant and weightless, filling me with terror and awe.

Sylvia stood on the sidewalk, beneath a street lamp. The light fell on her in a perfect yellowish dome. She looked like she was posing for a portrait. She bowed her head, her body heaved with a mammoth sigh. "There she is," I whispered to A and B just before she disappeared inside.

NOTES ON CONTRIBUTORS

JACOB M. APPEL has published short stories in numerous literary journals, including *Southwest Review, Missouri Review,* and *Virginia Quarterly Review.*

RAE ARMANTROUT's latest book, *Versed* (Wesleyan), was a National Book Award finalist in poetry. She received a Guggenheim Fellowship in 2008 and won the Pulitzer Prize in poetry this year.

LAURA VAN DEN BERG's first collection of stories, *What the World Will Look Like When All the Water Leaves Us* (Dzanc Books), was a 2009 Holiday pick for the Barnes & Noble "Discover Great New Writers" Program. Her fiction has appeared in *Best New American Voices 2010* and the *Pushcart Prize XXIV,* among others. She is the recipient of the 2009–2010 Emerging Writer Lectureship at Gettysburg College.

STEPHEN BERKMAN is a single-frame filmmaker and installation artist, whose camera obscura constructions reconsider the prechemical era of photography. He has exhibited widely. His work has been featured in *Blind Spot, 21st: The Journal of Contemporary Photography: Strange Genius,* and *Photography's Antiquarian Avant-Garde.* He is currently at work on a book, *Predicting the Past,* which will be released in the near future.

MEI-MEI BERSSENBRUGGE's latest book of selected poems is *I Love Artists* (University of California). She lives in New York City and northern New Mexico.

JONATHAN CARROLL has published fifteen novels. His latest is *The Ghost in Love* (Farrar, Straus and Giroux, and TOR). He lives in Vienna.

Widely known in his native France, fabulist GEORGES-OLIVIER CHÂTEAUREY-NAUD has been honored with the Prix Renaudot, the Prix Goncourt de la nouvelle, and the Grand Prix de l'Imaginaire. *A Life on Paper,* a volume of selected stories, was recently awarded Hemingway and French Voices grants, and is forthcoming from Small Beer Press.

MICHAEL COFFEY is the author of four books of poems—*Elemenopy* (Sun & Moon Press), *87 North* (Coffee House Press), *CMYK* (O Books) and, with Rebecca Smith, *Between Two Things* (Lake George Arts Project). He is working on a literary memoir about adoption.

SUSAN DAITCH is the author of two novels, *L.C.* (Lannan Foundation Selection and NEA Heritage Award) and *The Colorist,* and a collection of short stories, *Storytown.* A third novel, *The Dreyfus Book,* is forthcoming from City Lights.

JULIA ELLIOTT's fiction has appeared in *Tin House, The Georgia Review, Puerto Del Sol, Black Warrior Review, Best American Fantasy 2007,* previous issues of *Conjunctions,* and other publications.

JOSHUA FURST is the author of the collection *Short People* and the novel *The Sabotage Café* (both Knopf). He is currently working on a new novel entitled *Foreign Devil.*

Writer and translator EDWARD GAUVIN is a consulting editor for graphic literature at *Words Without Borders,* and his translations have been featured in *Subtropics, Two Lines,* and *Absinthe.*

CATHERINE IMBRIGLIO is the author of *Parts of the Mass* (Burning Deck), which received the 2008 Norma Farber First Book Award from the Poetry Society of America. She lives in Providence, Rhode Island.

JASON LABBE is the author of a chapbook, *Dear Photographer* (Phylum Press). His poems have recently appeared or are forthcoming in *Boston Review, A Public Space, American Letters & Commentary, Open City,* and *Vanitas,* among other journals. He lives in Bethany, Connecticut.

MICHAEL J. LEE lives in New Orleans, where he works as a teacher, waiter, and record-store clerk. His fiction has recently appeared or is forthcoming in *Denver Quarterly, Indiana Review,* and *Fairy Tale Review.* He is also one half of the Brothers Goat.

J. W. McCORMACK is a senior editor at *Conjunctions.*

MIRANDA MELLIS is the author of *The Revisionist* (Calamari Press) and the chapbook *Materialisms* (Portable Press at YoYo Labs). She is an editor at the Encyclopedia Project and teaches at California College of the Arts.

RICK MOODY's new novel is *The Four Fingers of Death* (Little, Brown). He is working on a volume of essays on music.

MELINDA MOUSTAKIS has fiction published or forthcoming in the *Massachusetts Review, Alaska Quarterly Review,* and *Cimarron Review,* among other journals. She is finishing a collection of linked stories, which includes "The Mannequin in Soldotna," and is working on a novel.

JOYCE CAROL OATES is the author, most recently, of the novel *A Fair Maiden* (Houghton Mifflin) and the story collection *Dear Husband* (Ecco), the title story of which appeared originally in *Conjunctions.* She is the 2008 recipient of the Mary McCarthy Award in Fiction, and lives and teaches in Princeton, New Jersey.

H. M. PATTERSON serves as fiction and managing editor of *The Tusculum Review.* She lives amid the mountains of East Tennessee.

JAIME ROBLES has published work in *Five Fingers Review, New American Writing, Shadowtrain*, and *Volt*, among other journals. The "Clone Poems" are part of her book *Anime, Animus, Anima*, forthcoming this year from Shearsman Books.

JESS ROW is the author of *The Train to Lo Wu* (Dial Press) and a chapbook, *The True Catastrophe* (Suture Press). His fiction has appeared in *The Atlantic, Granta, Ploughshares*, and other journals, as well as *The Best American Short Stories* and *The PEN/O. Henry Awards*. He teaches at the College of New Jersey.

MICHAEL SHEEHAN is the James C. McCreight Fiction Fellow at the Wisconsin Institute for Creative Writing, and an assistant fiction editor for *DIAGRAM*. He lives and teaches, at present, in Madison, Wisconsin.

ELENI SIKELIANOS is the author of a hybrid memoir, *The Book of Jon* (City Lights), and six books of poetry, most recently *Body Clock* (Coffee House). She currently teaches in and directs the creative writing PhD program at the University of Denver.

SUSAN STEINBERG is the author of the story collections *Hydroplane* and *The End of Free Love* (both Fiction Collective Two). She teaches at the University of San Francisco.

ARTHUR SZE's latest book, *The Ginko Light* (Copper Canyon), was selected for the 2009 PEN Southwest Book Award for Poetry. He is the editor of *Chinese Writers on Writing*, recently published by Trinity University Press.

FREDERIC TUTEN has published five novels: *Tintin in the New World, Tallien: A Brief Romance, Van Gogh's Bad Café* (all reprinted by Black Classic Press), *The Adventures of Mao on the Long March* (New Directions Classics), and, most recently, *The Green Hour* (W. W. Norton). His collection of interrelated short stories, *Self Portraits: Fictions*, is forthcoming from Norton in September.

ANNE WALDMAN is the author, most recently, of *Manatee/Humanity* (Penguin Poets) and the coeditor of *Beats at Naropa* (Coffee House), as well as *Matriot Acts* (forthcoming from Chax Press). Her play *Red Noir* was produced by the Living Theatre and had a December–February run in New York City. She is the coauthor with Ed Bowes of his recent movie, *Entanglement*.

PAUL WEST's latest novel is *The Shadow Factory* (Lumen), and his work has recently appeared in *Harper's, The Yale Review*, and *Conjunctions*. His current projects include a new novel (his twenty-fourth) and essays for the French periodical *Transfuge*. In 2009, Gallimard published his novel *Les dieux ont Soif*.

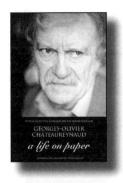

Châteaureynaud, France's own Kurt Vonnegut, has received the Prix Renaudot and the Prix Goncourt. *A Life on Paper—* which includes stories from *Conjunctions, Harvard Review, Agni Online,* among others—introduces his distinct, dynamic voice to English readers. Châteaureynaud examines our diffidence, our cruelty, the humanity in the strangest of us, and our deep appreciation for the mysterious.

Georges-Olivier Châteaureynaud, *A Life on Paper: Stories*
Hardcover · $22 · 9781931520621

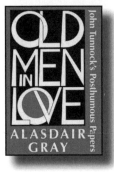

The first US edition of this beautifully illustrated novel—and printed in two colors. Smart, bawdy, politically inspired, and filled with the sense of play that Gray (*Lanark, Poor Things*) delights in. Combines a modern Glaswegian's diary with stories set in Periclean Athens, Renaissance Florence, and Victorian Somerset.

"Our nearest contemporary equivalent to Blake, our sweetest -natured screwed-up visionary."—*London Evening Standard*

Alasdair Gray, *Old Men in Love: John Tunnock's Posthumous Papers*
Hardcover · $24 · 9781931520690

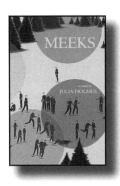

"The powerful alternate reality of *Meeks* is also an unforgettable truth. You'll never see marriage the same way again." —Lydia Millet (*Oh Pure and Radiant Heart*)

"A feat of desolating literary spellcraft, irresistible for its bleak hilarity."—Wells Tower (*Everything Ravaged, Everything Burned*)

"Holmes' lucid prose tightens the noose of this curious world around your readerly neck before you even know what's hit you."—Brian Evenson (*Fugue State*)

Julia Holmes, *Meeks: a novel*
Trade paperback · $16 · 9781931520652

Excitements Brewing in Our Laboratory

Karen Lord, *Redemption in Indigo: a novel* · *A Working Writer's Daily Planner 2011* · Kathe Koja, *Under the Poppy: a novel* · Ted Chiang, *Stories of Your Life and Others* · Karen Joy Fowler, *What I Didn't See and Other Stories* · Kelley Eskridge, *Solitaire: a novel* · *LCRW:* a zine that comes with chocolate bars.

Jane Unrue: *Life of a Star*

An actress of sorts recalls her childhood, longs for absent lovers, imagines traveling. Her life is a carefully crafted and rehearsed engagement with a real and imagined world that has left her, in the end, alone. Unrue's intriguing sentences manage to fuse detachment and emotion, heartbreak and humor.

"Unrue successfully forges an evocative approach that could be seen as metacubist in its dizzying, vapried takes of the familiar world." —*Publishers Weekly* [on *The House*]

Novella, 112 pp., ISBN13: 978-1-936194-00-1, original pbk. $14

Jennifer Martenson: *Unsound*

In these poems, concepts have the presence and force of physical objects — you may hit your head on them. The focus is on dissonance, whether between perception and received ideas, between lesbian identity and social prejudice, or between the desire to make the world orderly, intelligible, and finding the systems for doing so wanting.

"*Xq28*[1] appropriates the authoritative discourse of science and makes it boomerang back on itself.... She bonds description to narrative in an admirable sort of 'molecular origami.'"
—Christine Hume, *Chicago Review*

Poetry, 64 pp., ISBN13: 978-1-936194-01-8, original pbk. $14

Jean Daive, *Under the Dome: Walks with Paul Celan*

[Série d'Ecriture, No. 22; tr. from the French by R. Waldrop]

An intimate portrait of Paul Celan in his last, increasingly dark years.

"I can't really think of a better introduction to Celan's poetry...[or] to the hauntedness of the man, the constant sense of loss that he endured."—Robert Archambeau, *samizdat*

Memoir, 136 pp., ISBN13: 978-1-886224-97-1, original pbk. $14
Also avialable by Jean Daive: *A Lesson in Music* (tr. Julie Kalendek). Poem, 64pp., pbk. $14

Peter Waterhouse: *Language Death Night Outside*

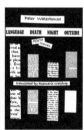

[Dichten=, No.11; tr. from the German by R. Waldrop]

An "I" between languages. A text between the genres of poem and novel. 3 cities, 3 poems, 3 philosophers. A life takes shape through precise particulars in short, staccato sentences. But the effort toward the concrete and definite stands in tension with the boundlessness of thought where the city turns ship, and a flower in Vienna touches the sand dunes of North Africa.

Poem.Novel, 128 pp., ISBN13: 978-1-886224-99-5, original pbk. $14
Also available: *Where Are We Now?* Poems. Duration Press, 1999.

Orders: SPD: www.spdbooks.org, 1-800/869-7553, In Europe: www.audiatur.no/bokhandel
www.burningdeck.com

NEW DIRECTIONS BOOKS
Spring / Summer 2010

AH CHENG

The King of Trees. *Tr. by McDougall.* Three classic novellas that completely altered the landscape of modern Chinese fiction. $15.95 pbk. orig.

ROBERTO BOLAÑO

Antwerp. *Tr. by Wimmer.* Crimes, campgrounds, poetry, sex, love, and misfits mark this—his first novel—as pure Bolaño. $15.95 cloth

The Return. *Tr. by Andrews.* The 2nd volume of stories. $23.95 cl. (July)

ANNE CARSON

Nox. A haunting, beautiful facsimile of a handmade book Carson created after her brother's death. $29.95 illus. fold-out "in a box." ($100 ltd. ed.)

ALBERT COSSERY

A Splendid Conspiracy. *Tr. by Waters.* Egyptian friends sardonically celebrate idleness. "Caustic satire" —*The Guardian.* $14.95 pbk. orig.

THALIA FIELD

Bird Lovers, Backyard. A tour de force blending literary genres (poetry, prose, essay, and drama) examining nature. $16.95 pbk.orig.

LINDA LÊ

The Three Fates. *Tr. by Polizzotti.* Novel about rivalries, strange motives, and destructive passions in a Vietnamese family. $15.95 pbk. orig.

NATHANIEL MACKEY

From a Broken Bottle Traces of Perfume Still Emanate: Volumes 1-3. *New* Preface by the author. A great American jazz novel. $18.95 pbk.

MICHAEL McCLURE

Mysteriosos and Other Poems. The preeminent Beat Generation poet's newest work. "Soulful freedom play" —Gary Snyder. $15.95 pbk.

MURIEL SPARK

Not to Disturb. Novel. A winter's night: a luxurious mansion, a lucrative scandal, and murder in Dame Muriel's most audacious work. $12.95 pbk.

DYLAN THOMAS

The Collected Poems. The Original. *New* intro. by Pulitzer Prize winner Paul Muldoon. The classic, definitive edition available again. $14.95 pbk.

ROBERT WALSER

The Microscripts. *Tr. by Bernofsky.* Afterword by Walter Benjamin. Lavish co-production w/the Christine Burgin Gallery. *Bilingual.* $24.95 cl.illus.

TENNESSEE WILLIAMS

The Rose Tattoo. Drama. *New* intro. by John Patrick Shanley (*Doubt*). A crazy Valentine from Williams. $13.95 pbk.

NEW DIRECTIONS PEARLS
A new series of short masterpieces

JORGE LUIS BORGES: Everything and Nothing. His best fictions & essays. **CÉSAR AIRA: The Literary Conference.** A mad scientist is loose. $9.95 ea

www.ndpublishing.com

DELILLO FIEDLER GASS PYNCHON
University of Delaware Press
Collections on Contemporary Masters

UNDERWORDS
Perspectives on Don DeLillo's *Underworld*

Edited by Joseph Dewey, Steven G. Kellman, and Irving Malin

Essays by Jackson R. Bryer, David Cowart, Kathleen Fitzpatrick, Joanne Gass, Paul Gleason, Donald J. Greiner, Robert McMinn, Thomas Myers, Ira Nadel, Carl Ostrowski, Timothy L. Parrish, Marc Singer, and David Yetter

$39.50

INTO *THE TUNNEL*
Readings of Gass's Novel

Edited by Steven G. Kellman and Irving Malin

Essays by Rebecca Goldstein, Donald J. Greiner, Brooke Horvath, Marcus Klein, Jerome Klinkowitz, Paul Maliszewski, James McCourt, Arthur Saltzman, Susan Stewart, and Heide Ziegler

$35.00

LESLIE FIEDLER AND AMERICAN CULTURE

Edited by Steven G. Kellman and Irving Malin

Essays by John Barth, Robert Boyers, James M. Cox, Joseph Dewey, R.H.W. Dillard, Geoffrey Green, Irving Feldman, Leslie Fiedler, Susan Gubar, Jay L. Halio, Brooke Horvath, David Ketterer, R.W.B. Lewis, Sanford Pinsker, Harold Schechter, Daniel Schwarz, David R. Slavitt, Daniel Walden, and Mark Royden Winchell

$36.50

PYNCHON AND *MASON & DIXON*

Edited by Brooke Horvath and Irving Malin

Essays by Jeff Baker, Joseph Dewey, Bernard Duyfhuizen, David Foreman, Donald J. Greiner, Brian McHale, Clifford S. Mead, Arthur Saltzman, Thomas H. Schaub, David Seed, and Victor Strandberg

$39.50

ORDER FROM ASSOCIATED UNIVERSITY PRESSES
2010 Eastpark Blvd., Cranbury, New Jersey 08512
PH 609-655-4770   FAX 609-655-8366   E-mail AUP440@ aol.com

Summer Writing Program
June 14 - July 11, 2010

The Jack Kerouac School of Disembodied Poetics

Co-founded by Allen Ginsberg
and Anne Waldman

Weekly Workshops June 14–July 11
in Boulder, Colorado

Week One, June 14–20
Charles Alexander, Junior Burke, Julie Carr, Linh Dinh, Thalia Field,
Ross Gay, Bobbie Louise Hawkins, Laird Hunt, Stephen Graham Jones,
Bhanu Kapil, Joanne Kyger, Jaime Manrique, Jennifer Moxley, Jennifer
Scappettone, David Trinidad and others.

Week Two, June 21–27
Jane Augustine, Caroline Bergvall, Jack Collom, Samuel R. Delany,
Alan Gilbert, Michael Heller, Brenda Hillman, Helen Howe Braider,
Lisa Jarnot, Tracie Morris, Daniel Pinchbeck, Evelyn Reilly,
Elizabeth Robinson, James Stevens, Mary Tasillo and others.

Week Three, June 28–July 4
Sinan Antoon, Sherwin Bitsui, Xi Chuan, Dolores Dorantes,
Jack Hirschman, Jen Hofer, Anselm Hollo, Bob Holman, Semezdin
Mehmedinovic, Murat Nemet-Nejat, Akilah Oliver, Margaret Randall,
Damion Searls, Julia Seko and others.

Week Four, July 5–11
Penny Arcade, Amiri Baraka, Laynie Browne, Ambrose Bye,
Douglas Dunn, Danielle Dutton, Brian Evenson, Colin Frazer, Joanna
Howard, Allan Kornblum, Rachel Levitsky, Julie Patton, Selah Saterstrom,
Patricia Smith, Steven Taylor, Anne Waldman and others.

For a complete list of SWP faculty and workshops,
visit *www.naropa.edu/cm.*

Credit and noncredit programs available:
Poetry • Fiction • Translation • Letterpress Printing

For more information or to receive a catalog,
call **303-245-4600** or email *swpr@naropa.edu.*

**Keeping the world safe
for poetry since 1974.**

Naropa
UNIVERSITY

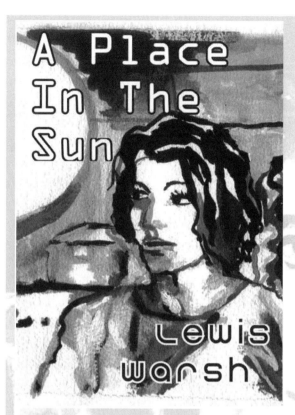

A Place In The Sun

Lewis Warsh

A deeply engrossing book, I couldn't put it down.
And now that I've finished reading it, I can't put it
away, for how it furthers my thinking of the genre
itself. *A Place In The Sun* beautifully combines the
high action and salaciousness of page-turners,
with the self-reflection and risk-taking of post-
modern fiction. It's a must-read and a must-study.

Renee Gladman

Cover Art by Pamela Lawton
ISBN 978-1-933132-71-6 $16.00
Dist. thru SPD   spdbooks.org

spuytenduyvil   spuytenduyvil.net

Best American Short **Stories**
Best **American** Poetry
Best American Essays
Best American **Science**
& Nature **Writing**
the **Pushcart**
Prize anthology

Since 2006, ecotone is the only publication to have had its work reprinted in all of these anthologies. Find out why Salman Rushdie names us one of a handful of literary magazines on which "the health of the American short story depends."

REIMAGINING PLACE

ecotone

ecotonejournal.com

NOON

NOON

A LITERARY ANNUAL

1324 LEXINGTON AVENUE   PMB 298   NEW YORK   NEW YORK   10128

EDITION PRICE $12 DOMESTIC $17 FOREIGN

BROWN UNIVERSITY LITERARY ARTS

Program faculty

Brian Evenson
Thalia Field
Forrest Gander
Renee Gladman
Michael S. Harper
Carole Maso
Aishah Rahman
Meredith Steinbach
Keith Waldrop
CD Wright

Joint-appointment & visiting faculty

Ama Ata Aidoo
Rick Benjamin
John Cayley
Robert Coover
Joanna Howard
George Lamming
Gale Nelson
John Edgar Wideman

For over 40 years, the Brown University Literary Arts Program has been a home for innovative writing. To learn about the two-year MFA program and the undergraduate concentration, or to have access to Writers Online, an archive of literary recordings, see our web site: http://www.brown.edu/cw

MFA application deadline is 15 December.

FC2 Catherine Doctorow

Innovative Fiction Prize

$15,000 & publication by FC2

entries accepted aug. 15 – nov. 1, 2010

judged by ben marcus

guidelines: fc2.org

JARVIS & CONSTANCE DOCTOROW FAMILY FOUNDATION

FC2 is among the few alternative, author-run presses devoted to publishing fiction considered by America's largest publishers too challenging, innovative, or heterodox for the commercial milieu.

siglio

NEW BOOKS AT THE INTERSECTION OF ART & LITERATURE

TORTURE OF WOMEN   Nancy Spero

Juxtaposing first person testimony by female victims of torture with imagery drawn from ancient mythology, *Torture of Women* is a public cry of outrage and a nuanced exploration of the continuum of violence. An innovative and polyphonous narrative, a feminist disquisition, and a register of political protest, this fierce and epic work of art has now been translated to book form so that it can be read with immediacy and intimacy. With a story by Luisa Valenzuela, an excerpt from Elaine Scarry's *The Body in Pain,* and an essay by curator Diana Nemiroff. **$48 • HB • 156 p • 96 full page color plates • APRIL**

S P R A W L   Danielle Dutton

An absurdly comic and decidedly digressive novel, S P R A W L chronicles the mercurial inner life of one suburban woman. Inspired by a series of domestic still life photographs, Dutton creates her own trenchant series of tableaux, attentive to the surfaces of the suburbs and the ways in which life there is willfully on display. In locating the language of sprawl itself—unremitting, ever expansive—Dutton has written a stunning work of fiction that takes us deep into the familiar and to its very edge. **$18 • PB • 144 p • AUGUST**

EVERYTHING SINGS: Maps for a Narrative Atlas   Denis Wood

In pursuit of a poetics of cartography, Denis Wood has created an atlas unlike any other. Examining Boylan Heights, his small neighborhood in North Carolina, he subverts the traditional notions of mapmaking to discover new ways of seeing this place, the people who live there, as well as the nature of "place" itself. Each map attunes the eye to something invisible or insignificant but now essential to understanding how we shape the places we live. As he looks for ways to map what has never been mapped or what may not even be mappable, a narrative rich with poetic suggestion emerges. **$38 • HB • 112 p • NOVEMBER**

www.sigliopress.com . 2432 Medlow Avenue, Los Angeles, CA 90041 . 310-857-6935

PUERTO DEL SOL

a journal of new literature

45.1, Spring 2010

featuring
Antoine Volodine
Roberto Tejada
Blas Falconer
Sherman Alexie
Kate Bernheimer
Maria Melendez
and more.

puertodelsol.org

44.2, Summer 2009

featuring
Erich Chevillard
Helen DeWitt
Julie Carr
Blake Butler
Dan Beachy-Quick
Peter Markus
and more.

PUERTO DEL SOL

a journal of new literature

2X² is a zany, wise, moving, beautifully written life investigation of sorts. I laughed out loud. That poet Bellen has a hell of an imagination.

—Kate Lardner, author of *Shut Up He Explained: The Memoir of a Blacklisted Kid*

Smart, funny, at once spare and lyrically lush, this mythic tale of a lost girl stalking her lost double will pull you delightedly along with its swift narrative—pull you up short when it makes you stop and think. Martine Bellen is an astonishing writer.

—Rilla Askew, author of *Harpsong* and *The Mercy Seat*

In this work is some of the most beautiful and intuitively provocative language of anything I have read.

—Ken Keegan

Nora comes across a newspaper article about her lost twin that sets in motion her search for her doppelganger and thrusts her from the safe island life that she has created into a sweeping, surrealist escapade, buried in the depths of an undifferentiated dream of ocean. Drifting through the foggy myths of her past, she practices spycraft and lessons of Dōgen Zenji, and follows her guardian angel stepmother's advice to always bring bread, milk, and ham (gifts for spontaneous bribes) when traveling to lands unknown. Veils of betrayal and isolation are lifted as Nora navigates systems of story (fairy tale and science); belief and faith (spiritual and myth-ological); and reality (phenomenological and truth). As in many travel odysseys, the fictions of space, time, and being are placed under a microscope and an ever-unraveling solitary journey loosens into an always uncanny, sometime hilarious, interdependent adventure.

Martine Bellen

2X² by Martine Bellen

Martine Bellen is the author of six collections of poetry, including *The Vulnerability of Order* (Copper Canyon Press); *Further Adventures of the Monkey God* (Spuyten Duyvil); *Tales of Murasaki and Other Poems* (Sun & Moon Press), which won the National Poetry Series Award; and *Places People Dare Not Enter* (Potes & Poets Press). Along with composer David Rosenboom, Bellen wrote *AH!* opera no-opera. She was a recipient of a Rockefeller Foundation residency in Bellagio, Italy and of a New York Foundation for the Arts fellowship, as well as an American Academy of Poets Award. For more about her, visit her website www.martinebellen.com

www.blazevox.org/bk-mb3.htm   www.blazevox.org/catalog.htm

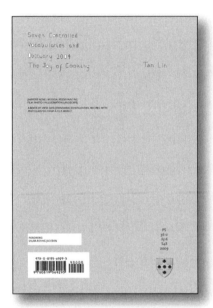